TRANCE ADAMS: MAN OF MYSTERY
(a Satire)

BY

KEVIN PERSELL

For Amy, Emelia, and Hailey. And thanks to Marsha for the first edit and pushing me over the many years to finally publish this darn thing.

Cover design by Kristyn of Drop Dead Designs

First published September 2017

Chapter 1: Greetings

Another day had gone, and the sun followed it. It was a yellowish half orb sinking in the mountains to the west of the town of Hunter, Washington, when Trance Adams, public employee number 10897-0678, closed the back door to his office and began to shamble down the now dimly-lit alley toward the parking lot where his trusty and reliable Ford Astrocruiser waited for him patiently. He didn't know it at the time, but he was entering the final moments of a normal life.

Trance's office, a branch of The Document Security Department, sat in a squat building at the edge of town. The DSD's sole purpose of existence consisted of providing documents for use in other Washington state agencies. Their motto coursed briefly through his mind as it always did at that time of night as he walked toward his car: "We Serve: Documents." If you wanted a G-6 10 A form for tracking the migratory patterns of banana slugs for instance, or perhaps a box of ten thousand of them, the DSD was the place you contacted... as long as you were willing to fill out a Z-10 14 B (rev) Document Request form, that is. Heaven help the poor sorry sap who ran out of Z-10 14 B (rev) forms!

Trance possessed the type of job that had required him to develop a very specific set of skills. If the world ended suddenly, he would have been left totally confused and completely helpless. Until then, however, he was sitting pretty.

His primary duties at the DSD were to reroute D29-16A Applications for Clemency from one arm of the agency to another. Due to a minor clerical error several years before, applications intended to go to the Henter, WA branch were permanently routed to his office in Hunter instead.

A little known fact is that State law requires all D29-16A applications be processed by Grade 10 Processing Staff, and these staff were all located in Henter. So, it was Trance's job to gather all of the Clemency Request forms coming in daily and mail them in bulk.

Unfortunately, the Henter office staff administrative assistants followed their printed directives very well; they sent all the applications right back to the Hunter office.

Naturally, not a lot of criminals got released under this system. But on the positive side of the equation, Trance kept permanent employment and the post office (in Hunter, anyway) had been in the black for years. So Trance had little reason to complain.

Off in the distance, on the hill above the town, Trance could see the brand new high school, home of the Raging Butterflies. It sparkled majestically in the sun's rays and made him proud a little town like Hunter could have something as exciting as a new high school, even though it was mostly made of recycled tires and other trash.

All the aforementioned thoughts were floating around pleasantly in his mind as they always did at the end of the day. Neither clockwork nor bowels could be more regular. But that was about to change.

Since Trance had just gotten off work, he was also thinking dully of the night ahead when a blue beam of light split the evening sky and lanced into the ground scarcely ten feet in front of him. The event shocked him because beams of light hardly ever came out of the sky, especially in his vicinity. This was especially true in the quiet town of Hunter, WA where nothing out of the ordinary ever happened, at least since Cheap Barney, a regular over at the Sailfish Bar, had drunkenly proclaimed "All drinks are on me!"

Trance was the product of ten years of service to the state, and routine guided his life. There were no unforeseen events or unplanned circumstances… until now. So, even as long underused synapses and neurons began firing spasmodically but frantically over the strange occurrence, his body, given no real direction, decided to return to comfortable everyday routine. Regardless of what the eyes, notoriously unreliable in the best of circumstances in his body's estimation, had seen it was back to business as usual. This meant a quick trip to the car, an hour-long commute and a short evening at home punctuated by deeply satisfying top ramen and possibly a cold beer. Best to get started.

However, when his body had shambled forward ten feet to the approximate location of the terminus of the beam, a new sight assaulted his senses causing his body to pause. The previously smooth plasticrete now bore a charred pockmark. Nestled in this tiny crater, a shiny silver-colored ring with a single blue diamond-shaped gem set in the outside face glinted at him smartly. It appeared to be glowing slightly.

The ring looked very valuable, especially with such a deep dark blue stone. In fact, it seemed like the kind of ring emperors or kings might wear when they wanted to impress each other; something best turned over to the local authorities to be claimed by its rightful owner.

He bent down and grasped the ring, which was surprisingly cool to the touch. As he was standing, he grunted. Something had just occurred. Had the ring flashed just now? He peered at it. It looked… blurred.

Suddenly, the ring melted, shifted, and flowed from the palm of his right hand to his middle finger where it solidified into its original shape around the digit. And then a disembodied voice spoke to him, breaking the stillness of the alley. "Just a second….. ahem…. Greetings, Protector," it stated metallically in a bored voice.

"Ahhhhhh. Hello?" was all Trance could manage given the circumstances.

"Greetings Protec….. Oh. I already said that," the voice muttered to itself.

Trance noted dimly the stone in the center of the ring, which now faced outwards from his finger, glowed softly in conjunction with the voice. "Well, Trance Adams, we can't be bothered by tradition, unfortunately. I'm supposed to introduce myself and explain your new purpose, but there just isn't much time. Right now, as I speak, we've got an 08-802 sentry drone headed for our position. Its intent is to procure me and obliterate anything I am attached to at the time.

"By the way, when I said 'obliterate' just now, I meant completely destroy, and when I said 'anything I am attached to,' I meant you. I always try to be helpful, and I wanted to make sure you completely understood."

"I figured out the meaning, thanks." Trance's head was spinning. Was he hearing voices? Did he respond to them? What was happening?

"So, I need you to get us out of here or hide us, or something. I can supply more power than you'll ever need, but I can't make decisions unless you're in direct, immediate danger. Even then, I can only react. In other words, I can't think on my own."

"Well, get off me then. I don't want any part of this." Trance shook his hand vigorously, but the ring held on.

"Sorry, Protector." The voice shifted down an octave. "'Once a candidate has been chosen as a Protector, the Protector's ring –that's me – cannot be removed, without dire consequences, until all duties have been dispatched in a successful manner, or the bearer is dead.' It's in the manual you recei…." It coughed and returned to its previous timber. "Well, you should have gotten a manual. I'm certainly not doing well tonight, am I? But that can't be helped. I'll just have to explain things as we go along.

'Now come on! Remember the sentry drone I mentioned, the 08-802? I have it tracked, and it's just now entered the atmosphere of this puny planet. I estimate we have about three minutes before it lands on your head. When it does, If I were you I'd rather not be in that head, because it's going to be mighty flat. It's going to be lights out, chum."

"You're joking, right? This must be a joke. Seriously, get off."

"No joke, and I can't get off your finger. I thought I explained."

"I wasn't paying attention at the time."

"Well, you'll have to accept it as fact, then. Look, Protector, I can't spend all my time repeating myself. You've been chosen, and accepted the contract by picking me up. I'm not going anywhere… unless you go somewhere."

Trance sputtered. "Contract -- I did not accept a contract!"

"You did. It's in the manua… Oh. You never got it. Well, it's too late now, and if we don't hurry we're both going to be in a load of trouble."

"Well, shit."

"Are you giving me a command?"

"No," Trance grunted. "I was just mulling over my choices. I guess Top Ramen and a beer are out of the question at this point."

"Tell you what. If you can take care of this little 08-802 issue, I'll find you something that will make your ramen and beer seem like a bunch of noodles soaked in fermented juice. What do you say?"

"Will saying 'No,' result in my death in the near future?"

"Oh, most definitely," the ring responded happily.

"Will saying "Yes" end up with pretty much the same results?"

"Probably! But you'll most likely live a few moments longer." It paused. "At this little bar that I know towards the galactic rim, wagers are being made even now. Currently, the odds are even that you'll be able to fit into a doggy bag within the next three minutes. I have much more faith in you than the odds makers do. I just bet that you'll last at least four minutes. Maybe if you last longer, I'll share the winnings with you."

"Thanks. Let's get going, shall we? What are my options – Hiding or fleeing? Can I fight it?"

"Any of those are certainly options. However, at this point, I would advise against fighting or fleeing. With your current level of experience, if you attempt to stand up to the 08-802, it will most likely crush you like an antari filchere berry, and I will be out a ton of money."

"What kind of berry?"

"It's a... well... never mind. On the other hand, if you try and flee, it will certainly find you... with the same results."

"Hiding, then. How is it tracking me?"

"Excellent question. I'm impressed. The 08-802 model is approximately ten of your earth years old. Its tracking system involves energy signatures and visual cues. Frankly, it's quite antiquated. However with your skills and experience it is still more than you'll be able to handle."

"Thanks. Tell me more about this energy signal."

"Each entity has a unique energy signal or aura. Mine is quite powerful. It can be seen, like a candle across the breadth of a football stadium, as far as a galaxy away. Granted, you have to be looking for my signal specifically to find me, but I know the sentry droid is doing just that. Of course, he can't tell it's me specifically. He just sees a ring is here on the planet. When he gets closer he'll be able to pinpoint the signal."

"So... can you mask your signal somehow? Put your candle under a bushel in other words? Make it look like my energy signal?"

The ring managed to look doubtful. "I can, but only for brief periods of time."

"Now we're getting somewhere. Can you also mask yourself visually?"
The ring brightened. "Oh, yes. Indefinitely."

"Okay, so, can you do both?"

"You'll still be able to see and hear me, but for all intents and purposes, I will be invisible and untraceable. For about ten minutes, that is. You can probably guess what will happen after that."

"Yes. You've told me," Trance responded dryly. "Go ahead and take care of the masking thing now then. We'll talk about this 'contract' later."

The ring seemed to dull briefly, and then blur. Trance began walking toward his hover car as if locked in the throes of everyday life. Unbidden, his lips began to whistle the famous ditty "I've Done Nothing Wrong, Officer (That You Can Prove)," by the Bakersfield Dozen Trio.

Suddenly, a shock wave hit him from behind, followed closely by a WHUMP. Everything turned white momentarily. When his vision cleared, Trance found himself face down on the plasticrete.

"Uh, the sentry droid is here," the ring whispered conspiratorially into his ear.

Trance jumped to his feet and looked back. Standing where he had been seconds before was the ugliest hunk of metal he had ever seen. It could only be the 08-802.

"It's only good for one thing," the ring whispered again. "Search and Destroy."

"That's two things," Trance replied irritably as he backed away from the monstrosity. It blinked at him owlishly.

"Whatever. It's good at both of them."

The 08-802 sentry droid stood a good eight feet tall and five feet wide in Trance's estimation. Its trunk was divided in two, with the lower half parallel to the ground. Four small segmented legs branched out from the lower section and pierced the ground in sharp and deadly points. The upper half curved straight upward. It had a tiny head at the top end and two huge arms on the sides. The arms were easily twice the size of its legs and would have been highly muscled had they been made of flesh rather than metal.

Two massive gun barrels seemed to have sprouted from somewhere on the droid's backside and arched over his shoulders. Both barrels pointed solidly at Trance.

The moment seemed to drag on for hours. The droid contemplated Trance silently, as the human continued to back away. Then, it dropped to its "knees" and investigated the pit the ring had created when it fell from the sky, completely ignoring him.

Trance turned and ran to his hover car, a black Ford Astrocruiser, jumped in and hit the juice.

They rocketed into the evening sky, merging with the other air traffic, which had already begun to clear out; the evening rush nearing completion. Trance sighed and wiped his forehead, realizing he had been sweating profusely, then concentrated on the task at hand.

The traffic zone consisted of stratified lines of traffic. With a flick of his wrist, he activated the "Up" signal on his vehicle, and shot into a higher level. This resulted in honks as outraged drivers angrily made room for him. "Air hogs!" he yelled out of habit, shaking his fist. Several responded by waving at him. "Use all your fingers, jerks!"

Meanwhile, the ring did nothing, other than pulse faintly. It was obviously under a lot of pressure. "How much time do we have?" he asked it.

"It depends. How fast does this bucket of bolts go?"

"I modified it about five years ago," Trance replied smartly. "It tops out at three hundred."

"Huh. Well, then, we have about five minutes; about how much longer I can keep masking my signal."

"I think I have a tire iron in here somewhere. Maybe I can bash its eyes out," Trance said seriously.

The ring snickered. "Fella, you have a death wish."

"OK. Does it have any weaknesses?"

"Let me consult the diagrams I have. Give me a moment... OK. This model is meant for operation in space. You probably noticed the tiny legs. It doesn't do too well when it is on terra firma. For one thing, it can't walk too well, and tends to overheat when it is flying for extended periods of time. This doesn't matter in deep space but it is a big problem here, because it can't effectively cool down.

'It does have passive intake vents which cool its circuits while on planet. These help immeasurably but are only good if it is moving, and still aren't a complete fix. It will still have to leave the atmosphere eventually. If these vents could be clogged with something viscous, or we could keep it from moving for, say an hour, it would overheat and slag itself.

'The other thing is it gets dumber and dumber the hotter it becomes. Keep it busy long enough, and it might just blow itself up accidentally."

"Great," Trance grunted as he activated the "Up" signal again, rocketing higher. There were only a few cars at this level, and he merged without having to use profanity.

Once they were at sufficient height, he tapped a key on his steering unit. A light bearing the words "Auto Pilot Engaged" began blinking on the dash. The car's speed also registered … a robust 295. Trance glanced over at the On-Board Holographic Automobile Representation device. The OB-HAR showed various colored dots in a sphere around a central green dot, his Astrocruiser. By touching individual dots, he could pull up information relevant to the vehicle in question. The dots generally seemed to stay parallel with him, although some would break off and fly out of range, while others would enter the area to take their place.

Muttering to himself, he touched the keypad near the hologram emitter. It responded audibly. "Display set for 5 mile radius."

"Five miles should give us a least a little notice," Trance said, apologetically. "I wish I could put it out further."

"Yes," the ring responded wearily. "It is becoming much harder to keep this up. I've had to turn off some functions. The less I have to do, the longer I can hide us."

"Can you spare the energy to give me some pointers on what else you can do?"

"Yes. It's really quite simple. I can do anything you can will me to do."

"OK, I will you to destroy that sentry droid, and then get off my finger."

"Well, it isn't that simple. Firstly, you have to successfully dispatch all of your duties before I can be removed. Generally, what I mean by 'duties' is completing one tour of duty. The second is –"

"Tour of duty? How long is that?"

"Well, it varies…." The ring flickered with embarrassment.

"How long?"

"Heh. It's a thousand years. But don't blame me! I didn't design the rules; I'm just here to enforce them!"

"A thousand years! My race doesn't even last to a hundred and ten usually! We turn into prunes when we reach seventy! How in the heck am I going to last a thousand years?"

"More to the point, how are you going to last the next three minutes?"

"Yerg. I guess I got a little ahead of myself. Tell me more about this "will" thing. Why can't I just command you to destroy the sentry drone?"

"Because, you have to 'describe' with your mind how to destroy it. You know I can read the thoughts you direct at me and pick up what you want me to do mentally, right? That is how I can speak your language and describe things in ways you can understand, usually. I have been speaking to you with a voice you think you hear with your ears because it is more comfortable and familiar to you. But in reality, I have been speaking directly into your mind this whole time. You have also been speaking to me mentally, besides verbally. You just didn't know it."

"Hmm." Trance tapped his fingers on the console, momentarily lost. "So I need to picture what I want you to do in my mind, and hold the thought in there for how long?"

"It depends. If you want something constructed that is real, you only need concentrate on the subject as long as it takes me to make it with available real-world materials. If you want something made out of energy, such as a construct, then you'll need to concentrate on it for as long as you want it to exist."

"Do I need to understand the inner workings of something in order to get you to create it? I mean like say I wanted to make a nuclear bomb to blow up the robot, would I need to take a physics course at the local college first?"

"You'll be dead first if you take that route. But, no, not necessarily. There are huge exceptions, but it would be enough if I understand the basics of what you need me to do. However, what about the other consequences? The weight of sentient lives must be measured and accounted for in everything you do."

"Yes, and other life as well of course," Trance muttered. "However, I only used an example. How much time do we have?"

"Two minutes. Maybe less. This is creating a huge strain on me, Protector."

"I know. But at least you won your bet."

The ring brightened visibly. "Say, you're right. I'll have to collect when this is all over. Speaking of, can we practice a little? I'd rather still be on your finger when I get my money. And I would even more prefer to have the finger attached to the rest of your body at the time."

"Sure." Trance closed his eyes and began to envision a sphere.

"How big a sphere, Trance? I need perspective. For all I know you want to encircle a gnat!"

Size then. Perhaps the size of the sentry drone. In fact, exactly the size of a sentry drone.

"Where, you big dope? I need everything. Location. Size. Color. Texture. Everything. We are so dead."

"We're not dead yet!"

"We will be if you don't concentrate, Protector."

"Right. Good point." Let's start small. In fact, I want a sphere the size of an egg. Except in sphere-form. And I want it right here in my hand. It's blue, with little speckles glinting in the light.

Trance opened his eyes. There, resting on the palm of his hand was the sphere! Shocked, he blinked, and it was gone.

"Not bad for a first timer. Maybe we'll get by this after all."

"You just made another bet, didn't you."

The ring looked shocked. "I never! Ok. I did make another bet. Double or nothing." It chuckled, then looked worried. "Shit, boss. It's on to us. You better take evasive action, now."

Suddenly, proximity alarms began to shriek as the OB-HAR registered a blip heading straight for the Ford. Trance flicked the alarm off irritably and looked out the windows waiting for death. There was no time for evasive action. No time for more tiny spheres.

In a blink of an eye the sentry droid shot past the vehicle, its retro jets firing madly. Abruptly, it stopped, several miles away. Trance envisioned it shaking its tiny head in confusion wondering where its prey had gone. The stupid fucking machine. It thought it was so cool with all that technology, all those guns, yet it had no room for brains. Who did it think it was coming here with a chip on its shoulder? Trying to kill him? For nothing! A stupid fucking ring with a big fucking mouth. He screamed at it.

The anxiety and fear washed away in a flood of pure berserker rage. Instinct took over, and Trance felt himself doing things that he had seen only in comic books as a child (Ok, he still read them--but only to look at the pictures).

The car melted away from him, peeled back by a field of pure energy. It solidified a few feet away, and became a missile shooting straight for the droid propelled by pure will. Unerringly it struck his target, pulverizing into it in a cloud of fire, ash, and late –model Ford parts. The shock wave tossed cars as far as a mile away off-course. It blew through Trance's hair like a hot wind, feathering it lightly. He scarcely noticed.

The droid was still there, and it looked pissed.

It flew straight at him, both barrels of its back gun blazing. Shells the size of VW's exploded around him, singing the air with their heat. With a grunt, Trance materialized a shield out of nothingness that blocked the missiles, reflecting them away.   Then he cocked a fist, creating a huge boxing glove.

The 08-802 shot straight at him. He waited for what seemed like an eternity, and then struck with lightning quickness, landing a blow in the center of its massive chest. The detonation was incredible. It stopped the sentry-drone mid-flight, and flung it like a paper doll far into the evening sky.

"Cool."

The single word drained the berserker rage from his body. He found himself floating calmly a mile up in the sky, surrounded by a thin aura of smoke. He stepped out of it as if he were on solid ground and watched as the mist dissipated. The physical remains of the battle, including the few sorry pieces remaining of his Ford had long since rained down upon the unsuspecting city. "Thanks ring," he said, half to himself. This Protector gig might not be so bad after all.

"You knocked the droid out past the moon."

"That *was* pretty cool huh?"

"That's not what I meant. What you did was cool it down. It is now smarter, faster, and meaner. Look, you have done surprisingly well for a novice, but you certainly didn't damage it. Don't get ahead of yourself."

"Oh."

"So, Protector, are we going to hover here and wait for it to come back and really pulverize your ass, or do you have a plan?"

"I guess I have to make a plan."

"Are you going to share your plan with me when you make it, or do I have to just pretend?"

"I thought you could read my mind."

"I can only capture the thoughts that you direct at me. Even we rings have privacy clauses built in. For another thing, I can't sell your private information to outside entities. It's Section 98987.189987.1921A in the manual."

"The one I didn't get."

"Right," it said smugly. "Not to change the subject, but remember that little droid problem? My sensors show the 08-802 now is turning around and heading back here, surprisingly enough."

"Sarcasm does not become you," Trance grunted, looking upward.

The night was peppered with stars, each one winking and glowing crisply in the cloudless firmament. One of the stars seemed to be getting bigger and bigger with unsettling speed.

"Think Think Think, damnit!" Trance muttered, tapping an index finger against his temple.

"We are so dead," moaned the ring. "Does your race believe in an afterlife? If so, you may wish to prepare for it."

"Shut up."

A strange sense of déjà vu began to wash over him as he watched the little dot become the massive 08-802 sentry-droid. Quickly, Trance formed the picture of a wall in his head, about five feet in front of the oncoming missile that was the sentry droid. It was a huge red brick wall, fashioned from pure energy, thirty-five feet high and ten feet thick. It popped into existence about ten miles from his present location.

The 08-802 plowed through the obstacle like it was butter, and the remains disappeared guiltily.

"Huh. Let's try the sphere again, but with some real ingredients."

A sphere much like the one he had temporarily created in his late, lamented Astrocruiser appeared around the droid, masking it from view. With a groan, it shattered from the inside, spraying a thick, yellow liquid and bright blue specks for miles in every direction.

"Let's get out of here!" Trance screamed at the ring. The droid was less than a mile away, and approaching fast. Trance was seconds away from obliteration.

With a thought, he created a small rocket- powered backpack that formed around him. Switches led from his back down his arms into his hands. He hit the switches savagely. "Go! Go! Go!" he screamed.

The resulting explosion took his breath away momentarily. When he had regained it, and the stars had cleared from his vision, he found he was speeding away from his previous location, the 08-802 nipping at his heels like a lost and very angry dog. Trance was in the race of his life.

The jetpack was extremely fast. But not fast enough. Trance knew the droid would beat him hands-down in an extended race. With a grunt, he hit the off button, and allowed himself to plummet like a stone toward the city below. The droid, taken by surprise, rocketed forward for several seconds and many miles before it turned around. By then, Trance had already fallen into the city.

Somehow, Trance willed his rapid descent to become a gentle one. He touched down softly in an alley somewhere in the business district, and stood there looking up into the night sky. On either side of him, gray brick buildings reached twenty-five stories into the firmament. Lights gleamed silently from several of the hundreds of windows. A single piece of paper floated between his legs, pushed by a gentle gust of wind.

"Now what?" the ring muttered.

"Is there anyone in these buildings?"

"No, they are empty. The last inhabitant, a janitor, exited the one on your left ten minutes ago. The nearest sentient being is a rat down in the basement of the edifice to your right. His name is Rex The Conqueror, and he likes to eat flowers in particular. There is, however, a busy road nearby."

"Any chance we'll get interrupted here?"

"Other than by the 08-802?"

"Yes."

"I doubt that any humans will wander into the line of fire here. There are several news droids flying around. We have already been filmed extensively, and five local stations are reporting on your battle thus far, however we are not being filmed right now. I think your sudden plummet from the air move lost them momentarily."

"Any police officers or CADP in the area?"

"No. Your police force and Civil Air Defense Patrol sure are slow. If we were on a more advanced planet, they would have already been here by now."

"We're a small town," Trance countered. "The police also deliver pizzas. It's probably a busy night."

"I see."

"I sure could do with a pizza right now," Trance sighed. "Ok, this is as good a place as any. Before it gets here, can you create a zone around this block that will blur the lenses of any of the news droids and keep the police out?"

"OK. No problem."

Just then, the stillness of the alley was broken by the scream of the sentry droid's retro rockets. It landed ten feet from Adams, and let loose with both barrels.

"What the…." Trance managed before being covered with what could only be thousands of red and yellow rose petals.

"I'll explain later," the ring said in a guilty voice. "Are you going to fight back, or what?"

Trance nodded and raised his ring hand, pointing at the monster before him, which had begun to stride forward. The ring spat out a silver glob of matter which expanded as it interacted with the air. The glob hit the droid in the chest with a splat and covered it, flowing and molding itself to the 08-802's body structure.

The droid looked down almost comically, and began to shake itself like a puppy dog. The glop just continued to spread slowly.

The droid was frantic now. It scratched at the substance with both hands, then began crashing into the walls in a futile effort to remove the substance, which soon covered its entire body in a thin film. It made no effort to fly away, too distracted to attempt to effect an escape.

"What is the temperature inside the droid?" Trance asked calmly, though his heart pounded furiously in his chest.

"800 degrees Celsius, and rising. It is turning into quite an oven in there."

"Increase heat by 10,000 degrees, but create an area around the droid with a lining that will keep outside temps at a normal level. I don't want to toast this part of the city."

"Yessir." Yet another sphere, this one clear, popped into existence around the droid, which continued flailing around mightily. The silver covering it quickly turned red, then white. Trance noted clinically the plasticrete within the sphere's circumference had turned to ash. Then, there was a tiny pop. With a sigh, the droid's four legs collapsed and the upper half of the body slammed into the ground, its barrels burying themselves in the ash.

"Delicate yet important circuits within it have turned to slag," the ring reported. "Congratulations. You won your first battle."

"Thanks."

"The glue you filled the air sphere with completely covered the passive vents. It was only a matter of time before it would have overheated."

"Yeah. But it might have killed me or someone else in the meantime. I thought it would be better if I sped things up a bit."

"True."

"Ok, let's get the body out of here. No sense creating any more of a spectacle than needed. Then, let's go to my place."

After he had disposed of the body by sending it on a one-way trip to the moon, Trance wearily flew to his apartment across the city, managing to avoid being seen by anyone.

Chapter 2: Lessons Learned

Trance lived alone in a small but clean apartment building at the edge of town. His apartment was a two-bed one-bath unit on the third floor. It had forest green shag carpet and light brown plasticast counter tops, which had been popular ten years before but now seemed overly dark to modern eyes. Trance was completely clueless when it came to such things, however. Fashion remained a murky and mysterious subject in his mind, when he happened to think about it at all. The fact his apartment could use a serious upgrade and possibly a complete razing was lost on him. To Trance, it was home.

The complex was dark, except for a lone light here and there, by the time he arrived. With a frown, he looked at his watch and shuddered. Quite late, indeed. He knew he would be calling in sick the next morning.

"I have a feeling you'll be calling in sick a lot from now on, Protector," the ring stated as if it had read his mind.

He trudged up the stairs outside his unit, glancing forlornly at the parking space that had housed his Astrocruiser for so many years. Now, all that remained was a spot of syntho-oil shimmering on the smooth, sanded, surface of the plasticrete. "I should probably wipe that up, one of these days," he said to himself, trudging upstairs.

Inside the apartment, it was dark. He could hear his downstairs neighbor's radio belting out a sloppy rendition of "Ain't Got No Sense Nor Feeling" by the Everly Twins. It matched his dark mood exactly.

Trance sighed and flipped on the light switch, illuminating the entryway. Straight-ahead was the kitchen. Off to the right lay the living room and dining area. Down a short hallway to the left were the two bedrooms and a single bathroom. Home.

Trance cooked Top Ramen in silence, too lost in the momentous change his life had gone through in the few hours since he left his office.

It all seemed like a dream. On the one hand, the prospect of gallivanting around the Universe excited him, but it also worried him just slightly. He'd always secretly believed there really were aliens despite overwhelming evidence to the contrary (namely the single fact no aliens had ever been seen or heard from), and had always wished, deep down inside, he'd been born during a time when extended space travel was possible so he could find out for sure.

He daydreamed during the frequent and extensive boring parts of his workday, and in those dreams he often lived as a famous rocket jockey solving mysteries and battling aliens at the ends of space. Like episodic television, he always solved the riddle in half an hour or less with plenty of time to reveal the conspirators or save kidnapped princesses. It was easy to be a hero in the safety of dreams – but how would he do in real life?

For the first time in a long while, he faced a great deal of unknowns. What would tomorrow bring? What exactly was out there beyond the clouds— beyond Earth's tiny sun?   What were aliens like? Did they have the same hopes and dreams as he did? Or were they aliens in every respect of the word – too foreign to his way of thinking to even comprehend?

Before him lay the adventure he wanted, but with it a caveat – the adventure might actually get him killed. In picking up the ring had he begun the first step on a path leading to glory? Or did each step lead inexorably to his doom?

A bomb disarmed with only a second left on the clock or a narrow escape from an oncoming train made for exciting theater, but how was the party involved really affected?   It was all fine and good on the silver screen; movie heroes dealt with those kinds of odds all the time and always came out on the winning side. Of course the story never told of the years of therapy and the powerful narcotics they had to take to deal with the stress. Not the stuff of happy endings… it just wouldn't do to show them like that. Much safer to have them ride off into the sunset, yes?

His life up until the point he had picked up the ring had been uneventful in the extreme, and he enjoyed it. He'd developed a safe and comfortable niche at work, and felt a certain level of respect from his supervisor and peers. His personal life wasn't lacking either. Though he wasn't dating at the moment, he had plenty of male and female friends he spent time with. Other times he read or watched TV or visited with his parents, his sisters, and brother. In short, up until he stepped into the alley that very night, it had been an idyllic life. Unfortunately, though he hadn't realized it until now, it had also begun to bore him.

He now knew he had been living a recycled life: the same commute every morning and night, eight hours of drudgery each day, forty hours a week, and weekends filled with a revolving door of friends and family. How long had he been living the same day over and over? He found himself longing for something new.

When he picked up the ring off the plasticrete he hoped, in the deepest corners of his unconscious, it might lead him on an adventure of some sort, even if it was just a trip to the local police station to turn it in.

Perhaps that was why he had been so willing to accept as possible and even natural the events occurring since then. But now in the safety of his home, he began to wonder: what had he got himself into? On the one hand, the prospect of a new tomorrow excited him, but on the other hand he longed for the safety of yesterday. The competing thoughts left him, if anything, slightly irritable. He glared at the ring, glowing palely in the light. It managed to look sincere.

He couldn't think about it now. He was too close, and way too new to the situation to fully comprehend it. Instead, he grabbed his beer and Top Ramen and collapsed into his couch, hand on the remote control. Perhaps watching the evening movie would dull his racing thoughts. If he remembered correctly, tonight's fare was a classic.

Instead, the news anchor from Channel Five swam into view. He was obviously excited. "…ief of Police Samuel Herbert of the Hunter Police department stated the two unidentified flying objects then landed in the alley between Second and Third Street in the Southern District. 'He explained the 'Mêlée In The Sky,' as the national media has dubbed it, happened so fast that authorities didn't have time to mobilize. When they finally tracked the combatants street-side, a barrier had been erected which prevented interference.

'There were witnesses, however, to what occurred next. For more, let's go live to the scene of the spectacular event. Sue?"

The picture shifted to Susan Jones, Trance's favorite reporter on the Channel Five team. Tonight she was wearing a cute purple outfit. She had her trusty "Channel Five - News When it Matters" microphone in her right hand, and had her left index finger in her ear. "Charles, I am with Fred Halberstam, who says he saw the whole thing."

The view panned out to show a man with glasses and a flannel shirt swaying slightly and nodding helpfully. "We are standing about a hundred yards from the mouth of the alley where the incident occurred." She said. "Unfortunately, we can't get any pictures to you of the scene itself. Every time our own Channel 5 Eye in the Sky goes in there, we lose clarity in the image."

"We've never let technical issues stand in the way of getting the news to our public, right Susan?" Charles' voice sounded over the feed. "Let's hear what Mr. Halberstam has to say."

Susan looked at Fred encouragingly and stabbed his nose with her microphone. "So, Mr. Halberstam, what happened tonight?"

Fred made a grab for the mic, but Susan quickly pulled it back, shaking her head. Trance laughed. What a pro.

Fred grimaced, but dropped his hands and was rewarded with the microphone being pointed in his direction again. "Well, Suthie, it's like thish," he sloshed, peering glassily into the camera, "I was walking home from er... work (hic), when all of a sudden, thegh two big bug fly out of the sky. They askthed for my schpare change, then tried to take all my money (hic). Well, I gave 'em a good uppercut with my right fistht, and they flew backward into the alley where they exploded. I think that I shaved the world tonight. Wanna get a beer or maybe some coffee? You and your friend sure are cute. Twins?"

At that point the feed cut back to Charles. "Well, there you have it folks," he said seriously, "Fred Halberstam saves the Southern District from Flying Bugs. We'll continue to bring you more on this late breaking story as we uncover the details. This is Charles Feist. Good Night."

"We now return you to the previously scheduled program, 'Attack of the Mutant Slugs,' starring Terry Allen and Jose Burns," the voice-over intoned. Trance switched the TV off in disgust.

"Are news reports on this planet always this accurate?" the ring questioned.

"I guess," Trance responded morosely. He'd almost forgotten he was even wearing the ring. He tried to wriggle it off his finger. It wouldn't budge. He sighed. "You're not going away, are you?"

"No. You'll get used to this eventually, Protector. I realize it is a lot to take in all at once."

"You got that right."

"In fact we're going to be together a long time. Why not just accept me? You'll be happier that way."

"I'm less than four hours into these thousand years of yours, and already I hate you."

"No you don't. In fact, you're starting to warm up to me. I can read you better than a book, remember? I'm part of you now." The ring looked up at him smugly.

Trance tapped his fingers on his thigh. Maybe the ring was right. He'd always considered himself a rational individual. The ring was there, he could see it. He could feel the metal band encircling his middle finger. He knew it was real, and believed it when it told him it wasn't going to leave. In short, the simple truth was whether he liked it or not he was stuck with the thing. Wasn't it Saint Bernard, or Saint Francis who said, "God grant me the Serenity to accept the things I cannot change, the Courage to change the things I can and the Wisdom to know the difference?"

"Actually, Reinhold Niebuhr wrote those words, in 1943," the ring said confidently.

"Huh? How do you know? Are you reading my mind?"

"No, you've been talking aloud to yourself for the past ten minutes, and there is an advertisement on your coffee table for a Serenity Prayer Hands keepsake medallion, only four easy payments of $25.99."

"Oh. Yeah, I was thinking about getting it for my mother for her birthday."

"Hmm. Not a bad price to pay for serenity."

Trance didn't respond. The ring had a point. Why not accept the path he was on? At least that way he might have some control over the direction it took. "So now what happens?" he asked.

"I suppose the Top Ramen you ate will be slowly digested as it passes from your stomach through your colon. However, that's a guess given what the stuff is made of. Do all humans eat as poorly as you?"

"That's not what I meant."

"What did you mean?"

"I meant, what do I do now? Are more of those sentry droids going to come looking for me?"

"Yes, but it should take some time. The 08-802 will have to be reported missing, no doubt. Then, a probe will be sent to determine the last known whereabouts, and then a couple of droids will be sent to finish the job. Or, they may just cut their losses and go after another Protector. So, let's say a week just to be safe. In the meantime, I need to get you trained."

"Yeah. But first, I need to know a little bit more about what I am up against. Who sent the droid in the first place?"

"Hmmm. Frankly, we're not sure."

"Well, what do you know?"

"I know a lot of things."

"Be more specific."

"I know the Top Ramen—"

"That's not what I meant!"

"What did you mean?"

"Piece of crap."

"Swear words are the most confusing piece of your vernacular. Is that a command of some sort?"

"No!" Trance glared at the ring in disgust. It was going to be -- check that, it had been -- a long night. "Start at the beginning. What are you? Who created you? Do you have any weaknesses, like kryptonite or yellow, or anything that I should be aware of before I run into it? Why did you choose me as a... a Protector?"

"Oh. You want a history lesson."

"Yeah."

"I was created along with thousands of other rings billions of years ago, by a race of beings so advanced as compared to your current civilization that they might seem magical to you. I am a machine, like one of your hovercrafts, yet I have no moving parts in need of fixing. I have what you might call a battery, but your sun will have burned out long before I need a replacement. In other words, to your perspective, I have nearly limitless energy."

"Energy which must be directed as I will it."

"Correct. I see you've been paying attention. Like all things, certain rules and laws govern our existence. I'll give you only the important ones for now. The first one is a ring's energies are directed by outside forces –that's you-- in most cases. The second rule is rings cannot be used in direct opposition to one another or their wielders."

"What do you mean?'

"I mean a Protector cannot form an energy construct –"

"Constructs are purely ring energy thingamajigs, like the sphere I created, right? I remember you mentioned something about them in the car."

"Right. I am impressed. It is an object created purely out of energy that may look like it has form but does not. When you create a construct, you must continue to will it to exist. When you stop willing it, the construct goes away. Constructs usually have a blue hue, and are translucent, but really excellent ones can be nearly indistinguishable from the real thing."

"So…"

"Ah. So, a Protector cannot use a construct against another Protector. Nor can a Protector attack another using energy beams or other direct means. There can be no direct opposition of rings."

"Direct opposition, huh. What about indirect? Could I create a real knife and stab another Protector if I wanted?"

"You certainly hail from a violent race. Why would you want to do that?"

"Well, I wouldn't, honestly. But could I?"

"Yes."

"Hmm. What's the next rule?"

"Heh. I'm quoting from the manual here…. 'A Protector's tour of Duty shall last a period of not less than 1000 years, unless the position is vacated due to death.' See, I didn't make it up."

"That version sounds different from the one that you quoted me earlier."

"You'll find the 'Declaration of Duty Length' several times in the manual. The Creators wanted to make sure no one would be deluded when they signed up. I was quoting from Section 1298.52.9887 before. The most recent quote was from page one, paragraph three in the introduction, entitled 'So You Want to Join the Corps... A Few Things You Should Know.' It's quite interesting and very informative."

"I'm sure. You said 'due to death.' It seems your limitless power would be able to keep a Protector from dying."

"Actually, it is near limitless, with certain restrictions."

"The rules that we've been discussing. But how does that apply to Protectors dying?"

"Weakness. It's the fourth rule.... But first, a little history:

'You see, originally the rings were created with no inherent weaknesses whatsoever. Of course, a Protector could still be overwhelmed, even then.

'At the very infancy of the corps' existence, a group of rogue Protectors defected and attempted to overthrow the Creators. They almost succeeded."

"Whoah. How is that possible?"

"If you shot Mr. Smith or Mr. Wesson with one of the rifles that they made, what would happen?"

"Huh. Point Taken. Please continue."

"A civil war waged throughout the known universe for five hundred years, led by the vicious golden dragon, Si-truc. Whole star systems were snuffed out in the battle for supremacy. We even lost a couple of galaxies. In the end, the rebellious Protectors were defeated in the Battle of Sector Brandenburg, near the moon of Korondor, though at great cost. As the last of the wounded and dying were removed from the sector, the remaining Creators decided there would never again be the chance for a rebellion. As the rings from our defeated comrades were recovered, they were given new directives: Number one, Rings can't be used directly against one another. You already know that. The second is each ring has a weakness, chosen at random at the time of impression with the new Protector. Only the Protector, his or her ring, and the Creators know what this weakness is. If the Protector is lucky, it is something unique to a certain sector, like the two-toed Pican of Sector Jugularam, or even a one-of–a-kind item such as a specific rock from a certain mountain range on the face of a moon circling the fourth planet of a solar system at the Universal Periphery."

"And if the Protector is unlucky?"

"It's completely random. You could get Oxygen, which is breathed by a good majority of the corps, or the word 'Hello' in any language. Whatever the weakness is, it disables the ring, leaving the Protector helpless. This is much easier than attempting to overwhelm a ring wielder with sheer power or inducing one to drop his or her guard, the other ways of killing a bearer. It's a safety valve of sorts.

'Once the Protector is dead, the ring can be drained and 'reformatted,' and then used to choose a replacement. A new weakness is instituted each time, and once chosen it can't be changed by anyone, even the Creators. It's hardwired into the ring's design and software."

"So, what is my weakness?"

"I'll get there momentarily. After the Battle of Korondor, whenever a tour of duty ended or a Protector died and his or her ring was recovered, the new rules and weaknesses were instituted."

"Yeah?"

"This system worked for many eons. But then something or someone began to wage a new war on the corps. Something has been discovering the individual weaknesses of the ring bearers and killing them. In the past two hundred and fifty years, we have lost one thousand members, and seven rings to this mysterious force."

"Huh."

"One month ago, the Creators decided that the next candidate who was chosen would receive a ring wiped clean of the rules and weaknesses that have guided the corps for as long as can be remembered." It paused dramatically. "I am that ring, and you are the chosen one, Trance Adams."

"So… you have no weaknesses, and I can use you on other Protectors…"

"Yes. My, you're quick. Except, of course you can still be overwhelmed and even killed. Especially given you are so green behind the ears."

"That's wet. Wet behind the ears," Trance sighed. "I have one question. Why me?"

"Because you were the next candidate chosen, and I was the next ring that happened to become available. If some other schmuck had been chosen, I'd be sitting in different living room right now. I wonder… do you think it would have been better decorated?"

Trance ignored the barb. "Why did you choose me and not somebody else?"

"Protector, I'm just a ring. I can't make decisions like that."

Trance grimaced and chose another track. "So, why remove all of the safeguards?"

The ring managed to look frustrated. "So you could find whatever has besieged the corps and put a stop to it, of course! We need to discover who is behind this, and how they are finding out what the weaknesses are. If you're just as vulnerable as everybody else, what good would you be?"

"And I suppose that sending a more experienced Protector would have been out of the question."

"That has been tried, numerous times to no avail." Trance sensed that 'numerous' was capitalized and had several squiggly lines under it. "You're a last ditch effort kind of thing. Rings in use can't be removed and reformatted, of course, without dire consequences, so they had to start with a fresh recruit."

"Dire? Consequences?"

"Pretty much in all cases the Protector suffered a mental breakdown, which would make it rather difficult to complete a mission such as this."

"Hmm. So, why don't the Creators just get involved with it? Swoop down from on-high and administer a righteous ass-kicking to whoever is messing with their crew? Surely they are more powerful and omnipotent than anybody else around here."

"Not really. Perhaps eons ago, when the first of the rings were created. In fact, they fought side by side with the loyal Protectors during the Revolt. But not now. They are an extremely long-lived race by your standards, but not an immortal or all-knowing one, and the technology to create new rings has been lost for just about as long as mammals have roamed this rock. All that is left is the ability to maintain the rings."

"Surely they can control them."

"Have you ever met a Creator?"

Trance thought momentarily of all of the strange people that he had encountered working for the State of Washington. "Um. Not that I am aware of. No, in fact, I am quite sure that I have not."

"They stopped wielding rings shortly after the rebellion ended."

"Why?"

"Who knows? They are the Creators. They make the decisions, not me."

"Oh." Trance nodded as though that explained it all. With a sigh, he cracked open another beer.

*****

Huge robots and tiny spheres stalked Trance throughout the night. Always a step behind, they taunted him ruthlessly and mercilessly.

"I'll get you my pretty, and your lovely ring too!" one of them screamed incessantly. Instead of laser beams or rockets they were armed with wicked-looking knives and blunt objects.

In the background, urging the robots and spheres on, a figure lurked, cloaked in darkness. Though he could not see its face across the length of his dreamscape, the shape looked suspiciously like his Astrocruiser.

Chapter 3: Good Morning!

The beeping intruded into his consciousness like a thief in the night – slowly but insidiously. Only when it reached a crescendo did it finally wake him. "What the heck…" Adams grunted, one eye peering dimly at the TimeDisc on his bedside table. Above the disc a glowing 3:05 AM could be seen. He hit "Snooze" several times in rapid succession, then with a sweep of his arm he sent the TimeDisc and his bedside table lamp crashing to the floor. The beeping continued unabated.

Trance vaulted out of bed nearly entangling himself in the sheets, then realized the source of the commotion was the ring. "What?! What?!" he yelled incoherently.

"You know how I said that whoever is behind this probably wouldn't attack for about a week?"

"Yeah," Trance responded, dread sinking in.

"So, we need to practice."

"What?! I thought this was an emergency!" Trance glared at the smugly glowing ring.

"You'll know it's an emergency one week from now when an angry troupe of sentry droids does a foxtrot on your ass."

"Forget that. I'm going back to sleep. I'll practice tomorrow morning." He scooped up the Timedisc, replaced it on his bedside table, and vaulted back into bed. He was asleep before his head hit the pillow.

*****

When Trance next awoke, the sun's rays were slamming themselves angrily against his window shade.

"Ohhhhhhhhhh," he grunted, holding his head in his hands. One fatigued, bloodshot eye crawled over to his clock. 12:30 PM floated brightly over the TimeDisc.

He crawled out of bed, and shuffled into the living room, glancing guiltily at the answering machine. It was blinking.

Somehow, he summoned the energy to hit the "Play" button.

"Greetings… owner's name," a sexy female voice called from the machine. "You have four new messages. Should I play them?"

"Yes, please," Trance responded, scratching his backside and yawning. Satisfied with those efforts, he twisted his neck around until his vertebrae crackled like a bowl of crisped rice. Ahh. Morning pleasures.

The answering system, meanwhile, had begun speaking in a male's voice. "10897… uh… 10897…" there was the sound of paper shuffling. "-0678," the voice rallied, "this is your supervisor, CX1089-69875. It is my duty to inform you that it is 8:03AM. As you know, your position requires that you be here at 8:00AM, promptly. Though it gives me no pleasure, I must inform you that your pay will be docked for the three… now four minutes that you are tardy. Please remember in the future that we here at the Document Security Department, and the State of Washington., wish to provide the best customer service possible, between the hours of 8:00 AM and 5:00 PM, and we can't do that if we arrive at…8:0… 8:05. Thanks."

"Delete message. Play next message," Trance grumbled.

"10897… uh… damn … 10897…" there was the sound of paper shuffling. "0678," the same male voice spoke, this is your supervisor, CX1089-69875, again. It is my duty to inform you that it is now… 8:15 AM. As you know your position requires—"

"Delete message. Play next message."

"10897-0678, this is 15898-7898, down in Human Resources in Olympia," a bored and rather peevish female voice spoke through the machine. "It is now… 10:16 in the morning. The D15-R16 Attendance Report from the Hunter, Washington office indicated your lack of attendance for today. Since a check of our files shows you did not fill out the 1458-H-190 Sick Leave Request form one week in advance, I must assume that you wish to take this time as unpaid. Could you please call me at (555-898) 458-5589 so that we can discuss the overpayment resulting from your negligence of duty? Thanks so much, and have a nice day!" She signed off, and the answering machine beeped soundly.

Trance sighed. How come bureaucracies only moved fast when their own money was at stake? "Delete message. Play next message" he said as he moved to the kitchen and poured himself some cereal.

"10897…." It was his supervisor, again. "10897… Oh for heaven's sake, Trance, this is Barry. Look. It's 10:30. I've called several times. Where the heck are you? God, I hope you didn't get caught in the attack last night. I heard a swarm of bugs killed several people, and set half the East Side on fire. Good thing Fred Halberstam was there. Now that's my kind of hero. Anyway, if you're still alive, get here when you can, will you? If you did die in the attack, well, err… I guess I'll see you later."

Trance sighed again, and around bites of Lieutenant Crunch Berries instructed the answering system to delete the final communication. "Messages deleted, owner's name," it said helpfully. "Is there anything else that I can do?"

"Call work," he said munching happily.

"That's a long distance call," sexy voice said doubtfully. "Are you sure that you want me to complete it?" Due to the regulation cuts made by recent federal administrations, the cellular and local telephone companies were able to choose any rates they wanted. The apartment across the hallway was now a long distance call.

"Yes Please."

"I can do that, owner's name," sexy voice replied.

"Patch it through to the dining area," Trance yawned. "Voice only."

"Thanks for calling Document Security,"

"Yes, this is 10897-0678 -"

"Your call is very important to us which is why we use this answering system instead of real people. Please listen carefully to the following 75 options before choosing. Choosing before listening to all of the options will restart this message….. If you would like to request forms be sent to you, please press or say 1, then 89998, then 45B2…. If you would like forms sent to someone else, please press or say 2, then 878857 then 46B1…. If you would like to make a complaint regarding forms, please press or say 3 then 88987 then 658HI…"

Trance yawned again, and after tossing his bowl and spoon into the sink, stumbled into the bathroom and took a long shower. After getting dressed, he wandered back into the dining area. "…if you would like to leave a message regarding forms, please press or say 75 then 588 then 15B. If you wish to speak with a human, please stay on the line. "

Several minutes passed. Trance spent the time preparing himself to speak with his boss by sniffing and coughing and working up phlegm. While doing this, he wandered around the house looking for props. Then a peevish voice came on the line. "Thanks for calling the Document Security Department. This is Mimi Saberhagen. How may I help you?" She was the old man's secretary; the guard dog.

Trance quickly stuck his finger down his throat, gagged and coughed. "Hey, Mimi. This is Trance…Hurgh… Belch."

"Trance! Where the heck are you? The old man is riding everybody! Do you think that the D29 dash 16A's get out of town on their own?"

Trance sneezed. "Can't you tell I'm sick?" he asked irritably, working up more phlegm.

"Hmp. I sure hope you filled out a 1458-H-190." The rest of the conversation didn't go any better. After several minutes of begging, he finally got Mimi to put their supervisor on the phone.

"Hey, boss," Trance wheezed when they were finally connected, "This is 10897-0678."

"Who?"

"Trance. Trance Adams."

"Trance! By gosh, you did make it through the attack!"

"Uh, yeah. What attack?" He faked a sneeze.

"Just turn on the news on your way in here. It's all over."

"Actually, boss, I'm sick. Can't you tell from my voice?"

"How could you be sick? I don't have a 1458-H-190 on my desk." Trance heard the distinctive note of papers being shuffled.

"I just found out this morning. Also, I am going to have to request all my vacation time and sick leave…. I uh… lost my grandfather." The papers stopped shuffling.

For a heartbeat there was silence on the line. Then, "Your grandfather died three years ago."

"No, we only lost him. He turned up, eventually."

"Huh. So is he dead or just lost this time?"

"Boss, that's a heck of a question to ask someone who just lost his grandfather," Trance sneezed. "My feelings are hurt."

"Look, I'm sorry. I am really, really sorry. Please don't sue me over this, Trance. It's been busy here, and I just wasn't thinking clearly. What can I do?"

"Well, like I said, I need to request some time off. How much do I have?"

"Just a sec. Let me pull up your files…."

Trance managed to work out a deal with his supervisor. After some wrangling, he agreed to forget the slight that Barry had perpetrated upon him regarding Trance's grandfather. In return, Barry would give him the full sum of his vacation and sick leave -- one year in total.

It was a dirty trick, but an effective one. In his mind, Barry avoided a lawsuit, which Trance could have won but never would have filed anyway, and Trance got the time he needed.

Unfortunately, life in the United States had become overly litigious, and everyone was extremely wary. Trance himself had been sued twice that week – once for accidentally cutting a person off on the freeway, and another when he mistakenly had twelve items in a ten-item checkout lane.

After signing some papers Barry instafaxed over, Trance ended the call. "Boy," said the ring, "I can't believe you got away with that."

"Oh? It's really hard for a state employee to lose his job. I've heard of folks setting their desks on fire, and still getting to go to work the next day."

The ring thought for a moment. "Are they hiring?"

"You already have a job. It's to annoy me."

"Yeah. I'm good at what I do."

"So, Now what?" he asked the ring.

"Well, now we start training," the ring said in a voice hinting at lots of work and sweating.

"So, is this all you do? Make wisecracks and train people?"

"No, you forget. I also make bets."

"Oh."

"Look, it's my job to get you started on the path to being a successful ring bearer. I have to teach you the basics like elementary construct building and flying. Once I feel you're ready for the next stage, we'll call in more advanced Protector who will train you in higher theory."

"Oh yeah? A real alien -- wow."

"May I remind you, Protector, that you have already met an alien?"

"Oh, yeah, the Sentry droid or whatever."

The ring continued unperturbed. "You may choose him or her as your mentor. A lot of candidates do. Once a bond has been sufficiently established, the real training begins with the introduction of the squad instructor."

"Your Creators sure are excited about me learning how to use you," Trance griped.

"Protector, I say this without sense of boasting: I am the most powerful weapon in the entire Universe. You are the Universe's newest Protector, a being representing one of the most backward and unintelligent races the Universe has yet known. You have been given the most difficult task ever assigned to one of the corps. You need training."

"Well, when you put it that way…"

"So, as I was saying, after we get the training started, it's off to Monidad for the Great Tour."

"Monidad?"

"Yeah. I'll explain that one later. OK, first, let's go to your moon."
Trance nodded, formed the familiar jet pack in his mind and started to will it into being. "Not like that!" the ring barked irritably.

"Huh?" The pack disappeared with an audible pop.

"You can fly without the aid of that. Create an invisible bubble of air and heat around you, and then use your will to force that bubble to lift off the ground. It's actually pretty simple."

This "pretty simple" task took more than an hour to complete. He discovered the hard way that just creating a bubble and adding some heat and oxygen wasn't enough.

One also had to add more oxygen as the initial supply was used up and continually heat the enclosure without cooking his body. The ring snippily informed him of this necessity when reviving him after he passed out from carbon monoxide poisoning. It also let him know that it could regulate and replace oxygen and monitor heat for him if he wanted. He heartily agreed.

That settled, they worked on getting him airborne. Flying was a lot harder without the crutch of the jetpack, at least at first. With the pack in place, he'd had the luxury of relying upon technology that was proven, reliable, and comfortable. His faith in the thing had provided the necessary stability to make the construct work. Now he was faced with the prospect of relying on his own willpower and the "magic" of the ring's energy rather than known equipment. He had to find the faith quickly in order to survive.

Several near misses and a painful bruise on his tailbone later, Trance was finally airborne for good. Once this task had been completed, he discovered it was easy to direct his flight path. At this point he also asked the ring to teach him how to mask his radar signature so he might avoid an embarrassing encounter with his country's Civil Air Defense Patrol fighters. The CADP had notoriously itchy trigger fingers on a normal day – he could only wonder how they would react the morning after a "major" attack like the one the night before. He made it out of the atmosphere without incident.

Chapter 4: Second Contact

He landed on the moon and discovered it was more or less like he had expected it: silent, gray, and dusty. What caught his breath, however, was looking up at the Earth, sparkling like a gem in the night sky. It was the most beautiful thing he had ever seen.

"There are other worlds out there, Trance," the ring whispered into his reverie. "You'll see sights that will make you ache for all their beauty."

"But those sights could never replace this one," Trance responded.

"That's right. There is nothing that could do that."

Trance sat there for awhile, taking in the sight of his beloved planet while feeling the sand of the moon rush through his fingers like a stream. Somehow, the bubble around him allowed his fingers to feel the coarseness of the individual grains but kept the bitter cold at bay.

Eventually, the ring spoke again. "Sorry to interrupt, Protector, but we really do have to continue the training. There is only so much time."

The ring then proceeded to run Trance through a series of increasingly complicated exercises designed to increase willpower and stamina. Through this training, he found he could easily increase and decrease his speed when flying with no ill effects.

He had initially been afraid sudden bursts in speed might cause his brain to pulp itself against the back of his skull, but the ring showed him this was not the case. When asked why, the ring gave him a strange long-winded explanation which sounded like, "You don't actually move. I move space around you." But the answer sounded so silly and preposterous he laughed at the joke and dropped the subject. He didn't notice the ring failed to laugh with him.

They practiced after that for nearly ten hours straight with occasional breaks so Trance could eat or expel waste. Every minute he was using the ring was a new and exciting moment. He learned far more in those few hours than he had learned in his entire life, and yet he knew he had only just begun. He discovered again what a tremendous joy it was to learn new things. He drank the knowledge like a man dying of thirst, soaking in as much as he could.

They started with constructs. Trance found that while creating simple things like a sphere, or a jetpack had been fairly easy in the heat of the battle with the droid, they were much more difficult during practice. It was exasperating. He could see in his head the image the ring asked him to create, but getting it to form was difficult. Things kept intruding in his concentration: the achingly beautiful disk of the world in the corner of his eyes, the tiny pinpricks of the stars – it was all too much to bear.

He could hardly believe his good fortune to be alive now, with the ring as his guide to new worlds, new adventures. Yes, certainly there was a war on somewhere, and there were mysteries to be solved and lives to save, but here and now there was only him and the ring. And practice.

The ring berated him constantly, complaining bitterly that he wasn't concentrating as hard as he should or working as hard as he could. But in its voice he noted a deep sense of satisfaction with his efforts.

When they finished practicing for the day, back at his apartment, after a warm Top Ramen and a cold beer, Trance asked it what it thought of his progression thus far.

The ring grudgingly admitted he had done fairly well for his second day. "But don't get excited, Protector. We're still in deep trouble," it grunted. "I have only a few days before I need to pass you off for more advanced training. Usually, the entire process can last at least ten of your years or more, but we just don't have the time."

"Why the rush?" Trance asked. "I thought we had some time."

"Protector, that is a story for another time. Right now, it is late. You need to get to sleep. Tomorrow, we are going to study simple knives and stabbing weapons and how to create them using me, your Ring."

"That sounds exciting."

"It's not. Trust me."

"Oh." He thought for a moment, then looked at the ring again. "There is a lot of crime on my planet," he said, "a lot of pollution and many problems that need fixing."

"Yes. A lot of things are at this very moment going horribly wrong. People are being robbed by other people, there are two natural disasters about to occur, and global warming progresses unchecked."

"So, maybe I need to fix some of those things."

"I am really sorry, Protector, but this sector is a Restricted Zone, which means 'hands off.' We absolutely cannot interfere."

"Why not? I evidently have the power to make some real and lasting changes."

"Yes, your statements make sense. Start with bank robbers for instance. Stop the murders, take all the pollution and trash and send it on a one-way trip to the moon. But what next? What real changes have you made? You certainly haven't given the companies reason to stop polluting. In fact, you've just given them an open ticket to keep it up, and what important lesson has your race learned? There aren't any consequences, no reason to change. There is no motivation to grow, and that is a step backward."

"But what about problems like hunger and war?"

"Humans hate it when someone with more power comes in and changes things. Look at your own country's involvement in Iraq and Afghanistan and Iran during the past hundred years. Your leaders felt they were doing the right thing by going in there and making changes."

"They got rid of dictators who had killed thousands."

"How many thousands more did they kill in the effort? If you were living within the society, would you have seen heroes or invaders?"

"Ah. Point taken."

"And how do those people feel about your country now?"

"They still hate us."

"You can't change a society from the outside with an iron fist. You'll risk strengthening the bonds of society rather than dissolving them. You must work from within. It is perhaps better that you become involved by volunteering and encouraging your friends to donate time and money to causes they believe firmly in. That's the real way to make lasting changes."

Trance sighed. "Maybe you're right. But I hate to sit on the sidelines and not act."

"How many hours did you volunteer last week?"

"Um. None."

"What about the past year?"

"I made a small donation to the local food bank..."

"My point exactly. Look, your race has to figure things out on its own. It's still in its infancy, and if you interfere too much, it may not grow and reach its potential.

'You're on the Restricted List because you have the raw materials and the drive to become a space-faring race. The Conglomerated States has been very careful to shield you from the true nature of the Universe so as to not unduly influence or frighten you."

"We have to find our own way to you."

"Yes. Granted, you might blow yourselves up in the meantime, but that's a decision you have to make on your own."

*****

Two more days of practice slipped by like they were on greased wheels. Trance spent a majority of the time on the Moon, but ventured out as far as Mars once. The sheer beauty of space awed him, and left him in a philosophical mood frequently. When they were taking a break late in the afternoon of the second day, Trance looked down at the ring. Perhaps now might be as good a time as any to talk.

Trance was sprawled out in a Lazy Boy with his feet up. He'd been forced to create a simple seatbelt to stay in the thing, but it was worth it. The Lazy Boy had patches in several places and the gearing needed some attention- it was his first major purchase out of college many years back and had seen a lot of use - but it fit his body perfectly. He let it gently rotate in the silent vacuum of space. It was dizzying but fun to see the stars spin around. They were nearly half-way between Mars and the Earth.

"It sure is beautiful out here," Trance said, commenting on the stars glimmering in the firmament. "Except for the bad guys we're hunting, is everyone pretty much enlightened?"

"Explain." The ring sounded a little grumpy.

"I mean, do all the different races sit around and drink tea together and talk about how to solve the Universe's problems?"

"Not really. Everyone is too busy living life."

"Oh." Trance mulled this over in his head a moment. "I guess I had hoped you all might have been more advanced than us hicks," he grumbled.

"Oh, we're much more advanced than you, don't get me wrong. But, nonetheless we still have mundane worries like war, taxes, and sales quotas."

"What about the corps of Protectors?"

"What about it?"

"I guess I imagined the corps is this highly skilled and perfect police force traveling around the universe saving people from crime and helping get cats out of trees," Trance said tentatively. "It's more of a working theory, though. I'm open to revisions."

"Currently, the corps is spread mighty thin," the ring said in a serious voice. "We've had to reposition to more effectively cover the border between the Conglomerated States and the lawless regions."

"The what?"

"Look, space is pretty vast, with about two trillion galaxies, and we don't actually cover the entire universe, per se. There are vast areas our influence has yet to touch: the lawless regions."

"I thought you'd all be above calling people outside your society 'lawless.' Are they also called barbarians?"

"The names vary depending upon the people. We call them 'lawless' because many of them are."

"I bet the inhabitants of those regions don't call themselves lawless."

"True. The largest region calls itself 'The Cluster,' and is ruled by an Emperor, if you can believe the rumors."

"Why not just talk with them and find out for sure?"

"Protector, I don't mean to sound rude, we've already tried that. You see, we've had a lot more time to think about the situation than you have."

"Oh?"

"In fact, we've made numerous entreaties in that regard. We stopped sending live ambassadors several thousand years ago when our last emissaries came back in little boxes."

"Oh."

"I mean really little boxes."

"Gotcha."

"I mean boxes so little that—"

"OK, ring, I get the point."

"Just making sure."

"So there is a lot of the Universe that you haven't encountered. A lot of people that you haven't met."

"That's right."

"So, how can you say that you're the most powerful weapon in the Universe? You don't really know for sure."

"True, but you have no reason to complain. Your own race makes assumptions. I only need to cite your 'World Series' which is only played in one country. The winner of the contest is called the 'World Champ.' How real is that?

'Anyway, if I may continue," the ring said, "In the past thousand years we've encountered more and more skirmishes along the border. In the past three hundred years we've experienced outright raids. We're starting to get them by the hour now.

'Something or someone is encouraging them. With each and every ring lost, the attackers become more brazen.

'The outer regions just aren't safe right now. As a result exploration and colonization are down, and the economy is headed in the same direction. Economic experts are predicting a recession at this point. If we don't do something quick, the Conglomerated States could spiral down into a depression."

"Come on," Trance said sarcastically. "What can one man do to stem the tide of the Universe?"

"I think that we're going to find out, yes?"

"Sure, but—"

Just then, everything exploded in fire. He found himself spinning out of control, the Lazy Boy shredding itself around him. His ears were ringing, and his vision hazy. He jettisoned the chair, trying to right himself. Just as he had freed himself of it, it exploded completely in a perfect sphere of fire and debris.

He righted himself quickly using a trick the ring had taught him in lessons a few days earlier. He used the ring again to track his attackers as he strengthened his shield around him. There were two blips coming at him. He enhanced his vision so he could get a good look at them.

Both of the attackers shone slightly in the starlight. They were both gunmetal gray, and resembled something he had once seen in a children's fantasy book. Or perhaps he had seen something like them in a nightmare.

One had two arms and two legs, each ending in four sharp looking claws. It had a barrel-like torso, atop of which sat a moon-shaped head with two bright yellow eyes, a strawberry-shaped nose, and mouth splitting the face from ear to ear. Dozens of razor sharp teeth protruded from between its lips. Two evil looking horns jutted from the top of the head. It also had a busy tail.

The other looked like a cross between a goat and a robot. It too had a couple of horns jutting from its head. It had an elongated snout, two beady coal black eyes, four short segmented legs, and a stubby tail which was wagging furiously.

"These are Battle Droids, Protector," the ring said in a worried tone. "They are a step up from the sentry droid, in a big way. Watch yourself. The only reason you're still alive right now is because they are playing with you."

"Right. I was going to let them just pummel me into submission, but maybe I will fight instead," Trance responded bitterly, his heart pounding between his ears as he watched the two approach, one high and the other low.

Bushy Tail struck first; a missile screaming soundlessly out from one of its arms. Trance created a large calloused blue hand with the ring, reached out, grabbed the missile, and sent it shooting at Goat-bot. He then used the hand to smack back Bushy tail, landing a shot directly on the strawberry shaped nose. As he did so, he raced upward, narrowly avoiding two more missiles and a dozen laser shards.

The missile exploded harmlessly in front of Goat-bot, burned out of the sky by shots fired from its horns. The horns then twisted and centered in on Trance as he flew upward. Trance turned this way and that, relying on luck and speed to avoid being lanced by the beams Goat-bot was shooting.

It was hard concentrating on avoiding two different attacks at once. "What do I do?" he screamed to the ring.

"Fight back!" the ring yelled. Helpful bastard.

Just then, Trance ran into the remains of his Lazy Boy. "Aaargh!" he yelled again, trying to wipe the powdery debris from his face. Of all the ignominies he'd suffered, being felled by his own recliner was the worst. Unfortunately, both Battle Droids used that lost moment to their advantage, and he was rocked again and again by tremendous blasts that impacted his personal shield. The darn thing seemed to stop missiles better than it did pieces of chair, thank goodness. It held, barely.

He shook his head. His eyes were finally clear, now. The Battle Droids were only a hundred yards away, hitting his shield with everything they had. His shield groaned in abject terror, and he knew it wouldn't hold long. He bellowed in frustration. What the heck did they think they were doing ruining his favorite chair and trying to kill him?

Two massive hands snaked out of his ring and wrapped themselves tightly around the two robots. Before they could react, he drew the hands a dozen yards apart and slammed them together as hard as he could. Both of the droids looked at him owlishly and began struggling furiously. He held on tightly and spread the hands again. "Have you two met?" he asked rhetorically before slamming them together.

This time, he was rewarded by the sight of Bushy Tail's head popping off. Tiny wires in its neck sparked dimly, and some sort of fluid pumped itself out into the vacuum of space before freezing into tiny globules. Bushy Tail's arms flailed randomly, and then set about twitching. It was dead.

Goat-Bot's eyes narrowed suspiciously, and it began to fire what appeared to be rose petals at Trance. They shattered harmlessly against his shield. Trance laughed in spite of himself, and squeezed the bot until he saw it shatter. The threat was over, for now.

"You know, it's funny," the ring said.

"What's funny?"

"When you're angry, you make things happen that I've only seen veteran Protectors do, and I think maybe, just maybe, we have a chance."

Trance felt warm all over. "Hey, thanks."

"I wasn't finished."

"Oh?"

"What I was going to say was that, when you're not angry, you suck really badly. In fact, I start to make plans on how I'm going to train the next individual who wears me."

"You have a real way with words," Trance said, the warm feeling evaporating into space.

"Oh, yes. I know many of them."

Chapter 5: Dexter

One day, their training regimen led them back to Mars. Trance felt like he was slowly getting the hang of things. He had moved beyond knives and onto constructs containing hinges and other moving parts. Most of his creations were simple and rough around the edges, but each day he saw small advances in their form.

He was also learning a finesse of sorts – the ring was massively powerful, and needed only a fraction of its energy to make a single construct. Too much energy into a construct would cause it to explode, decimating the local landscape. Not enough energy and his idea would never form.

Currently, though, he was resting comfortably in an air enclosure on Mars' surface. The half- bubble of air he had made was approximately fifteen feet across, and ten feet high. It was a balmy seventy degrees inside, and Trance was wearing Bermuda shorts and a white Hawaiian shirt. He was lying in a soft lawn chair and sipping a piña-colada he had brought from home for just this occasion.

It had been a bruising morning. He had asked the ring to create imaginary droids to spar with, and they had given him a sound thrashing. As a result, he gained several welts along his side and chest, and his arm felt as though it had been ripped from its socket, which it very nearly had. He gingerly felt his left eye – it too was developing a twinge and even now threatened to swell shut. He groaned. "Those droids were tough," he said. "It felt like they were really trying to kill me."

"Oh, they were," the ring responded seriously. "In fact, I lost quite a bit of money when you eventually beat them."

"Sometimes, I think you are far too honest."

"You want me to lie then? I can if you want."

"No. I think lying would be much worse. I always want you to be honest with me."

"Okay then…." The ring said in a voice that suggested it might have a great deal of difficulty keeping its promise.

Trance tried a different track. "Those droids came awfully close to seriously hurting me. I've been practicing my ass off, but I never seem to beat what's thrown at me with skill…. Just plain dumb luck."

"Well, you let your guard down for just a second, and they pounced. It was a simple mistake, but in a real battle you would have been killed. Here, you just got some bruises."

"I wish I could go back in time and fix my mistakes," Trance sighed wistfully.

"But then, you'd never learn," the ring replied smartly.

"Is time travel even possible?" Trance asked. "I mean, you can do pretty much everything."

"That's one of the few things that I can't do on my own. It just takes way too much energy," chimed the ring. "In fact, it's actually quite difficult and rather unproductive even in conjunction with other rings."

"Yeah? How so?"

"This is another one of those manual issues, but I'll let it slide on account of you still don't have one."

"I figured you might. One of these days I will need to get one."

"Probably." It slipped into the lawyer voice. As it spoke, fiery words appeared out of thin air five feet from them. "Many of the following rules are universal physical laws that cannot be broken even by me. Here they are:

1. Due to energy constraints (see below), the only way to travel back in time is to do so as an apparition. This means you can only be passive observer, because you aren't really solid. Others can see you, so Protectors are encouraged to be cautious.

2. Time travel is extremely difficult and requires a great deal of ring energy. In fact, rings have just enough free energy to record the event being witnessed, and keep up life support.

3. Time Travel is very dangerous. It should not be attempted by someone new, or alone. Large groups are encouraged but not required.

4. Travel can only occur during the time that you, the traveler, have been alive. The reason is there are two points of reference which must be held by the traveler: Present and Past. A string is created between these two points, and the Protector travels along it.

5. The oldest person of the group provides the time reference generally.

6. For every person that goes back, one Protector must hold their string in the present. Another person can act as a backup in case one string breaks.

7. Using your ring for anything other than holding the string (besides the aforementioned other tasks) will break the string.

8. Traveling too far from the physical location will break the string.

"Whoa," Trance broke in. "Even I know locations change over time. Isn't everything traveling at millions of miles an hour?"

"First of all, it's not polite to interrupt," the ring responded petulantly, slipping into its normal voice. "Second of all, you're not even close on the speed. Metaphysical and physical get all twisted up when you journey through time. I can't explain it in a way that will make sense to your small mind. Just believe it is possible. Now," it slipped back into lawyer mode, "as I was saying (ahem):

9. If one string breaks, the rings automatically return the remaining strings to starting point.

"Only nine rules? Hmp."

"Don't be rude. It doesn't become you."

"You have to abide by a lot of rules, is what I mean."

"Of course. Not to change the subject, but our company is almost here. However, before he arrives, I have to warn you about something."

"What? He's an alien?" Trance snickered. The thrill of seeing aliens had worn off after the last three aliens he had met had tried to kill him.

"No. There's really no good way to say this: one possible theory is the saboteur is a Protector."

"Really. Dissention from within. Hmmm."

"I am being serious, Protector. It's happened before. It is within the realm of possibility that it could be happening again."

"Oh?"

"Unfortunately, there isn't time to fully explain the history of the corps now. You'll hear more about it during the Great Tour."

"A tour? Like in a museum? I don't really care for those."

"No, *The* Great Tour. Pay attention, Trance."

"Oh."

"Now listen carefully, we have only seconds. Creator MasTho, the head of the Council, believes the saboteur is a Protector, and there may actually be more than one. He further believes the rogue may be a member of your squad. That's why you are joining this particular one. Also, your inclusion into the corps was handled exactly like every other Protector. Your stated weakness is rose petals."

"I wondered why roses kept coming up."

"Yes. Interesting, huh? That's part of the mystery. How did they know?"

"I have no idea. Why does, uh, MasTho think a member of my squad is involved?"

"He is a Creator."

"Yeah. And?"

"There is no more to tell: he's a Creator. We don't ask 'Why?'"

"Oh."

"As I was saying, there is some dissention within the council. Many theories abound. One theory is that threat comes from outside the corps.

Another is that it might actually be someone on the Council. Another is there are multiple Protectors involved from many different squads. No one knows. Just keep this in mind: anyone you meet now and in the future could be a friend or an enemy, and there is no way to tell which is which."

"Ugh. Talk about pressure."

"Yes. Other squads are suspected in containing a rogue Protector. They have been called to Monidad for various contrived reasons, and will be present when you are there. This should help in your investigation. You should make an effort to meet them. Oh! He is here."

Trance's jaw dropped in amazement. Landing a few feet before him on all four paws was what appeared to be an orange and white striped male tabby housecat. Dexter.

As the orange cat sauntered slowly toward him, the ring confidently corrected Trance saying Dexter was an Emilian from the planet Emilius rather than a feline from Earth. "Emilius is in a twin star system," the ring said knowledgeably. "Non-ring bearing Emilians only live to an average age of 25 years. The species is in the early pre-industrial period of existence, and are in Restricted Zone XX9767.0123. They are an extremely peaceful race, unlike yours. Many believe that given time, Emilius will join the Conglomerated States. This will probably not be the case for thousands of years, though."

"So, what are the chances of Earth joining this Conglomeration?"

"You mean if/when it develops interstellar space travel?"

"Yeah."

"It's possible, though at this stage doubtful. Like I said a few days ago, you have all the raw materials. But frankly, your species is just too war-like. It would have to change drastically in order to be seriously considered for inclusion."

"We're a lot more peaceful than we used to be."

"I shudder to think. Do you know that at this time, I count four major wars, and seventy-five minor skirmishes?"

"Power hungry dictators," Trance scoffed. "Those folks are always bad. I live in the United States of America. The good old US of A. If any of them get really serious, we'll go in there and clean up. Everything will be ok in the end."

"I thought we already talked about this. Your United States started most of those wars! The countries at the heart of all of the skirmishes are headed by rival dictatorships that your own Central 'Intelligence' Agency set up less than ten years ago! How can you possibly say such things?"

"Yes. Well. You can't be right all the time. Bad eggs breaking omelets, and all that. Shall we meet Dexter?" The cat had finally reached them, providing a welcome break from yet another lecture.

Trance liked Dexter immediately, though he constantly had to strike down the desire to scratch him behind the ears and offer him catnip. Dexter was 12 years old, middle age for Emilius, but was almost as youthful as Trance relative to the thousand year commitment. He had only been wielding a ring for two years.

Dex appeared to be both intelligent and observant, but had a fun-loving streak and general disregard of the law that tended to get him in trouble. He loved to drink and joke, but he was the kind of Protector that you might like to have behind you in a close quarters fight-- regardless of whether or not he started it. Unfortunately, also in close quarters you might note with some dismay that the cat had ambivalent feelings at best about cleanliness.

"So, you're the newest recruit," Dex said as way of introduction. He offered a paw to shake. Trance bent down and grasped it warmly. He noted Dexter had a furry, opposable, thumb. A smaller version of his ring graced the cat's other front paw.

"Oh! You speak English?" he asked in amazement.

"No. I speak Emilian Standard. Your ring translates for you automatically."

"That's odd. Your mouth even looks like it is saying English words."

"Another trick, I'm afraid. Your ring protects your brain – it shields the stimulus of hearing and seeing the real language interlaced with the translation. It makes everything really smooth for your mind."

"Oh. Neat trick."

"It works the same for written words, too, by the way. Every word you see will be translated automatically into English, though there might be a delay when your ring is under pressure or in action."

Trance smiled. "Nice to meet you," he said. "So, you're an Emilian."

"Yup. Don't hold it against me."

Trance laughed. "Don't worry. I won't."

"Alright. And you're a human. I don't think there's anything wrong with being from Earth, but unfortunately, I'm in the minority. There is a lot of disrespect out there for Earthlings, so watch out. You'll never catch any of that crap from a fellow Protector, but you will from some of the other quarters we'll land in."

"On account of our war-like nature?"

"No. Humans in general are seen to be... how do I put this... you're like the cousin nobody likes to invite to the party on account of he's a little weird."

Trance, who had such a cousin, shuddered. "I see."

"Aw. Don't take it too badly, fellow. I never get invited to parties either, on account of my being too sexy to handle. I ooze sex appeal, you see. It disarms the ladies and offends the men." He sighed. "It's tough being me."

"Oh. So that's what that smell is. I could have sworn it was kitty litter."

"Maybe that, too." He smiled. "So, I've been assigned to walk you through the ropes, a little."

"Oh? Yeah, the ring mentioned something along those lines."

"It's part of the first rate training schedule Aura, our squad trainer, set up for our squad: let your ring introduce the basics, then bring in another newbie to soften the edges before getting to the more advanced stuff with a Protector who has been around for a good long while.

'In a month or so, Aura will meet up with us. He'll be your official trainer. We've both been educated on the pre-emergent worlds in this sector. In fact, he's made quite a career out of studying your Earth's history."

"Anything in particular?"

"Please don't get him started. His favorite topic is the Middle Ages."

"Don't worry. I suck at history."

"And politics," his ring snipped, "among a great many other things."

*****

After running Trance through some basic exercises that tested his speed and agility, Dexter decided they needed to do something fun for a change. "I know this great bar," he explained. "We can go there and put up our feet and trade dirty jokes."

"I don't suppose it is the same bar that you were taking bets out on me with," Trance grumbled internally.

"Nah, I don't think I'll ever be able to get there, the way things are going here," came the reply. "Besides, I had them transfer the money to a special account I have."

"You don't even use money. What possible need do you have for it?"

"I use it to make bets with. What else is there?"

"Never mind."

Meanwhile, Dexter had been talking quietly with his ring. He looked up at Trance. "OK, that bar is just a short hop from here. It'll take just a few seconds. You ready?"

Trance nodded. "Sure. I'll just follow you, I guess. Don't go too fast for me."

The cat laughed. "No, we're traveling by Gray Space," he said.

"Oh. How do I get there?"

"Sit back and relax, if you can. I'll have us there momentarily. Just remember, though, none of it is real." Dexter's ring glowed briefly, sending out a disk that slipped through the night and came to rest a few feet in front of them. It constricted to a dot, then exploded, sending streams of light back toward and then around them. Behind the streams of blue, a deep and formless gray bled around him, obscuring Trance's vision momentarily. Suddenly, it was impossible to tell distances. He was sure Dexter was right next to him, but the cat seemed as if he was hundreds of miles away. When he reached out to touch Dexter, the tip of his finger seemed to stretch into infinity, a thin human colored strand the thickness of a human hair, (and yet as wide and deep as a river) connecting it and his hand. He tried to call out to Dexter, but the words just wouldn't come out, and then they did and they had form, little "Hey"s floating around momentarily. But then they slipped to the side and flew away behind the two Protectors.

Dexter turned, and his mouth formed as if saying something, his jaw dropping down like a puppet's, little screws on either side, and a wooden grain throughout. The cat pointed ahead, to a single dot of black amidst the formlessness; a single point a million miles away or maybe close enough to touch. It rose up to meet them, and then they were through.

Normal space never looked so full, or so inviting. Trance groaned in appreciation. "The first time I went through Gray Space, I threw up," Dexter commented. "If you can manage to relax, it won't be so bad next time."

"Erg," Trance said. "That took forever."

"Nah. Just a few seconds. And look how far we've come."

Sure enough, they had traveled a long distance. Looking around, Trance could see the same familiar constellations from his night sky, but here they looked warped as if someone had come along with a stick and jumbled them around a bit. "Neat," he replied.

Chapter 6: Legs

Dexter's favorite bar turned out to be a seedy joint set into an asteroid floating aimlessly in a nameless star system near to where they had popped out into normal space. A large neon sign on the front of it stated in alien letters "Legs" could be found inside. A large blue and white holographic tentacle with a fishnet stocking wrapped suggestively around it bent and flexed provocatively around the letters. "Great. An alien strip club," Trance sighed. They stopped before the airlock and the cat floated up and tapped on the door. It opened with a creak.

"Watch yourself. It's best that no one knows what we do for a living," Dexter whispered to Trance as they stepped inside. "They aren't too keen on Protectors here, but they serve an excellent brew and the entertainment can be exquisite." He thought for a moment. "I've asked my ring to create a closed circuit between us, like we're in space. It will be in effect whenever we want to talk. That way, we'll be able to hear each other perfectly no matter how noisy it is."

The airlock opened into a short hallway with one door at the end and a naked light bulb hanging by a wire in the middle. The door had probably once been bare wood, but now was covered with a greasy slick sheen one might expect in such an establishment. A 2-D depiction of the same fishnet-clad tentacle had been stenciled on its surface.

They pushed through and discovered the interior to be smoky, dark, and filled with a stench Trance couldn't quite describe but reminded him of fried fish, formaldehyde and gunpowder. Off to the left was the bar. To the right was a stage. In the center was a huge circular platform. Connecting the platform and the stage was a walkway. A fat little blob with a whiskery face, thick glasses and a bright blue and red necktie was strolling along the walkway toward the platform, bathed in a spotlight. A whistling sound escaped from a slit on its chest. The raucous crowd sprinkled throughout the room in an assortment of tables and chairs chittered appreciatively.

"Is that a stripper?" Trance asked Dexter. "Ug."

"No, the comedian. It's family hour."

"Ah. I can't believe they allow their kids in here."

"No way. Some of the most hardened criminals in the galaxy frequent this establishment. If any of them have reproduced it has been asexually or by accident."

"But I thought you said it was fam... never mind."

Trance peered at the being on the stage. Its chest was whistling again, and here came the translation: the comedian was saying, "Take my wife…. Please!" The crowd groaned.

A beer bottle the size of a watermelon tumbled lazily out of the darkness in an arc clearly intended to terminate in the vicinity of the blob's midsection. Suddenly, it vaporized as it met an invisible force field around the perimeter of the walkway. The air sizzled briefly as a tiny mushroom cloud formed and then dissipated.

"Whew. Even I've heard that one before," Trance said as they ambled toward the bar.

"You wouldn't believe how old that joke is," Dexter replied.

They reached the bar and sat down on a couple of stools that happened to vacate themselves as they approached. Dexter stood with his back legs on the cushion and his front paws on the countertop. Trance looked around appreciatively.

In front of them stood a tremendous dusty mirror running the entire length of the bar. Hundreds of shelves containing thousands of varieties of colored liquids were set in its surface.

The barkeep, a huge greasy, thick, and swarthy individual with six arms and four eyes was wiping the countertop further down the rail with one thick hand, while supplying three other customers at once with his others. He was a dynamo of constant motion and smooth skill. In the midst of a graceful pirouette, a tumbler somersaulted quietly over his head from one hand to the other, its contents spraying magically into three glasses before him. Trance suppressed the urge to clap wildly.

The bartender was ostensibly purely for entertainment value. Robotic dispensers lined the bar supposedly to dispense beverages according to taste. However many of these were broken down, so the barkeep kept busy.

When he had finished on the far end of the bar, he smoothly stepped over. "What'll it be gents…" he started in a voice sounding of gravel, then realized who stood before him. "Well. Dexter. Nice to see you. Same thing as usual?"

Dexter glanced at Trance with a guilty expression. "No… I'll have something legal. Give me a beer… a Chojo, please. In a little dish."

"Ah. Best Yvarian drink this side of the Galactic arm. Coming right up. And you sir?" Two of his four eyes peered at Trance. The others kept track of his hands as they went about their business.

"What do you have?"

The bartender smirked. "Everything in the galaxy. Name it, we got it."

"Quick, ring," Trance thought, "What won't kill me?"

"Get the Budweiser. I hear it's excellent."

"I'll have a Budweiser?" Trance said aloud, a surprised look on his face.

"That particular delicacy comes from one of the Restricted Zones, sir. I'm not saying we have it, but if we did, it'd be illegal, and rather pricey." He looked rather pointedly at Dexter with all of his eyes, though his arms kept dancing, filling orders.

After a heartbeat, Dexter shrugged and passed over some credits. "He's with me. I trust him."

"Ok, then: Budweiser coming right up. I must admit I am impressed, young sir. You know your exotic vintages." He reached down, pulled out their orders, and then moved down the rail.

"That's Melvin," Dexter said of the bartender. "All two thousand pounds of him. Melvin's a nice chap, but I certainly wouldn't want to make him angry. I've seen him put the hurt on people." He winked at a female cat at the other end of the bar and gave her a little wave. She turned away pointedly; ears suddenly flat against the top of her head. Dexter sighed and glared morosely into his Chojo.

Trance looked around in wonderment at the bar. It was a noisy and tumultuous environment filled with sights, sounds, and smells he had never before imagined were possible. Off in the distance, a four-mouthed lizard with a pinhead top and six bright orange eyes caught his attention. It was grinning at him, licking its teeth in a suggestive manner. Trance grimaced at it nervously.

"I wouldn't go there, if I were you," Dexter grunted. "You won't enjoy it much, and she'll eat you afterward."

"Yuck. I wasn't planning on it."

"Good man. So, as I was saying—"

"Excuse me, gents." It was Melvin again, holding a cup that frothed and bubbled at the rim. Dexter and Trance eyed the mug suspiciously. The liquid within was giving off sparks, which singed and pitted the counter. "Young lady over there —" he pointed to the lizard that had been eyeing Trance – "wants to buy the young feller a drink."

Trance looked toward the lizard who waved and winked. She licked her chops hungrily. "You better take it, or there'll be trouble," Dexter whispered across the conduit between them. "As you grab the mug, accidentally spill it all out. Who knows what that stuff will do to your insides."

"Sure thing," Trance whispered back. He thanked Melvin, and grasped the mug gingerly. That's when the plan went horribly awry.

As he brought the mug down to the tabletop, a spark jumped out of its mouth and landed in the middle of his thumb blistering the skin instantly. He bellowed in pain and surprise, involuntarily jerking his hand up and letting go of the mug in one florid motion. The mug sailed behind his shoulder, its contents spraying everyone in a five-foot radius behind him. Screams filled the air in their vicinity as the acidic liquid splattered unprotected skin. One patron exploded in flames, and began running around in circles squawking like a chicken. Tables were knocked over as aliens of every size and shape tried to escape the spitting, spraying, venomous gas forming wherever his beverage touched something other than itself. In the midst of all of the chaos some clever individual pulled a gun and began firing randomly into the air. This resulted in a new stampede in which several beings were crushed and mauled. Individual fights broke out all over the bar, but quickly became an all-out row, a tumultuous clash of arms, legs, knives, bottles, and tentacles. With a sickening crunch, a crumpled and broken body catapulted out of the mêlée, sailed through the air, and smashed into the great mirror, shattering it and sending row upon row of expensive and exotic alcohol bottles into the sky. Most of them rained down upon the combatants in a deadly storm of liquor, beer, and glass shards.

Trance glanced at Dexter nervously before ducking a random punch thrown his way. The ham-sized fist in question bounced with a thud off the ornate countertop. With a practiced hand, Trance returned the favor, landing a blow where he guessed the alien's solar plexus should be. He was rewarded with a faint cracking sound as the combatant folded like a newspaper and collapsed onto the slick floor. It didn't get up.

"Shouldn't we do something?" Trance asked the cat as he moved again to avoid a chair that had been aimed at his skull. It, too, crashed harmlessly against the rail.

Dexter looked around owlishly as if trying to pretend the events going on around him were his imagination, and sipped his Chojo tentatively. "If they find out we're Protectors, I'll never get back in here," he grunted. "Besides, these things happen all the time. If the Protectors don't get called in, the fight never happened; you know what I mean? It's not like we started it or anything."

"Yeah.... Maybe you're right. Still, I can't help feeling we did actually start it."

"What? Oh, you mean the flying cup of death?" They both watched as Melvin, the bartender struggled under the weight of ten flailing patrons. He was winning. "I don't think anyone would blame us for that," Dexter said hopefully.

Just then, Melvin flung one of his attackers away like a rag doll. Unfortunately, the poor sap crashed into what remained of Dexter's Chojo, sending the dish it was in spinning to the ground. The man lay face down over the counter groaning; oblivious and uncaring about the destruction his flight had wrought to the cat's favorite beverage.

Dexter sighed. "Well, that's it, then. Shall we?"

Trance grunted. "Yeah. My Bud was flat, anyway."

Before they could move, however, they were encased in a grip as strong as steel. They looked back to see all four of Melvin's bloodshot eyes peering at them murderously from behind a ton of muscle, fat, and lethal determination. He had obviously taken care of his other assailants, and his recent tussle hadn't even caused him to break a sweat. "Where do you two shits think you're going?" he spat venomously.

Dexter managed to look both incredulous and surprised the bartender would even think to ask such a silly question. "Now, Melvin, what makes you think we're going anywhere?" he croaked, trying to extricate his windpipe.

Melvin pulled the two even closer to his face. From this vantage point, Trance could see the millions of individual clogged pores making up the angry being's hide.

He could also smell what could only be pig barf emanating from between mandibles that, from the green tint and general look of decay, had not met a toothbrush or bit of floss in decades.

Trying desperately not to pass out from the awful stench, Trance listened numbly as Melvin provided them with a laundry list of activities he had planned for them to return the favor of ruining his bar. Most of them involved acid, hot tongs, and Barry Manilow music. With each item, he shook them angrily. Suddenly, however, he grunted around a curled lip and slowly toppled over onto his back, pulling the two Protectors with him.

They hung there for a moment on Melvin's stiff arms, watching the bartender blink at them furiously, and then Trance used his ring to give their now immobile captor a slight shock, causing his fists to open like tulips. They tumbled to the floor.

"Don't worry, Melvin," Dexter said as he caught his breath, "It'll wear off. In no time you'll be back up bashing heads and mixing drinks."

Melvin blinked rapidly. A small stream of drool escaped from his lips and cascaded down across his cheek to splash wetly on the sticky tiled floor. Despite his rigid posture, the bartender's fetid breath continued to whistle through his nose.

Fifteen minutes later, they managed to make it through the ruckus and to the door leading to the airlock. Before entering, however, Dexter handed Trance a ring-generated concussion grenade. "Toss this in there, will you?" he asked. Trance obliged him, and threw the thing as far as he could, before following the cat out. As the greasy wooden door clicked home behind them, Trance heard the grenade go off with a WHUMP that shook the doorframe and rattled his teeth. The explosion was followed shortly by the sound of more glass shattering. "That'd be what remained of Melvin's fine liquor," Dexter sighed. "Well, at least the fight is over."

"Nothing like a grand exit," the ring quipped.

"That's Entrance," Trance grunted. "You want to make a grand entrance. Nobody cares about making grand exits."

"Whatever."

Trance rolled his eyes, and followed the cat into the airlock.

Chapter 7: Aura

"Well shoot. I'll never be able to go there again," Dexter growled as they flew away from Legs.

"Melvin sure turned out to be an angry chap," Trance teased. "Wonder what his problem was?"

"I don't know. Some people just aren't happy people, if you know what I mean." Dexter thought for a moment and then laughed. "His breath sure did stink! Even my eyes were watering, and I clean my ass with my tongue!"

"Not nearly enough in my estimation," the ring said to itself.

"Y'know, we have a place back home for people who don't take care of their teeth," Trance laughed.

"Yeah?"

"Yeah. It's called Europe."

"Huh?" asked Dexter.

"It's a... never mind."

*****

They flew for a few minutes in silence, happy to get the debacle that had become Legs behind them. Then Dexter stopped up short.

"Yeah, OK," the cat said aloud. "I'll set a beacon. We'll see you in a few minutes." He turned to Adams. "Remember my good buddy Aura?"

"Yeah."

"He's going to be here in a few minutes. Let's hang here." Dex looked around for a moment, and then used his ring to grab a nearby rock floating aimlessly in space. As the rock neared them it began to change. At first it started to look like a pockmarked mushroom, but then it grew a dimple at the top. This dimple elongated, became a translucent blue, and then began blinking.

A flash nearby notified them of Aura's arrival a few minutes later. He was big -- perhaps even big enough to take on Melvin, the bartender from Legs, single-handedly. Trance would find out later he was tough, too.

Aura stood just slightly over seven feet tall—short for an Orian. He had golden-colored skin stretched thinly over taut muscles, and a serious but friendly and good-natured personality. His blue eyes twinkled in unison over a flashing white smile.

Aura was proud of his heritage -- Orias was one of the founding planets in the Conglomerated States-- but he didn't let it go to his head. He was extremely intelligent but a little dense and unimaginative, a trait that tended to get Protectors killed. These traits had served Aura well, however, as he had been a ring wielder for just under three hundred years.

Orians were a long-lived race, by Trance's standards, and tended to be scientists and historians by nature. Aura was no different. As a civilian, before accepting the Duty, he had indeed been a historian whose primary subject was Earth's middle ages. His love for the period had since spilled over into his life. While he did have a tendency to be chivalrous and noble toward everyone, and possessed a very defined idea of right and wrong -- and these were very helpful things -- he tended to get excited about quests and crusades. In fact, when he wasn't working he was off exploring the Universe looking for lost damsels in distress. He couldn't quite reconcile the fact that said damsels could actually rescue themselves most often.

Aura oozed good will, geniality and sheer and utter wholesomeness. He was the kind of being you might like to introduce to your daughter, knowing full well she would never ever date him.

The ring filled Trance in: the Golden Protector had recently been promoted to Trainer. His first charge had been Dexter, and that had gone fairly well, except for the cat's tendency to get into bar fights. But after a lot of work, and quite a few man-to-Emilian discussions of responsibility to the ring and respectability of the corps, he'd broken the cat of this tendency. It had been at least a month to his recollection, and that was Progress, with a capital P. "Obviously, he doesn't know about your recent encounter," the ring said snidely.

The prospect of training a human excited Aura. Besides being an excellent source of information regarding the Middle Ages from sheer dint of having grown up on the planet, he believed Trance to be an exciting addition in many other ways. The corps needed more ring bearers, for example, and it was refreshing to work with an individual from so far outside the Conglomerated States –Trance might bring a new perspective to the job, which was always nice. "He's a really nice guy, Trance," the ring said in conclusion, "but he has a few quirks. I just thought you might want to know."

"Anything you want to tell me?"

"No. You'll see."

"I could have sworn I heard you smirk just now," Trance grumbled internally. The ring chose not to respond.

After he introduced the two, who shook hands warmly according to Trance's customs, Dexter asked: "So, I knew we were going to meet up with you eventually, but I thought I'd have more time. What's up?"

Aura frowned. "Yeah, sorry to interrupt, but we have been asked to pick up and detain a known criminal in this sector, one Anad Grebstein. That's her real name, anyway, but she goes by a several aliases. She escaped from one of the prison systems about a month ago and has been recently spotted nearby. She's wanted for murder, destruction of public property, pillaging, and an assortment of other major crimes. This lady is one bad guy."

"Isn't she also a member of the Order of the Foul Dragon?" Dexter asked. "I heard reports of activity in this area."

"You're right," Aura replied. "They consider Si-truc to be their hero," he said for Trance's benefit.

Dexter brightened visibly when Aura began speaking. "Alright!" he cheered. "Finally some action!"

"What about Legs?" Trance asked innocently. Dexter glared.

"Funny you should mention that," Aura said.

"Oh shit."

"No, it's actually a bar, Dexter," Aura responded. "That's where we have to go. She's a regular there, apparently... works behind the counter sometimes."

"Oh, boy, this just gets better and better."

Aura put his hands on his hips. "You're not telling me something. Did you destroy another bar? I think it's best if you just tell me right now. It will save me time and energy later."

"Well, it's actually still standing, thank you very much."

"Not too many bottles left in it, though," Trance snorted.

"You really aren't helping anything by opening your mouth," glared Dexter.

"Sorry. I thought Aura might like to hear the truth from an unbiased observer."

"What?" Dexter pretended to be hurt. "You're the one that caused it, my furless friend, not me. I only helped extricate us from an untenable situation caused by your inability to hold your liquor. I should be thanked rather than vilified." He sniffed with his little pink nose in the air.

"Oh? Deserve a medal do you?" Trance laughed. "And what's with all the big words?"

"OK," Aura grunted. "Break it up. It sounds like there is a story to be told and I'd like to hear it sometime before the end of my term."

"Don't you have over seven hundred years left?" Dexter said.

"That's why I'm worried. Now come on. I'm getting tired of playing around here. You can't distract me forever." He put his hands on his hips in mock seriousness.

They quickly relayed what had occurred at Legs to the Golden Protector. He whistled, but kept his comments to himself until the end. When the story was complete, he said: "You took care of things this time, right Dexter?"

"He sure did," Trance piped in. "You should have seen the look on Melvin's face."

Dexter glared at Trance again. "OK, enough already. Let's get going," he grumbled.

It only took them a few minutes to get back to the bar. They cycled through the airlock together, but Dexter stayed behind as the others walked toward the now-familiar door with the neon leg. "Just a sec," the furry cat said.

When he rejoined them momentarily, Dexter acted amazed at the state of the bar. "Wonder what happened?" he said half to himself, looking furtively at Aura and then more pointedly at Trance.

Most of the patrons were still slumbering, though a few had evidently roused early and made their way out of the bar. Given the further degradation of the interior, it appeared that everything not nailed down or completely destroyed had been taken in the exodus.

Nonetheless, there were still quite a few awake individuals left (easily five hundred remained), and most of them were drinking heavily from cracked bottles and broken glasses.

Quite a few of the patrons were in need of serious dental attention and medical care. They looked at the trio of Protectors in a surly way as the three passed. Many an eye noted their lack of armament with pointed interest.

Up at the front of the bar, the three found Melvin. All of his eyes were decidedly bloodshot. Whether this was a result of his bout with Dexter and Trance, or because he had recently been crying, or maybe even sheer murderous rage, Trance could only guess.

"Maybe he just woke up from a nap," the ring whispered hopefully.

"Hello citizen," Aura said by way of greeting, "We're looking for a criminal known to frequent your establishment." Behind him, the four closest tables suddenly vacated as their inhabitants raced unsteadily for the airlock. Anyone who was as obviously unarmed as the three newcomers and looking for criminals was either completely insane or had a ton of guns hidden somewhere very nearby. Either way there was about to be some serious trouble.

Rather than chase them down, however, Dexter smirked and stood his ground. Trance looked at him inquiringly. Then he began to hear the cursing clearly even across the room and down the hall.

"I sealed the airlock," Dexter snickered. "They ain't going nowhere."

"Done this kind of thing before I take it?" Trance asked the cat.

"Yeah. They always try and sneak out behind us. It's kind of funny, really."

They both looked toward Melvin who appeared to be trying to blow a gasket, sputtering words Trance didn't recognize, but Aura blushed a nice shade of orange.

The golden man held up his hands in supplication. "Easy, there, citizen," he said in a friendly voice that said 'We don't want trouble,' "We're just here to talk; just a couple of friendly Protectors here for a visit. We don't want trouble."

At this point, some of the more aware and hardened patrons cocked their heads. Several more cocked guns. Dexter sighed. "He just had to use that word. Bad enough, him using the word 'criminals' but this—"

"What? 'Trouble'?"

"No, the 'P' word."

"Huh?"

"He used the P word, Trance; 'Protector.'" Dexter muttered. "Remember when I said they weren't exactly keen on Protectors here? Well, I made a bit of an understatement. In truth, they hate us with a passion. Things are going to get messy, real quick. Do you know how to create an invisible force shield? We don't want to alarm anyone, but do it now before we get cheesed. I'll do one for Aura. He probably doesn't know what a firestorm he created behind us."

"Yeah. I put one up already," Trance replied.

Just then, a beam the thickness of an arm exploded from behind them, impacting Aura's backside, and splashing around Dexter's hastily erected shield. Aura turned to the crowd, looking disappointed. "Now why did somebody go and do that for?"

"Sorry," someone shouted. "I had the safety off, and it just accidentally discharged!"

"Oh, well then, don't let it happen again, citizen. You might hurt someone." He turned back toward Melvin. "Now, as you were saying, sir –" This time, at least a half dozen beams of varying color and width struck him from behind.

Trance took one step and fell over. "What the—" he managed, seeing that he was still floating several inches off the floor.

"Ugh," the ring groaned. "Haven't you learned anything? You can't be shielded and walk around, Trance! It just doesn't work that way."

"Well then, why do I want to even have a shield for?" Trance asked, trying to rock himself over so that he could see what was going on. He turned his head and saw that pandemonium was going on – people were running, slithering, and jumping this way and that, and most of them were firing at Aura, Trance, and Dexter. The rest were firing at each other or at the floors and ceilings. Melvin stood rock solid in one place bellowing incoherently.

"Well, if we really need a lesson right now," the ring said moodily, "shields work great in space or when you are flying because you're not really moving. I can create a solid shield around you, and move space around the shield. But on land, it's a lot more complicated. You're essentially immobile when you are shielded. Get it?"

"Point taken," Trance said, and dropped his shield. He landed on all fours, and crawled forward until he was hidden by an overturned table. He peered over the edge.

Trance knew if you must be in a gunfight, the best place to do so is in a bar. Mix alcohol, firearms, and enhanced emotions such as fear and anger, and you're usually going to get a lot of missed shots. The thought cheered him until he looked into the barrels of several dozen massive handguns.

As a child Trance learned a tremendous and wonderful fact he had never been able to fully appreciate until now. Overturned tables, according to the movies, are almost universally adept at stopping even the most ferocious barrage of fire power. He'd seen a single sheriff take on dozens of armed bandits from the safety of a quickly unfolded card table, and come out unscathed. Usually, this was the same sheriff who went into a gunfight with a single six shooter, and still managed to fell everybody in the room.

The sound of all those guns being cocked in his face brought his attention slamming back into reality. The table in front of him obviously hadn't seen all of the old Western movies he had; it withered instantly in the barrage of laser fire that followed. Trance only had time for a single "Ulp," before....

Before a shield absorbed the power of the lasers. "Whew, thanks, Ring," Trance sighed. Talk about a close one.

"I didn't save your bacon," the ring said. "I can't do that kind of thing, remember? Thank Dexter."

"Oh." Trance looked at the cat, who had created a massive metal snow shovel, and was using it as a club. He had already laid out three individuals, and piled them in front of him. Dex nodded back at Trance, then resumed his shoveling.

Aura was something to behold. The golden Protector had formed a massive silver broadsword and was using it to great effect. He was incredibly lithe for such a large fellow-- fast on his feet, and deadly accurate with the blade. The sword seemed to slip through the air in front of him, hewing metal, wood, flesh, and bone – decimating anything that stood in his way.

Rather than simply lopping off limbs and heads however, Aura was using a technique unavailable to his knightly counterparts in the middle ages, his favorite time period. His blade, while neatly slicing whatever metals it came into contact with simply deadened live flesh. When the broadsword passed through an arm, for example, the combatant reacted as though he or she had lost control of the limb. When it passed through a head or torso the being collapsed on to the ground and started snoring peacefully.

The damn thing reflected laser, too. Several times in the brief moment Trance glanced at Aura, he saw the fellow use the broadsword to block shots that would have been fatal had they connected. He sidestepped other shots, bent his body just slightly so they missed him completely, or simply teleported away from them, only to return almost instantly swinging his blade. The effect was one of a whirling silver and gold tornado.

Aura also appeared to be screaming incoherently. Later, Trance discovered this was a battle cry. Something to the effect of "Death to infidels," or "Remember the Santa Maria!"

Trance whistled, then looked back at his attackers. They were still shooting, evidently hoping they might somehow break through his shield. Using the ring, he formed a wood grained baseball bat. It was a slick construct; he could see the individual grains and the famous "Louisville Slugger" emblem. It was about six feet long, and as thick as his thigh at one end. He caused it to twirl rapidly in the air above his head, and then brought it down like a mallet on the gunslingers in front of him. They folded like a pack of cards. He was rewarded by the sound of breaking guns, bones, and bodies. The head of the bat buried itself several inches into the floor sending cracks crisscrossing this way and that.

A few of the more adventuresome attempted to get up. One sputtered gamely before collapsing back onto a pile of his own teeth. Trance rapped them all smartly on the head one after another. Then, after ensuring no one was aiming directly at him, Trance vaporized the shield, stood, and then reformed it in one fluid motion.

From his new vantage point, Trance noticed a couple of things that hadn't been apparent from a prone position. Number one: Aura was way too much into this whole knight in shining armor thing. He was still screaming incoherently... now his bellows sounded like "God Save the King!" Trance shook his head.

Number two: the bar was taking most of the damage. Nearly all of the tables had been reduced to toothpicks, and most of the chairs had been used as clubs or deadly projectiles. And all the beautiful booze—gone, seeping into the floor and what was left of the orate countertops. Between his two visits, Trance had seen the bar nearly completely destroyed.

"This has to stop," Trance growled to the ring. "Can I gas everyone?"

"Unadvisable," the ring replied. "There are many different physiologies here. Any knockout gas you used might be effective only for a small part of this population. Others it might energize. Still others it might kill. We're going to have to think of another solution."

Trance looked around. Aura and Dexter were too involved in their own adventures to be much use. Their solution seemed to be knock everyone out individually. Effective, eventually, but there were so many combatants even with more than half the bar emptied, that it might take hours or even days to complete.

"What about a concussion grenade?" Trance asked. "It worked well before."

"That would be a great idea, however you don't know how to create one," the ring responded gamely. "I can create something if you know the general workings of one. But right now, you've got a nuclear bomb pictured and I know you don't want one of those babies going off in here."

"You're right. I have no idea how a concussion grenade works. Are you going to help me out with this one?"

"No. Besides, look around. Do you really think that this bar could withstand another one of those being lit off in here?"

"No," Trance admitted. "I'd be willing to bet that if anybody as much as sneezed against one of the outer walls it would collapse."

"You got it. I estimate if we don't stop this fight within about two minutes, the structural integrity of the bar will be compromised to the vacuum of space. That means everyone dies. Except of course the Protectors, unless they are caught off guard. And with how intent they are at destroying everything in sight, I wouldn't make any bets."

"I thought you bet over everything."

"Ah, yes. By 'I', I meant you. You shouldn't make any bets."

"Oh. Well, then." Trance looked around again. Nothing had changed, except a few more combatants lying stunned at the feet of his new friends. Dexter had a more impressive pile—he was standing at the top of it grinning from ear to ear and swinging his shovel furiously.

In front of Trance, a slimy looking and obviously completely plastered fellow with gold chains strung over his barrel chest had begun to pound on Trance's shield. "Come out, youse!" he exclaimed. "Some of us here want to use that there shield!"

"Shut him up, ring," Trance growled. "Can't he see I'm thinking?" He willed a big fist into existence and slammed it into the generous proboscis in front of him. The drunk flipped end over end for several yards, bowling into several other beings, then landed in a wet heap. He didn't get up. Trance grinned, momentarily satisfied.

"Less than a minute, Protector. You'd better hurry."

Trance snapped his finger. "Of course!" he yelled. He needed two big hands. They appeared before him. One of them was empty; the other had a large pair of brass knuckles firmly in place.

It took less than thirty seconds for the two hands to travel the entire room. The first came screaming in, ripping the weapons from startled hands; the other came immediately after with the brass: cracking chins, breaking noses, and dislocating jaws.

One poor specimen managed to hold on to his handgun – he screamed as he was pulled through the entire course before being deposited none too gently beneath a pile of broken guns and other armament.

Trance surveyed the damage, seeing a lot of broken bones and bruises, but everyone seemed to be alive and snoring. And the battle was over.

Aura shook his head as if coming out of a trance and stumbled over. "Yes, well, good show," he grunted. The broadsword became smoke and dissipated.

Dexter scowled in disappointment. He'd evidently been having a lot of fun. But he stepped down from his pile of bodies, shambled over on all fours, and then sat in front of his two friends and washed one of his paws with his little pink tongue. "So, now what?" he asked between mouthfuls of fur.

"Well, now we sift through all this refuse for Anad," Aura said, sweeping a hand along the expanse of the bar's interior.

"Um, I don't suppose that's her over there?" Trance asked, and pointed toward one of the corners. There, they could see a figure hunched over. Trance got the impression of shapely curves and long flowing brown hair, but that was about it. In the now quiet room they could hear a faint buzzing noise emanating from her corner, and could see flashes of blue and green. She was so intent on her mission she didn't know the mêlée around her had stopped.

"Missed one, didn't you, Trance," the ring groused.

"She's trying to cut her way out of the room!" Dexter exclaimed in amazement. "Talk about brazen. If she made it out everyone in the bar would have died."

"Well, you did block the only exit, and she is a criminal," Aura said.

"Yeah. Aren't you glad I thought of sealing the airlock? I'm good, aren't I?"

"I wouldn't go that far," the ring muttered to itself.

"She must have a breather on her somewhere," Dexter said. "Either that or she better be good at holding her breath."

"Trance, she's a pretty violent criminal," Aura said, "and I'd hate to get you hurt on your first mission. Why don't you stand by the bar, or what's left of it, and we'll go talk with her? You'll have a good vantage point if we have to take her down. Maybe you'll learn a thing or two."

"Sure, Aura," Trance agreed. Besides, that would give him a chance to observe the pros in action. Perhaps he'd pick up a couple of great moves. He walked over to the bar. Because there weren't any stools left, he stood and leaned against the wood rail.

Anad was only a few feet away, and from this perspective, he could see she was indeed using a laser gun as a torch, trying to burn through the thick outer wall of the establishment. A substantial area had already begun to glow white hot, and rivers of molten metal were running down the expanse of the wall. She didn't seem to mind the heat.

In the few seconds it took the Protectors to reach her, Trance was able to get a good look at Anad. She was pretty enough, at least the side that he could see, with what appeared to be blue eyes and a fierce look of determination that was almost sexy. Her skin was flawless; a delicate shade of pink. Her breasts looked perky and not overly large or small – in short, she was perfect in every way that he could see. He couldn't believe his eyes; the woman could have been a supermodel on his planet, or any other.

By this time, the two Protectors had positioned themselves behind Anad. Aura reached out and grasped her shoulder in a friendly but firm grip. "Ok, Anad," he said, "why don't you set the gun down, and we'll all go outside and discuss this in a civil manner?"

She responded by dropping forward on her hands while simultaneously kicking back, striking Aura in the crotch with her foot. In the same smooth motion, she spun and landed a solid blow on the side of Dexter's head with the other foot, sending him flying as if he were a soccer ball. Aura went down with a gasp, his face turning a delicate shade of blue. Dexter sailed end over end, and landed on his head, splayed up against a table, with legs up in the air and his tail wagging furiously.

Anad didn't stick around to see them fall, however. She instantly turned again, and ran as fast as she could toward the exit, raising her gun as she ran and firing it wildly in every direction. Unfortunately for her plan, she happened to be running right toward Trance. She hadn't seen him.

"She's getting away!" the ring exclaimed. "Do something!"

Trance leaned over, stuck his leg out, and tripped her as she attempted to pass him. She went sprawling on her face, sliding forward a few feet before coming to rest, momentarily stunned. She groaned. Trance walked over and kicked her gun away. "You're under arrest pardner," he growled in his best Sheriff's voice, forming a pair of handcuffs around her wrists and ankles.

"You got me," Anad sighed in supplication. Her pretty face turned in a scowl.

"Good work, Trance," Dexter clapped, sitting up. "Whew, I am glad that's over." He stood and began to hunt for a beer.

Aura grimaced and wheezed, and flashed a 'thumbs up' before slowly getting to his feet and limping over. "In the end, good triumphs over evil again!" he exclaimed, looking around pleased. Just then, a section of the beautiful ornate bar behind him collapsed under its own weight with a loud crash. "Excellent job, everyone," Aura said to Trance and Dexter, then walked over to Melvin the bartender who had appeared again and was trying unsuccessfully to keep from turning purple with rage.

Trance formed the image of a sugar bowl in his head, complete with a flower press top and a spoon sticking out of it. His ring flashed, and the construct appeared around Anad, encasing her. Of course, he left it opaque enough so he could see the prisoner inside. Nice.

"Don't forget air holes, junior," the ring growled.

"Oh, right," Trance said, taken down a notch. He made the change.

Meanwhile, Melvin was explaining to Aura just exactly what he thought of Protectors, especially ones who seemed to go out of their way to destroy his establishment. Aura explained to him that he was very much willing to pay for the damage they had just caused, but really the bar was in such disrepair, it couldn't be much. Trance noted clinically that for some reason, even though they had already discussed the earlier carnage with Aura, Dexter started began shifting on both his feet, and looking desperately at the door.

It took Melvin fifteen minutes to describe in detail all of the items destroyed between the two visits. He was very eloquent. Aura listened placidly, one eye twitching in tune as Melvin counted on his fingers the damage they had wrought.

"Actually, that sounds pretty expensive," Aura said at last, looking to Dexter with a glare in his eye. The cat by now looked downright panicked. "Truthfully," he said, every word striking like hammer blows on an anvil, "I'm surprised you had enough money to cover the check."

"What?" Trance felt like he had been hit in the chest. Superheroes didn't have to pay for the damage they inadvertently caused in the line of duty, did they? Wasn't there some superhero bank account taking care of stuff like that? But then a little voice inside him reminded him that he wasn't in the line of duty was he? In fact, he was thinking seriously about getting drunk at the time, and you usually didn't see superheroes doing that, either. "Shut up, ring," he grumbled.

"Oh, yeah," Dexter was saying to no one in particular. "I guess we forgot about that little part."

"What are you teaching him – to run out on bar bills, now? Sheesh. I don't suppose you have any extra money." Dexter shrugged and gave his best 'Who Me?' impression. They both looked at Trance. It was obviously up to him. Melvin cracked his knuckles suggestively.

"Don't they have superhero insurance policies?"

"You mean policies against sudden superhero attacks?" Aura sighed.

"Uh. Yeah. I guess that does sound stupid."

"Hm."

"Well. What do I do, ring?"

"Don't look at me. It's not like I have tons of money just sitting around."

"Really? Wait a minute... remember all those little wagers you've made on my performance?"

"Oh. Darn."

"So you forgot."

"No, I remember everything. I was hoping maybe you had forgotten."

"Nope. Don't I deserve something for having gotten you through the fights and earning you all that money?"

"Yeah. I guess. A pittance."

"Maybe eighty percent?"

"Eighty percent! Why, you're trying to charge me an arm and a leg!"

"Well, considering you're on my arm, I don't think you have much choice in the matter, do you?"

"Sixty percent?"

"Done!" Trance looked up at the two Protectors and Melvin who was still glowering. "My ring is going to transfer over everything I have into the bar's account. Can you two cover anything? I'd hate to spend the rest of my life paying this bill."

Melvin pulled a little red disk out of one pocket, looked at it, then smiled. "No, this will do," he said toothfully. "I appreciate your... generosity. You can come and drink here anytime."

"Hey, thanks."

"As long as you pay, of course." Melvin's eyes darkened perceptibly, his brow wrinkling in a manner suggesting all the threats his mouth avoided making by staying closed.

"Of course."

"I wouldn't want anyone to get the wrong idea, you understand. My customers really don't like your kind here. You're bad for business. obviously."

"I understand."

Aura looked over at Dexter, then back at Trance. "Do you mind guarding the prisoner for a few moments? I want to discuss this mess with my good buddy here."

"Sure, I got things covered here," Trance responded. The two walked fifteen feet or so away, and began having an animated discussion which consisted mainly of Aura pin-wheeling his arms wildly like a windmill and whispering words that made Dexter blanch.

Melvin meanwhile had turned and traveled away from him in the opposite direction to a telephone set behind the bar. He too was talking animatedly to someone on the other end, but this sounded like the happy arrangement of the purchase of more liquor and other supplies. Trance thought idly about asking the bartender if he could use the telephone to call his mom back in Washington, but then realized that might not go over too well. Who knew what timezone they were in, for one thing, and the rates would probably be murder even if he could make it happen.

Trance remembered he had been left alone with the prisoner. He looked at her. She glared at him.

"You know, I've never met an inter-galaxy criminal before," he said conversationally. "What's it like?"

"Shut the filchereberry up," she spat.

"Really." He thought for a moment. "Why are you a criminal, anyway?"

She looked surprised at the question. "The only reason, I am labeled a criminal," she said heatedly, "is because you're the one with the power. It's a nomenclature thing, see. The people with power define the words. Maybe you're really the criminal here. You busted this bar up, not once, but twice, and yet I'm wanted for destruction of public property. I'm out of a job now because of you."

"You're wanted for a whole list of other things, too, I believe, like murder, for example," he pointed out helpfully. "Besides, I paid for what we destroyed."

"With my money," the ring groused. "Do you know how long it's going to take to win back all those credits?"

"Shut up, ring!" Trance growled to himself.

"Hmp." Anad turned up a lip. Luckily she couldn't hear him.

"Shutting up," the ring said in a small voice.

Trance tried a different track. "Say, what an interesting tattoo you have." Down by the base of the neck, he could see what looked like the head of a dragon biting into something. She turned away from him before he could get a closer look, trying to replace the cover of her shirt which had evidently been torn when Aura attempted to grab her.

"Mind your own business, prick, unless you want to get me one of those swords your friend uses," she said. He left her alone after that.

A few minutes later, Aura and Dexter returned, the golden Protector looking peeved, and the cat looking chagrined. "Let's head out," Aura growled.

They left silently, towing the bound and silent form of Anad behind them. Outside the bar, Aura's ring glowed briefly and Anad disappeared. "I've sent her to the nearest Outstation," he said to Trance. "They'll process her there and return her to the penal colony she escaped from."

"Oh? Do Protectors run those, too?"

"The Outstations and Penal colonies? No. Those are run by private companies from the Conglomerated States. Protectors act as a free-ranging Police corps. We're so thinly spread as it is… it would be a waste to lock a ring down in a desk job."

"And boring, too," Trance's ring affirmed.

"So, now what?" Dexter asked.

"Now, we find a place to practice," Aura grunted. "That was embarrassing, to tell you the truth, and I don't want to run into the same problems again. We were lucky this time… next time one of us might get killed."

Chapter 8: Practice Makes…

After finding a cozy planet with an atmosphere they all could breathe, they spent the next week practicing. Aura started them off on the first day by telling them to forget everything they knew about using a ring ("That wouldn't be much," the ring snipped). Then, he started them on theory. Then followed teamwork, in which he gave them tasks to complete which required them to sweat furiously without being able to use their rings.

Trance wasn't sure what the point of these tasks was, but he enjoyed them, and enjoyed the camaraderie. Time lost all meaning for him. Minutes bled into hours; hours into days.

On the fourth or fifth day, Aura finally let them use their rings, but only to complete the mundane tasks of boiling water and digging a latrine. Trance was the only one who felt some relief at the second activity; Dexter found a sandpit the size of a small island on their first day and Aura evidently processed foods differently for he never expelled waste that Trance could tell.

On the sixth day, they began anew with constructs-- nothing moveable or containing parts, however-- Aura expressly forbid complicated designs. Now that he was completely out of practice, Trance could only muster a large blue beach ball which popped loudly the moment it touched the ground. This elicited a tremendous theatrical sigh from the ring, which, Trance surmised, was actually quite glad to be in use again, albeit ineffectively.

Dexter, who had been a Protector for much longer, started off with a life-sized version of himself complete with a single furry-claw that saluted Aura resolutely from the middle of its paw whenever the golden Protector wasn't looking at it.

Aura put up with the faux Dexter for about five minutes. Trance swore later he could hear the Golden Protector count to three thousand more than once in that span. Once the five minutes were up, Aura formed a menacing blue pit bull, which chased the energy cat up a tree with a loud bark. Both constructs gave guilty pops as they faded away. Feeling better, Aura allowed Dexter and Trance time to play.

Chapter 9: To Monidad

One morning as the sun was breaking over a hill in the distance, Aura gently woke Trance and Dexter with the tip of his shoe. "Hey," he grunted to them. "It's time to get a move on."

Dexter, who had stayed up late drinking the night before, sat up and groaned audibly. "Turn out the light!" he cried, shading his eyes with one orange and white paw.

Trance, who generally only liked to imbue with Top Ramen jumped to his feet. "What's going on, Aura?" he asked.

"We're going to go to the System," Aura declared. "It's about time you met some other Protectors, and saw what the whole corps is about. Besides, I think we all need a good sonic shower. Especially you, Dexter; you stink."

"Hey," declared Dexter in mock seriousness. "I really hate it when you falsely accuse me of—" his nose wrinkled. "Oh, never mind. I do stink."

"So, what is this 'System?" Trance wondered aloud.

"I guess you could say it is the current base of the Creators," Aura responded. "They have been there for countless millennia, though no one knows where they hailed from originally"

"Hmm," Trance said. "Where is it?"

"Right now, it's in the Delta sector," Dexter said. "More specifically, I guess you could say that it's on the planet Monidad."

"Right now. You mean its location could change."

"Duh," the ring muttered in his head.

Dexter and Aura smiled at each other cryptically. "You'll see when we get there," the cat said knowingly. "In about three days."

"Why three days? Can't we just warp there?"

"Didn't you read your manual?" Aura asked curiously.

"I never got one," Trance shrugged.

"Ooh. Too bad. At the very least you would have had something to throw at evildoers if your ring ever goes out." He chuckled. "I don't think anyone really manages to read the whole thing. It's over fifty thousand pages long.

'Anyway, the short answer is: 'Because it's designed like that by the Creators,' of course."

Trance raised an eyebrow. "And the long answer?"

"Whew. He's got a lot of questions, Dexter."

"You don't know the answer, do you Aura?" Dexter responded.

The large golden Protector grimaced and laughed. "No. You're right, I don't!"

"I'll field this one while we fly to the nearest entry site," Dexter said. With that, he launched himself from the ground. The other two followed in concert.

Once in space, Dexter created a ship of energy around them. Inside, they found three lounge chairs designed to fit their individual frames. Trance groaned appreciatively as he sank into his. Immediately little fingers within the fabric began to massage him, quickly working out the knots in his tired muscles. "Hey, this is pretty cushy," he murmured. Aura grunted his acquiescence from his own lounge.

Dexter, meanwhile, plotted a course. His ring glowed briefly, energy coursing through the translucent walls of the ship and to a point several yards in front of the spaceship. There, it seemed to swirl and coalesce into a point of intense blue light which shattered and streamed past them on either side of the ship, to be replaced by the now familiar endless gray. They had entered warp.

Even though he had seen it before, the light show still amazed Trance. His mind tried to catalog where they were in relation to the rest of the known universe, but the concept kept on slipping away like a vapor. It made his head hurt. At least this time he didn't suffer the nearly vomit inducing side effects of travel through gray space. Perhaps being inside the ship had something to do with it. "You get used to it pretty fast," the ring said knowledgeably.

"We'll get to the nearest entry site in a few hours," Dexter said, turning his chair to face the lounging Protectors. "In the meantime, looky here." He pointed to a small cylindrical dais rising soundlessly from the floor. It stopped, and a holographic yellow orb coalesced over its smooth surface. Trance could see the sphere was alive; it burned and pulsed. Occasionally, a stream of flame would arch off the surface, fling itself into space, and splash back into the exterior again. "You both know what this is," Dexter said. "Right? No? It's a star, Trance. Pay attention."

The star shrank noticeably, and eight paper-thin rings sprang from its center, moving so they were fairly evenly spread across the radius of the dais. On each of these rings appeared at least one planet; ten in all. The second ring had twins, each appearing to revolve around the other as they spun slowly around the sun. The third and seventh rings from the star contained planets bearing rings of their own, like Saturn.

"This is The System," Dexter intoned, pausing dramatically. "Notice the planet on the fourth ring from the sun, Trance?" The indicated planet became bigger and bigger, washing away the other holograms on the dais. "This is Monidad, home of the current base of the Creators."

Monidad spun sedately on its pole. It appeared to be a barren world; gray and desolate, and pockmarked with meteor craters. The only thing of interest was a beautiful and delicate silver spire lancing through the top of the world. It appeared to reach several miles into the atmosphere, if there was one.

"Show Trance a cutout," Aura said languidly from his lounge chair.

The world stopped rotating. Then half of it sloughed off, revealing, what looked at first glance remarkably like the inside of a striped hard-boiled egg. In fact, where the core of the planet should have been, there was a green sphere. "They capped the core, and use it as an energy source," Aura commented. "As you can see, the entire planet is hollowed out. The silver tower that runs through the entire thing is a vent of sorts. It also serves as a central elevator shaft for transporting goods and personnel because it reaches every level."

"It's also an emergency exit," Dexter said, "and a hotel for Protectors and visiting dignitaries." Meanwhile, the planet grew its surface back, and shrank to its rightful size in the diorama.

"So, why can't we just *go* there?"

"I'm getting to that, Trance," Dexter replied, unhurried. "The Creators didn't originate in this system. We don't know where they come from originally. They just found this place, and have since taken it and shaped it to suit their purposes. In fact, this whole solar system has been re-engineered. It has become a spaceship they control.

'One of the safety features they created to protect Monidad and the other planets is a force shield surrounding the entire system. The shield bends the space-time continuum. If you tried to warp directly to Monidad from anywhere outside the barrier, you'd be flung so far out of the way, you'd grow old getting back."

"So, instead we have to warp to the edge of the system." Aura said.

"The force shield does allow entry at one of several junctures, and these are all at the very outer edge," Dexter continued. At this point, the tiny solar system shrank again, moving off to the side, pulling orbs that Adams hadn't noticed previously into the center. One whizzed silently past his nose.

Soon, all that remained was a single tiny orb, about the size of a gray pea. "This is one of the entry points. In fact, this is Transport station Alpha, the one we are going to." The sphere in question began to grow until it was the size of a tennis ball. It was steel-gray and unassuming. "The real Transport Station is the size of Earth's moon, Trance."

"Oh goody, I'd hate to have to fit my ass into something that small," Trance responded wryly. "So, why take a transport ship? Why not just enter the station, and then warp the rest of the way with our rings?"

"It's possible," Dexter said, "but we'd have to get permission, first. Otherwise the automatic defense systems would make mincemeat out of us. Besides, this is more relaxing, and will give us more time to train. After you have been in the corps several hundred years, you'll see that three days isn't that big of a deal here and there."

"And the defense systems only work one way," Aura grunted. "We can beam out instantly if we need to, for example, to pretty much anywhere." He stretched and yawned. "Now come on! Let's practice making some stuff! I got a couple of cool tricks to show you, Dex."

They spent the rest of the time in Dexter's spaceship relaxing and practicing creating small, though complicated constructs with their rings. Trance found designing and creating each one was easier than the last. The week of practice on the nameless planet really paid off.

Just shy of three hours after entering Gray Space, they broke out of the warp bubble, bounding back into real space with a flash. Fifteen minutes of sub-light traveling took them to the Transport Station Trance had seen as a holograph just a few hours earlier.

In person, Transport Station Alpha was even less inspiring than it had appeared as a tiny sphere. More impressive were the many ships orbiting the station. Big spacers and tiny tugs formed complicated but beautiful patterns as they orbited the tiny station.

Once they had passed through the airlock, they found the interior of the station to be brightly lit and sterile. A gray walled hallway with a somber blue carpet bearing a thin red stripe down the middle sheltered a long queue of patiently waiting beings of various shapes sizes and smells. The line terminated in a desk with an individual Trance recognized without introduction: a bureaucrat.

The bureaucrat had several tentacles, which were waving about in pursuit of various rudimentary tasks while he inquired in a bored voice as to whether or not the creature in front of him, a merchant, planned to transport any homegrown fruit or vegetables within The System. The creature indicated that she did not, and had nothing to declare other than the packages already stored and waiting for transport with the shuttle. Both inquiry and statement had the air of formal ceremony. "Your person and your goods will be thoroughly scanned for explosives and other contraband, of course," the Bureaucrat intoned. "We don't take lightly to anyone who tries to sneak illegal items into the System."

"I know, that's why I didn't bring any," the merchant smiled toothfully.

Ritual complete, the merchant accepted a ticket, and moved on. At this point the Bureaucrat glanced that the trio of Protectors and smiled. "Hey fellows. Welcome back. That'll be three tickets to…"

"Monidad," Aura said pleasantly.

"Ah. Working? No pleasure trips to Minius for you three, huh?" He laughed. Minius, the smallest planet in The System, shared an orbit with Ludite, one of the ringed planets, approximately as far from their sun as the Earth to its sun. Minius was designed by the Creators to be a vacation planet for the hard working Protectors, and all others employed by the Creators. It was warm and tropical, and filled with scantily clad female cats, which is why it was Dexter's favorite vacation spot.

"No, not this time," Dexter sighed wistfully.

Aura nudged Dexter with one huge elbow. "You're supposed to show Trance the ropes, right? Maybe it's your duty to make a proper introduction to all the planets in the system in due order."

Dexter brightened immensely. "Yeah. Maybe so!"

Aura smiled at the Bureaucrat again. "Maybe we'll go there later. For now, business before pleasure!"

"Fair enough. Three tickets to Monidad!" A tentacle shot over to them, and dropped a ticket into each of their upturned hands. Then the bureaucrat turned back to the queue. "Next?" he sighed.

As the next shuttle was at least an hour away, they relaxed in one of many crowded waiting areas sipping exotic drinks and swapping stories. Aura became mildly concerned when he discovered that Trance, an extensive ocean of information in regards to Washington State documents, was a dry desert when it came to the Dark Ages. He did brighten, however, after Trance promised to take him to visit the ruins of the Castle Leeds in England, the only location the human remembered from his collegiate History 101 course.

Chapter 10: Mollie

The transport ship, when it arrived, proved to be clean, tidy, and well lit. It consisted of a hundred cabins (each programmed to mimic the home environment of its resident), a galley, a large dining area, a media library, exercise and recreation rooms, several entertainment lounges, and a small bar. The cabins were tiny but comfortable, containing a bed, a tiny desk with a phone, artwork, and a porthole.

Trance spent most of the journey in the accompaniment of Aura and Dexter. They played games in the rec areas, drank at the bar, and generally had a stress-free and enjoyable time.

Between bouts of play, Aura found time to drill both Dexter and Trance in hand to paw combat for those times when using your ring just wasn't an option. Dexter protested that using your ring was always an option, but deferred to Aura in the end when the golden Protector threatened jovially to crush him and stuff his body in the nearest waste receptacle. Trance felt this might actually be a good thing because it would certainly improve the cat's smell, but he chose not to add his comments to the conversation.

They used a rec room for their lessons. Aura programmed the room with a gray mat floor, brown stone walls, and a white ceiling. The computer even supplied torches guttering from strategically placed niches along the wall. Aura said this was the traditional setting on his home planet. He wanted things done right, and doing things right started with the doing them in the proper environment. It was all about Tradition, he said. That and good old fashioned Sweating. Aura had the amazing ability to capitalize words in his speech somehow.

Trance had taken some karate lessons back home, and as a result picked up Aura's methods quickly. In fact, he found himself giving pointers to Dexter, who hadn't had any prior courses because he generally despised anything that involved exertion. Trance didn't mind coaching Dexter, although he sometimes thought the cat wasn't really paying attention.

When they sparred during practice, Trance and Dexter were pretty much evenly matched. Trance was larger and more knowledgeable, but Dexter was faster and had claws. In addition, he had a secret weapon that came into play frequently: he shed. Whenever Trance would grasp the cat in preparation for a throw, Dexter would shed furiously, becoming very slippery and filling the air with fur. Trance would invariably find himself gasping for air and holding nothing but two fistfuls of orange and white hair.

*****

On the evening of the first day, as they were taking a break from sparring, Trance found himself deep in thought, nursing a deep scratch on his arm, and rubbing his hands together rapidly to get rid of fur. The stuff was everywhere – in his eyes, lungs, and plastered all over his shirt and pants. He glared at the cat. Where did all of it come from?

Dexter took no notice of Trance's glare. He was too busy relating a raunchy story about one of his past conquests. Aura was doing his best to appear interested.

"Aura, Dexter?"

They both turned. "Yes?" Aura asked politely, although he seemed relieved for the interruption.

"I was wondering—how do you get along with your rings?"

Aura wrinkled his nose. Dexter looked surprised. "I never really thought about it, truthfully," the cat said. "Mine's OK. Not much of a personality, though."

"Hmp," Aura said. "I like mine too. It's a little talkative, though. It keeps me up at night sometimes, but it's good in a pinch. Why?"

Trance shrugged. "Mine is rude, boorish and loves practical jokes."

"Hello, I'm right here!" his ring cried in mock sadness. "Couldn't you wait until I left the room?"

Trance sighed. "Other than the fact it has a tendency to make wagers against me and crack stupid jokes, it's ok, I guess."

"That's better, I think," the ring said.

"Oh, one of those rings. Well, we all can't be lucky in the draw," Aura chuckled. "One poor fellow I heard about had a ring that would set his feet on fire when he wasn't looking. I imagine you're doing better than that."

"Not much, to tell you the truth," Trance grunted.

"Heloooooo! Ring here!"

"I heard about one unlucky fellow," Dexter said. "His ring liked to tell all his enemies what his weakness was! Can you imagine that?"

Aura nodded sadly. "Yeah, he didn't last too long."

"Maybe I'm not so bad after all," the ring snipped.

"It's early," Trance thought. "Really early."

*****

On the second day after lunch, the three ran into another Protector, Mollie.

Mollie was an Emilian, like Dexter. She also looked like a house cat, but instead of orange and white stripes she was a long haired calico, with brown, gray, and white patches of fur and green eyes. She was beautiful and smart.

Mollie was the second oldest of the Protectors, having been a ring bearer for nearly two thousand years. She had stopped going back to her home planet over fifteen hundred years before, at the ripe old age of 490, when she had realized that nothing that she had known remained there. Typically, Emilian's lived to be only twenty-five, so 19 generations had passed by that time. This filled her with a sense of deep sadness, and could have been one of the reasons that she felt such a deep kinship with Dexter; a single link to a home long lost. In truth, they were closer than friends – but not lovers.

Mollie was a fastidiously clean individual. She was talented with the ring, though quite skittish and prone to run rather than fight. Despite this inclination however, she had saved the lives of many Protectors through quick thinking and a deft paw, and for that she had the respect and admiration of the corps.

Trance found he like the female Emilian immediately. The urge to dangle bits of yarn in front of her and Dexter was almost overwhelming, but he successfully fought the inclination off. ("What is it with you and cats?" the ring moaned.)

He quickly discovered Mollie was the supervisor of his squad, though she was not the oldest member of it. Aura explained that each squad consisted of seven Protectors. Each squad reported to a Creator, and each Creator looked over 130 squads. It was an extremely loose affair – squad members seldom saw each other, sometimes going years at a time between encounters. Some squads were more active than others. The only hard and fast rule was that when a member joined the squad, everyone traveled to Monidad to welcome the new Protector.

Chapter 11: Monidad

Monidad loomed large in their view ports on the afternoon of the third day. Knowing this was the first visit for Trance, the Captain, a Green Dragon from B'tahi whose name he forgot immediately after she introduced herself, invited the four Protectors to the command center of the ship to view the approach and landing. As a favor to the four Protectors, the Captain offered to orbit the planet once before beginning landing procedures. Trance watched, impressed, as the endless miles flashed by before his eyes on the multiple view screens. The planet was impressive in its size, perhaps twice as big as Earth, but unremarkable and unassuming, and utterly frozen. Grayness covered everything, from the deepest chasm to the highest mountain tops. The surface was entirely pockmarked by craters, a barren and lifeless world.

When they were still hundreds of miles away from the North Pole, Trance began to notice a glow about the horizon. As they got closer and closer, he began to see the Spire itself. It was a thing of such pure and total beauty it made his heart ache.

The Silver Spire appeared airy and impossibly thin in contrast to its height; an impossible structure Adams was sure would collapse at any moment. ("It has been standing here longer than your sun has given breath," the ring said softly.) The outer surface of The Spire seemed to twist slightly as it reached toward the stars. Though it was smooth and polished as a mirror, it seemed to cast no reflection. It exuded an aura of vitality and welcome.

The ship circled The Spire once near the top, and then shot upward into the atmosphere, joining a horde of other ships that seemed to be congregating at random over the North Pole. This far up, Adams noticed the top of The Spire wasn't a single point. Rather, it was peppered with hundreds of entry and exit points through which poured a steady flow of traffic. He only had a moment from this vantage point, however. Almost at once the ship plunged into the warm and inviting maw of one of the entrances.

Lights flickered past his eyes in a steady stream, and he had a sense of passage through countless layers of smooth striated concrete, and then out, into a cavern of such immensity he couldn't see the floor or the sides at first. The captain knew what she was doing, though, for she soon landed the transport vessel.

After thanking the captain effusively, the four Protectors exited the ship with the other transportees. With amusement, Adams noted the merchant he had seen being grilled by the bureaucrat at Transport Station Alpha had made the journey with them. Currently, she appeared to be munching happily on a bit of fruit. Feeling his gaze, one eye swiveled to meet his, and she smiled wetly displaying a mouthful of sharp teeth. He smiled back uncertainly: the last alien smiling at him like that had apparently wanted to eat him. Without a word, though, the merchant stopped, letting the crowd wash over her and effectively obscuring him from seeing her.

Trance looked to the other Protectors. Aura and Dexter were bickering happily as they looked around the cavern. Mollie was listening quietly, looking at nothing in particular. Since he was left to his own thoughts momentarily, he let his eyes wander around the brightly lit, though sterile hanger.

It was a vast space, so vast that it seemed to curve out of sight in the distance. In fact, he couldn't see the walls; just ceiling and floor racing into eternity. It made him slightly dizzy.

As they moved along the concourse, Trance kept his eyes downward when he wasn't looking back and forth between his three friends. The floor was interesting: it appeared to be the equivalent of white plasticrete, or perhaps white concrete, divided neatly into squares each approximately ten feet by ten feet. The surface felt just rough enough to allow for a steady step.

Inset into the floor was a stripe of blue-green light that stretched about a hundred yards from the ship to a short squat building in front of them. The building was of a non-descript color, and consisted of a flat roof and many flat sides each with a door. It bored Trance immensely just looking at it. In fact, it seemed to exude boredom from every pore. The blue green light at their feet raced straight up to this building and then around it at a distance of five feet.

By this time, Trance had noted the landscape was peppered with buildings just like the one his group was headed for. There seemed to be a ship assigned to each. "This is the biggest of the hangars," Aura commented to him as they walked. "There are tons more, but this is by far the largest. Impressive, no?" He winked at Trance.

"It's the biggest room I've ever seen," Trance admitted, risking a look upward. Off in the distance above them, he could see the tremendous entrance they had come through; at this distance it was the size of a dime. It seemed to hang in the sky like a dark round moon. Around it flitted little pinpricks of light he guessed were starships. The sheer immensity of the layout made him shudder again.

They rapidly approached the structure in front of them, and headed for one of the entrances. Though the four Protectors stayed together, most of the rest of the group fragmented into ones and twos and began heading to doors of their choosing. On impulse, Trance looked to see which side the merchant chose, but she was nowhere to be found. He gave a mental shrug and followed the other three Protectors through one of the doors.

Inside was a small square room with another series of doors with strange symbols on each. Trance was surprised that he couldn't read them and asked the ring about it.

"Those are symbols, Trance. It's different than written words. I can't translate for you because you decide what the meaning is by seeing the symbol. It's kind of like the color red for your species, yes?

"Well, it means 'Stop.'"

"Sometimes. It can also mean 'Danger,' or 'war,' or a hundred other things depending upon how it is used."

"Hmm." Sometimes Trance wished he could have a simple "Yes," or "No." With a start, he realized he'd fallen behind the group. The doors were elevators – the three other Protectors were inside one of them looking back at him expectantly. Aura had one massive hand out keeping the door from closing, despite an alarm bell clanging softly. Trance grinned at them, sidestepped several individuals waiting for other lifts, and jogged forward and in.

Chapter 12: Sigfried and Kameko

The ride was uneventful. They were alone for its entirety. Trance got the feeling they were moving extremely fast over a great distance in a generally downward angle. Occasionally, though, it seemed like they were going sideways in several different directions at once. When the doors opened again, five minutes later, his breath caught in his throat. They were outside again! But they couldn't be outside, could they? What he was seeing just didn't make sense.

"No, we're not outside at all, not in your usual sense of the word," the ring replied. "Everything in Monidad is inside the planet's crust." Trance squinted into the sky, which looked like one might expect a sunny sky to look like as he followed the others out of the elevator.

"It sure looks real," he said aloud. The sky was bluish, and tiny clouds appeared to be flitting across its length and breadth. He couldn't see the sun – there were too many tall buildings in the way. "So, what's the secret?" he asked Mollie who looked amused.

He felt like a country bumpkin gawking for the first time at the city. He realized he probably looked the part. She smiled at him, all teeth and whiskers. "It's an illusion. The ceiling is about a mile up in this section, and the light is diffused. Each section, or cavern, if you could call it that, has its own weather. This section is… 75 degrees and sunny. At noon it will rain for ten minutes and thirty seconds, and then it will be nice for the rest of the day."

"The rain cleans the buildings and the air," Aura said knowledgeably. "It rains each night, too."

"Where does the water go, anyway?" asked Dexter. He'd evidently never taken the time to wonder. The cat looked mildly interested, a surprise given the fact the subject had nothing to do with females or alcoholic beverages.

"Into the drains in the road. Everything is recycled and purified, and used again, of course," Mollie stated matter-of-factly.

They were walking along a sidewalk of sorts at this point. On their right, shiny new buildings with mirrored windows lanced out of the pavement and reached into the sky. To their left was a street, but unlike any that Trance had seen before. Across the street were more buildings.

The road consisted of three raised metallic rails running parallel to the sidewalk. Traffic was one-way in direction and traveled along the central rail, hovering centimeters off the ground. The metal bands on either side of center were for vehicles that had reached their destinations.

When a car pulled to the side of the road, its passengers disembarked quickly, abandoning their transportation. Anyone was free to take an empty vehicle, and if no one did within a certain about of time, the car moved on to other places. The system seemed to work very smoothly; no one owned a vehicle in this society.

The vehicles didn't seem to be using combustion engines – they were too quiet, and didn't emit any visible gasses. He first guessed they were electric in nature, possibly magnetic. Aura said something about an inertial field, but Trance's mind couldn't grasp the concept and the Golden Protector gave up. He said he didn't fully understand it either.

The streets were set in an exact grid. The buildings to their right, and across the road, were of varying heights, but the city blocks were exactly the same distance in length. At the end of each block, another three-band road cut through from other caverns. You were able to cross the street at the corner -- the path bridged the road at a sufficient height so as not to impede traffic.

Everything seemed vaguely familiar. They walked by department stores, office buildings, a grocer, several fast food restaurants, and a movie theater. Finally, they reached a building shorter than many of the others they had passed. It appeared to be made of red brick and had a sloped roof, green eaves, two windows, and a glass door. "Boutique," had been stenciled in white on its eaves and on the door. "Open All Day, Every Day" it proclaimed haughtily. "We're here," Mollie said in satisfaction.

Aura raised his eyebrows but didn't say anything. Dexter scowled. "I knew we were going to stop here, I just knew it."

"There's this really cute pink collar that I've been wanting," Mollie said in way of explanation. "It has a little bell that jingles when I walk. I'll just be a minute."

"Can't you create one?" Trance asked.

"Sure," Mollie replied, "but what would be the fun in that? Besides, even though I could create something similar, I'd never be able to get all the details exactly right by using my ring."

"Well I'm not going in there," Dexter said with a darkened brow. "The last time I went in there somebody tackled me and put a bright red bow on the tip of my tail! I was mortified!"

"But you looked darn cute," Aura said. I think they shampooed you, too, come to think of it."

"Yes. And they curled my hair." He turned to Trance. "Have you ever seen a cat with a full-body perm? It's not pretty."

"I thought it was," Aura laughed, "and worth every credit."

"Fine, you go in with Mollie. Trance and I will stay out here, thanks. Right, Trance? Help me out, here, fella."

"I really wouldn't mind seeing you get a perm, Dexter," Trance replied. Certainly, you need a bath of some sort. My God, you attract flies like you're having a shit sale!"

Dexter laughed. "Yeah, it's all part of my natural charm. Hey, there's a bench over there." He pointed to a large grayish wooden bench at the corner of the boutique. "Why don't we sit there while they are inside getting pretty?"

"Alright," Trance replied. "I really don't have any money to spend anyway."

"And you're not going to extort any more credits from me," the ring sniffed.

"Well, great," Mollie said as she and Aura opened the door, "keep a look out for Sigfried and Kameko, will you Dexter? They are supposed to meet us here."

"Reading you loud and clear, Gray leader," Dexter said smartly to their retreating backs. The door closed behind Aura and Mollie. "Come on, Trance," the Orange cat said.

They walked over to the bench and sat down. Trance appreciated the time to sit there. It gave him a chance to watch the masses of Monidad as they went about their business. It was kind of like lying on a grassy hill as a child and watching the clouds as they slid across the sky – strange and wonderful shapes crossed his vision, and he played the game of trying to turn them into something familiar.

Many of the shapes were carrying shopping bags with bits of bright cloth tucked safely within, just enough sticking out to catch his eye. Some of them moved on four legs, others on eight, ten or twelve. Occasionally, there was even a biped. Some looked at the world with a thousand eyes of every size and shape, others with just one. Some laughed with one another as they meandered this way and that, others slipped quietly through the crowd, men and women and things with a definite purpose and direction.

At home, he might have called it a river of humanity. Here, that phrase would have been insulting. Instead, it was a river of... color.

There was no definite form of dress unifying the masses. They wore every conceivable color and pattern. Some seemed to be naked. Others were completely clothed without an inch of skin showing. Some wore bright purples and yellows, others were clad in gray. Some were even dressed in a rainbow of swirling colors that changed as they walked. One appeared to be a six-foot tall gerbil running on all fours within a large clear plastic ball. Somehow it made its way down the sidewalk without crushing anyone.

They sat there for five minutes, talking about nothing in particular and watching the traffic as it walked or drove or slithered by them. Then, Dexter jumped to his feet. "Great, they're here," he said. "Come on, Trance, let's meet them." He raised himself up to about six feet off the ground in a pale blue nimbus of energy, and started waving wildly as he floated down the sidewalk.

A small dainty hand rose out of the crowd and waved back. Trance stood and followed Dexter.

He first saw the pair when they were several yards away. One looked like a human female, and the other could only be described as a gigantic, cute, garden slug.

The slug was a good three feet long. It had two feelers that arched out of the top of its head. This was typical of slugs that Trance had known (stepped on) back home. The thing that made it different, besides the size, was that it had huge dinner plate eyes that were blue in color, and a large pink tongue that hung from its mouth like a tie. It also had a cute pink button nose, and small jowls. The rest of it was shaped like a slug – tubular and flaccid looking.

The woman was easier to look at. She had shoulder-length light brown hair, golden brown skin, hazel eyes and a small nose. She was lithe and muscular, and moved fluidly through the crowd. As she approached, Trance heard a smooth voice, like silk. She smelled like wild flowers after a rain storm. She seemed oddly familiar to him, like he had met her before.

She was wearing a gray-green short sleeve shirt with the customary Spiral Galaxy patch of the Corps on the breast. Her arms were bare. A lower edge of a colorful tattoo could be seen on her left shoulder beneath her sleeve. She was also wearing denim pants and black combat boots.

The slug wasn't wearing anything. But given that it was surrounded in a blue haze of energy and floating three feet off the sidewalk, Trance guessed it too was a Protector.

"It's good to see you two!" Dexter exclaimed happily when they were within arm's length.

"Hi there, Dexter," the slug said clearly in a masculine voice. "Who's this?" he asked, looking at Trance.

"Trance Adams. He's a human and the newest member of the squad. Introduce yourself, guys."

The woman spoke first. "My name is Kameko. I'm from the planet Tas'numg." She saluted smartly. "Welcome to the corps, Trance Adams."

Trance smiled and returned the salute.

"Hello. My name is Sigfried. I'm what you might call a slug. I'm addicted to salt. It's my weakness and my devotion," the slug said.

"Mighty upfront, aren't you Sigfried?" Trance asked pleasantly looking for a hand to shake. Of course, the slug had none.

"It's stage three in a twelve step program," Kameko replied helpfully.

"Hmp. I guess some things are universal," Trance decided.

"Yes, and different," Dexter added. "It's the first twelve step program where he is the higher power!" Somewhere cymbals crashed.

Trance looked around, and then back at the slug. Evidently, there was a cymbal sale going on somewhere nearby. "This is really an incredible place," he offered.

"Oh yes," replied Sigfried. "I agree. This is my fourth trip, but it's new every time."

"You been here long Sig?" Dexter asked jovially.

"No, I just arrived this morning. In fact, Kameko and I flew in on the same ship. We did a bit of shopping, and then made our way here."

"Pick up anything interesting?" Trance asked.

"Actually, I found some great cigars," Kameko said. She pulled one out of her purse, smelled it, and popped one end into her mouth. "Ahh," she said, "there is nothing like chewing on a fresh cigar in the morning."

The ring explained that Kameko had been a commander in the armed forces of her home planet before becoming a Protector. She had been in the corps for nearly fifteen hundred years, though she still had the military bearing. She exercised regularly, lifted weights in the gym, and ate a fastidiously healthy regimen of mostly vegetables and grains. She liked to say her only known vice was chewing, not smoking, thousand credit cigars. She had a blue streak and had a tendency to swear, liked playing cards and drinking whiskey. In short, she had a tendency to bring out the worst in Dexter.

Sigfried was an artist known, throughout his galaxy, for his clear vision and ingenious use of color. His favorite medium was oil-based paint on canvas. His subjects varied from fields of green and gold to a still-life of fruit in a crystal bowl, and he was comfortable with each.

Sigfried could take an object and with a few simple strokes capture its essence for all time. His art seemed to jump from the canvas. His works lived and breathed like only true masterpieces could.

A "Sigfried," as his paintings were called, could go for thousands of credits, if you could find them for sale anywhere. You weren't anyone unless you owned one, and the rarest of rare owned two. But that wasn't enough for Sigfried. He didn't want the fame, the glory. He was a philosopher, a dreamer, and found fame far too confining.

He longed to live a simpler life away from the flashing lights, the cameras, the paparazzi. He shunned society, turning away from it, exiling himself. When the ring came to him, he embraced it. He faked his own death, and left, never to return.

Sigfried still painted from time to time in the privacy of his own room, but his true masterpieces were the constructs he created with his ring. They were his specialty, and they seemed to breathe with the same fire and passion seen in his paintings. Some whispered he was unequaled in the creation of constructs – they were indistinguishable from the real thing.

Just then, Mollie and Aura approached them. Mollie had her collar on and looked smashing. Its tiny bell jingled pleasantly as she walked. Aura wasn't carrying anything, but his bald head looked as though it had recently been polished, and his golden skin shone like the new sun.

After pleasantries were exchanged, they found a nearby café and ordered lunch. The service was excellent. They were seated quickly at a long table outside where they could see the road. At least, it felt like they were outside. Trance realized he was having trouble reconciling the fact that they were miles beneath the surface of the planet. He shook his head to clear it.

Overhead was a blue eave flapping slightly in the gentle breeze. If he closed his eyes, he might still be at home.

The café, like all of the eating establishments on planet was designed to suit a tremendous variety of tastes. Trance was pleasantly surprised to discover Protectors ate free on planet. This was nice to know because he was beginning to regret spending all of the money he had muscled out of the ring on his substantial bar tab at Legs.

The menus were digital in nature, on a single sheet of what felt like paper. They were easy to use; you simply typed in your origin, and the selections changed to suit.

Trance even discovered a small sub-menu for humans. It consisted mainly of pasta dishes, but there was an attempt at Mexican, with several burritos. To his delight, he also found a hamburger and French fries. He ordered that.

At exactly noon, the sky darkened and raindrops splattered in the streets and tapped gently on the overhang for ten minutes. Then the sky cleared again. It was quiet during that time – just the sound of the rain. The world seemed to shut down as everyone stopped to watch it – conversations ceased and traffic slowed. It was peaceful.

Trance's hamburger consisted of a slice of meat shoved into a bun, but tasted suspiciously like it had all the fixings. He caught a strong taste of lettuce, fried onions, tomatoes, onion rings, bacon, ketchup, mayonnaise, blue cheese, thousand island, fried mushrooms, cheddar, Swiss, American, and Gouda cheeses, mustard, pickles, and relish. His fries tasted like they had been dipped in vinegar, ketchup, barbeque sauce, ranch, and an assortment of other strange flavors. It was all a bit much to stomach, but he was so hungry he ate every bite.

Chapter 13: Blue Sky

After lunch, they made their way back to the nearest lift. When it opened several minutes later, they found a blue carpeted reception area complete with comfortable looking couches and a desk with attendants. Behind the desk, a sign hung which said "Blue Sky Extended Stay Apartments." It was a simple foyer, but it had a striking feature – a large floor to ceiling window which looked out at the pockmarked and gray landscape of Monidad. Trance walked over and looked out. The view was spectacular; he could see all the way to the horizon. There wasn't a single sign of life out there -- no greens, no blues, no yellows-- just still, gray, and scarred soil. "Where are we?" he asked the ring.

"Two point five miles up. We are in the spire," the ring replied.

"Oh."

After a moment, Mollie tapped him lightly on the back of the leg. He looked down to see her sitting there looking out the window. "It's quite a sight, Trance, isn't it?"

"Oh yes. It's amazing."

"I never get tired of seeing the view," she murmured. "Well, we're ready when you are, Trance."

He looked back to see the others waiting patiently at the desk. Sigfried had a sad little smile on his face as if he were remembering times past. The others looked bored. Trance nodded and followed Mollie back to the desk where he was presented with a small piece of paper with a number on it indicating his room. It was in between Aura and Dexter. The other Protectors were just down the hall.

They entered another elevator, which only operated a few seconds. They stepped out into a long silver-gray hallway with green doors spaced evenly along its long expanse. Aura, Dexter, and Trance turned to the left, the others turned right. They followed the numbers, which were written above the doors until they came to the three they were assigned to. After agreeing to meet for dinner, the three separated. Dexter and Aura both said something about their rooms being preprogrammed – they stepped right into their rooms and closed their doors. But when Trance's door opened, he stopped.

Before him was a large 20 by 20 foot metallic room. Everywhere Trance looked; the walls, ceiling, and floor were covered in circular holes. Most of the holes were the diameter of a pencil, except for the holes in the far corner which varied in size from a dime to several inches. There wasn't a light source but Trance could see clearly the entire length and breadth of the enclosure. It didn't look comfortable.

"Don't go in just yet, Protector," the ring said as his foot crossed over the threshold. "Instead, address the room."

"The room?" Trance said aloud.

"Yep. Ah, here we go."

"Greetings, Protector," a voice said from within. A figure, most likely a hologram, had appeared in the center of the room and strode toward him about six inches off the floor. The hologram was bipedal, six feet in height and asexual. It had gray eyes, a tiny nose, and a Spartan mouth with overly bright white teeth. It was dressed in a gray pinstripe suit with an off-white shirt open at the neck, which seemed to fade into its chalk-like skin. It had no visible hair. "I am your domicile representative, here to help set up your room."

"Oh, of course," Trance mumbled. He should have expected that.

The Domicile Rep stopped when it was about five feet away, and hovered there pleasantly. "Yes," it said. "May I ask you some questions?"

"Yes, but nothing hard. It's been a long day."

"Good. Your outer appearance, and internal temperature, organ layout and chemistry all indicate Earth - Human specifically. Is this an accurate statement?"

"Yes." Trance admitted.

"Excellent. Do you require any toiletry facilities other than standard human?"

"Hmm. No." Trance had no idea what the question meant but he preferred not to have adventures in that arena. Best to play it safe.

"Excellent. Our standard human bathroom suite consists of a toilet, bidet, sink, shower, and a mirrored cabinet. Will such accommodations suffice?"

"No bidet," Trance grunted. He'd do his drinking out of a glass.

Behind the domicile representative, a lime green liquid had begun to ooze from the floor. In seconds it covered the entire surface and had filled the space between the rep's feet. "No bidet," the rep repeated sagely. "And your living quarters: a bed, desk, computer station, media center, and a bureau. May I include a holo viewer? It's not Earth Standard, but many visitors request one."

"Sure. That would be fine. I don't know if I'll use one, but sure, why not?"

"Excellent. That rounds out the living area. Next the bedroom—"

"What about a kitchen of some sort?"

"All meals are consumed at the commissary in this section," the rep replied. "However, as you know, you can eat at any establishment on planet free of charge."

"So, no kitchen then. Well, maybe it's for the best. I'm a horrible cook anyway."

"Excellent," the rep smiled and nodded.

The lime green liquid had begun to shimmer. Suddenly, streams of the stuff jetted up to the ceiling, flowed across it, and then down the three walls Trance could see. Then new walls began to form: two in the back corner and a third jutting from this junction, reaching across the center of room and meeting wall to his left. "Would you like a window in your sleeping area?" the rep asked.

"What will it look out to?"

"All rooms are on the outer edge of the spire," the rep replied. "You can see a great deal."

"Ok, I'd like a large window, then."

"Excellent. One last question: what type of floor covering would you prefer?"

"I'd like the thickest damn carpet you can give me."

"Is gray acceptable? It's my favorite color."

"Yes." Trance nodded. His head was spinning just a bit.

"Excellent." Behind the representative, the wall had solidified then turned white. A wood-grained door formed and opened revealing a fully furnished bedroom. A large picture window slid across the far wall. Stars twinkled in the black sky beyond.

Trance tore his eyes from the window and realized that a living room had grown out of the lime while he was momentarily distracted. He now saw the thick gray carpet he had requested. To his left, he recognized a media center, with a tele-screen and a cabinet of electronic components recessed into the wall. A comfortable looking couch had grown out of the carpet and faced the tele-screen. On his right was a computer desk. It had an old-fashioned bendable OLED 16K monitor, a keypad, a headset, and what appeared to be a mouse, though he could only guess having just seen them in high school history texts. In short, it was a nice apartment. He nodded in satisfaction.

"Done!" the representative exclaimed. "Your choices have been recorded for your next visit. If you need any further assistance please address me again." The hologram faded.

"Now you can step in," the ring said.

Trance walked in and explored the nooks and crannies of the apartment, then used the bathroom. The facilities worked perfectly. After he was done, he sank wearily into the couch.

He was awakened by a furry paw tapping him on the shoulder. "Hey Adams, wake up!" It was Dexter. The cat was sitting on his chest. "Hope it's ok, but I let myself in. You sure do sleep hard!"

"Uh, sure, anytime," Trance said, wiping his hands across his eyes. "How about getting off my chest?"

Dexter was washing one of his front paws with his tongue. "Huh? Oh, sorry. Just a minute; I'm busy here."

"Don't put yourself out, or anything, on my behalf," Trance grunted.

"So, you ready to eat?" Dexter jumped down to the floor, leaving tiny claw marks and large clumps of orange and white fur on Trance's chest.

"Yeah, I am hungry," Trance said, sitting up and rubbing his chest to dislodge the fur.

After breakfast, the two met Aura near the set of lifts closest their living quarters. Together they traveled to the deepest part of Monidad – the core. The lift trip took only a minute or two despite the tremendous length, and opened to a sight almost unimaginable.

Chapter 14: The Tour

He stepped out of the lift with the others. "Look down," Aura said, pointing at their feet.

They were standing on a narrow catwalk. If he raised his arms from his sides, he could just touch the handrails on either side. He stepped to one side, looked down, and then jumped backward quickly, his heart falling into his stomach. After a couple of breaths to calm himself, he was ready to venture another look.

The heart of the core had been completely capped. He could see the outer edge less than a hundred yards away below him, curving away from him in all directions; a dull lusterless metallic surface of ridges and rivets. The thing was massive; he couldn't get his mind around the dimensions. The sheer size of it ruined perspective. Feeling slightly dizzy, he looked around rather than down.

To his left and right he could see, well, more catwalks. The ring informed him that each successive row down was angled just slightly from his perspective, to account for gravity and the curvature of the core. It was impossible to tell, frankly, but in matters of education, Trance had to trust the ring. In all other matters, the jury was still out.

Easier to see was that the catwalk curved as well along its length so that it followed the plane of the core. Suddenly, it hit him that everything within Monidad followed this pattern, but the closer that you got to the outer surface, the harder it was to tell due to the sheer size involved.

With a start, he realized Aura and Dexter had walked a short distance away to a platform where a group had formed. He followed their lead.

The platform was easily a hundred feet by a hundred feet square, and like the catwalk had a slightly curved bearing. On one of the four sides there was a lift much like the one that his tiny group had taken. Two of the sides exited onto catwalks. The fourth had a flimsy looking handrail with the same stunning view of the core. Trance shied away from the edge and joined his friends.

"Is this where the tour starts?" Trance sighed.

"You don't like tours?" Dexter asked.

"It's not that I don't like them, exactly," Trance said, which was the truth of a sort. In fact, Trance despised tours.

His hatred, because that was really the only name for it, toward tours had started early. Growing up, his parents had frequently dragged him along with them on vacations to wonderful (they thought) and exotic (they claimed) locales. Naturally, these locales' main feature tended to be a museum with gift shop firmly attached. Just as naturally, Trance usually ended up with a shirt from said establishment proudly stating, much to his horror and embarrassment, that he had indeed survived a visit. He usually got these t-shirts as presents at Christmas time. He'd force back a shriek of "Gee, where did you get this?" or "Oh, what a coincidence, look where Santa's been!" because he knew bloody well exactly where the gift had been purchased, and by whom. He loved his parents dearly. He just hated tours. They were dry and uninteresting-- a plague on his otherwise happy youth.

The one tour he enjoyed had been a guided trip through a wax museum somewhere in Canada. The museum had been filled to the brim with famous persons and re-enactments of battles that tore the periods displayed right out of the textbook and into his active imagination.

Each figure had been lovingly created and included actual real hair, though probably not the actual real hair of the person portrayed. Since he had been a teenager full in the bloom of puberty at the time he secretly wondered if the sculptor had given as much attention to the parts beneath the clothing. Trance smiled at the thought.

He was more than willing to put his feelings about tours aside in this case. Everything he had encountered thus far had fascinated him wholly, and he was actually looking forward to finding out more about his new environment.

The group consisted of several Protectors, but most of the people here were not ring bearers. Some of them lived in shapes familiar to him, as his mind liked to make familiarities wherever it could.

One shape looked vastly like a small dolphin in facial features. Its head was encased in a clear plastic bowl filled with liquid; its body had been surrounded with a bipedal exoskeleton, which it appeared to be manipulating with its fins. It saw Trance looking at it and nodded to him. "Hey, how's it going?" it asked from speakers on its shoulders.

"Nice to meet you," Trance replied, and let his gaze slide onwards.

There were cockroaches the size of cats, amphibians with large yellow eyes, and even what appeared to be a family of fur balls. Some were taking pictures; others were gnawing on snacks or talking quietly. Just about everyone had an "I've been to the CORE (And ALL I Got Was This Lousy Shirt)" t-shirt.

They stood there for a few minutes before the lift opened and their guide walked out. Trance knew instantly she was the guide because she had the look of a guide complete with a name tag that said "Edlani Vitleksky – Guide." She stood about five foot four, but must have weighed less than a hundred pounds because she was rail thin. She had four legs and two arms. In one arm she carried a stool.

Edlani stepped forward until she was an arm's length from the group. She was wearing a blue coat with a purple and yellow striped tie around her neck, and brown slacks. Her feet bore black shoes with flat soles.

She carefully placed the stool on the ground and then climbed aboard. When she was comfortably situated, she began speaking. "Welcome to the core of Mondidad," she said. "This is the first step of our tour tonight. What you see before you is the heart of our planet in more ways than one. This is where most of our power originates, and where we recycle matter and energy. Now, if you will all file into the lift, we will travel to our next stop."

"She talks like she's been giving this tour a long time," Trance whispered to Aura.

"That's right," Aura responded. "At least five times a day, probably about a hundred times a month. She is the same guide I had nearly three hundred years ago."

"Really?" Trance scoffed.

"This tour has been around for millions of years," Dexter said, "and it's always the same. I imagine it gets quite boring. Besides, she's a Protector. I'm sure she can handle it."

"I thought the corps was too thinly spread for desk jobs," Trance asked internally.

"Edlani's been retired for some time," the ring said. "She doesn't want to give up her ring, though, so the Creators keep her around to give tours and answer questions. It works well for both parties."

They were now all in the lift. After the doors had been closed momentarily, Trance felt the familiar tug of gravity. One of the littlest fur balls began to whine softly and was cuddled by its parents. But other than that, the lift was quiet.

The doors opened again in a nondescript hallway. The guide allowed everyone to file out, then stopped in the middle of the hall, climbed aboard her stool and addressed them again. She pointed back over her shoulder as she spoke. "Behind me is the most secret room on planet. You can see it is guarded by two of the meanest and most highly trained sentries we could find. They are very observant and incredibly smart, ready to kill at a moment's notice to protect our planet.

'Between those two doors they guard, of course, is the machinery running the force shield protecting the System. I can say no more." She paused for a moment as if waiting for something, and then looked witheringly back at the two guards. Both of them looked at her mutely like deer caught in the glare of an oncoming car. "I SAID," she said, "I can SAY no MORE!"

The two looked at each other, and then back at the tour guide, who appeared to be making secret covert gestures at them both. Then one of them stirred as the sunlight of comprehension slowly dawned across his face. He stepped forward, caressing the butt of his holstered pistol with one meaty hand, his lip curled around a snaggletooth, and growled, "Move along youse guys. Nuthin' to see here." Unfortunately, the effect was ruined when he turned back and smirked at his companion who flashed him a thumbs-up sign. They gave each other high fives.

"Mommy, those guys don't look mean or smart," one of the smallest fur balls said in a loud piercing voice. Its parent shushed it. A couple of the adults chuckled but held their tongues.

The guide looked mortified, but kept to the script. "Yes, sir," she said between gritted teeth as she stepped down from her stool and led the group back into the lift. Before the doors closed, however she leaned back into the hallway and glared at the two guards again. They smiled innocently.

When they were on their way again, Trance called to Dexter on their shared connection. No one else could hear their conversation. "Why not staff that door with Protectors if it's so important?"

"It's really just for show, Trance. Nobody has ever attacked Monidad directly, ever. Not for billions of years, and besides there aren't enough Protectors to go around as it is."

Trance, who worked for the Government and knew something about misdirection, said, "That's probably not even the real door. I bet it's just a mop closet."

"Oh, it's the real door, alright," Dexter said. "Behind it lies just about the most important equipment this side of my penis."

"OK, that's a disgusting picture," the ring groused.

"Huh," Trance said, trying to forget what the cat had just said, "it seems awful brazen of the Creators to show everyone where it is, if it's so important."

The cat shrugged. He was rapidly losing interest in this line of thought.

"May I make a comment?" the Ring asked, and then continued on unabated, "what you are saying makes sense."

"Hey, thanks ring. Why don't the Protectors see it as a potential problem?"

"Because you're talking about a concept that is foreign to them in every way; an idea so foreign as to be completely 'alien' to their society... their way of life."

"I... I... I guess I don't know what you mean," Trance replied.

"The Creators are super-powerful beings as compared to pretty much everybody, right? They have an incredible, pretty much impenetrable security setup, from the force shield around the System, to the alarms that go off if someone tries to sneak aboard Monidad, even to the Protectors."

"Yeah?"

"I wouldn't say the Creators have become complacent, but I would say that even the thought of someone breaking through their security system, with all its backups, is so alien to them as to not even be considered." This conversation lasted for several stops in the tour.

Over the next hour, they visited a training room for Protectors, science and research laboratories, and a library staffed entirely by glowing energy beings. Trance liked the library best: he was glad he had taken the time to participate in the tour, because he wouldn't have recognized it as such otherwise.

The sights were incredible and the stories even more so. They heard about the carving out of Monidad, the terraforming of the other planets in the system; about the recent discovery of a new race of sentient beings in a previously uncharted realm of space, and the creation of new and amazing inventions that could possibly revolutionize life in the Conglomerated States.

The guide was very informative, using her ring to create visual aids in order to enhance her stories. Though Edlani Vitleksky was diminutive in appearance, she had a great speaking voice, and used her ring to affect stunning and lifelike visual aids. The result was a slick and fascinating look at the inner workings of Monidad and the System.

Comment []: a little on the nose

Comment []: what does he mean by this?

Chapter 15: History

Eventually, they made their way to the Hall of History. The "Hall" was actually a massive museum dedicated to the history of the Corps. It had a combination of large open areas filled with murals, paintings, and sculptures, and also long corridors of exhibits, statues, and other memorabilia. It was easily twice the size of the Louvre in Paris, France, which Trance had visited with his parents as a child. Sure enough, this museum had a gift shop firmly attached.

Because it was so big, there wasn't any hope that they could see the entire thing in a single tour. To give the museum even half the attention it deserved, a solid month could be spent, maybe more. Many individuals had given their lifetimes in pursuit of cataloging, labeling, shelving, and guarding its contents. The curators had done an excellent job – each item had a label with a tiny plaque bearing an inscription. Trance promised himself he would return one day and spend whatever time was needed in order to see every single item.

There were tons of relics both ancient and modern: everything from concept costumes - a green and black model with a lantern as the symbol emblazoned across the chest- to weapons (all carefully "sterilized"); murals, portraits of the famous and infamous, and even land and space vehicles. The guide told stories about a select few, and answered questions about any when prompted. She really knew her stuff.

They spent another hour wandering about in what seemed to be a random fashion. In truth, they were skillfully being led to exact center of the tremendous building, to the Reliquary of Truth.

The Reliquary could be best described as a separate museum within the Hall of History. It was a building within the building, complete with a single locked door and no windows. Trance commented about the lock and was told by Aura the section they were in had been designed specifically for a guided tour. The Creators wanted absolutely no confusion regarding the subject within. For this was where the Museum got its name: it contained the true History of the Corps; a story at times dark and murky. As he listened, Trance began to appreciate the Creator's care to ensure it was properly relayed.

The lights were already on when they entered. They saw the building was actually a single room with many corridors of statues and dioramas. Edlani gave the group a moment to gape, then pulled out her stool once again and climbed it like a pulpit. "What you see before you is the sum total of our existence – from our tense past to our bright present, and hope for an even brighter future." There was a flash behind her like a firework, lighting her from behind in an aura of warmth. It was a good effect, obviously ring created, and the non-Protectors ate it up.

"In the beginning, there was chaos," she said, and the light began to turn into a sickly gray, darkening by degrees into an inky blackness. "Pirates roamed the space ways, preying upon the innocent and the ill-prepared." At this point, a sleek white vessel rocked out of the black, and zoomed through the group zigging this way and that. A much larger, and somehow swarthy, ship pursued it. The smaller vessel didn't have a chance.

When it reached the rear of the crowd, it was destroyed in a harmless flash. One of the little fluff balls jumped, emitting a small squeak. The rest of the group showed its approval by grunting.

The guide continued on. "A union was created to hold back the night; two species from different systems bound together for protection. They prospered, and invited others to join. Slowly their influence spread over millions of years.

'It is unknown when the Creators joined the fledgling Union. But we do know that they brought the law with them. Through their machinations, a cobbled together group of barely lawful member fiefs became what we now know as the Conglomerated States. Their tools were the Protectors."

At this point, she stepped down from the stool, carefully folded it up, and began walking down the first corridor they came to. On the left and right were marble statues of Protectors who had served with honor at the infancy of the corps.

"Originally, the corps of Protectors was created to police the fledgling Conglomerated States," Edlani said. "As the corps grew, its mission changed to protect the neutral races and the developing ones as well… to keep them from becoming unduly influenced by outside forces while they developed naturally." She pointed at what looked to Trance like a squid. "Protectors such as

T'ruk'mons-sim, under the guidance and direction of the Creators led the Universe from the brink of chaos to where it is today."

"The middle of chaos," Dexter said, nudging Aura. They both winked at Trance.

"For countless millennia, the corps has existed in harmony," the guide continued. "Except for one brief and tragic period…." She paused dramatically, pointing to the statue of a cruel looking dragon standing defiantly on various skulls, which were piled upon the north pole of a planet. It was beautiful, yet ghastly.

"Si-truc," Trance whispered to himself, looking at the figure in disgust. The statue had fallen into extreme disrepair, unlike the others they had seen so far. It was pitted and crumbling in places and had acquired a fine layer of dust. The pedestal it sat on had cracks in many places, and one of its arms had broken off and fallen to the floor where it lay undisturbed.

"Si-truc." The guide spit the word out like a rotten grape. "The foul dragon." She paused, apparently gathering her thoughts. "The dragon's goal was the destruction of The Conglomerated States and the return of chaos to the universe. In pursuing this twisted goal, the foul one subverted many Protectors to his cause through deceit and manipulation. But he could not trick them all.

'Foul Dragon would have been triumphant had it not been for the gallant efforts of the remaining corps members and all of the Creators. They battled him without rest for five hundred years before ultimately defeating him and the other rogues at the Battle of Korondor in Sector Brandenburg. He was tried and punished: cursed to a prison without walls for all of eternity."

Most of the crowd gave off appropriate "ooh's" and "ah's," but Aura made a gagging sound. "Plantarshit," he said to Trance and Sigfried. That's just legend, guys." They looked at him inquisitively.   "Don't believe it. They probably shipped him off to a deep dark black hole and dumped him in without a breather. He certainly wouldn't have lasted an eternity, that's for sure."

The guide didn't notice Aura's mini outburst. "Though Si-truc was unable to destroy the States, he weakened them immeasurably. Though they did not fall, it took eons to recover economically and even longer to restore their faith in the power of the Protectors, their guardians. Even now we must work diligently to erase the stench of the Dragon and his ilk."

Though Trance was thoroughly enjoying himself, Dexter was quite bored. In fact, he had plans for an interlude. He saw a figure further down the hall, engrossed in what appeared to be the task of restoring a statue. She was currently brushing it carefully and filling in cracks with a tube. Her task looked complicated and time intensive, but one she appeared to be thoroughly enjoying. "C'mon," Dexter said to his two friends. "There's somebody I want to introduce you to, Trance."

Aura squinted at the figure, and smiled cryptically. "Oh, you'll get a kick out of her," he gushed. "Talk about history!"

Chapter 16: Taa'lien

They quickly broke off from the main group. The guide droned on, unaffected by their desertion. She seemed to be discussing the exploits of Elle'inad, who had apparently led the corps during that famous battle. It was through her guidance the corps had made a final stand around Korondor, and ultimately defeated Si-truc's forces. Trance glanced back at the statue the guide was pointing at. His jaw dropped. She looked very much like an angel, with two large bird-like wings and a flowing robe. It was a beautiful depiction. He wished he might have had more time to study her.

"Excuse me, Taa'lien," Dexter said as they approached the woman. She turned and looked at the cat politely. "Yes, Dexter, how can I help you?"

"I'd like to introduce you to someone. Taa'lien, this is Trance Adams, from Earth." Her eyes widened momentarily when she looked at the newbie from Earth. "Nice to meet you, Trent," she said, in a musical voice, smiling demurely. "I've always wanted to meet an Earthling."

Taa'lien's smile, while light and fresh, did not match her face, which bore hundreds of little scars and several rather large ones across a patchwork quilted of gray and discolored skin.

The rest of her features were pleasant, an odd contrast to her scarred visage. She wore sandy long hair that framed her face and enhanced her crystal blue eyes, and her figure was breathtaking. "That's Trance," Trance muttered underneath his breath as he shook her hand, taking her in with a glance.

"Sorry... Trance! My hearing isn't so good anymore. I'll remember it forever once I get it right though!" She laughed pleasantly. Despite himself, Trance found he liked her. "What do you think of the tour so far?" she asked.

Trance looked around the hallway, at the statues and finally at the ornate ceiling. "I'm speechless," he admitted. "It's all so magnificent and mind blowing. It is quite a lot to take in all at once. But it's nice to see some of the history and tradition of the corps, and the rest of the tour has been simply incredible."

Her smile grew wider. "Trance, I have been a Protector for longer than I can remember. Even I still haven't seen this entire place!" She winked. "Relax. You'll never take it all in. There's too much! That's why I designed the tour; so new recruits could get a brief overview of Monidad and the corps without becoming overwhelmed."

"You designed this tour? But the guide said..."

"Oh yes, I know," she winked at Sigfried and Aura. "These two fellows will undoubtedly tell you all about it while you catch up with the rest of the group," she laughed, pointing down the hall at the retreating backs of the rest of the party. 'Tell you what, I have to finish a few things here, but after that, I'll join you three for the culmination of the tour." Her eyes sparkled. "They show the final battle of Sector Brandenburg." With that, she turned walked toward another corridor.

"She's the oldest of the Protectors, Trance. From the beginning, just about," Aura whispered as they watched her withdrawing backside.

"Really? She looks like she is in her late twenties, except for the scars on her face," Trance contended.

"If she were human, perhaps. But don't let her outer appearance fool you. Her interior anatomy is much different, I'm sure."

"Taa'lien was at the Battle of Sector Brandenburg," Dexter offered knowledgeably, "or at least part of it. She was nearly killed by a rogue. Did you see her ring arm?"

Trance squinted. "Yeah, it looks slightly odd, like it doesn't belong with the rest of her."

"It's mechanical. Her real ring arm was ripped off sometime during the battle."

"It was later recovered, though," Aura said knowledgeably.

"Yeah, they found it floating about ten feet from her unconscious body, apparently," Dexter shuddered. "I heard that she tried to swim to the ring before her body gave out."

"I didn't think that was possible," Trance said.

"Many races can swim through space without a breather." Aura replied. "Her race just doesn't do it very well, it appears."

"Oh."

"The ring could be easily taken because the flesh around it, specifically her entire arm, was deceased," the ring spoke into his mind.

"They say the whole experience, especially losing her ring, was so traumatic she has no memories of anything that happened before it," Aura stated as they hurried to catch up with the touring group. "She didn't even know her name when she woke up, or where she was from."

"Poor thing," Dexter grunted. "Still, I don't know why she doesn't just get a new arm, and fix that face…. Yuck. It gives me the willies."

"She likes the pain," Aura replied.

"Hey, that's just nasty," Trance murmured.

"Not like that," Aura returned. "She likes the pain because it keeps her going. It keeps her alive while she hunts for clues to her past."

"Surely she's thought to check the public records," Dexter mused.

"She's a pretty smart lady. I'll bet she checked and didn't find anything," Aura responded. "Besides, a lot of solar systems just disappeared during the revolt. Unfortunately, a lot of records have disappeared too."

"Why doesn't she just go back in time and look around then? She was alive during that period," Dexter sniffed.

"There is some sort of injunction against traveling that far back." Aura said. "She's tried it several times."

Trance brightened. "I bet somebody is practicing Revisionist History," he said. "My people know all about that!"

*****

The rest of the tour proved uneventful. The group was treated to several stories that were definitely worth repeating but which were forgotten immediately by most who heard them. They saw hundreds of cool paintings of battles and statues of heroes long lost to antiquity.

Frequently along the route, Trance saw individuals putting up signs indicating a joust would be occurring in one of several training rooms later that evening. "Come One, Come All!" The posters proclaimed in bright orange letters. "Come and Test your Mettle! Prove your ***Strength*** and ***Wit*** in the Battle Room! Who will be the Champ? Will YOU?"

"Hey, let's check that out," Trance said.

"Feeling adventuresome, Champ?" Aura chuckled. "Maybe you can try and match wits with Perridan."

"Perri -who? Nah, I just want to see other Protectors in action. I'd like to see what they can do with their rings."

"Perridan's the best," Dexter said. "Maybe we'll have enough time to check it out."

Chapter 17: The Battle of Korondor

Four hours into the tour, when they were entering a large auditorium, Taa'lien joined them again. "Hey, fellows. Still enjoying yourselves?" she asked. The three nodded wearily. "That's great. Whenever I'm in town, I try to catch this show… I keep hoping that watching it will bring some sliver of memory back…" she smiled wistfully.

"I also try and catch this memory record whenever I am around," Aura said. "It is my favorite part of the tour. As a historian, it is fun to see other cultures' history. As a Protector, it is intriguing to see my own."

"I heard somewhere that this film shows the actual battle of Korondor, not just a reenactment of it," Trance offered conversationally.

"Sort of," Taa'lien replied. "It is actually a mem-rec, or a memory record.
A mem-rec is the actual memory of an individual, recorded at a later date. In this case, the memories of Creator Farouk, the head Historian of the Creators at the time of the Rebellion, were used. He was a witness and an active participant in the battle, as you'll see."

"Memories are notoriously flawed," Trance scoffed. "How are we to be sure this is actually what happened, rather than just his faded recollection of it?"

"Your brain records everything that it senses flawlessly, Trance," Taa'lien responded. "It just has trouble accessing memories it creates. This system creates true records of events. They are accurate in every way. Everything Creator Farouk saw and heard that day is perfectly preserved. The only difference between the battle of Korondor mem-rec and the ones that are made today is that this one doesn't have smells. They didn't add that feature until several hundred years later."

"I'd hate to see one of Dexter's mem-recs," Aura commented. "The general stinkiness of the whole thing would be unbearable."

"Well, at least it wouldn't be boring like yours," Dexter snipped back. "Mine have action in them…. And ladies. Beautiful ladies." He sighed longingly.

At that point, they had found their seats. Though the floor beneath his feet was sticky, Trance was surprised to find his chair had no gum deposits upon it (though it was an awful shade of brick red); a rather pleasant deviation from what he was used to experiencing from going to the Planetarium Cineplex in Hunter.

The four Protectors conversed among themselves and with the other ring bearers and citizens around them for a few minutes before the room's lights flickered once and began to dim. At this point, everyone began placing headsets with goggles of a sort Trance had never seen before over whatever passed for their eyes.

Hanging on a peg sticking out of the chair in front of him was a set of the same type of goggles. From their appearance, with six eyepieces and over a dozen wires, Trance seriously doubted they were meant for his anatomy. But, with a mental shrug and a silent prayer he wouldn't make a complete ass of himself trying to get the set on, he reached out and grabbed them.

Amazingly enough, just as the wiry monstrosity touched his head, it beeped into his ear, and said quite clearly in English "Adjusting for human." It seemed to shudder around him, blurring and changing. Momentarily, the six oddly –shaped goggles had been replaced by two rather ordinary looking ones which hung over his eyes. Some sort of tubes had extended into his ears, but the whole outfit remained surprisingly comfortable, so he left it as it was.

After a moment, the theater darkened fully, causing the crowd to go completely quiet. Suddenly, Trance realized he was completely alone. Impossibly, he was standing on a small, insubstantial planet with gray features and a pockmarked surface. Though initially disturbed by the sudden transfer of perspective, he quickly relaxed after realizing it was part of the show. He couldn't control his body or his viewpoint, so why not sit back and enjoy it? In front of him, a few feet away, large green letters appeared: "Creator Industries Presents, in association with Monidad Films, The Battle of Sector Brandenburg." They quickly faded away. He began to suspect he was on the moon of Korondor during arguably one of the most famous battles in all of recorded history. That meant it was about to get really busy.

But, just then, it really wasn't busy. In fact, the moon was silent and barren, broken only by rolling hills, and off in the distance, the peaks of several mountains rising above the landscape. The mountains were only a slightly darker gray than the other parts of the moon, ragged and sharp at the peak. Above them, stars twinkled in the clear night sky. Korondor hung nearby; it filled the sky. Trance couldn't see much of it because the Creator never looked at it directly, but Trance got the impression it was fertile; a mixture of golden butter and deep greens and blues.

Among and between the stars, Trance could now see flashes of lights ranging through all the colors of the rainbow. The battle, it seemed, was joined. It was so far off, though, he doubted seriously that he'd be witness to it.

But then he saw his body --or rather Creator Farouk's body since it was his memories -- had a ring on the right hand and it was glowing with power. His vision shimmered, and suddenly he was in the thick of the mêlée, deep in space. It was everything that he had imagined and more.

Everywhere he could see destruction reigned. He was in a single star system, whose inhabitants had somehow become embroiled in the combat. Trance wondered if they had even been noticed when they were obliterated. Their spaceships, the parts he could see anyway, had been shattered. Bodies floated here and there, seared to perfection by the heat of explosion and cold of space. Perhaps a whole race had perished like a colony of ants crushed beneath an uncaring, unknowing boot.

A planet hung in the distance; it too had borne the punishment of close proximity to the battle. It was permanently scarred, a dark fissure running through it like a lance. Closer though, he could see the fight itself, in all its unorganized glory.

There were thousands of them. Here and there, Protectors screamed silently and perished as they burned beneath the onslaught of their brethren. It was hard to see which side, if there was a side, was winning. It was a chaotic and deadly dance. Energy streams flowed like rivers, and constructs flashed and faded as they burst into being, slammed into their objectives, and quickly dissipated. The sight alternately excited him and overwhelmed his senses, sickening him. So much death, so much destruction – it all seemed senseless. Then his perspective faded again.

Time had passed; how much time was uncertain. Korondor hung in the sky, and closer still its moon, and around and between the celestial bodies the battle raged.   All he knew was it felt different, now. Before, the mêlée had seemed ruthless, disorganized and deadly. Now, he began to notice a clear sense of organization.

There were two sides now. He looked for the dragon Si-truc, knowing the foul dragon's presence would give him an idea of where the bad guys were. The dragon was nowhere to be found, but Trance did see a few more of that race, among the smaller side.   He also saw the famed Elle'inad. She seemed to be guiding the group like a unified weapon, and her strategy appeared to be working. Though clearly outnumbered, her side was inflicting heavy damage. In fact, it was slowly pushing back its opponent.   Then everything blurred again…

More time had passed. Now Trance could see the battle was nearly over save for mopping up here and there. The victorious true Protectors and the remaining Creators landed on the moon to celebrate. Once hundreds of thousands of Protectors had guarded the Galaxy; now little more than a thousand remained. As one, they landed on the gray surface of the moon of Korondor to regroup and celebrate their victory. One of them created and then planted a flag; a piece of blue cloth upon which a galaxy spun in the center.

The flag was beautiful; it seemed to fill his entire vision with its grandness. It shone from its pole like a beacon in the evening light, warding off the night. Its presence spoke of strength and of righteousness; of goodness and of truth.

Just then, twin beams of energy split the sky, arching over the flag and striking the ground behind it. Creator Farouk's vision shifted, and there was Si-truc, the foul dragon, attempting one last feeble attack. Why he bothered Trance could only guess, outnumbered as he was a thousand to one. Two hundred energy streams arced out and grabbed him – two hundred beams of light brought him down to earth, encapsulating him with a cold embrace.

At last a voice spoke into Trance's ear as he watched the final moments of the show. "For his crimes against the Conglomerated States, Si-Truc was sentenced to be imprisoned for all eternity. His prison keeps him just enough alive so that he can forever ponder the evil of his actions. Though he can never expect a release, it is hoped he will seek redemption nonetheless."

Like a mist the presentation faded away and the lights began to slowly come on. Trance shook his head and placed the headset back on the peg jutting out from seat in front of him. It seemed to have reverted back to its previous state.

Everyone else around him was quietly standing and leaving the theater. The previously boisterous crowd had been silenced by the import of what they had viewed: the near destruction of the corps could not be taken lightly.

As he stood, Trance glanced over at Taa'lien . She looked worried. "Everything OK?" he asked her.

"Every time I see this, it makes me wonder," Taa'lien said.

"What's that?"

"Have you ever had a crazy feeling that you couldn't quite let go of?"

"All the time, I guess," Trance shrugged. But the look in her troubled eyes gave him pause. "The movie seemed OK to me…"

"Today, watching it… I got a premonition… there is something wrong there, Trance. I know it. But I just can't tell what it is."

Chapter 18: The Battle Room

Taa'lien shrugged palms up. "Isn't that strange?"

"Hmm. Well, you were there, right? Does any of this look familiar?"

"I was knocked out well before this record begins."

"Is there any way to fake a mem-rec? Enhance it with computers, or something?"

"I suppose. Obviously they added music, but I believe that is the only change." She thought for a moment then looked up at Trance again. "My ring says that there are no computer enhancements. It's real."

Trance tried a difference tact. "Is it true you have no memory of anything that happened before the battle?"

She hung her head. "No memory whatsoever. They said that it might come back, or it might not. It never has. But, nonetheless some spark, some fragment of a memory perhaps, tells me this story isn't quite right."

Trance shrugged noncommittally. "You're the expert, I guess. You're the only person still alive from back then." He started to get up, but she put a hand on his arm and smiled winningly.

"Maybe I'm just too close to it," she said suggestively. "Perhaps it would help to have someone else look at it... from an outsider's point of view."

Trance looked around to Aura and Dexter for a bit of moral support, but the two had jumped up quickly and vacated the theater. "I suppose," he said doubtfully, a sinking feeling settling nicely into his stomach.

"Great. It's settled. I'll send a copy to your cabin. I'm sure it has a holo viewer you can use."

"A holo viewer? What's that? It sounds familiar, but..." he shrugged.

"You've never heard of one? That's odd. They usually come with the room you're given."

"Well, maybe the fellow who set up my room mentioned it, but it's hard to remember. He asked me a lot of questions."

"Oh yeah. I keep forgetting how new everything is to you. A holo viewer allows you to see memory records and entertaining movies in 3D. Like I said, you probably already have one, but I'll bring you another."

"Neat. If you send me it, I'll sure check it out, I guess."

"You'll have it tonight, Trance," she promised. "Thanks again."

Trance looked back at the exit. "OK, Taa'lien. I have to get going. We're going to the Battle Dome."

"Yeah, I know. Most of the squad is going."

"Why don't you come with us now, then?"

She smiled. "I'll see you there," she said. "I have to meet up with Mollie and some of the others first."

Outside the theater, Trance found Dexter and Aura wearing smug but guilty faces. Together they walked down one of several wide corridors that branched away from the theater. "Thanks, guys," he grumbled.

Aura laughed and clapped him on the back. "She already got both of us, chum."

"Yeah, I've seen it a thousand times, probably," Dexter seconded. "I still don't see anything noteworthy."

The corridor they were in was brightly lit, like everything else. The carpet was a beautiful shade of medium blue, and the walls were a light grey. Periodically, other paths bisected theirs and branched off. They continued moving forward.

There were hundreds of other people using this corridor, but it didn't seem crowded. In fact, it seemed warm and inviting to Trance. Aliens of all shapes and sizes meandered by his field of vision. Most of them glanced at the trio; some of them joined them in conversation briefly before moving off in divergent directions. Aura and Dexter spoke jovially with a good number of them, and introduced several as friends, but Trance lost their names quickly in the hubbub.

"Well, hopefully you'll enjoy the Battle Room, Trance," Aura said at one point, clapping Trance on the shoulder. "We still have time to visit it before dinner."

Trance brightened. "Do they have any special shows or anything? I'm hoping for the cosmic equivalent of 'Sigfried and Roybots' here."

"Huh?" Dexter asked.

"You know, the robots with the white tigers. They were in Las Vegas or some place for many years. I've never been, but I hear that they are pretty cool."

"Oh, the white tigers," Dexter said. "Why didn't you say that in the first place?"

"So, you've seen the show?" Aura looked bemused.

"You could say that. I had a thing with one of the girls for awhile. Wow. Rarrrr. Fsstt! Fssstt!" He swiped the air with his claws extended. "She was a tiger! Unfortunately, she was way too into herself, though. Being a huge star does that, I guess." He shrugged.

"Oh." Trance looked at Aura for support, but the golden Protector only grinned. It was hard to tell if they were pulling his leg or not. It was best to move on, he reasoned. "So, is there something special tonight?"

"Just the all-time champ, Perridan, remember?" Aura said.

"Oh."

"He's been undefeated for about three years, I think. That's the longest anyone has gone, ever."

"Wow," Trance said. But he remained unimpressed.

By then they had reached a juncture of sorts. The corridor widened substantially, and branched off to the left and right. At the head of each branch were two doors, one on either side of the path, so there were eight in all. Each of them bore complicated symbols Trance reasoned were directions. They doors obviously led to elevators.

Aura chose one and the group moved into it. Inside, he keyed a series of instructions into a keypad inset into the wall about chest high to Trance. "You can't use your ring on these transports," he explained to no one in particular, "because they are used by everyone, even non-Protectors. This lift will get us where we want to go." He hit a final button and Trance began to feel the steady pull of gravity. They were moving.

When the elevator stopped, the doors opened to a busy street much like the avenue they had been on the day before. It had the familiar three-banded road, tall buildings, and crowded sidewalks. Most of the people appeared to be going in the same direction – the Protectors joined the river, and began to move with it.

The river poured into the strangest building Trance had yet seen. Most of the edifices Trance had seen thus far had been placed so closely they appeared to be attached. Most were rectangular in appearance.

The Battle Dome, as it was called, was a large octagon-shaped building sitting by itself at the end of a block. It was surrounded by a tall wrought-iron fence, which had several gates that varied in size. All of the gates were open and admitting customers.

Rather than being smooth, the Battle Dome had bumps and outgrowths over its entire surface. It was the color of rusted iron, and looked to be two dozen stories high. Several paths corkscrewed up its sides in a haphazard fashion.

Normally, Trance had seen bridges at each of the street corners so foot traffic did not impede vehicular travel. The Battle Dome had many bridges that spanned the two streets forming the corner it sat upon. Vehicles were pulling up by the second and disgorging their inhabitants. Foot traffic flowed through the gates and into the dome smoothly.

A sense of excitement permeated the air. Babies were crying and children cheering, laughing and skipping under the watchful eyes of parents and loved ones.

Trance saw several t-shirts proclaiming "Perridan – All Time Champion," and "Perridan: He's the Man." Not a few cried out, "Marry Me, Sexy Beast!"

An equal number were wearing anti-Perridan memorabilia. Dexter pointed out a squid-shaped individual bearing an "I'm Down on Perridan" hat. Another proudly displayed a "Let's Make Perridan a Chump. Go Challenger!" bandanna.

Trance was mildly surprised to see there were no guards taking tickets at the gates. Apparently, the gates acted as DNA scanners. Bills would be automatically sent to account for each fan in attendance. Of course, Protectors could attend free of charge.

The ramp they took terminated near the top of the dome. Inside was a wide, well-lit concourse, which curved to the right and left. There were no windows, but every thirty feet a set of doors punctured the interior wall. Queuing ropes snaked out from each set of doors in a maze-like formation allowing for maximum usage of space. Each of the queues Trance could see was filled.

When they were in the hallway, Dexter stopped and pulled them over to the side against the outer wall. "Let's hold up for a moment," he said. "Mollie and the rest of the gang should be here soon."

"Oh, yeah, Taa'lien said she was meeting up with them," Trance said. "Maybe we can sit together."

"They'll be here in a few minutes, Trance," Dexter said. He was true to his word. Less than five minutes later, Taa'lien, Mollie, and Kameko met them and together the group walked to the nearest set of queuing lines. Sigfried wasn't with them; Mollie explained to Trance that the slug hated the chaos and pain of the Battle Dome. It just wasn't in his peaceful nature to witness violence.

Though the line was fairly long, it moved fast. Periodically, the doors would shut, and the line would stop for less than twenty seconds before the doors opened again.

When it was their turn to enter, Trance was mystified. "Where did everyone go?" he asked. They were now standing in small room that was open to the air. Ten rows of ten seats met a blue painted guardrail. Trance couldn't see much beyond the rail... there seemed to be a blue haze preventing seeing more than a few feet in any direction.

"Just wait," Dexter said mysteriously.

The group was able to sit in a single row. Trance and Aura took up seats on his right and left, with the others spread evenly in the rest. The individual chairs seemed to be reactive – they changed to fit the individual anatomy placed in their confines. Strangely enough the row length didn't change, but Trance suspected the number of seats did to account for the space needed.

When all of the rows were filled the doors closed, and Trance could feel a slight rumbling below his feet and along his backside. The rumbling went on for less than a minute, and then the blue haze lifted. Trance's jaw dropped. The room had floated into what Trance had previously thought of as the Battle Dome's interior and had positioned itself so the fans within could see vast swaths of the sky.

In Trance's estimation, the name "Battle Dome" was an entirely unworthy appellation. "Arena," or perhaps "World" might be more appropriate, because that was how big it seemed from the inside.

He knew empirically that the room was entirely encased in the cool embrace of metal deep within the confines of Mondidad. His eyes and other senses told him another story entirely.

In fact, the room seemed to go on forever. Strategically placed throughout the arena, glinting in the sunlight as they floated in space, were more viewing stations where the relaxing crowds lounged waiting for the match to begin. He guessed that perhaps a hundred thousand beings were already present, and the seats were still half full.

Adams glanced past the viewing stations toward the mountains off in the distance. They were capped with a light dusting of purple snow. Overhead, he could see, impossibly, three suns orbiting around one another in a complicated dance. Closer still, a ringed planet loomed. It encompassed most of the sky. All of the sights gave the illusion of immense space.

By that time his attention was diverted due to the arrival of the current champ, Perrridan. He materialized with a thunderclap, and bowed toward each of the viewing stations, a faint smile painted across his purple lips. The crowds appeared to be quite enamored with him, giving him a standing ovation. Trance stood halfheartedly and clapped along with everyone else.

Several rows back, someone was selling confections out of a large box connected to a shoulder strap. He or she – Trance couldn't tell—was braying in a loud voice, "Kepplers! Kepplers! Getcher Kepplers right here! Ten credits! Wot a Deal!" In one hairy hand (for the being closely resembled a large blue hairy ape), it held a rectangle with purple straw-like material jutting out of one end. The straw was wriggling violently enough to shake the ape's hand slightly. Trance grimaced and turned back feeling slightly ill. Dexter ordered two portions.

By that time, the first of the challengers had floated up to join Perridan and a golden orb. They spoke for a few seconds, and then flew in opposite directions.

Each Protector squared off facing one another and fired constructs for a few seconds to show the crowd they really couldn't hurt each other with them. This was purely for show. Everyone on Monidad knew that the rings were unable to oppose each other directly. Trance turned to Dexter, who was munching happily on his purple straw. Bits of it were wriggling at the corners his mouth. "So, how are these things decided?" he asked the cat.

SMASH! Trance looked back up at the two combatants. One of them had been flattened between two pieces of gray marble. The other, Perridan, was bowing to the crowd, which was clapping hysterically. "Just like that," Dexter said sagely.

"How'd he do that? I thought we couldn't use our rings in, uh.. direct opposition of each other."

"Yeah, I know it's confusing for newbies. That's real marble. After they cart the loser off to the hospital, Peridan will turn it to dust, or back to air particles, or whatever he made it out of. He is really good at metamorphosing things out of the air. I think that's why he has been a champ so long."

"Are the matches always so fast?"

"Not usually," Dexter replied. "Sometimes it goes quicker."

"Not much to it, then."

"Basically, no. But it sure is fun to watch. You want some?" He offered Trance one of the boxes of purple straw. "I got extra so I could share."

"God, no. How can you eat that stuff?"

"Well, I put it in my mouth, and chew, if you'd really like to know."

Trance scowled at the cat in mock anger, then crossed his arms and settled back into his chair to watch the show.

The second contestant fared much better, lasting enough time to scream as it was encased in a large handgun and shot at one of the planets off in the distance. Its departure left a thin smoke trail which quickly dissipated. Perridan bowed again as the crowd cheered wildly.

After about five rounds, all of which ended in victory for Perridan, a voice came over the speaker system. It said, "The champ will now entertain challengers. Does anyone dare to face the great Perridan?"

Trance chuckled. "I feel sorry for the poor sap who takes up that offer."

Kameko smiled around her cigar as she leaned over her seat and looked at Trance. "I don't think you're a sap, Trance," she said.

"Hah, Kameko that's funny. No, I meant that I feel sorry for anyone silly enough to volunteer."

"You can also nominate someone," she said. "Hint. Hint."

"Ladies and Gentlemen," the announcer said just then, "We have a nomination! Trance Adams, Earthling! Give him a hand, folks, he's come a long way!" The crowd screamed its approval.

Chapter 19: First Strike

"You what?!" Trance couldn't believe his ears.

"That's right, I signed you up," Kameko said. "It will give you experience. Plus, I thought it might be fun to see how you do."

"I'm going to get crushed, that's how I'll do."

"Well, it's too late now," Kameko said bluntly. "The crowd is chanting for the next victim – er -- candidate. If you step out now, our squad will lose face."

"Why don't you go instead? Or maybe you, Dexter?" He pointed at the Tabby, who had been guffawing.

"You're joking," the cat sobered. "He'd kill me."

"What do you think he's going to do to me?"

"Yes, well, he won't really kill you, but it might hurt a lot. Either way, I think I'll enjoy it more from this perspective," the cat snickered.

"Thanks, Kameko. You too, Dexter." Trance glared at the other Protectors for assistance, but each of them happened to be looking away at the time.

Aura was the best actor; he was examining a piece of lint on his uniform carefully. He looked up, and seemed surprised to see Trance looking at him. "Pardon?" he asked.

"Nothing," Trance snarled.

Dexter smiled sweetly. "Go on. It'll be fun." He prodded Trance with one orange paw.

Trance glared at the cat and then back at Aura and Taa'lien, but it was no use. He knew Perridan would humiliate him like the Protector had humiliated all the other challengers who faced him, but even embarrassment was better than losing face because he refused to try. He sighed and willed himself to float up to where Perridan was waiting in the playing area.

"Anything you can tell me about this joker, ring?" he asked. But for once, the ring ignored him. In fact, it had been relentlessly silent the past few minutes, uncharacteristically so given its usual diatribes. This meant it was up to something shady; something he'd most likely disapprove of. Probably even now it was making bets against him in some seedy bar, trying to gain back some of the money it had lost in Legs.

It took him a moment to reach the champion, who was listening raptly to the crowd cheer and scream his name. While the champ reveled in his applause, Trance studied him carefully looking for defects.

Perridan looked like a cross between a human and a purple octopus. He stood well over six feet tall. Four tentacles with little suckers took the place of legs, and two more tentacles sprouted where his arms should have been. ….A small, thick neck supported a large bulbous head that bore three eyes (each with two pupils), a single nose, and a small, expressive mouth. Spikes punched through his skin in several places; three on each shoulder, three along each side of his torso, and one near the terminus of every tentacle.

Instead of hair, yellow and white feelers grew out of the top of Perridan's scalp, moving according to his mood. When he was happy, they hung limply. When he was angry, or concerned, they had a tendency to stand straight up and undulate wildly.

"So, you're the current champ of the Battle Room," Trance commented once Perridan had swung his attention back from his fans. Perridan sneered, his upper lip curling from one end to the other and back again like a wave.

"That's right, human. And I'll probably still be champ tomorrow. If there's a change in my stature, I doubt the cause will be someone as green behind the ears as you." He laughed loudly.

"That's wet behind the ears," Trance sighed.

"Huh?"

"Never mind. It's not important."

Just then, the referee, the golden orb, floated down from somewhere above. "Greetings, Protectors," it said in a warm female voice. Are both of you familiar with the rules?"

Perridan nodded smugly. "Er. No," Trance gulped.

"There are none, chump," Perridan grunted. "I can crush you any way I want."

"All ready then?" the referee waited until they both nodded.   "On the count of three. One... two... three..."

"Maybe you better just hit him with something, Trance," the ring said helpfully. "Just remember, don't use your ring against him directly. You'll blow your cover."

"OK."   Trance leaned back and let his fist fly. His fist impacted on Perridan's small nose. It gave a satisfying crunch, and snapped the being's head back soundly. The rest of the body tumbled after it, end over end like a Ferris wheel. The crowd went wild.

The ring wasn't so ecstatic. "I meant use me to create something to hit him with, you moron! Why do you always have to use your fists to solve problems?!" In fact, it sounded peeved.

Perridan came to a stop a dozen yards away. He shook his head and raised a hand to his nose. It was bleeding. He shook his head again, trying to erase the fog, and then looked up to see Trance barreling toward him, ring blazing. He didn't have time to react.

Trance hit him midsection, arms wrapped around him in a vice, and rocketed toward the nearest grandstand. Perridan looked backward, his eyes popping and his feelers waving wildly, and said, "Oh shit."

They hit a hastily constructed pillow, which popped into existence just before they impacted the grandstand. Perridan then used a gigantic spatula to pry Trance off him, and flipped the human over his head and into the crowd.

"Hey, watch it, fella! You spilled my Keplars!" a rotund fan yelled in his ear as it pushed him away.

"Sorry," Trance said, as he slid back into the arena. Instantly he began to fall – he'd forgotten monetarily that the viewing stations floated throughout the playing area.

He poured on the juice, and just missed being swatted with a ten foot long Billy-club that sprang out of the air. He varied his speed, flying randomly as he tried to get a bead on Perridan while avoid being smacked. Most of his attention was on the other Protector, but a small part of him couldn't help but be impressed by the exquisite detail of the club with its wood grain, and dozens of silver spikes that had grown out of the head.

"You really pissed him off, Trance; be careful!" the ring advised, breaking its silence again.

Suddenly, a red brick wall popped up in front of him. "Holy Shit!" he said, realizing that he couldn't avoid it. It was at least a mile long, a hundred stories high, and twenty feet thick. Compounding that, the club's head was right behind him, bearing down, the murderous spikes glinting in the light. He could feel them whizzing toward him, pushing the air with them as they came.

The only solution, then, was through, not over. He extended his hands above his head and formed a drill bit there, increased his speed, and bore into the wall with such force that his impact site vaporized and cracks crisscrossed the entire length and breadth.

Then he was through. The bat crashed into the wall behind him, shattering bricks and sending mortar flying. Trance turned, still barreling forward but on his back facing the wall. He detonated it, with the ring, and was satisfied to see the Billy club shatter with it.

But he wasn't out of the woods yet. Where was Perridan? That flashy bastard was somewhere around here – he was too much of an egomaniac to hide. He'd be out in the open somewhere, thinking he was orchestrating things. And so far, he had done exactly that.

Suddenly knives were shooting everywhere, hundreds of them; blades of every conceivable size and shape slicing toward him, cutting the air. But they didn't cut him. He'd anticipated that one, and had already begun to plan for it. He was ready with a simple but effective magnetic shield; a shield with a diameter of ten feet held by an arm of equally tremendous stature. The knives slammed into the shield, and stuck there.

He was learning to program the ring in series, literally on the fly. It took equal parts anticipation and luck, but it seemed to be working. Unfortunately, it would take a lot more than that to net Perridan, especially when the other Protector couldn't even be found.

And then he saw his quarry. He was just a flash of light several miles out, but right in the open where Trance guessed he would be. And that meant he was vulnerable. Maybe he'd like to play catch. Trance willed the construct arm to flex, and it tossed the shield at Perridan like a Frisbee.

That done, he stopped willing the arm to exist, and it vaporized. He flew diagonally, tracking the disk as it rocketed forward, and then detonated it with a blast from his ring when it got close enough. Perridan, who had been attempting to flee the discus was caught in the shockwave of the explosion. Trance was rewarded by the sight of the other Protector spin out of control. Unfortunately, too quickly, he righted himself.

And here came the biggest friggin missile that Trance had ever seen. It came screaming at him like a banshee. The ring was kind enough to translate the letters on its sides: "DANGER – RADIOACTIVE."

He let himself fall. The missile flew past him, missed him by several miles, and began a tight curve so that it could track him again.

He fell a dozen stories, flipped over again so that he was facing Perridan, and kicked himself into high gear. The missile hadn't even finished turning. He stopped and waited for it just a fraction of a second, then poured on the juice, rocketing forward. He didn't even see Perridan's shocked face as he blew past the other Protector. Two-dozen yards away, Trance stopped and turned so that he could see the show.

Even taken by surprise, the Perridan was too good to be beaten like that. He shimmered briefly, and the missile passed right through him, still targeting on Trance. It was too close to evade this time. There was only just a moment before it would impact him. It was definitely going to be messy.

He released his will into a beam of energy that vaporized the missile instantly. Unfortunately, the beam also struck Perridan with full intensity. The crowd gasped as Perridan flew end over end backwards; spun out of control by the force of Trance's blast.

"Oh, well, there goes your cover," the ring griped. "Did you forget that you weren't supposed to let anyone know that you could use your ring directly against another Protector?"

"Oh, yeah. Damn. Well, maybe no one will notice."

Before anyone could react, however, something occurred that took everyone's attention away from the amazing thing that had just happened.

Suddenly, a powerful explosion ripped through the largest seating area, tossing splintered bodies and debris into the Danger Room's arena. A second explosion tore into the crowd, and then a third in the space of a heartbeat. The crowd surged backward from each, reacting to the explosions like a stunned and wounded beast seeking to escape the pain, heat and force.

In the next heartbeat, the corps sprang into action to stem the flow of carnage. Nameless Protectors flew into the air, rings blazing: supporting the balustrade of the tottering wall, rushing the wounded to safety and medical aid, and attempting to help the uninjured safely exit the observation decks.

Screaming filled Trance's ears -- pleas for assistance from the wounded and the dying. And then he was moving, one with the corps, helping where he could.

But somehow as he worked his mind picked out an oddity, like a tremendous moving puzzle piece; a single island in an ocean of confusion. A female, standing stoically as others rushed around her. And in an upraised hand... a switch. Her thumb came down, and he heard and felt the heat of a fourth explosion nearby, and a fifth. And then she was gone.

"Holy shit!" Trance called out concentrating on the void left by the bomber.

"It's a site-to-site transport!" returned the ring. "They only work at short distances!"

"What's the nearest most likely destination point?"

"Docking bay 10-70-A. It's only a short distance from this locale."

Trance sent a pulse message explaining his discovery to Aura, and asked the golden Protector to follow him.

Trance looked sadly at the chaos. There were so many who needed help. He wished that he could stay there. His ring might be the difference between life and death. But then the bomber would get away. He could not stand by knowing that he had done his best to stop her. She would pay for her deeds.

The fastest direction was down. They rocketed hundreds of stories downward in the blink of an eye. He began to notice things as they plummeted, things like the true shape of the Dome. The Dome was a Bowl with an interior surface that curved in to meet them as they fell. He also caught the impression of an infrastructure that had been seriously damaged by the bombs. Engineers and Protectors were even now working to repair what the terrorist had undone. He hoped they would succeed before the Dome crumbled around them. It would be a close race.

And then they reached the bottom. At the southernmost point was a set of massive double doors. The observation modules passed through on the way to each of the entry points. Food carts, and other service vehicles also came through these doors. Currently they were blocked by tons of debris.

Aura swore at the delay while forming a large plow; he quickly pushed aside the refuse. Trance used his ring to pry open the doors, which refused to budge on their own. And then they were off, racing through a small section of the series of service halls, piping, and other infrastructure, which connected all of the buildings on Monidad.

Very quickly they exited the service areas and entered a main concourse of sorts near the Dome. People were already pouring into the same hallways trying to escape the carnage; a stream of the terrified and confused. The two Protectors flew over the crowds in an effort to make the best speed.

"Is she in there?" Trance asked his ring, as they got closer to the hanger in question.

"You'd better hurry," it responded. "She's powering up a ship. Oops. It just took off. Oh man, she's torching everything in her path. What a mess."

"There's the door!" Trance exclaimed, willing his ring to go faster.

Chapter 20: Race against Time

Perfect. Everything was going excellently. Soon, sirens would screaming somewhere nearby, and he imagined people would be screaming too. Unfortunate. But perfect.

As he walked down the corridor, he twisted his neck just slightly, feeling the vertebrae crack, popping and releasing pressure. He felt alive and dangerous.

The package in his hands excited him with the possibilities that it promised. It had been waiting for him on his bunk as the Master had promised. He fingered it as he walked.

Closer to his objective he began to worry. Just slightly, of course; his faith could move mountains. But the worry ate at his resolve with tiny bites each and every step he took closer to his destination.

The Master told him that the resulting chaos of the bombs would pull the guards away from the door. But would they return before he could complete his duties? He chided himself for his fear. If he were truly faithful, were truly one with the dragon, his fear would be gone. He would be invincible.

The cowl over his head shrouded his face and blanketed it in shadows. He knew no one would remember seeing him here, in this hallway. Hopefully, not even on this planet.

The ground shook just slightly. It shook again, and again and again. That would be his companion leaving her calling cards. And there were the sirens, the flashing lights. They painted the corridor a dull red and filled his ears with music. And there, there was the door, partially open, and unguarded. He praised the dragon and slipped through.

*****

Seconds later, the two Protectors burst through a set of large set of blast doors and into the docking bay proper. In a flash, Trance saw this bay was much smaller than the cavernous structure they had landed in that morning. It was perhaps one-tenth the size; only able to hold about a hundred ships.

The room was curved so the far wall met the ceiling. At the top very top, at least a half-mile up, Trance could see the gaping hole that surely led, as all Hangers did, to the central spire. Fully a quarter of the ships were engulfed in flames or already smoking wrecks. One ship exploded as they flew over it, sending debris and ruin skyward around them.

Trance's vision was momentarily obscured in the heat and smoke. "Hurry!" the ring said in his ear, "She's exiting the hangar!" Trance gritted his teeth and flew toward the ceiling. That piece of shit was not going to get away.

*****

Delicately now. No sense in killing himself. To die in battle; aye, there was a heroic act. But to die from foolishness or clumsy fingers… there was another matter entirely. The Dragon would give him sure hands and a steady heart—the Dragon would ensure he would die in battle rather than here on this godforsaken planet.

The machinery in this room gave off quite a hum. It vibrated his bones and set his teeth chattering. It was hot, too. A bead of sweat ran down his creased forehead, slid the length of the bridge of his pencil thin nose and plummeted from its tip. He scarcely noted it, concentrating instead on the task at hand.

The final package was set, an innocuous cylinder the size and shape of a large tube sausage. It had a small keypad and screen, and attached to the wall with a series of suckers along its back side. It could hang there until the end of time if his master desired it to. But it would be used much sooner than that.

He keyed in a special code. The screen flashed "ARMED" in tight red lettering. He entered a second code and the entire surface darkened and then blurred. In seconds, the package had completely disappeared from sight.

*****

"Son of a Bitch!" Trance exclaimed violently. He had just managed to avoid a screaming yellow laser beam shot from one of the many guns that peppered the surface of the vessel they were pursuing.

"She's shooting at us, Protector," the ring said matter-of-factly. "I'd watch out, if I were you."

"Thanks. Let's give her something to think about." Trance flew sideways positioning himself so he could fire a shot across the fleeing ship's bow, while still matching speed with his quarry. The ship rolled left, avoiding his beam. Turrets on its stomach fired shards of light at him, and he was forced to drop speed and fly erratically to avoid them.

They were up against an experienced pilot. She had managed thus far to avoid Trance and Aura who was also attempting to disable the ship without destroying it completely. Trance could hear the Golden Protector through their shared link, commanding the occupant of the ship to pull over and let them board her. His entreaties were answered with missiles and radio silence.

Trying to get a bead on the ship was nearly impossible. He imagined it was like trying to shoot a fly with a .357 Magnum; it was moving too fast and without any real pattern to key into in order to hit it solidly. Add to that a magnificent force shield that caused their glancing blows to slide harmlessly off into space... he found himself getting frustrated with every second that passed. "Hold still, damn you!" he yelled, increasing speed.

He willed a large hand that shot out and grabbed the ship around the center, and stopped flying, willing himself to stop. The line continued out from the hand, slack tightening rapidly. In his mind's eye, he saw himself standing solidly on air, holding the vessel in his energy hand, beam taunt, maybe even shaking the damn thing like a Yahtzee can until the occupant tumbled out like a dice and apologized for the destruction. "I'm sorry," the bomber would say. "Please forgive me."

Instead, a little voice intruded into the picture saying, in the ring's patient timber saying, "Um... Protector, I hate to think this might be the time for a physics lesson, but—"

With a snap, the line became rigid. His arm jerked forward, his shoulder screaming in pain as it was almost ripped from its socket. When his vision cleared, he found himself flying behind the ship, skimming on the atmosphere like a stone on the surface of a pond.

"We're in for a bumpy ride!" the ring finished.

*****

"Did you...?" They were standing in another room now, him and the master. The room felt musty and old. Furniture was minimal-- a table recessed into one corner, and a single wooden chair-- and diffused light seeped weakly from the ceiling. Perhaps it was a trick of the light, but his master's face blurred and danced before his eyes. And his master's voice; another trick prevented him from hearing its true timber. But no matter, these deceptions could be attributed to the projection belt worn at the waist, a tool he was very familiar with. If the master wished him not to know the true identity... well, that was the master's prerogative.

"Aye, by the dragon," he nodded. "They will feel the heat when the time is ready."

"When I am ready. Remember that." The voice was soft and dangerous.

"Yes, master. When you are ready."

The being before him smiled, pleased. It was good to please the Master. But, there was just one thing. One thing missing. He hesitated to ask, knowing the fear was a weakness, and a sign of his lack of faith. Nonetheless...

"Master?"

"Yes?" The smile grew wider, predatory.

"You said a reward would be waiting when we met, but I see it not."

"Ah, yes. A reward for a job well done." A small box flipped end over end in a tight arc and landed in his large grey hands. It was two inches to a side. Each side was segmented into two triangles. The triangles were red, blue and yellow. His fingers felt along the edges looking for seams and hinges. He could not open it, though many feared his strength.

He looked, questioningly to the master who was leaving the room, stepping into the hall. The master nodded. "Wait ten minutes and then leave. Your reward is within. Enjoy." The door closed, and he was alone.

*****

"Let go!" Trance screamed, and the hand released its grip on the hull of the ship, and dissipated.

He tumbled for a few seconds, dizzy and nauseous. Eventually, he shook his head, righted himself, and looked for the ship. Flashes of blue and yellow nearby showed him where to go.

Aura, with an energy wall here or a glancing push off the force shield there, was still doing an excellent job of keeping the ship within the minimal atmosphere of Monidad. He smiled at Trance gamely as Trance rejoined the party. "I thought you had gotten bored and decided to leave us," he said over their shared link.

"You'd be surprised at how hard it is to find a bathroom up here," Trance joked.

"Yeah, especially at this time of night," Aura grunted, forming a net. The ship blew through it easily.

"This is getting old, fast," Trance grunted, flying hard to the left to avoid more shards of light.

"Yeah, OK," Aura said. "I'm going to disable the engines if I can. I had wanted to avoid this, but the pilot's not cooperating."

"What do you need me to do?"

"Well, it's a little tricky. It's taken me awhile to get the feel for this model. I think that it is a Mark-10, or maybe a knock off of the 'Mark' brand. It's pretty sophisticated, but can be beat. With this type, the force shield sends more power to the area that is hit. It's kind of a reactionary thing."

"Yeah?" Trance dodged more light beams and sent a half-hearted shot toward the aft of the ship. The force shield sent the beam out into space.

"So, the energy has to come from somewhere. Generally, it's pulled from the opposite side, and then flows back toward the spot it was drained from. But the spot it pulls energy from is just temporarily the weakest spot of the shield."

"Gotcha."

"So, working together, we may be able to land this thing. When I tell you, hit it as hard as you can from the front. I'll try and sneak in through the back."

"Sounds good. Let me know when you are ready."

"It will take a second to set the program I have in mind. You'll have to distract our quarry in the meantime."

Trance gave Aura thumbs up, and poured on the energy. In the few seconds that they had been in discussion, the pilot had managed to get to the very outer edge of the atmosphere, and the vessel was picking up speed. He reached the ship and formed a large hand again, but this time he used it to slap the ship down rather than try and grasp it. He was rewarded with the pleasant sight of seeing the ship tumble back toward the ground momentarily, but it soon righted itself and began another ascent. So, he slapped it again. "Take that, jerk-face," he growled.

Just then, Aura called to him. "Ready?"

"You Bet!"

"Now!"

Trance rocketed ahead of the ship, and flipped around so that he was facing it. When he had accomplished this maneuver, he concentrated on the forward hull and released his will in one solid stream of energy. The beam struck out hard, momentarily stopping the vehicle, but then it began to slide around the shield, and forward momentum slowly returned.

He could feel the ship fighting against him, pushing back with increasing force. Even in the thin air he could hear the thrusters laboring as they fought to regain speed. Sweat beads slid down forehead, and his arm began trembling with the effort. But the stream of energy remained steady. "I hope you've got a plan going, buddy," he gasped to Aura

"Keep it up, Trance, almost there...." Aura said, tentatively. "I got it!"

White flash. Trance grimaced as he lost sight of the ship momentarily, and then the shockwave him like a hammer, knocking the wind from his lungs and sending his body flying backward as if he had been struck by a thousand blows simultaneously.

He lost consciousness.

*****

The man turned the box in his hands, feeling it. It was soft, yet he could not crush it. When he shook it, it did not rattle, yet he knew that inside his reward awaited. He had even tried several choice curses. They'd had no effect. He peered at it intently, and then held it up to his ear again.

Click.

One of the edges opposite his viewpoint had sprung open.

He turned the box quickly so that his reward did not tumble out.

Inside, a single point of white light so intense that it hurt his eyes flowered and grew with a speed that might have amazed him had he lived more than a millisecond longer. All he had time for was a single "Oh," as his life ended in fire.

WHUMP.

The box vaporized as the tiny fusion bomb inside of it ignited, sending radiation, heat, and debris exploding out into the hallway.

Chapter 21: Crash Landings

The sound of air rushing past his ears like a jet woke him up. With a shudder, he willed his descent to stop, and tried to get his bearings. Off in the distance, he could see a smoke trail dissipating rapidly in the thin air, but his companion was nowhere. "Aura," he called, "Are you there?"

"Yeah," came the weak reply. "I must have blacked out for a second there. I'm OK, now. Are you?"

"Whew. That blast threw me for a loop, but I'm alright."

"Great. I'm setting a beacon. I just found what's left of the ship. Can you find me?"

Trance asked his ring to home in on Aura's signal, and flew the direction it guided him in. He found the Golden Protector momentarily. Aura was about a quarter mile up in the air, staring at the ground. Trance followed his gaze, and whistled. "What did you hit it with?" he asked.

Below them, the landscape of Monidad was barren in every direction; a virtual carbon copy of all of the landscapes that Trance had seen since being on the planet. Except that it had one addition: the smoking hulk of a spaceship, thrusters pointing toward the sky at a thirty-degree angle. Its fiery descent and bouncing, gouging, travel across the terrain to its final resting place had left a debris field that stretched for several miles.

"I didn't hit it with anything," Aura responded. "I was trying to safely cut its engines and then bump it, sending it into a controlled spin. I didn't mean for that to happen. What a mess."

"Well, I'm not reading any life signs," Trance said. "I hope they left plenty of evidence before they died."

"Like a big smoking 'I DID IT' sign," the ring grumbled.

They landed just next to the downed vessel. Aura had placed a containment field around the ship to keep more air from escaping. The Golden Protector had hoped that there might be pockets of air that the bomber could have survived in, but given Trance's scans that likelihood was minimal.

Just as they were about to enter the ship, Trance's ring chirped notifying him of an incoming call. It was Taa'lien. She appeared before Aura and Trance in the form of a holograph. They could see clearly that her normally bare face bore fresh bandages. "You boys OK?" she asked.

"We're doing alright," Trance said in his best cop voice. "We got the perp grounded, and are about to investigate."

"Good," she said. "Kick him really hard for me, will you? I lost some acquaintances in that bombing, plus I think that I added a few scars, which really pisses me off."

"Is everything OK?" Trance asked, thinking of the people that had been at the Battle Room.

"Everything is mopped up, and medics are treating the survivors," Taa'lien replied somberly. "We only lost about ten spectators, thank God. The wounded will be fine in a few hours."

"Is everyone OK from our squad?" Aura asked.

"Oh, yes. Dexter's fur got a little singed, but I was the only one that sustained actual damage." She pointed to her bandages, and Trance noticed that her hand was also wrapped up. "I haven't seen Kameko since the first explosion, but I am sure she is OK. Truth is, I've been so busy, I haven't had a chance to check."

"That's a relief. A little time under the Re-Gen, and you both will be good as new," Aura said, pleased.

"You know I don't like using those machines," she said. "But that's not important right now. I have some bad news: We lost five Protectors. One more is unaccounted for."

"What happened?" Aura asked

"Blue-10 squad was the hardest hit: they lost three. Looks like one of them had a weakness to wood splinters, and the other two got crushed trying to brace one of the viewing areas by hand."

"And the others?" Trance asked.

"They paid the price of sitting directly over bombs, I'm afraid. I doubt they even felt a thing."

"They will be missed," Aura said sadly.

Taa'lien nodded somberly. 'I have no idea what happened to the missing Protector. We'll find him eventually, I'm sure. There are several search parties involved."

"Oh." Aura said softly.

"We'll talk later," Taa'lien said in response. "You both have a lot of work to do."

After they signed off, Aura transformed a pile of dirt into two metallic robots and sent them sniffing for fires to put out around the crash site. Satisfied with these efforts, he and Trance found a hole large enough to fit through, and entered the ship.

Trance let his hand run along the jagged yaw as he followed Aura in. The ship felt dead to him; cold and barren. The hull was at least three feet thick. Inside the outer skin was a pocket of empty space; most likely it had been filled with air. Inside that was another hull and then wires and piping. Finally, another two walls with a pocket of air between, and they were inside.

The interior was dark and murky. Trance caused an orb to appear which lit their way as they traveled down hallways tilted at thirty-degrees. It was a small ship, in comparison to the others that he had been a passenger on. It could have housed only a dozen people comfortably. Most of the vessel appeared to be given over to storage and engines, though they found a large living compartment with a small kitchen and three bathrooms. There was also a multi-purpose room. Everything was in disarray; shelves had broken and disgorged their goods, and lighting panels had cracked or shattered.

Most of the mess didn't look as though it had been caused by the flight and crash. Much of the food that they found splattered in the kitchen looked as though it had gone sour some time before.

"Ring?" Trance asked, as they looked around, "Should I be concentrating on this?"

"Do you mean, is this taking you away from your primary objective?"

"Yeah. Is this somehow connected? Or do these kind of things happen all the time?"

"It's hard to say, Protector," the ring replied. "As you learned in the tour, terrorist events never happen here. This is pretty unusual. And keep in mind, several Protectors were killed. It's possible that this is connected to your secret investigation."

"Ok, let's see where this takes us, then," Trance said.

*****

After about fifteen minutes of fruitless searching, they found the control room, and finally, a body.

Debris had pretty much eviscerated the lone occupant of the ship, though the head seemed to be fairly intact.

"Why don't you check and see if it's anybody we know?" Aura asked. "We can at least scan his face and see if it matches any records."

"Ugh," Trance said.

"You never seen a dead body before?" Aura asked.

"No. Just on TV."

"Well, congratulations. In this line of work, you're going to see a lot of them."

Trance gingerly grabbed the top of the head and pulled it up revealing the face. The eyes were showing all white, and the tongue hung limply between two sets of sharp teeth. Blue blood began to seep out of the nose and down the chin. But despite these ravages, the visage was familiar.

"Why, it's the merchant that was on our transport ship!" exclaimed Trance.

"Are you sure?" Aura looked concernedly at the corpse.

"Yes. I'd recognize those features anywhere. I saw her first being grilled by the bureaucrat that gave us our tickets, and then later when we deplaned."

"De-who?"

"Never mind."

"Well, we won't be getting any information from her, I think," Aura decided.

"You mean because she's dead?" Trance responded dryly.

"Uh, yeah. Let's look around."

"Just a second. There's something else here." Down by the base of the neck, the edge of a tattoo could be seen. Trance used part of the corpse's clothing to wipe away gristle and fluids covering it to reveal the entire design: a dragon sinking its teeth into a spiral galaxy. It was approximately the size of a fifty-cent piece. At first glance it was quite beautiful, with the dragon's tail wrapped intricately around the arm of the galaxy, but the look on the dragon's face made him shudder: the artist had captured a look of pure evil that chilled him to the bone. "The lady we picked up at that bar, Legs, had some sort of tattoo right about here. I didn't get a good look at it at the time, but I bet it was the same as this one."

Aura frowned. "Yeah. Anad. She was with the Order of the Foul Dragon. You don't think they'd be so stupid as to tattoo all their members, do you?"

"It certainly gives us something to start from," Trance responded, letting go of the head. It fell to the floor wetly. Given nothing to wipe his hands off on, he used the former merchant's tattered shirt. "Well, shall we?"

The bridge of the ship was tiny. Trance suspected, looking it over in a glance, that it had been messy before the explosion that had crippled the vessel, but now it was a complete disaster area, with bits of paper lay here and there, and something was rotting in one of the corners. Several of the command consoles had blinking lights on them, so evidently power still coursed through them.

Much like the whole investigation thus far, it was hard to guess where to start. He scratched his head and thought for a moment looking at nothing in particular.

The merchant had traveled to Mondiad on a transport vessel much like everyone else. Trance had seen other ships arriving which meant that the transport ships were just a suggested means of traveling, not the required one. So, why go through all the trouble? Why not just fly her own ship there? She obviously had it to fly off planet with. Things just weren't adding up.

Aura broke Trance's reverie with a shout of triumph. This may help us," the golden protector said, holding up a gray cube. After sweeping off some refuse, he placed the cube in a receptacle on the command chair. It slid home with a click.

"Command?" a non-sexual, disembodied voice said.

"Computer, play most recent command log," Aura responded. "Let's see what this merchant has been up to," he said to Trance.

A figure appeared before them momentarily. The representation wasn't very good – it was fuzzy on the edges, and distortions frequently obscured the features of the speaker—but it was clear enough to see that it was indeed the merchant. She was dressed in a much different outfit, a flowing robe tied at the waist. "Things seem to be progressing nicely," she said to no one in particular.

"That's nice," Trance commented. He looked over at the corpse, which continued to do nothing. Things hadn't ended too well, he thought. He glanced back at the much livelier version. The holograph continued to speak, her face twisted in anger.

"...It smells here, and I will be glad to wipe my feet of this when this is over. I am glad I was able to make contact with local resistance fighters; the stories I had heard are true. This is the home of a doddering old men and women with little to do but stroke their own egos and play games. These 'Creators' make me sick, with their talk of responsibility to care for the weaker races.

'Phah!" She spat off camera. "They will soon be a pile of feces beneath my boot. When they see what my master has in store for them, they will quake in fear. I hope today's entrée of fire and death will give them a small taste of what is to come, and pray that it will not be visited upon my new friends." She spat again.

"Eww," the ring said, "Talk about mixed metaphors! Listen to that diction. She should be ashamed of herself."

"Would you please pay attention and quit joking around? This is serious stuff," Trance replied.

The hologram continued. "For too long we have waited in the shadows," she said. "People talk of destiny and of patience. Now, finally, it is time for action. I thank the dragon that the Master has allowed me to take some small part in His designs.

'The Master decided the best place to strike is the so-called Battle Room, the only thing that passes for sport here. A large portion of the population will either be present or will view the proceedings on television. This is the most ideal spot to begin our reign of terror."

"Well, she's certainly an angry one," Trance commented, disgusted.

"And not at all hygienic," the ring muttered. "Better watch your step."

They watched the holographic merchant spout like a broken sewer main for a few more minutes, then Aura spoke: "Computer, stop program." The hologram stopped mid-sentence, little bits of spittle frozen in a downward arc from her mouth. "Computer, what is the next previous file to this one?"

"The next previous file, saved twelve hours prior to this one is also an audio-video file. Would you like to display it?"

"Yes, Computer."

The merchant appeared again. This time, the audio and video were much less clear: every few moments the feed grew hazy and threatened to cut out, but the image never stopped playing.

The merchant was sitting in the Captain's chair, bent over the controls. Her head snapped up, and she smiled, all teeth. "Ah, at last," she said.

"Captain's log... No, that's not right." She thought for a moment. "Well, whatever. This is the first log of a new Captain—me."

The Merchant settled back into her chair, getting comfortable with her new ship and her new role. "This planet's stench is overwhelming. It fills my nostrils.

'I must admit that I was surprised to receive this gift from the Master—I had been willing to do the job for the price of seeing Monidad burn plus a small pittance, but if the Master wishes this extravagance upon me, I cannot decline."

She stood, straightening her tunic, and began pacing about the small cabin, here and there running a finger across a console in the manner of an English butler performing a white glove inspection. "I think," she said, "there is much to be done to make this boat truly worthy of me, but it will do for now— the engine is space-worthy, and the controls appear to be in good working order. I plan on putting this boat to the test in the next hour or so to ensure my getaway will be a sound one. But first... ah, right on time."

The door leading from the control room had beeped. "Come," the merchant said.

With a swish, the double doors parted, and a figure strode through. Startled, Trance froze and then belatedly tried to move out of the way.

Chapter 22: The Shadow

The figure passed harmlessly through Trance, focusing on the merchant. Seeing the newcomer as a 3-D holograph didn't offer Trance much in the way of clues. It was a 5' 10" humanoid, and appeared fairly solid in terms of muscle. Trance couldn't see any skin for the holograph was covered from head to toe in a brown robe with a hooded cowl covering the face completely with shadows. Both hands were gloved in black leather.

The merchant bowed deeply until Shadow touched her on the shoulder. "Report," came a voice Trance knew at once was modified. It sounded slightly masculine and very mechanical in nature, the edges smoothed and the word short and clipped.

"Coming together, Master," came the reply as she straightened, looking into Shadow's face. "There is much work to be done here, but I believe I will be ready."

Shadow nodded. "I am pleased," he said. "I had feared you would not be prepared for tomorrow."

"I will be ready, Master."

"See that you are." Shadow turned, heading for the double doors.

"Master?"

"Yes?"

"How… how was the trip in? I had heard you arrived today…."

"Long and boring. But worth seeing what is to come." Shadow turned again."

"Master?"

Shadow turned coolly.

"Well, I was wondering -- How can you work with and for these beings, these Creators?" Too late, she realized her brash words had been a mistake. With cat-like quickness Shadow turned and raised his arm, slamming the merchant into the bulkhead like a rag doll with a blue flash.

The merchant hung there for a moment, dazed, then slid to the ground. "Master! Master!" she wheezed. "I didn't mean—"

Shadow stepped closer, and leaned down so that his still-hidden face was inches from hers. "Never, never question my motivations," he said coldly. "I let you live this time because I have much work for you to do. But next time, make no mistake, I will kill you."

"Pause."

Aura's awed voice startled Trance. "What is it?" he asked.

"Did you see that flash, Trance?" The Golden Protector pointed at Shadow. "This fellow is a Protector."

"Hey, what do you know," the ring said, "We might have a huge lead here."

Trance whistled. "Oh."

"Well, that helps a lot," Aura said seriously.

"Yeah," Trance responded. "We also know this shadow person arrived the same day as the merchant."

"The same day we arrived, Trance."

"Right…." Trance thought a moment.

"Hmm." Aura responded hopefully.

Trance snapped his fingers. "Oh!" he exclaimed. "We also know alarms go off like crazy if someone tries to sneak on board the planet."

"Right!" Aura agreed. "So... Shadow had to arrive by transport. Unless he had special dispensation from the Creators," he amended. "Dispensation is so rare any such arrival would be easy to recall by the Creators; I doubt he would make it that easy."

"Right, we should check with someone anyway. Say... are arrivals and departures tracked in some way?" Aura nodded. "But more specifically, is there anyone who tracks Protectors?"

The Golden Protector brightened. "I don't think so, but it's a good question. Hold on." He paused for a moment, and his ring glowed slightly. "Well, I'll be. There's a little database that does just that. It's tied to the Transport Company which bills Monidad by the head for transporting Protectors and all other personnel who work on Monidad. I thought we were getting a free ride; evidently not. Hmmmmm." He paused again then looked directly at Trance. "It says that day was actually quite light for Protector traffic. Only nine Protectors arrived: Sigfried, Mollie, you, me, Kameko, Taa'lien, Dexter, Per'dita, Danitae, and Ne'lom."

"Who are those last three? I know the others."

Aura was silent for a moment consulting his ring. "Oh. Well, Danitae and Ne'lom who were in Blue-10 squad."

"What do you mean?"

"I mean, one of them had a weakness to splinters, and the other wasn't strong enough."

"Ouch. What about Per'dita?"

"Per'dita is in Yellow-5 squad."

"So pretty much everyone in our squad is a potential suspect. Well, that does narrow things down a bit. I can safely say that I was not involved in this."

"I'm reasonably certain you weren't involved either," Aura ruminated. "I know I wasn't; that leaves only four of our members and of course the others."

"Yes, but in every murder mystery I have ever read, the bad guy turns out to be one of the hero's best friends, and at just the right moment attempts to stab him in the back."

"We have those exact types of books on my planet, too," Aura laughed. "There is always a betrayal just when you least expect it."

"Just to be sure, can I see your neckline?" Trance asked. "It's not that I don't trust you, but why not just get that unpleasantry out of the way?"

Aura was unperturbed. "Sure, buddy." He peeled back the corner of his jumpsuit revealing the base of his neck and even his upper chest; they were bare save a smattering of golden hair. Trance noted with some jealousy that Aura's pectoral muscles looked as though they had been carved out of concrete.

In return, Trance bared his chest. It too didn't have a tattoo.

"Well, I feel better. At least we know we can trust each other."

Trance said nothing; he only nodded.

"Still, Trance," the ring cautioned, "can you completely count Aura out?"

"No," Trance admitted silently. "I can't. I have a gut feeling it is someone else, but I just can't count anyone out at this point. Frankly, though, I have to trust someone."

"Besides me, of course."

"Um, yeah, right," Trance responded. "So, I have to go with my gut. I need the help, and I feel like I could trust him to a certain extent."

"Be very careful, Trance," the ring cautioned.

"I will." Trance looked back at Aura who was waiting patiently. "My ring sure is talkative," Trance laughed.

"Tell me about it," Aura chuckled. "I was up till midnight because of mine last night."

Chapter 23: Investigations

They decided the best course of action would be to fully investigate the ship and the merchant's involvement in the bombing, then move on to the Protectors who had arrived on the day in question. They didn't have a lot of clues to work with, and hoped careful investigation would net them more. They figured they could move slowly – it was doubtful anyone knew that they knew that a Protector was involved.

In the engine room they found another surprise. The wall of the primary reactor had exploded outward in a curiously even pattern suggesting, to Trance's untrained eyes, a bomb of some sort. "Maybe you really didn't cause this crash, Aura," he said.

"I told you, buddy," Aura exclaimed. He peered closely at the jagged rupture, running his finger carefully around the edge. "Hmmmm," he said thoughtfully. "What do you bet this was on a timer?"

"No bets," Trance said. "If I was trying to get out of the area in a hurry, and I was in a ship, I'd probably jump into grey space almost immediately. I wonder if that is what she was trying to do."

"It sure seemed like she was trying just that. It was pure luck you happened to see her in all the commotion. If you hadn't happened to have seen her, she would have been off planet and into grey space immediately, I bet; untraceable and untrackable."

"And then, Whammo," Trance said. "Her engines go out in transit. What then?"

"Lost in gray space," Aura shuddered as they exited the engine room and resumed their search. "No escape."

"And no witnesses."

"Whew. Brutal."

"Yeah. On my planet, we have a saying: 'Dead men tell no tales.'"

"We have a saying on my planet, too, Trance."

"What is it?"

"Roughly translated, 'The Boleweavel of destiny always scrunches in the end.'"

"That's rough alright, Aura."

"It's true, though."

"Right."

They spent the rest of an hour inside the bowels of the ship. Unfortunately, they didn't get much further. When they were both completely frustrated, they contacted Mollie, the Captain of their squad, and filled her in without mentioning their belief a Protector was somehow involved. Mollie was pleased with their investigations, and told them to proceed as they deemed appropriate. "Don't worry about the ship," she said. "Go ahead and abandon it where it is. I'll send a team in to tidy up."

"I don't know if it would help our investigation, but this lady lived somewhere while she was on planet. I'd like to search there," Trance said.

"Good idea," Mollie responded. "Place a quarantine field around the vessel before you leave, Aura."

"I will, Mollie," Aura replied.

"By the way," she said, "Our squad is all accounted for."

"Oh?" Trance perked up. "Kameko is OK, then? Taa'lien said that she hadn't seen Kameko after the first explosion."

"Yes, Kameko spent a great deal of time ferrying the wounded to area hospitals," Mollie said. "She is definitely OK."

After they signed off, they went back to the Bridge and, using his ring, Aura scanned the Merchant's fingertips and some of her blood, and transmitted the the results to a central database where such information was stored. This was another reason crime levels were so low on the planet. All visitors were required to register upon entry, including providing an address where they would be staying. It only took a few moments to get a name, Y'lloh, and an apartment number. Armed with this information, they left the ship in silence.

Outside, standing in the soft and cold sand, Trance watched as Aura willed a containment field around the crumpled wreck. Aura also placed several beacons in the soil that flashed warning messages designed to scare off any beings who might want to investigate the ruins. "That'll do until the cleanup crew arrives," the Golden Protector grunted when he was finished.

With that, they leapt into the sky, and flew back toward the nearest entryway. Once inside the planet's crust, they flew down a series of crowded thoroughfares filled with shops, restaurants, and malls, then down several little side alleys that weren't very crowded but were certainly busy nonetheless. Finally, they flew down small alleys that were so crowded and dreary Trance doubted the powerful overhead lights set in the ceiling ever reached the ground.

The further they journeyed, the danker and darker everything looked. In this section, the restaurants had titles that, translated, made bold statements like "Pay First," or "Mostly Fresh." One promised, in green and blue neon, that it served "Genuine Pussburgers." Trance shuddered inwardly, but noted clinically there was a long line outside the establishment.

Finally they reached the district the central database reported to contain the merchant's apartment. Truthfully, it looked as though it served only the lowest common denominator on this planet or any other.

As they landed, Trance noted with some concern a couple of rather scruffy looking street urchins fighting over the still steaming body of a spider rat. When the pair sighted the two Protectors, however, they rapidly settled their differences amicably and scuttled off with the contested meat.

The next thing Trance noticed as his feet hit the floor was a pervasive smell of decay. This was perhaps the oldest section he had seen thus far, and it looked it. The soft and serene blue carpet that soothed the weary traveler in other sections of Monidad appeared green and sickly here, filled with stains and sections where it had worn down to rock. Trance knew the entire world had once been carved out of whatever the planet had been made of, but in the newer sections, one could hardly tell. Here however, everything from the walls to the ceiling had that look about it. The buildings in this area jutted out from the walls in a haphazard manner, and in some places seemed to blend and bleed together. Most appeared to be constructed of brick or stucco at first glance, but here and there Trance could see the façade peeling back to reveal granite.

In front of them was the apartment building they had been searching for. "Hmm," Trance said looking up. In this section, the ceiling was ten stories up. Halfway between the first and second stories a blue and pink neon sign hung on rusted metal rods. It was a nice contrast to the dirty red brick finish of the building.

The neon sign displayed the name of the apartment, "The Contested Arms." Below the pink and blue, next to a dirty window with the word "Manager" stenciled on it, was a tiny sign proclaiming "Hourly Rates Available," and below that, "No VACANCY." Inexplicably, the architect had chosen green and yellow neon for these two displays. Trance groaned, wishing he had a pair of sunglasses.

A set of steps led up to the front door of the Contested Arms. At the top, Trance rapped smartly on the door. It opened under the power of his tapping. The interior was dim and smelled of mildew. "I don't suppose we need a warrant, do we?" he asked Aura.

"A who?"

"A… never mind. I forgot: you only know about the Middle Ages."

Aura shrugged. "Shall we?"

Y'lloh's apartment was on the fourth floor. Because the lift was broken, with an "Out of Order" sign that had long ago faded into oblivion, they chose the steps. When they reached the second floor landing, they began to notice puddles of liquid on every other step. Halfway up to the next landing, they were avoiding rivulets of the same substance. By the time they reached the door marking the fourth floor, they were wading through a river cascading down the steps.

Inside the door, they found a large group of people milling about and talking excitedly about something that had happened in one of the apartments on the floor.

They pushed through the crowd, and found a mean looking guard standing behind a string of yellow tape with big block letters that said "CAUTION, CRIME SCENE" which had been stretched across the hallway. The guard was wearing a yellow raincoat and a scowl. His five red eyes peered at the crowd suspiciously from beneath bushy eyebrows. When they alighted upon the two Protectors they brightened visibly. "Oh – Protectors! Here to relieve me?" the guard asked hopefully.

"Sorry, chap," Aura replied. "We're here about another matter: we are apartment hunting."

"We just had a vacancy in this section," the guard said seriously. "My crew's cleaning up with tweezers." He gestured over his back. "Truthfully, though, it might be vacant awhile."

Over the guard's shoulder, they could see perhaps a dozen individuals of varying shapes and sizes in yellow raincoats. They too appeared to be soaked, but were going about their business in a quiet and professional manner. Several of them were carrying what looked to Trance to be Geiger counters, which were clicking mightily. A good number of them clutched vacuum cleaners. One appeared to be attempting, somewhat unsuccessfully, to suck up the gallons of water that covered the floor up to two inches thick in places. That poor fellow was whimpering to himself in a dejected tone.

Trance looked at Aura. "You don't think that's the apartment we're looking for..." he said.

"Nah. Not possible. Well, maybe. We better get a closer look."

The guard let them by but collared two onlookers who attempted to shoulder past him in the moment that the tape was down. "Hey, Assholes," Trance heard the guard say as he followed Aura down the hall, "see that word 'CAUTION' on the tape? It refers to me!"

Trance turned to see the guard not so gently introducing the two to his fists. He appeared to be getting a lot of enjoyment out of it. In fact, he seemed to have found the relief he was seeking.

Trance turned with a smile on his face and slogged after his companion. After about twenty feet, he began thinking dark thoughts at whoever had left the sprinklers on. His feet were soggy now, and he was having trouble seeing more than a few feet ahead, because the sprinklers in this section of the hall were emitting particularly strong streams of water. With almost every step he had to avoid a different clean-up crew member who, up close, Trance realized was working hard at doing very little. In fact, the crew members with the Geiger counters appeared to be making the clicking sounds with their mouths. He doubted the machines were even on.

He nearly ran into Aura when the larger Protector stopped suddenly. "Sorry, Aura," he said, then whistled as he saw what had stopped them.

They were now standing before a wall that had been perforated by a large explosive device. The edges of the central cavity had a singed look, and had been pushed outward. At the upper edge, bits of a doorframe could still be seen. Above the frame Trance could see the apartment number, 1158; a match to the numerals they had been seeking. It appeared as though they had found the Merchant's domicile.

Across the hall from the gaping maw, Trance could see more evidence of the explosion. Bits of door, cloth, blood and bone had painted a grisly portrait on the surface of the wall.

Inside the doorway, the remains of a small living space could be seen. From his current vantage point, Trance noted a living room, and off to the left, a kitchen. The kitchen had scarred yellow and brown linoleum; the living room had green shag carpeting and a six-foot diameter hole through which he could see the apartment below. A steady stream of water was pouring over the edge making things nice and damp for the inhabitants below.

They found more grisly evidence pasted on the wall around the door jam on the inside of the apartment. "Is that hair?" Trance asked rhetorically. "Yuck."

"My ring says it matches the stuff on that far wall," Aura said, pointing at the gore in the hall.

"What do you make of it?"

"Not sure. I'll send it to the database of known criminals."

"How long will it take to get a match?"

"Depends. There are literally trillions of 'known' criminals. It could take... Well, what do you know. We have a match."

"So don't keep me in suspense. What is it?"

"Another escapee, Trance, by the name of E'bbied. He was a bomber of some notoriety. Looks like we won't be booking this fellow again."

"Maybe we should read him his rights anyway."

"Go right ahead."

"Um. Maybe later."

"How do you figure this guy got plastered all over the walls? Maybe one of his bombs went awry?"

"I don't know. Given the fact our merchant also got blown up, and this is her apartment... it seems so clean and tidy, like someone is mopping up a little leftover mess."

"Maybe that person should have spent a little more time in the living room," griped the ring. "What a crap hole."

"Still, it makes me wonder how they even got the explosives. I thought it was impossible to get them on board the planet."

Aura shrugged. "I have no idea," he said. "But it sure is weird."

Trance grabbed one of the clean-up crew members by the arm, a bright orange and yellow fellow who bore a name tag that read "My Name is XCX. How am I cleaning? Call 77788777."

"What happened here?" Trance asked in his best cop voice.

"Well, boss," XCX squeaked, "It's like this, see, somebody decided to ventilate the place."

"I got that. What else?"

"Your guess is as good as mine, boss. All I know is that I'm on overtime at this point. We're the morning crew. I got called out of bed to do this job. All they tell us is that we need to clean. Know what I mean?"

Aura rolled his eyes. "We're not going to get anywhere with this crew, Trance."

Trance sighed. "Do you know who's in charge here?"

The worker looked at him uncertainly. "Um, you are, boss. You're the ring bearer. Or maybe the large yellow feller that's with you. Maybe he's in charge."

Trance looked at Aura again, who shrugged and said, "We're always in charge, Trance. That's part about being a Protector. But it is still unwritten protocol to check with the management on-site before pulling rank. Ask him who was in charge before we got here. That might work."

"You heard him—do you know who was in charge?"

XCX looked relieved. "Well, why didn't you say so? Gosh, of course I know that!"

Several seconds passed as Trance looked at the worker. "Well?" he finally asked.

"Well, what?"

"Who was in charge -- I mean, before we arrived?"

"Oh, heh, heh, heh. See, I thought…. Never mind. You want NKDKR over there."

NKDKR turned out to be just about as helpful as a door jam. He was a massive, inexpressive jackal with yellow-stained teeth and breath that smelled of stale coffee and cigars. When they first sighted him, he had a large dilapidated stogy clenched sadly between his mandibles. He chewed it steadily while they explained their mission, rolling in between his thick sausage-like fingers. But that was about the extent of his interaction with the pair. After they had politely asked his permission to search the apartment, he shrugged, and returned to work, all but ignoring them.

They started in the bedroom, which they found off of the kitchen. The sprinklers in this room had never come on, so everything was dry.

Three beds, a small television, and a closet filled the tiny enclosure. The closet was empty, and the beds were each bare save a disheveled and patched mattress. "Not much here, Trance," Aura said thoughtfully.

"If you discount the dust bunnies."

"Bunnies? Where?" asked Aura.

"That's just a figure of speech, Aura. There really aren't any bunnies here, just bits of dust."

A dejected look passed over the Golden Protector's face. "Your figures of speech sure are disappointing, Trance."

They voyaged back out into the living room / kitchen area. After poking around for a few more moments they made a discovery: there was absolutely nothing of any worth in the apartment.

"Hey, Trance," Aura said, "There's nothing of any worth here."

"Yeah. Sure seems like she was out of here for good," Trance replied.

In fact, just about every piece of electronics left in the apartment had been turned to slag in the blast or doused completely by the resulting shower from the sprinkler system. Whatever evidence that may have survived the fire and the water had been trampled, vacuumed or otherwise destroyed by the random and clumsy movements of the cleanup crew. In other words, the hole in the floor was the only thing of note in the entire apartment. Trance and Aura left feeling dejected and rather sodden.

On the way out, they noticed a smarmy, thin individual wringing his hands and moaning dejectedly while staring into the apartment's gaping front. "Let's talk with that fellow," Trance said. "I bet that he owns this apartment building," he said, "or maybe has some other vital connection to it."

They stopped, eyeing the individual who was standing still like a small and forlorn island in the stream of water and cleaning crew members. "What makes you say that?" Aura asked.

"Well, he's not wearing a uniform, yet folks are leaving him alone. He's not writing furiously, so I doubt he's a reporter. And finally, he's obviously distraught at the damage to this apartment. C'mon, let's talk with him."

Aura looked impressed. 'Sure, why not?" he said. "You take the lead, Trance."

"Excuse me, um, sir," Trance said uncertainly as they approached the fellow.

"Yes," sniffled the man, "What can I do you for?" Up close, Trance noted he was missing several teeth, wore glasses thick as coke bottles, and had thick greasy hair, all over his body. A slightly thicker sheaf of hair protruded from beneath his nose, giving off the impression of a mustache. He also gave off a steady powerful stench of raw and rather rotten wet fish. He was wearing a blue cotton robe tied at the waist, and fuzzy slippers that looked like octopi, but Trance couldn't be sure. He took it all in one disgusted glance, and then opened his mouth.

"Sir," he said, "We have reason to believe you are in some way connected to this apartment. Who are you?"

The man withered under the direct question. His lower lip began to tremble slightly, and beads of sweat broke over a wrinkled brow. Trance wondered momentarily if he were about to cry. But then the man rallied wonderfully and spoke in a tremulous voice. "I... I... I'm the manager of this building.... My... my," he sniffed and wiped an arm under his large nose, "my name is Lofrahd Croftban."

Trance looked at Aura triumphantly. "Lofrahd Croftban," do you know what happened here?"

"Well, somebody decided to ventilate the place," he said in a steadier voice.

"I mean, besides that," Trance said after a quick count to five. "Were there any witnesses to the crime?"

"All my friends call me Lofrahd," the fellow sniffled.

"Mr. Croftban, uh... Lofrahd, can you answer my question?"

"I don't know, but I am sure we got it on vid." He pointed over his shoulder to a camera hanging from the ceiling on a thin rod. It had a fish-eyed lens so that its view encompassed the entire hall. "We have so many problems in this sector that the owners installed these babies five years ago. Best decision they ever made," he sniffed, "besides hiring me of course, and crime's down fifty percent in the halls ever since then."

"Yeah, it's moved back into the apartments, where it belongs," the ring grumbled sarcastically.

"Know how a couple of Protectors with crime solving in mind might be able to see this vid?" Trance asked gently.

"Yes."

They stood there for a moment, and then Trance sighed theatrically. "Tell you what, why don't you take us to where we can view the vid. Then we can start the investigation and you can get back to worrying."

"With this guy, it's a full time job," the ring said.

"Oh! Well, why didn't you say so?" the manager sniffed despondently.

The manager took them to his apartment which was on the first floor. It felt good to Trance to be on solid dry land again, away from the clutter and bustle of the onlookers and the cleaning crews. On the way out, Trance nodded to the security guard who'd let them in past the yellow tape. He smiled pleasantly back at them and rubbed his knuckles. "Now there is a man who loves his job," the ring said rhetorically.

Chapter 24: The Shadow Moves

The manager's apartment was adjacent to the office. They stood outside in the hall while Croftban went inside and rummaged around in his domicile for a key, then followed him as he shuffled over and unlocked the office. Inside they found a small slightly dusty room with a dark wood counter upon which sat an ancient telephone, a monitor, and a keyboard. On one wall was a plastic container housing little brochures which cheerfully suggested they visit several tourist attractions in the area. "Genuine Pussburgers" had a large full-color advertisement complete with pictures. Trance shuddered and looked around the rest of the room.

Off to the right was a small kitchen with a microwave and a refrigerator. It seemed clean and sparse. Beyond that Trance could see an open door leading to what he guessed was a bathroom based on the roll of toilet paper in plain view. However, the fixtures he could see in the vicinity looked completely foreign to him.

Behind the counter a window looked outside the apartment building and into the hallway proper. Outside, Trance noted, the pair of scruffy looking street urchins they had scared off earlier were back… and were bickering over the spider rat again. He chuckled.

The manager, seeing Trance's reaction looked out the window and frowned. Rather than comment about the impending fight however, he turned, leaned over and flipped a switch beneath the counter. Behind him, outside, the "NO VACANCY" sign beneath the "Contested Arms" gave a shudder and a slight hum, and the "No" flickered and faded. The manager grimaced. "Do you know how hard it is to rent an apartment in this section?" he sighed. "I just rented the darn thing a few weeks ago. I don't suppose either of you two is interested in taking on the lease." He looked at them hopefully.

"Uh, no," Trance stammered looking to Aura for help, "I can't afford the rent on the one that I have back home," he finally muttered.

"Sir, you said you had a vid for us to watch," Aura said helpfully. The look on his face said he wouldn't be caught dead living in an apartment in this building.

"Oh, yeah," the manager brightened. "Maybe if you catch the bastard, you'll get him to pay for the damage? My deposit money just isn't going to cover this one."

"Oh, he'll pay alright," Aura said truthfully.

The manager smiled, and typed a few commands into the keyboard. Then, he swiveled the monitor so that it faced the Protectors as well. "What we are about to see is live footage from the camera. I'll focus in on apartment 1158," he said, tapping a key. "Ah there it goes." The monitor brightened, and the hallway appeared on its face. They could see the gaping hole, and around it the clean-up crew. They were all standing around drinking Chojos.

"Well, at least they have nice taste in beer," Aura said.

"Hmm. Can you give us some earlier footage?" Trance asked. "Nothing suspicious going on right now."

"Unless you're wondering where they got those bottles," the manager said suspiciously, looking into his kitchen. Nonetheless, he typed some more commands, and the image on the screen froze and then began to rewind. The figures stayed exactly where they were, but their arms became a blur as they traveled up and down to and from their mouths.

"Let's go back four hours," Trance said, after a few moments.

The monitor darkened momentarily and then the hallway appeared again whole. "OK, forward from here, not too fast, though," Aura cautioned.

The image sped up slowly. Bodies crossed the field of vision frequently in a rush, their arms and legs pin wheeling like crazy puppets.

Then an individual slinked into sight, hugging the shadows like they were close friends and he was going away on a long trip. "Go normal speed. That's our fellow I'll bet," Aura said.

The man oozed into the lighted area directly beneath apartment 1158 and fumbled at the door.

"Hit pause. Do you recognize that man?" Aura asked the Manager.

"No," the Manager said, disappointed. "I have never seen him before in my life, and I know, or at least would recognize all the people who live or frequently visit here. I pride myself on that."

"It's a fellow by the name of E'bbied. He just escaped from one of the penal colonies," Aura said firmly.

"Are you sure it's him?" Trance asked. "Last time we saw him he looked quite a bit different."

"Being plastered all over a wall will do that to you," Aura replied, "but yeah, I am sure. Remember the database I checked? They sent me a holographic picture with the file. It matches this individual exactly."

"Fair enough; can you please continue the film, Lofrahd? Thanks."

On the screen, E'bbied continued fumbling for a moment more and then eased himself into the apartment. The door remained closed for a period of less than two minutes and then it opened again.

A figure appeared in the doorway, turned momentarily, and then stepped out into the hallway closing the door behind it. It walked quickly away from the apartment and disappeared from their view. One minute later the camera shook as the apartment wall exploded outward in a rain of fire and debris.

There was a moment of silence as they processed what they had just seen.

"What the heck was that all about?" the Manager asked.

"I have no idea," Aura said truthfully.

"Look at the time, Aura," Trance whispered. Down in the left hand corner, the time and date were blinking a steady beat. "That's right when we were chasing the Merchant's ship. In fact, I bet it's right then that..."

"The bomb in the ship blew," Aura finished. "Hmmm."

"Well, we do know something," Trance offered. "The person that left the apartment right before the explosion was not the person that entered."

"True," Aura admitted. Physically, they are much different. In fact, unless I miss my guess, I'd wager this was the same fellow we saw on the ship's log."

The manager raised an eyebrow but said nothing. "Can you use the other cameras in the building and follow him out?" Trance asked. "And can you slow the vid down while you're at it? I want to see if we can catch his face."

"Sure. I can even make it a seamless presentation from camera to camera," Croftban boasted. He typed for a few seconds, and then pointed to the monitor. On the screen the door and wall of apartment 1158 were whole again. The door opened, and the dark shape stepped into the hall and turned briefly. At the slower speed, they could see that it was speaking with someone inside.

"Pause right there," Trance said.

"Looks like the Shadow is talking with E'bbied," Aura said.

"He's probably saying, 'There's a bomb in here, but don't worry, it won't bite,'" the ring said darkly.

"I was wondering when you'd pipe up with something," Trance thought, smiling inwardly. Out loud, he said, "Please continue the vid, Mr. Croftban."

"Uh, sure." The shadow turned, closing the door behind it, and walked down the hall in a smooth, though hurried gate. It didn't stop when the shockwave tore into the hallway behind it.

Suddenly, the empty hall became a mad rush of beings; mothers and fathers in terry-cloth bathrobes clinging to babies, singles carrying their pets, children hanging on to dollies – a river of bodies heading down the stairs and into the street in a chaotic rush. And Shadow swam with the current, became one with it, and was gone.

They watched the vid several times, finally resorting to viewing it frame by frame; the shadow simply disappeared without a trace. Never once was its face revealed.

"Can you do a search program with that thing? Find out if that exact shape entered that apartment anytime in the recent past? Maybe if the cameras captured the Shadow entering the apartment, we could get a face then." Aura asked.

"You're joking, right?"

"Not that I am aware."

"So, I take it you can't do that, then," Trance said.

"Sorry, Protectors," he said, a tear welling up in his eye. "I guess that's it then."

 "You've started worrying again, haven't you?" Trance asked.

"No! I... well... Y... Yes," Croftban said, lower lip trembling. "I'm afraid we'll never find out who did it."

"Hey, remember we said you can start worrying after we're gone," Aura said. "Besides, I have a trick I can use, if you can just show me where those files are stored."

"O.. OK," The manager rallied again, confidence returning. He pointed to a small box next to his monitor.

Aura concentrated for a moment. "Huh," he said. "Well, whoever it was must have used a site-to-site transporter, because I can find no record in the past year of that form entering or leaving that Apartment."

"Perhaps the Shadow used a site-to-site in the hall as well," Trance mused.

"Could be," Aura grunted.

"Of course, a Protector could use his ring to dematerialize any time," the ring said. "I shouldn't need to tell you, but it's wise not to let the Manager know we suspect the criminal is a ring-wielder. We don't want to start any rumors."

"Good idea, Ring," Trance said silently. He looked at Aura. "What about the merchant or our wall-hugging friend?" he asked.

"Wall-hugging... do you mean the fellow vaporized all over the corridor, first name E'bbied?" Aura frowned.

"Have they been visiting that apartment before?"

"Right. Let me check frequency... looks like the merchant just started using the residence during the past couple of days. E'bbied visited it for the first time today," Aura said. "There have been others in and out of there in the past couple of weeks. They seem to have been moving small packages out of there. But I can't get a read on what those packages contained. Oh, and there is no record of the Shadow."

"Hmmm. Well, I guess that's all we can do here. Can you copy the vid?"

"Already did. Got it stored in here." He pointed to the ring.

They thanked Croftban and asked the manager to contact them if any more information surfaced. He promised them he would let them know.

Outside, Trance looked at Aura. "What next?" he asked, leaning against the side of the apartment building.

"Well, next we need to start talking with all of the Protectors who arrived the same day we did. Unfortunately, I have no idea who to start asking first."

"We can discount Mollie, Dexter and Sigfried, right? I mean, they are nowhere near the size and shape of the Shadow."

"Unfortunately, we can't. It's pretty easy to use your ring to disguise your shape. I've done it myself too many times to count. It's handy at class reunions – I dropped twenty pounds in five seconds before my last one," he beamed.

"Oh," Trance said, crestfallen. "I'd hope to narrow things down a bit."

"Well, maybe we should examine the bodies of Danitae and Ne'lom. We can reasonably assume that neither is this "Shadow" person. You'd think he would be smart enough to avoid something like that. However, it appears as though the Shadow has a tendency to dispose of the help. Maybe they were involved."

"Uhh -- more dead bodies. I had hoped that we wouldn't have to do that. But, you're right."

Before they continued on, Aura attempted to smooth the way by speaking with the Captain of Blue-10 squad by hologram. After giving his condolences, the Golden Protector delicately asked the disposition of the bodies, and requested permission to examine them. The captain, obviously mourning the loss of two of his members told Aura pointedly to shove his request in the nearest orifice he could find.

Aura began to sweat as he protested feebly. He was stuck – he couldn't tell the Captain exactly why he needed permission because he knew the admission that they suspected a Protector was intimately involved with a murderous plot could throw the corps into chaos. Unfortunately, he couldn't come up with a good excuse, and he couldn't go around the Captain's wishes. Meanwhile, the Captain, a being that looked somewhat like a cross between a bird and a bottlenose dolphin, was working himself into a frenzy of accusations and threats. He wasn't having a good day and, by God, nobody else around him would either.

"Trance," the ring called to him.

"What?" Trance pulled his attention away from the verbal reaming his comrade was getting.

"Are you sure you trust Aura?"

"Yes, I do," Trance said seriously. "I have to trust somebody," he amended.

"Then tell him to ask the Captain to contact Creator MasTho if he has any questions."

"He can contact who? Did you say MasTho?"

"What?" Aura asked. Trance realized that both Aura and the fuming bird/dolphin were looking at him. He'd evidently spoken aloud. "Explain your statement, Protector," the Captain said in a cold voice, feathers ruffling along his sides and the back of his head.

"You can contact Creator MasTho if you have any questions," Trance repeated weakly. "My ring is relaying you the Creator's personal line. Tell him, um, members of Squad Red 26, under his special investigation, made the request."

"I'll do that," the Bird/Dolphin said, eyes narrowing, sharp teeth showing. "I'll tell him all about it. And if this cockamamie number doesn't check out, my next call will be to Dymin." He disappeared after telling them not to go anywhere.

"Well, now you've done it," Aura said peevishly when the Captain had faded away. "I hope you know what you're doing," he growled.

Trance sighed. He actually had no idea what the ring had gotten him into now.

Chapter 25: Dead Ends

"Do you even know who MasTho is? Do you know what Dymin will do to us if that Captain contacts him?" Aura sighed. "We'll be busted down to dishwashers in the dirtiest and dankest gallery he can find!"

"MasTho is the head Creator. Who's Dymin?"

Aura collapsed to the ground and put his head in his hands. "Dymin is perhaps the meanest, most vindictive son of a bitch that I have ever had the displeasure of laying my eyes on. He hates our squad with a passion."

"Good thing he's not the Creator we report to," Trance said.

"He is the one that we report to, Trance," Aura growled between his teeth.

"Huh. Well, my ring says not to worry." He sat down next to Aura and smiled to him. The Protector grimaced back. "Besides, Aura," Trance snickered. "I washed dishes as a kid. It's not too bad."

"I'm sure Dymin would make it bad," Aura said. "In fact, I – hold on, I have an incoming call, high priority. Ulp. It's holographic."

"Why don't you answer it, then," Trance smiled. His pulse raced a little. "I hope you did the right thing, Ring," he said internally.

The Bird/Dolphin was back. It frowned, with its sharp teeth covered. "I am really, really sorry," it said. "What can I do?"

Aura broke into a smile, which he quickly covered in a cough. "I accept your apology, Captain," he said. "What did our friend, Creator MasTho say?"

"Whew. My ear buds hurt. He said you were on a special mission, and if you asked for assistance I was to provide it without question. I have no idea what you're up to, but I wish you the best of luck.

'I am sorry about giving you a hard time about examining our squad members. It's just that... well, Nej'ifer was my... my... life partner."

"Oh." Aura said. "I am truly sorry. And I do appreciate the help."

"I am transmitting the coordinates of the observatory. They will be cremated tomorrow, of course so I suggest you hurry. I'll send a message ahead that you need privacy, and if there is anything else you need, please let me know."

They signed off. Aura looked at Trance for a moment. Afterward, he nodded to himself. "I have no idea how you managed to get MasTho to vouch for us. Maybe it's best if I don't know. But you are a member of my squad. I will help you as long as you need me, and that's all there is to it."

"I wish I could tell you, Aura," Trance responded warmly. "All I ask is that you keep this between us for now."

Aura nodded. "We better get going," he said.

They followed the Captain's directions. It took them over ten minutes by lift to reach travel all the way on the other side of the planet, and another ten minutes to travel by foot to the observatory. They chose the slow route so that they could discuss their investigation so far. Trance was warming up to Aura with every minute he spent with the large fellow. He had an agile and extremely inquisitive mind, loved a good mystery, and approached problems in ways that Trance would not have. In short, they made a good team. Unfortunately, as a team they weren't coming up with any solid answers.

"Boy, I sure hope one of them has a tattoo," Aura said seriously. "We'd at least have more direction."

Trance shook his head. "Do you really think that either of them will, though?"

Aura frowned. "No. Whoever it is has thought these things through really carefully. I can't help but think this is a dead end."

"My feeling exactly. Well, we still have to check this lead out."

They found both of the bodies in the same room along with the third Protector of that squad who had been killed in the bombings. It was tradition among the squads to honor their own in quiet solitude for twenty-four hours before final disposal in the form of cremation. To this end, the room contained three raised platforms and a small contingent of chairs. Currently, there were five members of Blue-10, and two members of another squad. Several were weeping openly. The three had been popular.

The Captain of Blue-10 had evidently radioed ahead. Although it was highly irregular, the observers silently filed out when Aura and Trance arrived.

"Let's get this over," Trance said. They approached the raised platforms, and prepared to investigate the bodies. Nej'ifer was the worse off of the two they needed to investigate; the wood splinters had serrated his body. The splinters had been removed, but out of respect his body had not been repaired. What was the use? Nothing remained but an empty shell whose memory must be mourned.

Nej'ifer was missing most of his skin, and four of his six eyes. The center of his torso had been split open, and some, but not all of his inner organs had come out. These were piled in a sealed container next to the platform. Trance saw the destruction, turned quickly and retched.

Aura tisked. "Not much here," he said. He performed a quick visual inspection, forming a pair of tongs to aid him.

Trance cleaned up the mess he had made and then joined his comrade. "Sorry," he said.

"I thought you'd be ok given you did so well with the merchant. But you're still not comfortable with dead bodies are you?" Aura asked kindly.

"No. Hopefully I never will get used them."

"You'll see a lot more before we're done, I reckon," Aura grunted. "Take a look here." He pointed with the tongs at a large hole, the size of a phone book, on the upper chest.

Trance could see through to the tabletop. The neck looked as though it had almost been completely separated from the rest of the body. "Great," he said, "right where the others had their tattoos."

They performed a quick visual scan on the rest of the torso and what remained of the five limbs with no results. "Not very conclusive," Aura said. "I had hoped at least to eliminate Nej'ifer as a part of the conspiracy, but I guess we'll never know."

There wasn't much left of the second Protector, just a sealed bucket. Trance was glad they didn't have to investigate her. They moved on to Ne'lom.

The body was bent in odd angles by Trance's standards. It was gray with over a dozen appendages, each splayed in a different direction. The head reminded Trance of an ant: it had two bug eyes a mandible, and two antennae. It was hairless and wasn't wearing any clothing. The total package looked to be just over five feet tall.

"Didn't you say Ne'lom was crushed?" Trance asked.

"Yeah, she looks pretty bad," Aura said. "Poor dear."

"What's wrong with her, then? She looks fine. Apart from being disgustingly ugly, that is."

"She's supposed to be over eight feet tall, for one thing," Aura said reprovingly.

"Ah. Yes. She does look a little mashed now that I think of it. And what do you know... no tattoos."

"OK. So, let's move on to Per'dita. I'll check and see where he is." Aura appeared to be thinking for a moment. In reality he must have been communicating with his ring. "My, my, my," he said, "looks like we were investigating the wrong Protectors."

"What do you mean?"

"Remember when Taa'lien said one Protector was missing? It's Per'dita."

"Really. That is interesting. What can we do?"

"There is a massive search going on right now. His body wasn't in the rubble of the Battle Dome, and oddly enough his ring isn't being used anywhere in the Galaxy. That's the distance limit we can scan, you know."

"I know. Does it leave a trail or something we can pick up?"

"Rings do, of course, when they are used. However his ring wasn't used to take him off planet."

"So he was onboard a ship, then. Can we check the ships that left in the past, say, twelve hours? Maybe he bought a ticket off planet."

"I checked that already. No Protectors have left the planet in the past twelve hours. Besides, we usually use transporters to beam off the planet. It's faster."

"Oh... can we physically check, then? Maybe he disguised himself. There can't have been too many ships that have left Monidad in half a day."

"Thousands, in fact. There isn't a speed limit for ships leaving the System, just entering. It's a safety thing, yes?"

"Oh," Trance said, crestfallen. "He's our main suspect, I bet. It seems there isn't anything that we can do about it, though."

"I'm sure we'll think of something. In the meantime, maybe it's best we proceed with our plans to check the other Protectors. Just because this Shadow is a Protector doesn't mean he is the only one involved."

They made their way back to the lift, and stood in silence for a full five minutes while it hummed away as it traveled toward their home, each lost in their own thoughts. Finally, Aura spoke. "I've been thinking about how we're going to proceed. We have to be careful that we don't alienate our own group, but we have to check them nonetheless. But, if one of our own is involved we also don't want to let that person to know you and I are on to them."

"I really wish we had more to work with as far as Per'dita is concerned. I mean, why bother checking our own group if he's still our primary target?"

"What can we do, then?"

"I think we should go search his apartment. Can we get away with that?"

"Good idea. It's a start, anyway. Hopefully we'll find something there."

By this time the lift had made it to the Spire, the location of most of the Protector Apartments. Per'dita's space was just one level below theirs. It had the same non-descript door which yielded after some prodding with the rings. Inside they found a cheery layout complete with a cleanly made bed, and a stack of Plexiglas shards, which turned out to be encoded with self-help and art instruction data. They were library books.

The apartment was filled to the brim with stuff. There were holodiscs containing representations of Per'dita's friends and family members on every flat space, framed artwork, and other knickknacks and memorabilia.

After a thorough search, which netted absolutely nothing in the way of evidence, they reconvened at the entrance to the apartment. "I don't care where the clues point, Aura," Trance said. "This is not the room of a saboteur. Why go to all the trouble to make a bed if you're not coming back to it later? Why put out pictures of friends and relatives? If Per'dita really was mixed up in all of this, I seriously doubt he'd have gone to the trouble of setting up his room. He only got here yesterday, for heaven's sake."

"Remember, decorating choices are held in memory by the Spire's computers. Any aspect, from the toilets to the framed artwork can be created at a moment's notice; even the holodiscs."

"Maybe so, but it still doesn't feel right."

"You have a lot of good questions, Trance. Let's pretend for a moment that you're right, and Per'dita really isn't a suspect. What now?"

"Well, I really had hoped to find a tattoo on one of those bodies."

"Frankly, Trance, I'm not surprised. Why would someone go to all the trouble to stage a bombing and then put themselves in a position to be killed by it? Besides, remember that Shadow left the exploding apartment after the events in the Battle Dome, and even if one of them had a tattoo, we would still need to be looking for other suspects."

"Right. Unfortunately, that means the saboteur is a member of our squad, if we forget about Per'dita, of course."

"Yeah." Aura thought for a moment. "That's not a pleasant thought. Until today, I would have told you I trusted each of them with my life. Now I'm not so sure."

"You have known everyone a lot longer than I have," Trance replied. "Who do you think it is?"

"I have no idea, Trance. Want to conjecture?"

"Kameko is a name that pops into my head, though truthfully I hope she isn't involved."

"Why do you think that she might be?"

"She disappeared during the bombings for an extended period of time. Maybe enough time to blow up E'bbied."

"Hmmm. Maybe it's Taa'lien," Aura responded. "She could have singled out Kameko to throw suspicion her way."

"Maybe it is one of the cats or the slug," Trance replied, "using their rings to create a human appearance. That's possible, too. In fact, Sigfried wasn't with us at the Battle Room. He's the only member of our squad who wasn't there."

"He certainly has the talent. Remember he was a famed artist before becoming a Protector, and constructs are his specialty."

"We're going to have to check everyone then. But, like you said in the lift we don't want to let the others know that you and I suspect them. It would ruin the trust they have in us, and make it mighty hard to work as a team. What to do?"

"I suggest that we contact your friend, MasTho. We may need his help in this."

Trance nodded and asked his ring to contact the Creator. Momentarily, MasTho appeared in front of them in the form of a life-sized hologram. This was the first real view of a modern Creator. They hadn't changed much in the millions of years between the mem-rec recording and now.

MasTho stood about five feet six inches tall. He had long gray hair, which was pulled back into a pony tail, bushy eyebrows and a smooth face with little wrinkle lines at the eyes and lips. His eyes were an icy blue. He wore a full-length robe with a hood, which was down. His ears were pointed at the top. The whole effect was that of a kindly elf. "Can I help you?" he asked pleasantly when he appeared.

"Creator MasTho?" Trance asked.

The Creator smiled and looked at the two Protectors. "Yes. And you are?" Beside him, Aura frowned in surprise.

"I'm Trance Adams, an Earthling. This is Aura. He's a…. an…"

"An Orian, from Orias," Aura finished.

"Ah. Yes. The Earthling! Can I help you, Trance? I am anxious to hear how you are progressing."

Trance explained the investigation thus far completely with nothing left out. Here and there, Aura jumped in to flush the story out. When they were done, MasTho nodded. "That was smart to check Per'dita's apartment," he said. He doesn't sound like an involved party, but we need to find him to make sure. Your next step should be investigating your teammates. I'll ask another squad to take care of the Per'dita aspect of this mystery. Good work."

"That's where we need your assistance," Aura said frankly.

"The tattoo will prove it, I bet," Trance said, but we need your help." He explained their concerns about revealing themselves to their squad mates.

"I see. Plan to meet Dymin in his office in one hour. I'll handle the rest."

"Yes sir."

"Oh. No one knows. Not even Dymin. No one." With that, MasTho faded away.

"What's that supposed to mean?" Trance asked.

Aura sighed. "We're to meet everyone in Dymin's office. We have to play along with whatever happens."

"One hour. That reminds me: I haven't eaten in a long time. Let's get something to chow on first. I'd rather face the unknown with a full stomach."

"Good idea," Aura chuckled. "I need to show you where Dymin is anyway. He is our Creator, after all, even if he is a complete jerk. I'll fill you in over dinner."

Chapter 26: Suspicions

Dymin was the oldest of all the Creators, by far. He had been born 8253 years after the Great Rebellion. Aura described him as a cross between MasTho (whom the Orian obviously respected a great deal), and a raisin. Trance guessed that all the Creators shared certain features and was correct: most had gray long hair, pasty skin, and short stature, and possessed an affinity for ponytails and long flowing robes. Dymin was no different in this respect.

There were eleven Creators on the Council, the ruling body that guided the Corps of Protectors and governed the System. MasTho was the head Creator, though he was not the oldest.

Many members of the Corps believed MasTho to be a good and wise ruler. He had been in charge for nearly twenty thousand years, and during that time the Corps had prospered... until recently.

Unfortunately, for past thousand years, things had been going very poorly for the Corps. Attacks by regions outside the Conglomerated States had increased, and the mysterious entity that was attacking and killing Protectors had begun to weigh heavily on the Corps' morale. A small, but rather vocal minority had begun to question MasTho's leadership during this period. A very few had begun to privately mutter that he step down so that another could tackle the problem. Perhaps the most vocal in this regard was Dymin who could scarcely contain his ill feelings toward MasTho and the Corps by proxy. His own squad, of which Trance was now a member, frequently bore the brunt of Dymin's ill will.

As a historian by trade, Aura knew something about the long story of the Creators. He believed wholeheartedly that MasTho was the only person capable of getting them through this difficult and trying time. He resented Dymin's accusations and insinuations, as he felt that they further degraded morale. Unfortunately, he could not publicly voice his feelings. One simply did not speak out against a Creator – it just wasn't done. And so he fretted in silence, and worried about the future of the Corps.

Dymin's office was toward the center of the planet, about a mile from the core. The rumor was he liked the heat - it was just slightly warmer near the core - but Aura suspected it was because he liked the solitude. There wasn't much else around his office, just interconnecting pathways, transport tubes, and assorted piping. Most of the rest of the Creators' offices were spread in clusters around the Great Spire.

They found the other members of their squad waiting outside the door to Dymin's office. It was located at the end of a darkly lit hallway in an otherwise deserted building. Mollie looked the most worried, but this wasn't a clue to Trance because he knew she usually worried. "Do you guys know what we're here for?" she asked.

"I have no idea," Trance said truthfully. What was MasTho up to? "Have you all been waiting long?"

"About ten minutes, Trance," Taalien said. "I was just eating dinner when MasTho's call came in."

"We think he called us all at the same time," Dexter said, sauntering out of the shadows. Trance had figured he was nearby on account of the general Dexterness smell that permeated everything within his vicinity. "Did you get the call about forty-five minutes ago?"

"Right around that time, I think," Aura said. "Trance and I finished eating first, though. Whatever it is can't be too important if we all had to meet here. They would have hologrammed us a message if it was that important," he reasoned.

"I came right away," Mollie sniffed disapprovingly.

"See, that's why you're the boss," Dexter said teasingly, "You follow the rules."

"I try to. That's what they are there for, after all. Why have rules if you can't follow them?"

"Oh, I can think of a good reason to have rules, to break them to piec -" Dexter started.

"Knock it off, you two," called a voice from inside the office, "and get in here."

"Oh, Geez, I hate it when he listens at the door," Dexter whispered to Trance. "Did you fill our new Protector in?" he asked Aura in the same voice. Aura nodded but said nothing.

"Oh, dear," Mollie said wringing her white paws, "here we go."

"I'm sure everything is fine," Sigfried said consolingly as they walked through the door. "We'll be out of here in no time."

The office was large and slightly dusty. Bookshelves lined the walls – the old fashioned books with actual pages. There were no windows, and it was stiflingly hot.

In the center of the room was a desk. Dymin sat behind it. MasTho stood behind him in the form of a hologram. The group stood about five feet from the desk.

MasTho spoke first. "I'm sorry that I couldn't be with you in person, but I have to meet with several other squads in the next few minutes. We have very good reason to believe that a rogue Protector is on board the planet. Please do not use your rings. I am sorry that I cannot tell you more. Dymin?"

Dymin looked at MasTho then turned back to his squad. "Please remove your shirts," he said with no preamble. He stood and walked around to the front of his desk.

Trance pulse quickened. Who would it be?

"You got to be kidding me," Dexter said. He never wore shirts.

"No, we're not kidding," Dymin growled.

"Creator, I must protest, Kameko said huffily. "This is an invasion of my privacy. Please don't ask me to do this without an explanation."

Mollie was already struggling with her pink collar. "Urf," she said, "Let's just get this over with."

Dymin looked at MasTho. "I told you this would be difficult," he said.

"The other groups understood, brother," MasTho said firmly, "when they heard the reason."

"They should do it without question!" Dymin growled. "They are our tools! The hammer does not question why it must hit the nail; it just strikes."

"MasTho looked at the squad. "We are looking for a specific tattoo," he said. "We believe that the Protector who has this marking is involved."

"Oh," Kameko said, somewhat mollified.

Taa'lien stepped forward, unbuttoning her shirt. Beneath she wore a lacy blue bra. Her breasts were exquisite, and her skin clear and free of scars. "Do I need to remove this?" she asked, pointing to her brazier. The view was incredible. She turned around in a complete circle so that Dymin and MasTho could see her entire upper half. She bore no tattoos.

"That is not necessary, Taa'lien," MasTho said. "The tattoo is at the base of the neck. I appreciate your cooperation."

Aura removed his shirt next. Of course, he didn't have a tattoo either.

Trance stepped forward, pulling his shirt over his head. He felt embarrassed showing off his skin in front of everyone, but he wanted to get it over with. His body was firmly sculpted – he worked out daily—but he felt a little silly underneath the scrutiny of his squad mates. When it was over, he put his shirt back on, his ears burning.

Mollie allowed Dymin to gently push back her fur around her neck. It too was bare.

It was Dexter's turn next. Mollie glared at him until he submitted to Dymin's examination. He said nothing while the Creator pulled back his fur, but his tail puffed up, and a ridge of fur along his backside stood at attention. Despite this resistance, however, The Creator nodded in satisfaction. "Nothing," he said.

There were only two left – Sigfried and Kameko. It had to be one of them. But Sigfried never wore shirts, and Trance could clearly see his neckline, or more appropriately the area below his head was clear of ink. So, if it wasn't Per'dita, the missing Protector, then it had to be Kameko. He held his tongue. She would be revealed soon enough. He was disappointed, in a way. There was something about her that took his breath away. But it had to be her, right? There wasn't anybody else.

But Sigfried was first, and this proved to be a brief and uneventful delay. After giving the slug a perfunctory once over, Dymin declared what everyone knew already, and then he was standing in front of Kameko, and Trance's pulse quickened again.

Kameko hung her head, refusing to meet the gaze of Dymin. "Let's not make this difficult," he said to her.

Kameko nodded mutely. Her finger tapped twice at the top of her shirt and slowly slid down the center of its seamless surface. Behind her finger, a line appeared as the cloth separated from itself. The shirt fell to the floor as she turned in a tight pirouette.

Trance's eyes slid over her six-pack abdomen and perfect chest; they raced toward the base of her neck when her body turned to face him. There was nothing there. "I picked the wrong day to forget to wear a bra," she growled, covering her nipples.

MasTho was a good actor; his face remained completely impassive. "I would appreciate it," he said, "if you not reveal the nature of our search to anyone else. We are checking all of the squads who currently have representatives on Monidad, and secrecy is of the utmost importance."

They quickly dressed and exited Dymin's office. Outside in the hall, Dexter turned to Trance. "Dymin sure is a dick," he said. "They're just tools," he said in a mocking voice, "they just hammer things."

Mollie snickered, then sobered. "Let's get something to eat," she said. Mollie had skipped dinner to come down to Dymin's office.

"I could do with a stiff drink," Kameko muttered. "That was embarrassing."

"I never wear clothing," Sigfried said proudly. "It's too confining."

"Are you coming, Trance?" asked Kameko.

"I'll catch you all later," Trance said. "I need to think a little first."

"Come on, Trance," Taa'lien said, "It wasn't so bad."

Trance smiled. "I know. I just need to spend some time by myself. It's been a rough few days."

"Ah you humans, such solitary creatures," Dexter joked.

"Fair enough, Trance," Aura said. "You know how to get home, right? We'll meet you there later."

Trance nodded and watched as the others walked down the hall and then out the door at the far end. He stood there for a moment, and then followed.

He spent two hours considering the clues that had presented themselves as he walked the streets and passageways of Monidad. His mind was racing and getting nowhere. The only conclusion he could be reach implicated Per'dita as the saboteur. But that just didn't feel right. There were too many questions, and not enough answers. He felt he was drowning in a sea of riddles. It was an uncomfortable thought.

Eventually, he found himself back at his apartment. He almost didn't notice the small disk sitting on his couch. He picked it up and opened the note attached. "The mem-rec as promised. Enjoy! – T. PS: Use the player on the coffee table," it said.

"You might as well watch it," the ring said to him. "You've been thinking about this way too much. You need a break."

"Oh very well," Trance grumbled. He had been about to set the disk aside. The truth was he did need a break, and he had a feeling Taa'lien wouldn't leave him alone until he gave it at least one viewing.

He grabbed the contraption sitting on the coffee table and walked into the bedroom with it, turning it in his hands this way and that. There wasn't much to it; just a single tiny lens, some colored wires and several buttons. It was the size of a small paperback book. He set it on the bed, and pressed one of the keys. Nothing happened.

There was a slot on the side. He pressed the disk against it, and felt a small thrill when the viewer accepted it with an audible click. But that's all the viewer would do—further prodding of the buttons resulted in nothing. With a sigh, he asked the ring to assist him. Following the directions, he was rewarded with a flash from the player as it powered on.

Sometime later, the door slid open, and a voice called into the room interrupting his reverie. "Are you going to sit around watching holo-films all day? We've got a rogue Protector to find and punish judiciously!"

Trance looked up wearily from the holo viewer and smiled. It was Kameko's voice he had heard, but Aura filled the doorway to his cabin. Just for a second, Trance thought the tremendous Protector was flexing his muscles adroitly, but then realized the fellow was simply just standing there. Then he noticed that Mollie, Dexter, Sigfried, Kameko, and Taa'lien filling the spaces between and behind his bulging manliness. They had all had more than a few drinks. "Taa'lien suggested we come over and see what you were up to," Aura said, slurring his s's.

"I'm ready to go out again," Dexter said. "Everyone wants to join the search for Per'dita, but I just want to go back to the bars!"

Trance smiled at Dexter, then immediately sobered. "In the auditorium the today, you said that the mem-record made you feel uncomfortable, Taa'lien," he said. "I think you're right. There's something about this that doesn't match up. I just can't put my finger on it. Looks like we've got another mystery."

"We've all seen it a thousand times, Trance," Dexter purred. "The only mystery, hic, is why we keep watching it. Now come on, we've got more drinking to do, and it's your turn to buy a round."

"Perhaps a thousand and one times would be in order," Mollie said. We've all had enough for tonight."

Everyone groaned. But, as the Captain of the squad, there was no way around her commands. The group trooped into Trance's room and plopped down in various positions staring at the wall. Kameko fell over.

"I might as well make some coffee," Aura grumbled to himself, and headed to the kitchen.

"See if there is any Shempoit, will you?" groaned Kameko from her position on the floor. "I have a massive headache."

"Why don't you lie on my be-- hey!" Trance yelled. "Get off my pillow, Dexter!"

"Heh. Sorry, force of habit," Dexter muttered. But he didn't move to a different area of the bed.

Trance glared at him for a moment. "Well, at least stop washing your ass, would you?"

Dexter sniffed. "You're the one that is always complaining that it smells. I thought you'd be happy."

Ever the leader, Mollie brought them back with a sharp retort. "Start the movie, Trance."

With one last glare at Dexter, Trance concentrated on the viewer. His ring glowed slightly, and a panorama opened around them.

They saw the battle as it had happened so many eons ago, watched as the nameless and the named fought for the final time for supremacy. Whole star systems flashed into nothingness, fuel for the fire of chaos. Pure light and energy danced around and through the combatants like a crazy, squirming snake. And Protectors and Creators alike screamed soundlessly as they died, eviscerated by the energy they wielded.

And then, it was over. On the moon of Korondor they landed, to count the survivors and celebrate the tenuous victory they had finally achieved at great cost....

Farouk's vision shifted to the new flag of the Corps... twin beams of fire screamed over his head and he looked back to see the rather easy capture of SiTruc rogue leader. The holo-presentation faded away.

"Looks like the Battle of Sector Brandenburg to me," Sigfried said helpfully. He was the most sober of the group.

"Yep, looks that way to me, too," Dexter seconded.

"Well, now that the mystery has been solved, let's go bash some heads!" Kameko cracked her knuckles and began flexing her muscles recklessly. She had recovered nicely during the span of the film.

Mollie smiled at Kameko, and then put a paw on Trance's arm. "Are you still getting that feeling?"

"Yeah. There is something wrong; I know it. I start getting uncomfortable when they land on the moon of Korondor."

"Let's see that part again, then," said Taa'lien, to groans from Kameko and Dexter. Aura sighed happily and sipped his coffee. He loved a mystery.

"Have your rings noticed anything?" Trance asked. Not surprisingly, none of the rings had been paying attention.

"You're not being helpful, here, ring," Trance scolded.

"What do you want from me? I'm a ring, dammit, not a film critic!"

Trance concentrated again, and the moon swam into focus around them. Farouk had obviously landed on the surface, which Trance noted seemed to be made of blue powder. A Creator constructed the flag, and handed it to one of the Protectors who planted it resolutely into the ground where it flapped somberly in a slight breeze. The flag filled Creator Farouk's field of vision momentarily.

And then twin beams of light shot straight overhead.

"Stop!" Dexter bellowed, leaping off Trance's pillow.

The group looked at him in concern. "What?" Sigfried cried.

"I get it. Finally. Why didn't I see this before?" He was talking to himself, muttering as he paced back and forth along the length of the bed in front of his companions.

"Tell us! What is it?" Trance asked.

Chapter 27: Red Flags

Dexter looked at them momentarily, before resuming his pacing. "I can't believe it. It's the flag. Concentrate on the flag, and you'll see it. Oh God, what a mess. What a friggin' mess."

"Put it back on the moment Farouk looks at the flag, Trance." Taa'lien said. "Let's see what Dexter is all worked up about."

The flag appeared, in all its poignant glory, swimming in full view... and then the twin beams of fire split the sky. Creator Farouk turned to see.... Trance froze the image in place.

"Don't you see it?" Dexter grumbled, "It's so clear."

"I can't see anything, other than a crazy cat and a stupid flag," Kameko retorted.

"Oh for heaven's sake. Start it again, and don't look at the cloth this time. Look at the pole that it's on. And play it slow, or you'll miss it."

Everyone looked at Trance, who shrugged, and willed his ring to begin the diorama once again.

The Protector planted his feet.

He raised the flag.

Then he slowly slammed the pointed end into the ground --

"Stop!"

The scene froze.

"Look at the shadows." Dexter sprang forward, pointing one furry paw at the base of the pole. There, faintly, in the outer range of Creator Farouk's vision, they could see the shadow the pole gave off in the dim sunlight. It was long and thin, and arched slightly to the left.

"Move it forward one second."

Trance and Mollie gasped simultaneously. The shadow had moved across to the right, a span impossible in a single second.

"I still don't see it." Aura complained, sipping his coffee. He looked to Kameko for support, but received only a shrug.

Taa'lien sighed, and patted Aura on the shoulder. "The show is rigged. Creator Farouk looked at the pole for only a couple of seconds, and yet the shadow traveled quite a distance around the pole."

"A good couple of hours passed, I'd wager," whispered Dexter.

"OK, so they are hiding something," Trance said. "But what?"

"It's a secret that has lasted this long, I don't think we'll ever be able to crack it," Mollie replied looking around the group. "You're the only one alive back then, Taa'lien, what do you remember about this?"

"Not much, frankly," Taa'lien sighed. "I nearly died during the battle and still have the scars to prove it. Though I guess we are nearly immortal, my race must be slow to heal. I … I was in a coma for nearly ten thousand years recovering from my injuries."

"What?" Trance scoffed, incredulous.

"You're just a newbie, Trance," Taa'lien sniffed. "Don't let your misconceived preconceptions of the cosmos trick you into seeing things as you think they should be rather than as they truly are."

"Sorry. Please continue."

She smiled softly at Trance and nodded. "When I awoke, everything was different. The Creators were… different, and everything else around them had changed. They offered me this arm," she flexed her mechanical appendage, "and a new ring."

Silence filled the room for a moment as they considered the enormity of what they had seen and heard.

"So," Mollie wondered aloud. "How are we going to find out what they are hiding?"

"Why don't we just go back in time and have a look-see for ourselves?" Taa'lien asked.

"Look, aren't we forgetting about Per'dita?" Trance asked. "It seems like his possible involvement is more important than this mystery."

"You're right, of course," Taa'lien mused, "but this somehow seems connected."

"How so?"

"Well, the rebellion, and the resulting Battle of Korondor plays heavily into the mythos of the Order of the Foul Dragon," she said. "We all agree on that, yes? Well, we also can agree something is being hidden from us. Perhaps if we can uncover whatever it is we'll be able to shed some light on current events."

"You may be right, but what about Per'dita?" Trance persisted.

"There is a planet-wide search for him going on now," Aura said. "Really, our assistance would not be missed."

Kameko nodded in agreement. "He's right about that, of course. Besides, I'm much better at bashing than I am at searching."

"Fine. Forget about Per'dita for a second. I didn't think it was possible to travel back to the battle, even though you were alive back then, Taa'lien."

"You're right, Trance," she admitted. "I have frequently tried to go back to that time, and been unsuccessful. There must be some sort of injunction that prevents us. However, you seem to be able to do things the rest of us can't do. I have a feeling you can do this."

"It seems pretty far-fetched to me," Sigfried said. "I would go if everyone agrees; however it seems like a waste of time."

"I don't know. It might work," Aura mused. "We all saw how he used his ring against Perridan. Maybe there are other things he can do that we can't." He looked around the group. Everyone nodded.

Kameko shrugged and then nodded too. It's worth a try, I guess," she said. "Even if this is a little crazy, it's an adventure. Count me in."

"If we are going to do this, we have to do it right," Aura said.

"That includes notifying the Creators what we're going to do," Mollie announced.

Taa'lien shook her head. "That's not wise. They have kept their little secret locked up for millions and millions of years. Don't you think that they would do anything to keep it that way?"

"Yes… I guess you are right," Mollie said doubtfully. "I just don't feel right about this endeavor. I'm worried something awful will happen because of it."

Dexter looked at Mollie thoughtfully. "It takes a lot of energy to time travel. We all know that. In addition, for every person that goes back, at least one other has to stay here with an unbroken connection to the past, acting as an anchor for the return trip. There are seven of us here. That's three back, and four staying, if this crazy idea works."

Aura stretched his arms and cracked his neck. "Taa'lien lived during that time. She has the point of reference, and is the most experienced. She is the most obvious choice," he said. The others nodded.

"Trance is the other obvious choice," Sigfried furthered. He appeared to be warming up to the idea.

"Huh?"

"You have to go, Trance," Sigfried said resolutely. "Taa'lien is right. You can do things that the rest of us can't. If this works, it will be because of you and your ring. You have to go." Again the group concurred.

"I volunteer to stay here and help manage the threads," Mollie said.

"I'll stay, too," Kameko said.

"Me too," Dexter nodded. "I'd rather not chance getting my fur singed, especially with how soft and clean it is now that I have washed it."

"Yeah, we all know it might be a long time before that happens again," Kameko retorted.

"Aura is the historian of this group," Sigfried said. "He should go. I'll stay on this side of the timeline with you all."

"So, who is going to be recording?" asked Aura, ever the historian.

"No one," Taa'lien said firmly. "I don't want any records. If we get caught, we'll be in enough trouble as it is. I don't want more evidence pointing to our involvement."

"Well, I think we should record," Aura argued, "for posterity." Trance nodded in agreement, but no one was looking at him so he kept his mouth shut. He looked at Dexter for help but the cat only gave him a furry shrug. Kameko didn't meet his eyes.

"I am sure the Creators have a good reason for the subterfuge and misdirection," Taa'lien said. "Maybe it is better if we don't record what we see. I'd hate for a vid to get out... there really wouldn't be a way to guarantee its validity anyway, and it would probably just hurt a bunch of feelings. And, of course we'd be drummed out of the corps."

"Yeah, there is that," Dexter grudgingly admitted, poking Aura gently in the ribs. "She's right. Let's play it safe."

Aura gave Dexter one of his patented withering looks which failed to produce a whither. "Fine. I agree," he scowled, "but only under protest. This is a tremendous opportunity, for me as a historian. But I bow to the consensus."

With their tasks clarified, the group separated, agreeing to meet the next morning to travel to the moon of Korondor in the Brandenburg sector. Once there, they would prepare for the jump back to the famous and now disputed battle.

An hour later, there was a soft knock on Trance's door. "Come in!" he said.

The door slid open revealing the form of Kameko. "Am I disturbing you?" she asked. Her voice was different, softer. She was wearing a green silken robe tied at the waist and fuzzy slippers. Her shoulder-length hair was tied back in a pony tail.

"Oh, hi, Kameko," Trance said. "Come on in." He was sitting on his couch with his arms up, and up until the door buzzed had been lost in thought. The disturbance was welcome.

Kameko sat beside him. He now noticed she was carrying a small bottle and two glasses. She set them on the glass surface of his coffee table. "It's the custom of my people to share a toast before going to battle," she said, opening the bottle and pouring a gray liquid into each. "I was hoping I could share this custom with you."

"It's OK, boss," the ring said. "The liquid is safe for you to drink. Believe it or not, your biological systems are remarkably similar."

"Sure, Kameko," Trance said, looking suspiciously at the gray liquid. It was giving off bubbles.

"Thanks, Trance. It means a great deal to me that you would join me in this." She handed him a glass, and just briefly her fingers brushed against his in the transfer. The touch warmed him.

She raised her glass, and he followed her lead. "May we die honorably," she said.

"Honorably," Trance mumbled. They drank a small sip together.

"I'd rather not die, thanks," the ring said sagely.

Trance set his glass down. "This is mighty tasty Kameko," he said. "What is it?" The liquid had slid down his throat smoothly and began warming his stomach. It had an aroma of vanilla and berries with the slightest hint of nuts.

"Its name is E'ihar. My people have been toasting to it since the dawn of time. It's nice, isn't it?"

"It's warm," Trance admitted. Heat was beginning to spread into his chest and out to his fingertips.

She chuckled. "Only one case is made each decade," she said, holding her glass to the light and watching the liquid dance within. "This bottle has been in my family for many generations. It was given to me when I was a baby." She looked at him and smiled. "That was a long time ago."

"You've been with the corps for about fifteen hundred years, haven't you?" Trance asked.

She smiled ruefully. "About that long, yeah." She set her glass back down and settled into the far corner of the couch. "It sure has been fun, though. It really only seems like a few days ago."

"Why did you join? My ring said you had been a military leader on your planet."

"I dreamt of better things," she said simply. "I grew weary of all the death and destruction I saw in my daily life. I longed for peace. When the ring came to me, I accepted it. I felt drawn to the possibilities it offered. What about you?"

"I thought someone had dropped it," he grunted. "I picked it up so I could turn it in."

She laughed. "It sucked you in; too bad. It's better if you go into this with open eyes. Nonetheless, I am glad that you're here." She was so pretty. Her smile brightened the room.

"Thanks. I am glad to have met you," he said truthfully. *Her eyes were the deepest green, like emerald. He felt like he could sink into them.* He was so warm.

She blushed. Had she heard him? Had he spoken aloud?

"It is said that all who share a toast from it are linked forever, no matter where they go," she said quietly. "I toasted with you tonight because I see in you a kindred spirit, a mighty warrior who is not afraid to dream of better things." She held her glass high again. "To dreams," she said. He wondered what it might be like to kiss her on those perfect lips.

"To dreams," Trance said, and drank again, finishing the glass. And then, the world seemed to slip away.

Where do you go to dream?

There is a heavily forested hill at the edge of town. In the center, at the very peak is a clearing. I go there to think when I need time away. The ground is soft, and warm, and the air smells of pine. When you lie there, looking up, all you can see are clouds, and when it is sunny, the sky is a blue gem. You can hear the birds chirping softly, and it is easy to slip away on a thought.

Take me there.

Now? We are so far away.

This is a dream, Trance. This is E'ihar, my gift to you before the battle. It is time away to reflect, to learn.

Where are you?

I am with you, now. You are part of me, and I of you.

Have you ever met someone, Kameko, and known that you had known them forever, that they had always been part of you?

Just once.

When?

Take me there, Trance, to the place you dream, this forest of memory.

It was dark, now. All around them the woods slept. It was quiet, and the ground was cool. Above, the stars twinkled merrily.

This is beautiful, a worthy place to dream.

I come here when I can. I wish it were more often.

Trance, no matter how far you travel, this place will always be with you. This is your core, your center. Never forget it.

I won't.

The E'ihar fades fast, I'm afraid. Soon it will be gone, nothing but a memory. You have to keep this moment in your heart. It will sustain you during the battle, and afterwards. This is the true toast of E'ihar: To remember the Peace before the Storm.

I will remember this always.

And suddenly, they were back in his apartment, the two of them, sitting on his couch, empty glasses in front of them. She smiled at him, and he knew that they had shared the dream together.

They sat there for hours on his couch, talking. They spoke of the lives that they had left back home; of their hopes and fears. He told her everything, during that magical night, and learned a great deal about her. And when she finally stumbled off to her own apartment in the early morning, he fell into a dreamless but peaceful sleep.

He awoke a few hours later in a warm fog. He stumbled into the bathroom, and somehow managed to make it into the sonic shower, where he let the waves of sound wash the fog out of his system. After what seemed like an hour, he willed the sonic waves to stop, and stepped smartly out of the stall and into the bathroom proper. There, he created a razor, and carefully scraped his face clean of any residual fuzz.

Pleased with his efforts, he dressed quickly and headed to the Cafeteria where he found Aura, Dexter, Kameko, Taa'lien, Sigfried, and Mollie sitting together surrounded by a sphere of silence in the otherwise crowded and noisy room. Grabbing a tray of food, he sat down with them and ate without comment. He wished that he could talk with Kameko alone, but pulling her aside just didn't feel right. He wanted to thank her again for last night. There were a thousand other things he wished to say, but couldn't.

When they had finished clearing their trays, they headed for the transport room nearest the cafeteria. It was just down the hall. The technician behind the console looked up at them inquisitively when they entered the station. To Trance, it looked like a cross between a vacuum cleaner and a wire brush, with a gallon of slime thrown in for added yuckiness. "Where to, boys and girls?" it croaked from what Trance generously attributed to as being a mouth. "Oh, hey, Taa'lien, how's it hanging?"

"Ralph. Good to see you, fellow! How are the kids?"

Trance winced and shuddered inwardly. The thought of anything so disgusting mating and producing offspring made him want to gag ("You really need to work on your pre-conceived prejudices and notions of beauty," the ring snipped. "You do realize that the human race is actually considered one of the most ugly of all the bipedal races? Hmm?"). He barely kept a straight face as he listened. It was speaking again, and its voice sounded to him like two angry cats being rubbed together. "Good, getting along nicely, thanks. In fact, they're pupating this evening. Say, you've got a big group here today. Where to?"

Taa'lien glanced back and forth as if she were being followed, and wasn't sure if this was the right place to talk. "Here and there, you know. Actually, we're going to go pick up some beer (she winked at Ralph conspiratorially) for a party I'm throwing tonight. Are you going to join us after the pupation? Trance is going to teach us to play Po... Po..." she looked at Trance.

"Poker," he muttered through clenched teeth, trying not to stare at the monstrosity before him.

"I wouldn't mind a couple of Chojos, truth be told," Ralph sighed wistfully. "I sure wish I could join you, but the misuses wouldn't have anything of it. As soon as I'm done with my shift, it's back to the nest. What are the coordinates?"

Taa'lien rattled them off, and Ralph keyed them in. Then he whistled. "Right on the edge of Sector Brandenburg. You wouldn't be planning an excursion into any Forbidden areas, would you? I mean, you've got a legal destination, of course, but it sure is close to a Restricted Zone." Everyone shrugged and glanced at each other with nervous grins. Mollie looked like she was getting ready to bolt.

Just then, Dexter piped up. "Nah, we're not stupid." Someone snickered in back. "Have you ever been to Nardy's Cantina?" the cat asked. Ralph shook his head. "No? You should go sometime. It's my favorite hangout.... Yeah...."

Ralph's eyes narrowed perceptibly. "Whatever. Hey, no bristles off my back if you want to venture in to forbidden areas. If you see some Chojo while you're out, or maybe even a six pack, pick some up for me, will you Taa'lien?"

Taa'lien nodded, relieved. "Sure, Ralph."

They hopped on the transport. Trance felt a strange pulling sensation, like he was being torn apart; diced into tiny pieces. It wasn't painful, but it certainly wasn't pleasant. He almost preferred the disjointed and confusing grey space to this. At least in grey space he could see where he was going. A blue haze colored his vision, and then quickly dissipated. They were standing at Taa'lien's coordinates.

Trance checked himself out quickly. To his surprise, all of his bits and pieces appeared to have been glued back in good order. Satisfied, he looked around.

They were standing on a dark and airless moon spinning lazily around a planet that reminded Trance of Neptune. He looked aghast at the rings as they silently spun around the planet's poles. Across a vast portion of the surface, flashes could be seen as the clouds boiled and churned. A storm was evidently brewing. "It's beautiful, isn't it Trance," Aura said in his mind through their two rings. "The storm you're seeing is called the 'Raging Jewel.' I studied it in high school. Did you know they think that it has been in motion since the dawn of time?" Mute, Adams shook his head. "Since the day I heard about it, I've always wanted to see it. This is truly a dream come true."

With one last look at the tempest above them, the group flew to the Korondor System. It took about an hour to transverse the five light years. Most of this trip involved flying through the darkness between solar systems. The silent dance of stars across Trances' vision became both achingly beautiful and extremely dull at the same time. He found himself relieved when they arrived at last.

Chapter 28: Korondor's Moon

They had agreed that the most likely spot to see the action was a hill nearby the spot where the final confrontation with Si-truc took place. Taa'lien, who had seen the Battle of Sector Brandenburg film the most, found the hill almost immediately and they landed together on it.

The moon of Korondor had not aged much in the untold millennia since it had been the subject of Creator Farouk's mem-rec. The rolling hills, the jagged mountains—even the dust at his feet was pretty much the same as Trance had experienced it during the film. The others seemed wary, but relaxed. Taa'lien looked pensive. Dexter was looking around for a place to pee.

"Before we start, I think I'll have a look around the moon, make sure that this hill really is the best vantage point," she said. "Why don't you guys stay here and relax? I'll be back momentarily." With that, she blasted off and was out of sight in the blink of an eye.

Trance used the breather to lie in the soft sand and look into the dark sky. "What a view," he thought to the ring. "Look! There's a shooting star!" A single point of light had raced across his field of view and disappeared in silence.

"It's not really a star—" his ring started.

"I know, but it is tradition to wish for something."

"I wish for more wishes."

"You can't do that."

"Why the heck not? It's my wish, isn't it?"

"Never mind. It's just a silly old tradition." Trance let his thoughts drift for a moment, just enjoying the silence and the beauty.

"So what did you wish for?" the ring asked quietly.

"To tell you the truth, I am perfectly happy right now," Trance smiled. "I wish for nothing." And he realized that he was happy, just then, the happiest that he had ever been, lying there on a moon with his friends and comrades all around him. And then he did wish. He wished that he could be that happy forever.

Just then, Mollie poked him with one white paw. "Hey, Trance," she said. "Wake up; Taa'lien is coming back."

She had only been gone for a few moments. "Yeah, this is the best spot," she admitted as she landed. "I saw a couple of other places, but this seems right to me for some reason."

"Hmm. That's odd."

"What's that, ring?" Trance asked as he watched the others nod in agreement to Taa'lien's words.

"I'm not sure. There is an awful lot of background radiation, but something is definitely up. I just can't quite pin it down."

"Is it enough of a worry that I should pull the plug on this mission?"

"No. However, I suggest that we proceed cautiously."

"Naturally. Just to be safe, record everything, in all wavelengths once we get to our destination. I don't care what Taa'lien said back at Monidad. I want to have a record of this."

"I wasn't going to say anything, but that is a really smart idea, Protector," the ring said. He could tell it was pleased.

"OK," said Taa'lien, "we're all pretty clear on our assignments." Everyone nodded in agreement. "Trance, Aura, you guys stand here and here, and the rest of you back up a little. Who knows what's going to happen here. I'll throw up a visual blind once we get to that time, to keep any of the combatants from seeing us—my ring should have enough energy left for that one. You want to handle the air and heat Aura? Good.

'Trance, I just sent you the temporal cues we need to get there, if your ring is able to blast through the blockade, or whatever is keeping us from traveling to that period. So, just concentrate and will your power to get us there. OK, I think we're set. That should keep us all busy and, hopefully, safe."

Trance now stood in the middle between Taa'lien, who was on his left, and Aura, his right. He glanced at both of them, smiled, and then drew his thoughts inward. "Now what do I do, ring?" he asked.

"Well, typically, in these kinds of situations, time travel, I mean, you're supposed to consider the temporal cues and go from there."

"What?"

The ring sighed. "Look," it grumbled, "imagine you are in this place, but in a different time. Think of the time Taa'lien lived in. Can you see yourself in there?"

"Yeah, it's odd. I can see the battle raging around me, kind of like the mem-rec, but more clear. It seems warmer there than here. I can feel it."

"Must be because of all the energy they were flinging around. OK, good. Now, imagine a singularity at that point of time. Your friends will create one here, and we'll be able to slide between the two points like we're on a rail."

"A what?"

"A rail. You know a—"

"No. A singularity. I've heard of it, but I have no idea what one is."

"Do you want the astrophysical definition, or the mathematical one?"

"Um, the astrophysical one, I guess."

"A singularity is a point in space/time where space and time become infinitely distorted due to huge gravitational forces. Of course, matter becomes infinitely dense, and has an infinitesimal volume all at the same time. It's simple, really."

"Of course. What was I thinking?"

"Good. You understand."

"No."

"OK, here's a simpler explanation imagine a point—"

"Forget it ring."

"But it's a really good analogy involving an fried egg and a watermelon—"

"Just forget it. Not important. You supply the picture—I'll imagine that."

"Well, it can't really be pictured."

"Have you 'seen' one?"

"Yes, if you could call it that."

"Good enough. Give me as much of the experience as you can."

"OK. Here you are."

Momentarily, the singularity appeared in Trance's mind. It was hard for him to grasp. Part of him "saw" it as a point as small as a period, but that was just the part of him that couldn't reconcile the fact it was infinitely smaller still. He willed his energy into it. The strain was immense.

At the same time he saw the single point, he could feel a vastness behind it, a tunnel opening up into the same place but a different time. Dimly, he could hear the sound of the universe being torn asunder, moving just slightly aside to make room for the two pin prick ends. Energy coursed from his ring, running the length and breadth of the tunnel, strengthening, it keeping it intact. "Nice job," he said, congratulating himself, and wiping his forehead. It had developed a sheen of sweat.

"Yeah, nice job, for a newbie," the ring sounded impressed. "That's about all we need to get you through. It's pretty much impossible to get it any bigger than that."

"Could we if I was stronger?" Trance asked curiously.

"Remember, it's an energy problem, not a willpower issue. Even if we got all the members in the corps to will the same thing, there just wouldn't be enough energy for the task. You'd need as much energy as a hundred corps the same size as ours."

"Oh, well, what if I was a lot stronger? What if I did have the power?"

"You humans sure are a curious bunch. Sure, I guess that it would be possible. But it's not, so do we need to talk about it any longer? I'm having enough trouble dealing with this thing as it is."

"OK, but—"

"Later, please?"

"Oh, alright, ring. If you say so."

"Well, I never really say anything, remember? I'm in your head."

"OK, then, point taken. Now what?"

"I can only guess that we do it the way it says in the manual. You have to separate your consciousness from your body. Close your eyes and imagine yourself splitting off from your body. Your consciousness is a separate entity anyway. Just make it more separate."

"Always so descriptive, aren't you?"

"I try."

"Ring, despite myself, I am actually starting to like you."

"Thanks, Protector. I do pride myself on my likeability."

"I'm sure." Trance closed his eyes and imagined. He saw himself as someone else might see him; standing with his eyes closed and his hands at his side, ring glowing softly. He imagined a point in the center of his chest, a circular disk six inches in diameter, and squeezed his consciousness into it. Now, he could see himself on the outside and from the inside looking out at the same time. If he had thought of it, he might have felt dizzy at the divergent perspectives. But he didn't have time. Instead, he began to imagine he could fully separate the two.

It was simple really. He used the ring's energy to create a spatula. The spatula floated above his chest area, then gently slipped beneath the point in the center and eased it out like a pancake. Suddenly, he lost all feeling. He noticed a single tendril of energy extended from his chest to the discus. He wisely left it alone. "Ready ring," he said.

"Alright. Nicely done, Trance. You sure you haven't done this before?"

"First time," Trance smiled, pleased with himself.

"OK, let your friends do the rest. Now, when we reach the other time, you'll appear to inhabit your body again. So will the others. But for now, say goodbye."

When Trance had fully separated from his body, he had lost its perspective. He could see it now, from above. It looked like a limp rag. "Yikes! My hair is thinning a bit on top!" Trance exclaimed.

"I noticed, but I wasn't going to say anything," the ring said cavalierly. He could hear its voice distinctly. It seemed to hover just above him. "Are you ready?"

Trance looked for the others. Below him, he could see them; Aura and Taa'lien looked like marionettes with cut strings. He could sense them nearby, however, very much alive. Kameko, Dexter, Mollie, and Sigfried were concentrating on the three travelers. He could see slightly down Kameko's shirt, and felt warmed, then guilty. She sure was cute. He felt the ring smirk above him.

Trance let his focus slide to the singularity. It was calling to him, and to the two other energy forms near him. He longed to be closer. He felt himself being pulled toward it, and the pinprick yawned wider until it encompassed the universe. All of space could fit in its confines. Then he was sinking into it, and it became a tunnel, and he got the impression of incredible speed, of light, and of heat... and of time, streaming around him like a river. It was overwhelming, yet peaceful. And quiet.

When they first entered, he had noticed what could only be branch points – other tunnels which seemed to fork off from the tunnel that they were in. The branch points were placed randomly on the tunnel, every few feet, it seemed on the floor, ceiling, and along the sides. At first, he tried to look down them as he passed, but all he got was a glimpse, and the impression of tremendous distance. But then they were going too fast to even see more than blips here and there, and then nothing at all, just the tunnel, and infinity.

Suddenly a dark circle appeared in the distance, up against the fabric of the tunnel. Just a pinprick of darkness, it came up fast, growing in size as they approached. It was clear this was their fork in the road, and their lives would be forever changed because of it.

They shot through it, leaving the previous tunnel behind. "It's not far, now, Trance. Get ready," the ring advised.

"For what?" Trance said. But then he forgot the question. Here was the end.

Quickly, now. Grayness began to infuse the light, a somber tone of nothing interspersed within the color. Coolness where once was heat. And then total gray. He felt like he was being stretched now, pulled from a thousand directions at once, then squeezed and pummeled and torn apart. The pain was exquisite, delicious, because it was a feeling, like the brief taste of vision for a blind man. But then it too dulled and then seeped into numbness.

His vision faded completely.   And then, the impression of lines could be seen. The feeling of movement, not of the universe, but of individuals within. And then... he found himself staring at his feet. He couldn't move his head or his arms, and he felt dizzy, disoriented, and just a little nauseous.

Momentarily, the numbness passed, and he began to feel again. Just a tingling at first, then a heat spreading from his center into the ends of his limbs. He looked around, and first saw his comrades. They were standing on either side of him, Aura on the left, and Taa'lien on the right. Both stirred as if awakening from a dream.

They appeared to be standing upon Korondor's moon but everything was very much different.

Chapter 29: After the Flag

The battle was mostly over. Here and there, small fights were being waged as the victors mopped up. Trance had seen the sights before, but now they seemed fresher. The perspective seemed off just slightly, and he wondered why before noticing a figure a few feet in front of them. It had to be Creator Farouk.

And here came the victors. A thousand Protectors landed upon the moon en masse, the closest less than a hundred yards away. They had just won the biggest battle the Universe had yet seen, and they were torn and weary. But yet, they had won. And now, they seemed to be waiting for something.

One of the members of the group held out its hands and mist formed like fine gossamer. The mist solidified and became a pole upon which flew the new flag of the corps; a blue cloth upon which a galaxy spun in the center. The being held it up to a ragged cheer, and then slammed the point into the fine dust of the moon. It caught the light and fluttered majestically in the slight atmosphere.

The flag was even more beautiful than it had appeared on the mem-rec. Trance realized now how important it was as a symbol for the corps. It stood against chaos; the antithesis of all that the Order of the Foul Dragon stood for. It had stood in the hearts and minds of the entire corps for untold millennia as a constant reminder of how close the rebellion had come to shaking the foundation of the Conglomerated States. It shone just slightly, as if glowing from within when the pole it was on was placed in the earth. Trance waited for what he was used to seeing next – the twin beams of energy. They never appeared.

Chapter 30: Machinations Revealed

Instead a Creator materialized in the sky and landed near the flag facing the crowd of Protectors. They bowed their heads in respect. "Who's that?" Trance asked the ring.

"Um, that is Creator Xiedi," it said. "She is the equivalent of Creator MasTho in our time. Do you want me to supply the names for you?"

"Sure, that would help," Trance said, thankful.

"OK, just concentrate on the person that you want to know the name of, and I will take care of it," the ring replied.

"Hey, Trance, are you getting this?" Aura said.

"That's your buddy, Aura," the ring offered, nearly drowning out what the golden Protector was saying.

"Make it smoother," Trance grimaced. "Less obtrusive."

"Oh. I see. OK, so you won't even hear me, you'll just know," the ring whispered.

"Hey, Trance, what do you think of this?" Aura repeated softly.

"It's amazing," Trance said, lost in thought.

Xiedi was not the only Creator present. There were eleven others now, including Creator Farouk, all dressed much like her in flowing gray robes with cowls. They stepped out from the crowd and turned to face it. The eleven stood behind their leader, giving her the respect her station demanded. She nodded at them once, and began to speak in a voice that was as dry and crisp as parchment and loud enough for everyone to hear. "I honor you, my Protectors," she said. "You who have fought for a cause you believe to be just.

'Five hundred long years we have labored to eradicate this stain upon our great states. Tonight, I stand before you weary, but hopeful for the first time that perhaps we truly can begin a new day tomorrow. Tonight, I know, that the War is over, our final battle won!"

The crowd cheered at that, a somber tone tempered by the knowledge that many had died so they might all succeed.

'We have fought friends," Xiedi said when the cheering died. "We have lost loved ones. Each of us bears scars that will never heal. But one of us bears even more: a secret that tonight must be revealed."

"Here it comes, Trance," Aura whispered. "Wonder where that damn dragon is?"

But Xiedi wasn't looking at the Protectors. She turned toward the Creators behind her, singling out one, a male by the name of Nesger. "Step forward, Nesger. There is no escape. If you try to use your ring you will be killed."

"Huh?" Aura muttered to himself. Taa'lien tensed, but said nothing.

"My lady, I do not know what you mean," Nesger protested, but he stepped forward, pulling his cowl down from the peak of his head with both hands. He had a simple face, a lined faced that showed intelligence, and perhaps, something more; something evil. His long hair was pulled back, as was customary, into a ponytail.

Xiedi turned to face him fully, but spoke to the entire corps. "Please, Nesger, you cannot hide from the council any longer. We have known for some time that this rebellion was led by one of our own. I must admit the clues were few and far between, and pointed very carefully to others besides you.

'Your machinations and intrigues from the shadows have served to nearly destroy the corps. Billions of innocents have been slain because of you. But ultimately, they have led you here to your defeat."

Nesger shrugged. "You have no proof."

"You deny these accusations?"

Nesger opened his mouth and then stopped, a cruel grin splitting his face. "What are the microbes to a God? They were not innocents, but animals fit for slaughter. I weep not for them."

"So, you admit your role in this rebellion," Creator Farouk said. "To what end?"

"I admit nothing!" Nesger screamed, his face turning red and spittle flying from his lips. "I proclaim it from the highest reaches!" Glee played across his features. It felt good to be in the spotlight.

"Brother, you have shamed us," Creator Xiedi stated sadly. "You have perverted our beliefs and soiled the traditions of our race."

Nesger smiled cruelly. "I spit on you and your tenants," he sneered. "I will defy you as long as I draw breath, and will not rest until I grind you and the rest of creation under my foot."

"You would enslave the universe?"

"I have the right, and the power!"

"You have neither," said Creator Sadiki. "You will spend the rest of eternity in a prison we have created for you. It will give you just enough energy to survive, but keep you on the razor edge of hunger. You will have until the end of time to ruminate on the results your destructive actions. Perhaps one day you will see the error of your ways."

Xiedi nodded once. "With the rebellion crushed," she said, "and its leader captured, we can begin the rebuilding process. Soon we will have repaired the damage you have done."

"We have weakened the Conglomerated States far more than you think, 'sister,'" Nesger spat. "When the rest of the universe finds out that a Creator, one of the beings chosen to protect them from harm, was behind the rebellion, chaos will reign. The fragile egg that is the Conglomerated States will shatter, torn asunder from within."

A high-pitched laugh escaped from between his clenched teeth. It had a bitter hysteria at the edges that chilled Trance to the bone.

"He's insane," muttered Trance. Aura nodded solemnly. Taa'lien pursed her lips thoughtfully, an intent look on her face.

"He is correct, unfortunately," Creator Maat affirmed sadly. "Word of his involvement will spread like wildfire. The Conglomerated States will topple and fall."

Protector Noucter, a greenish blob, slurped forward. "Then no one must ever know of your involvement," she said. "After you are gone, we must wipe you and your actions from our records and our thoughts. Your betrayal will go unnoticed in the annals of history. You will be less than nothing; not even a memory."

The Creators nodded in agreement.

"Others will wonder who the leader was," another Protector called out. "The Conglomerated States have been cut. Innocent blood has been shed and cries for justice."

"Justice…" a thousand voices called as one.

"I will bear the weight of retribution," a voice came from in back of the crowd. A thousand weary faces turned to see….

"Look!" called Taa'lien, pointing.

"Whoa!" blurted the ring. "Uh Trance, I just got a really nasty feeling that--"

"Shh…. Tell me later," Trance whispered. "Something is going on!"

The crowd parted revealing Si-truc, the golden dragon, floating into view. "An accounting must be made," he said resolutely. "A villain must be found where none can now exist. The way is clear."

"That way means damnation eternal for you and your race, Si-truc," Creator Maat murmured. "Are you prepared for this?"

"I am. There is no other path that does not lead to the destruction of the Conglomerated States. But in return, I ask a single boon."

"Name it," Creator Aletha said.

"My sacrifice is mine alone. Others of the B'tahi should be allowed to rectify the name of our race."

"As long as there are Protectors, B'tahi will be counted among the ranks," Creator Xiedi said. "My brothers and sisters will not forget a sacrifice has been made today by one of your own."

"Then I go to my oblivion with a clear conscience."

"And now that you have seen that your plans will not reach fruition, Nesger, it is time to enact your punishment," Creator Sadiki said. "We have created a prison for you of mind and of body where you will have all of eternity to regret your actions."

"Nooooooo! You have not seen the last of me, I swear it!" Nesger screamed as ring energy directed by ten protectors and seven Creators enveloped him in the prison that would bind him forever. His screams faded into the night as the prison solidified around him and disappeared. All that remained was his ring. It flew silently to the waiting hand of Xiedi.

Aura whistled soundlessly. "Wow. My stomach feels like Jell-o," he grunted softly, almost to himself.

"I think we have seen enough," Taa'lien sniffed. Aura nodded in agreement. Trance, too shocked to speak, willed his ring to follow the lines back home.

The moon of Korondor seemed to blur as the figures around them faded into shades and finally into nothingness. A gray haze surrounded Trance momentarily, and then coalesced into a whirlpool, which pulled him downward into nothingness. He floated there for what seemed like hours, but in reality was scarcely a millisecond, then the horrible stretching began... it pulled him from all directions, and twisted his insides like a wet towel wrung dry. Just when he thought he was being torn apart completely, the moon of Korondor began to fade into being again. It gradually coalesced and solidified. They were back.

Disoriented, and dizzy from the return trip, he wasn't prepared for what happened next. It all seemed to happen at once. Taa'lien stepped back, and aimed both hands toward her feet, releasing two tremendous blasts into the soil. The shockwave knocked them all off their feet, but the worst was to come.

The moon, tortured by the dual blasts by Taa'lien shuddered, cracked, and tore itself asunder, shaking the Protectors like die in a can. Then gravity took control, as Korondor began to pull the fragments to it like wayward children.

Dimly, Trance could hear screams, and realized that they were issuing from his mouth. He barely had time to create a shield around himself before losing consciousness.

Chapter 30: Korondor

"...in this corner, standing in at exactly six foot one inch, one hundred seventy pounds of pure muscle, Trance Adams, ladies and gentlemen, the cold stone knockout king from our own backyard, Hunter, Washington! Give it up ladies! Listen to the crowd gone wild! And in the other corner, our champion, Taa'lien! Pay attention, here are the rules: now at the sound of the bell I want each of you to come out swinging. And the rules? There are no rules here, gentlemen, no rules a-tall."

Trance awoke on his back with the taste of blood in his mouth, and ringing in his ears. He sat up and winced, then slowly and painfully stood. His ribs didn't feel right, and his left leg appeared swollen from the ankle to his kneecap. It was probably broken.

He looked around the landscape, if it could be called that. "Battlefield" might be more appropriate a description. Fires were everywhere. Even the grass was aflame.

With a start, he noticed he was standing in a narrow shallow furrow that stretched for what seemed like miles. On either side of the furrow, large chucks the size of VW Bugs spotted the land, and the molten lava spraying up everywhere from deep fissures painted the vicinity a bright orange-red. And above the plains…millions of meteors screamed silently across the sky.

"Welcome to the remains of Korondor and its moon," the ring said, unnecessarily.

"Where are the others?" Trance croaked, spitting a mixture of dirt and blood.

"I count four other life signs in this planet. They are so weak that I cannot tell who they are. There is also one dead ring."

"Take me to the closest one," Trance said, as he willed himself to fly.

He found Aura's feet first. His ring unerringly guided him to the massive golden Protector, who was stuck headfirst in a sand dune a short hundred miles away. Forgetting himself in his delirium and worry, Trance crash landed beside the immobile figure, and began digging with his hands. A short time later, he uncovered Aura's face.

Aura's helmet had borne the worst of the headlong plunge. Hairline cracks danced across the entire span at the top. Trance gingerly touched one of these fracture, and the covering disintegrated, revealing the crown of Aura's golden head. It was mottled with green and yellow bruises. Adams looked into the whites of Aura's eyes, and down to his mouth, which had a little stream of green blood issuing from it. "Ring," he said. "I feel a pulse of some sort, and he is breathing. What do I do?"

"I'd need to scan him to see what sort of injuries he received. But after that, I'm only good for minor first aid."

"Do so." A moment passed seemed to stretch into eternity.

"This Protector needs medical attention immediately. I suggest you put him in stasis until a proper health technician can attend to his injuries." Trance stepped back, aimed his ring hand at the motionless Protector, and concentrated.

A bluish mist seemed to envelope his friend. It expanded, and then solidified into an Aura-shaped casket.

By this time, the temperature had increased dramatically. Meteorites began slamming into the soil in a fiery downpour, incinerating everything not already aflame.

Trance willed himself into flight once again, hoping the next body that he found would not be in as bad a shape. "It can't get worse than this," he thought grimly as he towed Aura behind him. He was wrong.

The ring led him three hundred miles to Sigfried, or what was left of him. Tragically, the slug had landed in the biggest salt bed Trance had ever seen. For some reason, Sigfried's ring had been unable to protect him from the caustic salt. All that remained was his ring, and a bubbling pool of yellow slime.

"Why didn't his ring…" Trance paused as the first words the Protector had ever uttered to him came tumbling into his consciousness:

"Hello. My name is Sigfried. I'm what you might call a slug. I'm addicted to salt. It's my weakness and my devotion."

"Truer words could not have been said," the ring replied moodily.

"We can put him back together again," Trance said.

"You know I cannot do that, Protector."

"But you can do everything that I can think of."

"Bringing back the dead is beyond even my powers, Trance. I can protect life, prolong it even. But once it is gone, there is nothing I can do. I am sorry."

Sadly, Trance used the ring to form a little doggy bag, and scooped up the liquefied remnants of Sigfried, then pocketed the ring the slug had used until quite recently, silently cursing Taa'lien for the destruction that she had wrought.

He found Kameko buried in a sand dune less than a hundred miles away. It looked as though she had skipped like a stone along an expanse of several miles before coming to rest. "Kameko!" he bellowed, scraping sand granules away from her nose and mouth.

Thank God. She was breathing. Her eyes fluttered open and locked on his. "I knew you'd find me, Trance," her voice croaked. "I need to tell you something… tell you how I feel…that I…" her eyes rolled back into her head as she slipped back into unconsciousness.

"She can't die!" exclaimed Trance. "Save her, ring!"

"She'll live," the ring grumbled. "But we need another stasis field." Trance willed the field into existence around his friend and then jumped into the sky with the three Protectors behind him.

He didn't have to search long to find the remaining two Protectors. As he landed with Aura, Kameko, and Sigfried in tow, he saw Dexter first. The cat's back faced him. It was shaking.

"I hope you've had better luck than I have," Trance said wearily. "This planet is murd…" He stopped as Dexter turned toward him. The cat was crying.

"She's dead, Trance," he sobbed. "I couldn't save her…" he pointed behind him at the crushed and lifeless form of Mollie.

Disbelief and shock struck him in the stomach like a fist and crushed his heart in a steely grip. And yet it was true. Mollie, the calico cat who had guided and nurtured the corps during the past eight hundred years lay dead at his feet. "Damn you, Taa'lien," he said again as tears broke through the numbness that encased him.

"Whoops," the ring broke through his reverie. "I'm reading several consecutive detonations on the far side of this planet. I think Korondor is breaking apart."

At that moment a quake shook them like beans in a can. New cracks and fissures jetted through the ground releasing steam and heat. The sound of rocks screaming as they were torn asunder was deafening.

The quake lasted several minutes. Sometime during the event, an entire mountain range several hundred miles from their present position erupted, sending plumes of ash miles into the sky. "Yup," the ring muttered dryly, "This planet is toast."

"We have to get out of here!" Adams screamed to make himself heard over the din. Dexter stared at him dully too wrapped in his own grief to care.

Somehow, Trance gathered the grieving cat, Aura, Kameko, and the remains of Mollie and Sigfried, and lifted off Korondor as the planet crumbled around them.

Just as they broke through what remained of the planet's atmosphere, Korondor exploded from the center, ejecting dust, ice, boulders, and chunks the size of small cities into space. Almost immediately the first of the shock waves slammed into the weary party.

Everything went hazy for Trance in a fresh rush of adrenaline as he struggled to control his flight hampered by dead weight of the other four protectors. The sound was incredible – the scream of the planet expiring was awful, and the force of the blast, the shockwaves, buffeted him like a leaf in a tornado. But he gritted his teeth and poured on the energy, molding it and forming it and using it to protect his charges and guide his way out of the screaming debris. Twisting this way and that as he avoided chunk after massive chunk, he kept his mind from caving in to the fear he felt, and focused on getting out. Eventually he made it to clear space.

Without looking back, he sped to the farthest edge of the solar system, then stopped to catch his breath and check on his comrades. Dexter appeared fine physically, though he was utterly grief stricken and unresponsive. Aura's and Kameko's life signs were stagnant – the stasis fields they were in continued to work their magic in keeping the two alive. Sigfried and Mollie were unchanged.

Unsatisfied, but realizing he could do no more, he gritted his teeth and told the ring to summon Creator MasTho. "You sure have a death wish, Protector," the ring commented, but Trance could sense the connection being made.

Momentarily, the Creator's head appeared. It seemed to float in space before Trance, just slightly larger than real-life but much more vibrant in color and clarity.

"Yes?" MasTho said cautiously. Then his eyes widened when he saw who had called him. They widened even more when he took in Trance's disheveled and bloodied appearance and that of his silent comrades. "Talk," he said.

Trance quickly explained what had happened. When he finished, MasTho's features shuddered. "We'll discuss this further later, Protector," he said in an angry voice. "The wounded and the dead must be taken care of. Prepare for transport." With that, the face faded from the center and disappeared.

"Oh man, I hate this part--" Trance started to say to himself. But then the universe shattered into a blue haze, and he was standing in a transport station much like the one his party had left from. This one was much larger; there was room for easily dozens of Protectors on the single pad. His group fit easily onto one corner of the platform.

Technicians in dark blue jump-suits were running this way and that. One of them appeared to be in charge. She was snapping orders out as she stepped forward to Trance. Trance saw out of the corner of his eye that her underlings were gently seeing to his comrades.

The woman was speaking to him in a clear and calm voice. "Are you in satisfactory condition, Protector?" she asked, looking into a handheld scanner. It was beeping quietly. She was about six foot tall with aqua-blue skin, dark gray eyes, and yellow hair. She had thin, graceful fingers with no nails.

"Yes, I think, apart from a splitting headache," he said. "But the others— "

"Will be taken care of. Will you please sit down?"

Trance nodded numbly, and gingerly sat down on the edge of the platform, allowing his legs to swing freely an inch or two off the floor. Behind him, he heard five distinct hums as each Protector and his or her assigned orderly were transported elsewhere.

Trance nodded and concentrated on the woman in front of him. She was tapping her fingers on the scanner's keypad. "You've gotten a fractured skull, a concussion, broken ribs, cracked vertebrata, and a whole list of other ailments. Frankly, I'm surprised you're even conscious, much less alive. What the heck did you guys get into?"

"A huge mess," Trance sighed. He put his head in his hands. Everything was throbbing, and the lights appeared to be flashing red and blue and green.

"Well, your friends will need some work, but we'll have you fixed momentarily. How do you want to feel?"

"Pardon?"

Her eyes crinkled in surprise. "Mentally, of course," she said.
"Euphoric, happy, sad, angry. Feelings. How do you want to feel mentally? We
can fix that, too."

"Personally, I'd rather you didn't mess with that."

"Hmp. Suit yourself. One physio-job coming right up. Close your
eyes."

Trance did, and momentarily he began to feel a sensation of warmth
around the tip of his skull. The feeling radiated outward to the edges of his hair,
and then began to travel down his head, then into his neck and shoulders and on
down. The whole process took less than a minute. He opened his eyes. "Now
what?" he asked.

"Now I leave and you go find something to eat. You're healed
physically. Mentally, you can turn into a basket case, for all I care." She smiled
gently.

"What about my friends?"

"The golden one and the bipedal female should be fixed in about twenty
minutes. The male feline should be OK now. The female Emilian and the
bucket of slime are DOA, I'm afraid. There's nothing that can be done about
those two."

"Oh."

"I wouldn't worry about your friends. The best thing for you is a healthy
dinner and a long night's sleep. Don't do anything strenuous for the next forty-
eight hours, OK? Doctor's orders."

"I'd like to visit my friends in the hospital," Trance said obstinately.

"Where are you from? People don't spend enough time in medical
treatment to need visitors. By the time you reached the care facility they are in
and explained to the orderlies your intentions, your friends would be long gone.
No, the best thing for you is to rest and relax."

"Oh."

"Well, that's it then," the tech said cheerfully, putting her scanner on a
little clip hanging from her belt. "Be a little more careful next time, eh, champ?
We have to keep you healthy for the next challenger in the Battle Dome." She
turned and left the room with a smile.

Trance shook his head and cracked his neck. The head and body aches
were gone, and he could see straight, but he still felt a little numb inside. It was

hard to believe how many times his life had been turned over since he left his office just a few short days ago. He stood, and ambled out the door the technician had walked through. It swished open and he stepped into the hall. It was quite late in the evening. Maybe dinner would be a good idea.

It only took a few minutes to find a lift. He instructed it to take him to the spire.

He was surprised to find that all but one of the many cafeterias in the spire was still open. He forced a cold dinner consisting of something solid and unsatisfying down his throat then headed for his apartment. He kept his head down on the way, barely noticing the rushing crowds around him. If any of the tumbling gray mass called to him or recognized him in any way he would not have noticed or even cared. He was weary and sought the warmth of his bed rather than the companionship of others.

In the quiet of his room, lying on his bed, Trance let the tragic events in recent days wash over him like a wave. Tears came unbidden. He wiped them away savagely.

He was so weary, yet sleep would not come easily. After an hour or two of silent meditation, he looked down at his ring. "Your brethren certainly are capable of despicable things, ring," he said. "Awful things."

"We are tools, Protector. Nothing more."

"Hmp. I'm sure. You know a lot of people on my planet have said just the same thing."

Several minutes passed in silence. Trance willed the light to dim, looking out his window into the midnight sky. Stars shone back at him, crisp and clear and bright. Off in the distance, he could see a sliver of one of the moons of Monidad.

"Well , I guess we know who the bad guy is now," he said moodily.

"One of them, anyway."

"Yeah, I guess you're right. Why the heck do you think she did it?"

"I don't know Protector. I wasn't created to think on my own."

"Handy. You never seem to be able to think when I need you to." The ring remained silent.

After that, Trance stared moodily into the night sky, lost in thought. The sky was particularly dark that evening. Besides the moon, he could see the stars. They were beautiful, so full of promise. He could see the same dusting across the sky that at home he knew would signify the Milky Way. Here... who knew what galaxy he was in.

And then a shooting star traced its way across the heavens, momentarily pulling him back to the moon of Korondor, and his request for the ring to record the events in the distant past.

"Were you able to make the record like I asked?" he inquired thoughtfully.

"Affirmative."

"When we were back there, at the battle, something happened. You tried to let me know what it was, but I brushed you off. What was it?"

"I recorded a huge spike in radiation that did not seem to be of that time."

Trance's eyes narrowed. "Show me your recording. Visual only. But don't start it at the beginning. Start at the moment that Si-truc first spoke, and freeze it there."

The room melted away, replaced by the moon of Korondor, a frozen tableau. At the center of his vision, he could see himself looking at the crowd. Next to him on the right, Taa'lien stood, her hand aloft and pointing. To his left, Aura's mouth hung open in surprise. Nesger faced them, his mouth set in a twisted grin.

Some of the other creators and Protectors were looking intently on the face of the captured and bound rogue. Most were looking toward Si-truc who was emerging from the crowd, his face set in lines of determination.

The frozen image was crisp and clear, much more realistic than the holo-viewer had been able to reproduce. When he closed his eyes and felt around, he could sense his surroundings, and the illusion was ruined, but with his eyes open he could almost believe he were there again.

"Where is this radiation centered?"

"Protector Taa'lien."

"Move forward, slowly," Trance said thoughtfully. "Quarter speed. Scan for the specific source of the radiation."

The hand completed its upward arch, and the index finger extended. This time, Trance noticed that the hand seemed to sparkle just slightly and ever so briefly. Or, perhaps, something on it glinted in the sunlight. Except that there was nothing there to glint off of. "Stop right there." He said. What happened just then?"

"Just a wild guess here, but it looks like she is pointing at Nesger."

"In the excitement of the events, I just assumed she was pointing at Si-truc when she spoke. What else?"

"Perhaps examining this situation on the other wavelengths I recorded would be advantageous at this junction."

"Good idea, ring. Let's add sound."

"Suit yourself."

They listened to the audio track with and without the visual several times without any results. Trance felt himself growing more and more frustrated as the evening wore on.

After several hours, he found himself back at the brief moment that Taa'lien pointed at Nesger. He knew that he was on the verge of something. There had to be something there that he just was not seeing or hearing. At last, in frustration, he said: "Isn't there anything else that you can do with this?"

"There are other wavelengths, Protector. Not just audio and visual."

"Hey! Why didn't you say so before?"

"You didn't ask."

"Shit."

"Is that some sort of co—"

"Shush. Just do your thing. Examine the other wavelengths, or whatever, and tell me what you come up with."

"This is very interesting, Protector," the ring said after a short pause.

"What?"

"Her non-ring hand is actually giving off radiation."

"What?"

"I said, her non-ring —"

"I know what you said. What did you mean?"

"I meant, it is a form of radiation I am very familiar with."

"Meaning what, exactly?"

"You humans sure are dense. She is utilizing a second ring, Protector. It is located on her right hand, on her middle finger."

Trance's stomach gurgled unpleasantly, and sweat broke out on his furrowed brow. "You mean a ring like you," he grunted.

"Remember, before we went back, when I mentioned I had noticed something odd but couldn't pin it down? This must have been it – the second ring."

"Don't Protectors usually have just one ring?"

"Not usually. Always."

"Why didn't you recognize she was wearing it immediately?"

"It wasn't in use at the time, and the concept was so completely foreign that it didn't register."

"Oh. Did you notice it at any time before Korondor?"

"I wasn't looking for it specifically. However… no, I did not notice it."

"She must have planted it the moon beforehand, and picked it up when she went scouting. What do you bet it's one of the rings that went missing recently?"

"Your hypothesis makes sense. It appears as though we have found one of the missing seven, and perhaps the instrument of their disappearance in one fell swoop."

"Right. Looking back now, it is clear that she orchestrated the whole trip. This just seems like more proof. But why? Why put us through all that crap of traveling all that way just to kill us by destroying a freaking moon? She seemed like a pretty direct lady. All that subterfuge just for an attempted murder seems like a bit much."

"Unknown."

Trance jumped up and began to pace, walking through the scene as if it were smoke. "Wait a minute. What if she wasn't really trying to kill us directly? What if she blew up the moon to hide something? Something we saw or perhaps whatever she did with the second ring…."

"Since the three of you were essentially wraiths, we have a short list of activities to choose from."

"I think that's supposed to be a joke, but you're right." Trance thought for a moment, an intense look of concentration sculpting his features as he stared at the frozen tableau. "You know, it's kind of funny," he said at last, "everyone is looking at Si-truc, but not Nesger. In fact, it looks like the rogue is looking right at Taa'lien rather than at the Dragon… like he knows that she is there."

"Perhaps. It is conceivable. She was supposed to be preventing you all from being seen…"

The hairs on the back of Trance's neck stood up and began to dance the Tango. "You don't think she used the second ring to send him a message, do you?"

"Possibly," the ring admitted.

Trance made a fist and slammed it into the bed in frustration. "Is there any way to be sure? Scan the track again. This time, look for patterns… anything that even remotely resembles a message."

Several seconds passed. "I've got some good news and bad news, Trance," the ring reported at last.

Trance's stomach decided to take up diving. It twisted into a ball and leapt into the depths of his rectum doing several flips and a barrel roll on the way down. "Give me the good news first, then," he grunted.

"Well…. I lied. There is no good news. The bad news is that it **is** a message of some sort! It's directed right at Nesger…"

"What does it say?"

"It's highly encoded. Just a second…. Hmm. I think I have it, but most of the message is in a language I have never encountered."

Confusion played across Trance's features. "What do you understand?"

"The names of each of the members in our squad, and our planets of origin, and the date and time we journeyed from. There is a lot more though."

"What?!"

"I said –"

"I know what you said. I just can't believe it. We need to tell the Creators. We have a huge problem."

Chapter 31: In Observation

Trance quickly grabbed some clothing and ran from the room toward the nearest transport. On the way, he called to Aura through his ring. "Where are you?" he asked the golden Protector.

Aura's voice came back to him after a moment. He sounded weary. "I'm with Creator MasTho, and Dexter," he said, "we're in observation. Kameko left about fifteen minutes ago."

"Send me your coordinates. I'm coming up."

"What is it? You sound agitated."

"Not now. I'll explain, but not like this."

It took him ten minutes, two transports, and an elevator to find the three. When he arrived, he found MasTho and Aura sitting quietly next to two biers in an otherwise small and empty room. Dexter had worn a groove in the floor pacing behind them. On one bier lay the forlorn remains of Mollie. On the other sat a covered bucket which could only be Sigfried.

Trance approached them quietly, and laid one hand on Mollie who was cool to the touch. He refrained from touching the goo that had become his other friend. "I'm sorry," he sighed to them both, then turned to Dexter, Aura, and the Creator. "We have to talk," he said.

It only took a moment to explain what he had found. After swearing the three to secrecy, MasTho asked Trance to play the message. When it began playing, his face turned a ghastly shade of white and he trembled visibly. Aura and Dexter only looked confused.

When the message was done, the three Protectors looked at MasTho expectantly. He looked troubled. "What I am about to tell you must never be spoken of again. Whatever else occurs after this evening; no matter what secrets are revealed in the near and distant future, you must never repeat this. Do you understand?" The three nodded in affirmation. "What you have seen is the visual representation of the Creator language, the language of my people. It is known and spoken by only my brothers and sisters. Until this time, we believed no one else even knew that it exists. We use this language only amongst our own, and in communiqués that we deem too important to leave uncloaked."

Dexter whistled. Aura only nodded thoughtfully. "Are these secret messages coded in some other format as well?" he asked.

"No. The messages were in a language thought to be known only by the Creators. We assumed that further encryption was not necessary."

"So, what was the message she gave Nesger?" Dexter asked impatiently.

"She told him how to escape the cell he would be encased in," MasTho responded. "Furthermore -- as you said, Trance -- she indicated the members of your party and origin, and the date that you had traveled from."

"I guess I just don't understand her motive for assisting him," Trance said morosely.

"Maybe she wanted to go back to help Si-truc get out, and just modified her plan when she saw that it was Nesger instead," Dexter said.

"But she didn't have a tattoo, remember? We checked. That makes me think that she knew about Nesger all along," Trance replied.

"Your statement makes sense. But how the heck could she know that?" No one could answer that question.

"I thought Nesger was supposed to be locked up forever," Aura said after a moment's pause.

"In these cases we always leave a keyhole. Can you imagine if we had accidentally jailed an innocent? So, every jail has a door; every cell an exit," MasTho shrugged. "Taa'lien's message gave Nesger the key."

"Regardless, Neger is surely dead after millions of years," Dexter grunted. "How could he possibly affect us today?"

"You mean, why even bother setting him free after all this time?" Trance responded.

"Yeah, it doesn't make sense."

"Maybe, if he had the poor fortune to reproduce, his descendents are on the loose mucking things up," Dexter grunted.

"Several rings were never recovered after the rebellion," MasTho mused. "Anything is possible."

Trance thought for a moment and then snapped his fingers. "Wait a minute. When each of us gets a ring, our weakness is reported to the Creators, right? Does your language have anything to do with that?"

"Very perceptive, Trance. You are correct. The item chosen is broadcast back to Monidad in our language."

"But my ring said it didn't recognize the language."

"Not surprising. As you know, when a ring comes back, it is cleaned and reformatted. At that time, our technicians install the program that will randomly choose an item, which will be the ring's weakness, from the vast store of our knowledge base. Until the weakness is picked and relayed to Monidad, the ring is non-functional. Once the weakness is chosen, and the message relayed, the program wipes out all knowledge of our language and self-terminates; in essence deleting itself."

"But then how can the ring remember what its weakness is?" Dexter asked.

"It must translate the description of that single item, and store it before self-deleting that program," Trance ventured. The Creator nodded in approval.

"Knowing Taa'lien is somehow involved worries me more than it abates my fears," Aura said truthfully.

"She is the best of the best," MasTho grunted. "I fear she may have more planned than what is apparent now." He looked at the three thoughtfully. "You're worn out and exhausted. Get plenty of rest tonight. In the morning I want you to set out to find Taa'lien, and bring her back forcefully, if need be."

"Yes, sir," Trance said, and then snapped his fingers. "In all the excitement, I forgot about Per'dita. Has he been found yet?"

"Didn't you hear?" Aura answered. "Shortly after we left, a garbage crew found his body stuffed into a trash bin."

"Taa'lien again," Dexter grunted. "She knew Per'dita was a potential suspect. His disappearance kept suspicion away from our squad long enough to get us off the planet. I'm sure she knew he'd be found eventually. After we were gone, however, it wouldn't matter."

"She is the answer to all of our questions, I think," mused the Creator.

"Hopefully it's not too late to stop whatever she is up to," Trance said.

"Just try and make it back alive," the Creator said worriedly, "with her if possible."

"Do you not think we will be able to succeed, sir?" Aura asked politely. But Trance could sense the hidden meaning behind the question. Were they being sent to their deaths?

MasTho looked Aura in the eyes. "I do not know," he said. "But we must find out. You are the only ones that I can send… at this point we must tell no else what we have discovered."

"If there are more conspirators, we risk sending alarm," Dexter said.

"And if she acts alone we risk alarming the Conglomerated States for nothing," the Creator finished. "Either way we need to know, and she is the only one that can tell us. Hunt her to the ends of the Universe if need be, but I want her found."

They left the Creator together after promising once again they would remain silent about their planned quest. They quickly wound their way back to their apartments in the Spire, and before they separated agreed to meet at the usual spot the next morning: the Cafeteria in their section.

Once again, Trance slept fitfully, haunted this time by the ghosts of Mollie and Sigfried. "I can't feel my legs," Sigfried cried from his bucket. "Help me!"

"You don't have any legs, you fool!" Mollie scolded him, shaking a single white paw at the bucket. She turned to Trance, "Find our killer," she beseeched, "only you can stop her. Use your ring, and even your fists if you need to, but you must stop her!"

"I can't find her!" Trance screamed at them; tried to run from their mutilated bodies, but his legs had become encased in an archway of stone. He looked around wildly for something to pry himself free... there was nothing on the ground in front of him, and above the dark sky was empty save a trio of stars off in the distance.

"You're not looking in the right direction, you fool!" Mollie yelled as her voice faded away. Trance sat up with a start. During the night the sheets had tangled around his legs—he fell out of bed in a disgruntled heap and shambled into the shower.

Dexter and Aura were already eating when he found them thirty minutes later in the cafeteria. Dexter had a new black collar on. Aura was wearing the same type of golden-colored outfit that he usually wore. After a quick meal, they headed for the nearest Transporter room.

Inside, they found a technician waiting for them. "MasTho said that you'd be by," it said by way of greeting, speaking through two slits that served as its speaking orifices. They smacked wetly with each syllable.

"How the heck did he know that we'd be here?" Dexter asked bluntly. "We could have gone to nearly a thousand other transport rooms on planet." He sniffed.

"This is the closest station to our apartments, Dexter," Aura said.

"I hate being second-guessed," Dexter responded to no one in particular.

"Actually, according to today's staff meeting, all the transport centers in this region have been put on high alert that the three of you would be leaving the planet today, and to send you wherever you want to go," the technician replied. "Even the restricted zones," he muttered ominously and gave the international sign for warding off evil. "Although heaven only knows why."

"Oh," Dexter replied, somewhat mollified. He looked at Aura.

"Here are the coordinates, friend," Aura said, and handed the technician a piece of paper. The coordinates were entered into the console, and the technician appraised its readout. "That's just off Korondor's moon," it said. "If we move your destination over a single click, I can drop you planet-side. My screen says the Northern Hemisphere should be in the midst of summer right now. Nice and warm and comfy."

"There's nothing there right now but debris," Trance said softly.

"Are you sure?" The technician tapped the screen. "Korondor is in the Restricted Zone. Nobody has been there for more than two millennia. How could you know that?"

"We were there yesterday," Aura said. "He's right."

"Oh." The technician shook its head, four of its eight eyes blinking at once. "They don't make them like they used to," it said to itself. "OK, if you'll step on to the pad, I can get you on your way," he said to the three and pointed to the transporter.

Trance allowed himself to be ushered to the transport pad by the technician. He found himself dreading the feeling he knew that he'd get when he process was instituted—but this was the fastest way back to the ruins of Korondor.

Momentarily, the three appeared in the Restricted Sector. Trance felt sick to his stomach for just a moment when they materialized, but the feeling quickly left him. This trip had been the easiest of the three for him. Perhaps he was getting used to the effects.

He looked at Aura and Dexter. "This is right about where the moon was," he said. My ring says that based on energy discharges from Taa'lien's ring, she went that away." He pointed off into space. Trance knew all rings emitted a discharge during their normal use. When the ring bearer moved from one point to another using a ring as a means of propulsion, this discharge became a path other Protectors (and no other beings) could follow.

"Hmm." Aura thought for a moment. "Watch this," he said to Trance, and a light blue path appeared before them stretching in the same direction Trance had pointed. It was thin and wispy, but evident nonetheless.

"Nice idea," Dexter murmured. "That will make things a little easier.

'This might be a long trip... I scanned for her ring, and she isn't in this Galaxy, at least as far as I can tell." That was the upper limit of their scanning range for other rings. "Maybe if we follow this path for a while, we'll come within range and get a positive capture on her ring signal."

"Usually the darn things dissipate quickly. Looks like we caught a break this time," Aura mentioned, pleased.

They slipped along the path moving slowly and carefully. Here and there eddies skipped off and faded into nothingness, but the path remained. Sometimes it too threatened to dissipate; sometimes it faded to nothing but a single strand. Often they had to stop and search painstakingly for a road to follow.

Trance wished Kameko had been able to come with them. He felt a strange sort of emptiness when she wasn't around, as if something was missing. She excited him, and confused him at the same time… she was so complex, so beautiful she made his heart ache. What had she been about to say back on Korondor? Maybe he'd never know. He wished he had been able to speak with her at least, before they'd left, even just to say goodbye.

Trance found himself frustrated by the slow progression along the strand. He was itching for a fight – dying to find Taa'lien. Her betrayal ate at him like an acid, a slow burn into anger. How could she betray her squad? How could she betray the corps? Could his meager group defeat her? Was he enough of a hero to get the job done?

Ah, there was the fear-- it too ate into his soul. Who was HE? Was he… a hero? In all the serials he had read as a child, that's what being a hero was all about—one man against impossible odds; one last fight to the death. Would he measure up?

One thing was for sure: this sleuthing was crap. It was for… people other than TRUE Heroes. They could sleuth all they wanted while he was out saving the world. Check that. The Universe. Yeah. That was more like it… wasn't it?

And yet… and yet this was exciting in to itself, the hunt to find the killer. The mystery to solve; the intrigue to uncover. Heroes did that, didn't they?

Sometime later he realized that he really hadn't met any true heroes -- just read about them in the comic books, and seen them in the movies. But then he remembered he had met a "hero" once, a firefighter who had saved a small child and a puppy from a blaze engulfing a house in his city. He'd heard of the feat, seen it in the news. There'd even been a parade of some sort. And yet when he chanced to meet the lady on the street a month later, he had almost passed her by until his mother stopped him and introduced her to him.

In person she had seemed so … ordinary. For one she wasn't glowing with determination. She wasn't even glowing at all. Her chin didn't have a dimple. She wasn't ten feet tall. In fact, she was actually shorter than his mother!

Her voice didn't ring with strength – in fact, it was a soft voice filled with kindness. He hardly could believe she was even capable of the feats attributed to her.

He couldn't even remember what she had said. His mind was too busy reeling from the implosion of his sense of right and of might. The experience disillusioned him and disheartened him. What if all of the other stories he had been told were similarly flawed? What if right was left and up was down? What if there really was no Santa Claus? All those thoughts boiled together.

The experience seemed so different now, viewed from the untold depths of space and the even wider span of all those years. He realized now, following the thin wisp of Taa'lien's discharge that maybe just maybe the firefighter had been a bigger hero than everyone had made her out to be. Heroes aren't made, he thought; they aren't formed. They are normal everyday human beings who, when faced with a task bigger than themselves grow to the situation. The thought left him quiet and somber.

They followed the trail for several hours and through three systems to a huge blue and gray gas Giant. It was at least twenty times bigger than the planet Earth.

They battled through the upper atmosphere, braving turbulent storms of hydrogen and helium, and into a thicker layer of metallic hydrogen. Eventually they made it to a core of ice and dirt that while small in comparison was the still the size of several Earths.

Because they couldn't see through the muck, they allowed their rings to guide them and provide their customary link for shared communication.

"Nice, huh?" Dexter commented across their shared link. "I might like to have a summer home one day," he sniffed.

"How will you know it is summer?" Trance responded greyly.

"We'll just have to guess. I think I'll put the house right there so it catches the sun in the morning. You know I love sunbeams."

"Shut up, you two," Aura said. "I think I've got something here."

Trance was the first to react, sending a scan toward where he knew Aura was. His ring revealed a metal object embedded in the icy surface.

"Well, I'll be. It's Taa'lien's arm," Trance said.

Dexter grunted. "How disgusting. I can't bear to look."

"It's her metal arm, Dex," Trance sighed. "And it has a burned out ring on it."

"I'll be, too" Aura said, impressed. "This whole setup is just too perfect," he remarked. "Let's get out of here—with the arm."

They gathered the appendage and headed back into space. There, they stopped to confer. "Now what?" Dexter asked.

"I really don't know," Aura said, looking at the arm closely. The fingers were closed tightly in the form of a fist. He gingerly pried them open. "Hey," he said. "There is a second ring here!"

They gathered around the arm. Sure enough, there was a second ring clutched in the hand. It too had been burned out. Trance whistled. "Two rings. She must have a third."

"Yeah, at the very least," Aura said.

"Hey, I thought it was pretty much impossible to change rings," Trance pouted, "and here she's done it two times that we know of."

"Well in the cases that I know of, the Protectors went insane," Dexter responded.

"Maybe she already was insane," Aura replied. "Maybe it didn't affect her. Maybe it drove her completely bonkers. I guess we'll never know."

"Wouldn't they have communicated with Mondiad when she started using them?" Trance asked.

"Maybe not," Aura ruminated. "Rings always go back there for reformatting, remember? If she was somehow able to capture the ring before that process happened, the communication might not occur. And if the ring was not in use at all, it might be hard to find."

They searched around the planet for another ring trail, but this time there was nothing that they could pick up on. The trail just dead-ended on the planet's surface.

"I'm sensing a slight bit of ion radiation dispersed fairly evenly throughout this system," Aura said thoughtfully. "There was a ship here, but it's long gone by now, and so is she."

"We'll never catch her, and since we don't know what her new ring's signature is…" Dexter let the thought trail off. They all knew Taa'lien had managed to evade them, possibly for good.

Suddenly, Trance grabbed the arm from Aura. "Look at this!" he exclaimed. Scratched into the surface of the arm were two words. "Are you getting the feeling that she wanted us to find this?"

Five minutes later, Dexter and Trance waited quietly as Aura contacted MasTho with an update. Trance was secretly pleased the big Golden Protector was the one to do the dirty work of informing the Creator this time-- especially with all the other bad news they'd had to impart to MasTho in recent memory. Aura didn't do so willingly. In fact, they had drawn straws.

Chapter 32: Conference Call

MasTho was in conference with Creators Dymin, Dy-ranb, and Shra-nele when the call came in to him. They were sitting in plush chairs around a large polished mahogany desk that was clear save a small marble cube with a metal inlay that read "MasTho". Framed pictures of family members and close friends graced three of the four walls. The fourth wall contained a door and a light plate.

"It's about time," MasTho grunted, motioning the three to stay. He waved his fingers perceptibly, and Protector Aura appeared, a small holograph twelve inches high on the surface of the desk. The Protector looked weary. "Report," MasTho said. "This transmission is secure."

"We've lost the target, Creator," Aura said with no preamble. "Her trail went cold. But we did find two rings she abandoned—hers and the ring we believe she used to detonate Korondor and its moon."

Across the desk, Dymin's eyes widened in surprise but he said nothing. The other two Creators pursed their lips silently. MasTho grimaced. "Any clues we can work with? A message? Anything?"

"Hmm. Are you ready for this? There was a message engraved in the arm. I hardly believe it. None of us do."

"What is it?"

"OK. Here it is: 'Nesger Lives.'"

"Oh, boy," Shra-nele grunted. MasTho glared at her witheringly.

"A message meant to scare us, nothing more," Dymin growled. "What are your next steps?"

Aura looked uncertain. "We had planned to return. Is there somewhere else we are needed?"

"No." MasTho said to Aura. "There is nothing else you can do out there. Return at best speed." He signed off, and looked back at the others. "What do you make of this?" he asked.

"It's a lie," Dymin said haughtily. "There's no way."

"Even if he is alive, why haven't we heard from him?" Dy-ranb asked. "It's been untold millennia. You'd think he would have shown his face sometime in that span, or at least sent us a holiday card."

MasTho tapped his fingers on the desk, and then wiped an imaginary speck from its surface. "I think," he said, "it's time we came clean."

"But our forefathers swore they would never reveal this secret," Dy-ranb quietly demurred. "Is it wise to do so now after so long a time?"

"You're right. That was a much different time, and our silence then was required to save a fragile union," MasTho responded. He paused and glanced at the pictures of his family for a brief moment before looking back across the span of his desk. "Now, however, the same policy may result in the destruction of the corps and all it protects."

"Perhaps we do need to inform the corps. They will most likely hear it secondhand anyway," Shra-nele said. She smoothed her cloak. "I'd rather they heard it from us."

"I think," Dymin concurred, "that it is time to hold an emergency meeting. The things that must be revealed cannot be broadcast throughout the Conglomerated states. We must meet here." The other Creators nodded thoughtfully, and in full agreement.

"Contact the corps," MasTho said.

*****

Captain Lance Taggart surveyed his bridge with pride. The good ship CSN Townsend, one of the jewels of the Conglomerated States Navy's Exploration division, slid through space like a silver knife on a surveying mission. And he was the man who guided that knife like an expert surgeon.

Sometimes, in secret, Taggart wished that he could helm a battleship, but those hadn't been in service for untold years-- several millennia probably— because there was just no need for them. The Protectors had proved adept at keeping outsiders out, and stepped in whenever internal conflicts arose, so powerfully armed services just weren't needed. Which kept his taxes low too, he admitted grudgingly.

That left exploration, and that was kind of exciting too, in a dull sort of way. Still, at the outer edge of the known universe practically anything could happen. Though, he grudgingly admitted, frequently it didn't.

In fact, the Townsend had spent the last several months passing the time by counting nebulae, comets, and other assorted space debris. There had been a few Class 1 planets, but even those were few and far between. He'd set up markers and sooner or later another crew would be by to investigate colonization possibilities. Maybe they'd name one of the smaller planets after him, or possibly a moon. That'd be a riot. He sighed.

The extreme monotony of their mission had not done a thing to dull the sharpness of his crew, and that pleased the Captain immensely. Even though his senior staff appeared relaxed as they went about their duties around him, he knew they were on a high state of alert, mandatory when on the outer rim.

Still, he reflected, it was nice to get away from headquarters—naval ships were hardly ever given permission to voyage out this far anymore. To be given the okay to do some deep space exploration – now that was something nice.

And of course since things did happen occasionally out this far, the brass always sent two ships. Taggart glanced at the Communications officer. "Drawoh, patch me through to the Reliant, if you please."

"Yes sir," Drawoh said, his voice slightly warped by the breather that he wore. His six eyes blinked simultaneously, the nictitating membranes sliding up to dampen the irises as he turned back to his console.

The Reliant, a slightly smaller exploration vessel was currently in the next star system over, less than fifty light years away. Her captain, Naied Gerason, an excellent officer in her own right, was every bit his equal in grit and determination. If she were his own race, he might have made a play for her. But she was a Ren'rag; beautiful to look at, with her colorful modulating skin, but ultimately incompatible sexually.

Shortly, Naeid appeared on the forward view screen, the skin of her face a slight pink. She smiled warmly. "Captain Taggart," she said, "how can I help you?"

Taggart picked an imaginary speck of lint off his immaculate wool uniform. "Greetings, Captain Gerason," he said pleasantly. "How are your scans coming?"

"Excellent Captain. My Science Officer reports a Class 1 about fifty light years from our present position. "It might be worth checking out."

"Good news indeed. Perhaps you and your senior crew would be interested in joining us this evening for a cup of Fermo."

"I thought that particular beverage was on the prohibited list for all vessels," she smiled conspiratorially.

Taggart shrugged, the antennae on his head moving spasmodically. "Yes, however somehow a crate managed to sneak itself aboard when we were last at dock. Since the rule has already been broken, why not enjoy it?"

"It would be a shame, I'm sure, to destroy such a fine beverage," she winked.

Just then, someone called to her from off-screen. "Hmm. That's odd," she said. Then, "Are you sure?"

"What?" Taggart responded, the warm glow he had been feeling leeching away at the sound of her voice.

"Just a moment." She continued listening, her skin turning a slight shade of blue. Here and there, yellow flashes were evident. After another minute or two, she turned back to Taggart. "We've been scanning out beyond the Red Line, as you know, just to see what's out there. A few minutes ago, just at the edge of our scanners, we found what we thought at the time was an asteroid belt surrounding a system in the Vega quadrant – nothing to write home about. But now, I'm not so sure."

"Why's that?"

"Well first of all, a huge number of the asteroids, uh, over one hundred billion of them if you can believe it, seem surprisingly uniform in shape, size, and density."

"Huh. That is odd."

"Yeah, we're running some tests right now to make sure our sensor arrays are functioning properly. They've worked well so far, but this…." She let the thought drift away.

"Is there something else?" Taggart asked kindly, intrigued at the puzzle.

"Yes. Well, it seems as though a pair of the asteroids have just broken formation and are heading this way."

Taggart chuckled at the joke. "Wake me in a few thousand years when they get to you," he laughed, settling back into his command chair.

"Funny. But these blips were moving fast before they just disappeared. My science officer—"

"Wait. Don't you mean before you lost track of them? Maybe they just moved behind a planet or something."

"No, they disappeared," she said firmly. "Furthermore, my science officer just informed me that given the energy signatures those bogeys gave off prior to their disappearance; we can only assume that they entered gray space."

"If those sensors are accurate," Taggart said.

The other captain nodded. "As I said, we're checking on it."

"Captain, sir?" came the voice of his navigations officer, a hard working though young and imaginative fellow, by the name of Briggs, "Think we should contact headquarters?"

"For a couple of bogeys? No," he shook his head. "If we bothered headquarters for every unexplained blip we encountered, we'd spend more time doing paperwork than exploring! We aren't a war ship by any means, but I am sure we have armament enough to deal with whatever is out there."

"Still, just the same," Captain Gerason said by way of agreement, "it might be better if you did mosey on over here. At least that way we'll have more of a welcome wagon for whomever or whatever is controlling those blips," she said, worry etching her face and betraying thoughts that could not be spoken aloud.

"Maybe we'll make first contact," Taggart said hopefully, brightening for a moment. "We haven't had one of those in awhile. God knows we need one; the taxpayers are starting to think we don't do anything with their credits!"

"Maybe they'll give you a nice big medal," she joked.

"No, I doubt they'll want to waste the money. It will probably be made of plastic." He smiled thoughtfully. "We'll be there in less than an hour. Keep a light on for us." He motioned to the Com officer again, who cut the transmission.   Make it so," he said to his Navigation officer. "Maximum speed."

"Warming up the engines," the Navigation officer replied.

Forty-five minutes and ten seconds later, the Townsend broke her warp bubble and appeared in the system. They found the Reliant exactly where she should have been, basking in the interstellar winds.

"Greetings again, Captain," he called said when communications had been reestablished, "Did we miss the party?"

"No, Captain, you haven't missed much."

Taggart turned to his science officer, Dujy Ybrd. "Anything coming out of warp bubbles in this vicinity?"

"Nothing yet," Dujy said, tapping commands into his console. "Sure wish we could track stuff through gray space…"

They didn't have to wait very long. In fact, less than fifteen minutes later, Dujy called to Taggart from across the bridge at his post. "Captain, I am getting a huge energy reading nearby, I think it might be our friends coming out of warp."

Taggart told him to keep an eye on it. Seconds later, Dujy signaled again. "Sir, I got them… two bogeys, three light years away and out of warp, but heading here fast. Shall I put them on view screen?"

"Yes. Give me the clearest picture you can. I want to see what these fellows look like."

Shortly, the two intruders appeared on the screen. They were obviously robots, and a scan showed they were not alive. They consisted primarily of deutronium and tritanium and several other hard metals. The first looked like large bulbous dinosaur. It had two moon-shaped eyes with hard black retinas set into a long watermelon shaped snout. The eyes popped out from the face in a manner that gave it a perpetually surprised look.

Below the snout was a small mouth with no teeth that appeared drawn up into a permanent smile. It had two ridges of bumps that traveled down from its head to the tip of a short tail that jutted out from its rear end. It also had two stubby arms and two short thick legs. In truth, the thing looked extremely harmless except for the two massive shoulder guns that appeared to have been added as an afterthought. Taggart shuddered and examined the other.

The second robot was much more diabolical in appearance. It had a small head with tiny ears that sprouted from the top, eyes like dark pinpricks, and a long snout. The head was set upon a long sinuous neck. It two had a pair of massive shoulder guns.

The second robot's body was about twenty feet long. It had two large flat feet, and small arms. It also had a tail that fairly bristled with armament.

"Signal the Reliant," Taggart said. "Let's see if they are getting the same pictures we are."

"Sir," Drawoh said after a moment of typing into his console, "I can't seem to raise them. I'll try and boost the signal."

A tiny flicker of dread began to burn in Taggart's stomach but he doused it with enthusiasm and machismo. *Damn circuits never seem to work right*, he thought. "Keep trying," he said aloud.

The robots, or whatever they were, came into the system like they were in a big hurry, retro rockets firing madly. They slowed, and then stopped completely when they were within five miles of the two naval ships. The Reliant was just ahead and to the Port of Townsend. Its edge cut into their view of the robots.

"Signal them if you can," Taggart grunted, indicating the intruders.

"Not working, captain," Drawoh replied miserably.

"Hmm. Raise shields. And, uh, continue hailing them," he said doggedly.

The lights flickered just briefly as the force shields came online. Somebody let out an audible "Whew." Taggart found that he agreed, silently, with whoever had done it; those things made his skin crawl. He felt much safer with the shields up. Though he knew his ship alone could have easily destroyed the two in front of them, he wondered, just a little, how they would do against a hundred billion of the things. Caution might be warranted.

"We're being scanned, Captain," Dujy, the science officer, said somberly.

"Keep hailing them in all known languages. Tell them that we are on a mission of peace."

"Yessir," Drawoh sighed. His efforts still weren't working.

"Uh Oh –" the science officer started. But he didn't need to complete his sentence. They could see what was happening on the view screen.

One of the massive shoulder weapons of the lead robot turned lazily and fired off a single beam of purple energy. The beam wasn't even slowed when it passed through the Reliant's force shield and lanced into and through the Reliant itself. Large chunks of the ship blew outward with the beam, followed by bodies and pieces of equipment.

"What the hell was that?" yelled Taggart.

"It's some kind of focused energy beam!" called Dujy. "It cut right through the Reliant's force shield like it was butter!"

"I saw that!" growled the captain, taking a breath. The aim had been true: the command center of the Reliant had been vaporized. He knew that its commander was dead, but there might be time to save some of the crew. That lone thought tumbled into his consciousness as the commands flew from his mouth like bullets: "Hit them with everything we've got! Protect the Reliant!" He turned to the navigations officer knowing every second counted. "Hard to starboard! Ahead Mark Three!" To the Communications officer: "Keep trying to contact base!"

The crew was well trained. The officers knew their duties, performing their instructions like clockwork. It was not enough. "Communication's still jammed, captain!" the communications officer exclaimed over the din. "The message keeps bouncing back," he said half to himself as he frantically entered commands into his console.

On the view screen, Taggart watched as five bright green lights shot from the Townsend, leapt across the span of space, and crashed into the monstrosities. Meanwhile, his ship attempted to ascribe the route that he had instructed his crew to take it on.

The torpedoes, which were the most powerful weapons known to the Conglomerated States' Naval fleet, and could have easily destroyed similarly sized spaceships a hundred times over, had absolutely no discernable effect. The robots, or droids, or whatever the heck they were, simply stepped right through them. As one, they turned to face the Townsend weapons charging up. "Whoops," Taggart said. It was his last word.

*****

One thousand light years away, a white dwarf star silently burned. Around the star, five planets slipped through space following their paths with dogged determination. This solar system, long since abandoned by its original inhabitants was largely lifeless; the primary reason why it had been chosen.

The Reliant's scanners had been accurate, to a point. Specifically, one hundred and five billion, two hundred sixty-two million, six hundred fifty thousand four hundred and nine of the most powerful battle droids ever created, near exact duplicates to the ones that had destroyed the Reliant and Townsend, hung in the sky silently waiting a signal. Powered down, they floated aimlessly and without purpose. On each, a single yellow light blinked keeping the time and waiting patiently. Waiting patiently for…

….the signal.

As one, they silently powered up and began systems checks. Arms with joints flexed and turned in a full range of motion. Weapons targeted imaginary enemies and powered up. Shield generators cycled up and down.

In a matter of moments they turned and faced toward a single point in the heavens. Engines powered, and they were gone.

*****

"Huh." Boyd peered at his spectrograph screen again, tapping it lightly with one thick finger. Momentarily, just a brief moment mind you, he'd seen a mass the size of… well it boggled the mind… flit into existence. He blinked, and the mass was gone.

Boyd looked left and right. Nobody else had noticed it. They were all staring glassy-eyed into their screens like he'd been doing for the last twenty years and up until a moment ago.

It was probably a mistake – the damn thing had been buggy the last few days. He'd heard rumors that spectrographic stations all along the line had been reporting just the same thing. It was his opinion, and he'd voiced it numerous times (at night, in the pub, to the bartender), that the whole damn' system should be scrapped, especially this far from the Red line, where nothing happened to nobody.

"Did ja say somethin', Boyd?" His boss slithered up, wheezing. He was an asshole; so keen on himself. Not here a month and already bucking for promotion. This wasn't a dead end job for him. No sire, he'd probably be gone in six months, off to some other exciting locale, and away from this ass-end place. But not Boyd. He'd probably retire in this very chair, or maybe die in it from old age, watching this very screen, wishing for faeries, just to pass the time. Ah, it was probably a mistake. Not worth the paperwork.

"Nothing boss," Boyd said. "Nothing at all."

Chapter 33: Truth Revealed

Exactly seven days after the call had gone out, the central auditorium on the planet Monidad was filled with Protectors. Or nearly so, Trance realized after a closer look there were still hundreds of empty seats. The empties were spread out throughout the seating area, making it difficult to tell, but there definitely seemed like there could have been a lot more filled. His ring informed him that every Protector was there, though: ten thousand in total.

He was sitting next to Aura, and Dexter. Kameko sat on the other side of Aura. She had been distant the past few days, since returning from Korondor. He hadn't been able to get any time with her alone; there were always tons of people around, and so he hadn't been able to ask her what she was going to tell him on that planet. Besides, it hardly seemed appropriate to bring it up, given all the sadness that had happened there.

Something seemed to be bugging her, but what was it? Was it something he had said or done? Just then, she looked at him, noticed he had been looking at her. She gave him a shy smile that warmed him. He looked away, ears burning, pretending he hadn't noticed. She was so complicated, so mysterious.

The auditorium had an ancient feel about it. The entire room had been carved out of rock, probably at the same time Monidad had been. It was small and intimate, comparative with the baseball and football fields Trance had seen back home. In fact, this was the first room he had been in that wasn't bigger or better or gaudier than ones on Earth. Then again, he amended, it was the oldest room he had ever been in.

In the center of the room was a stage with twelve chairs set into the back half of the surface. Eleven of the seats were occupied, but Trance couldn't see who filled them. The entire platform was shrouded in gloom except for a podium set in the center, which was bathed with light.

Around the stage in a crescent formation was theater style seating set in fifty rows of two hundred. A majority of the seats were filled by humanoid-type Protectors, though of course most of them did not resemble anything Trance had ever seen. Some had more than two arms; a couple had three or more heads. He noted other shapes: one Protector looked exactly like a cardboard box replete with military style lettering in a language he did not recognize; another was paper-thin, a torso with appendages seeming to float just slightly above it. His ring told him there was even a Protector the size of a microbe in the audience. One Protector looked to consist of only fire.

Each seat seemed to have magically changed to fit the unique biological and physical requirements of each member. Here and there globes had sprung up filled with atmosphere suitable to supporting each life form.

The larger Protectors sat in back. One, a female of the same size and shape of a small mountain, anchored the very last row. She was the most amazing sight in the room; she appeared to have her own weather patterns. Currently it was snowing at her peak. Flakes the size of dinner plates dusted the seats on either side of her. The Protectors in them didn't seem to mind—they were talking animatedly with her and with each other.

Down at the stage something was happening. One Creator had stepped forward. It was Nelor, the Council's historian. He looked as serious as his station required. "Greetings to all," he said. Ten thousand voices called softly back in greeting. "I wish I were not standing here before you today," he said with regret. "But I must tell you of a terrible lie that has been perpetrated on you all. Our forefathers bore upon their shoulders a terrible shame that must now, in our time of need, be revealed."

"What?" a Protector in back scoffed, "impossible!"

"Not nearly," Creator Nelor sighed. A wave of silence filled the auditorium, as his words sank in. Then pandemonium followed in its wake as nearly ten thousand voices spoke at once in confusion.

"Silence!" Fester, a silver dragon from the planet B'tahi, called out. "Let us hear what Creator Nelor has to say!"

Creator Nelor hung his head for a moment in silence. When he looked up at last, he began to speak and his words filled Trance with dread, for he knew them to be true.

"I stand here today, frankly, against my wishes. This lie, though a regretful one, has served my people well. It has protected us and our name since its inception so long ago. It is weaved into a story you are all familiar with, the story of the great and terrible rebellion." Muttering rippled through the crowd in waves again.   "You see, the version of the Rebellion that you have heard is not complete."

Yet another murmur reverberated around the room. This time it was quickly silenced. The Creator seemed not to notice. Nelor continued. "The Conglomerated States were newly formed, but relations between the races were tenuous at best, strained at worst. Our fathers and mothers knew that they were rich in resources, and everyone knew that the Union could be prosperous, given time.

"From outside came a new threat: pirate races who wanted to pluck the fruit of the Union and keep it for their own. A defense had to be created that was fast, flexible, and powerful enough to meet the pirates, and other outside and inside entities, head on and drive them back. The development of this defensive force was left to the Creators. We were successful, and the corps was born into a golden age; an age of Light.

"But then, a period of great darkness fell upon our great golden state. A traitor lurked among us; one who endeavored to tear asunder all we had made whole. He rallied support from among the rank and file, subverted some of the Protectors against those who had shaped them."

"A Rogue--" MasTho said, standing purposefully, his face rising from the gloom of his seat.

"Protector…" the multitude whispered as one.

"OK, that was eerie, and kind of weird," Trance thought to himself.

Nelor and MasTho looked at each other for a moment, and something passed between them. Nelor broke contact, and stepped back into the shadows surrounding the center rostrum. MasTho strode forward, his floor-length ropes whispering in the silence. He looked around the auditorium, his clear gray eyes piercing into each of them at once.   And then he spoke.

"Not a Protector, but one of us. Your so-called Creators." A shudder passed through the crowd like a wave. "A foul and twisted beast named Nesger, who believed that the 'lesser' races should be ruled over with an iron fist rather than be allowed equal membership in the Conglomerated States. He believed the rings were a powerful weapon to be used to subject and enslave the other sentient planets rather than to protect them and nurture them as they evolved. He was verbose in his expositions, speaking at length before the council, demanding they see his way. The council disagreed.

'Stymied, he appealed to the individual Protectors directly, making promises of leadership positions in his new regime when he took over. He found many who believed as he did, and many more who were willing to follow for a price.

"When Nesger was unmasked as the dark entity behind the foul rebellion, our forefathers wept." He brought a fist into the air and began pacing back and forth across the stage. "That one of their own could be involved with so evil an enterprise was unfathomable to them, and unacceptable. In order to prevent a repeat of this tragic, and frankly embarrassing, event they swore our race would never again wield the power or create new rings to harness it. When Creator rings became available, they were locked away. When all were safely hidden, the blueprints were destroyed."

MasTho's eyes swept across the expanse of the crowd again, challenging them all with his strength before he spoke again. And when he did, he told them the true story of the Battle of Sector Brandenburg and Nesger's defeat on the Moon of Korondor, of Si-Truc's sacrifice, and the cover-up that followed. He also told them of Taa'lien's defection, and that the Council suspected that she was part of some new rebellion. In the end, he challenged them to find Taa'lien so that she might face justice for her crimes. It was a moving story, and filled them with resolve.

Unfortunately, though, Taa'lien would find them first.

As the last of MasTho's words reverberated inside the auditorium, a new sound they had never heard on Monidad began filling the air: the wild keening of klaxons. Additionally, at the same moment, the floor shook just slightly with a deep rumble and the lights dimmed momentarily.

Trance looked to the stage to see if these events were part of the show, but they evidently were not because the stage was now empty. In the brief moment he had been looking at the ceiling lights, the Creators had vanished.

Suddenly, the ring spoke to him in another's voice. "Protectors," it said, "We are about to be under attack. Do not panic. Please proceed carefully and calmly to the nearest exit and then to the central spire." All around him, Protectors were rising. Evidently, they had heard the same voice.

Outside in the hall, Trance could see that the normal lights had been replaced by red ones. A mechanical voice was saying in a very Star Trek like tone, "Red Alert. This is a Red Alert. Please report to the nearest emergency exit pod. This is not a drill."

The ring spoke in his mind again in the same dry and detached voice as Trance followed his compatriots toward the nearest transport tubes. "Protectors," it said, "the shield generators have been compromised by terrorist bombs. A large mass of attack vehicles is entering this system. Please hurry."

He began running like many of the others. Ahead of him, the hall ended in a T. Some of the group turned left, and others turned right. Because this floor had been designed as a grid he knew there were many ways to get to The Tubes. He turned right, easing into a fluid and easy jog that allowed him to increase speed and maintain it. Here and there Protectors faded away as they used their rings as miniature site-to-site transporters. They disappeared with pops of blue and white light.

Ahead of him, he could see the doors leading to The Tubes. A steady stream of Protectors was pouring through them.

The tubes in this area were part of the main artery that moved goods and products through and around Monidad. The Creators had purposefully situated the central auditorium near this artery to allow for ease of getting large numbers of people to important meetings.

The Tubes was a room aptly named. The space was cavernous large, and square. It contained perhaps fifty doors, each leading to a different hallway. The centerpiece was a section of several hundred grey-colored cylinders stretching from floor to ceiling: the transport tubes.

Each tube bore a dark silver ring about fifteen feet up its steely grey exterior. When a lift arrived, fifteen feet of the cylinder rose up to this ring revealing a bluish rug-like disk beneath. Each time a disk was revealed, Protectors poured onto its surface. The cylinder closed, and then opened again, revealing another disk, a twin to the first. More Protectors jumped on, and the cycle began again.

Trance didn't have to wait long. Soon he had entered one of the tubes with nearly a hundred other Protectors. It was a tight fit, but there were no complaints. Everyone was nervous about the upcoming battle, but confident the corps would be triumphant. He watched as the walls slid down around them, closing off their view of The Tubes. Then a slight shaking began, and there was a hum as the disk they were on slid up the cylinder and toward a destination unknown.

Trance took the ride in silence. Miles and miles of tube passed before his eyes. At one point, the wall seemed to slip away diagonally, and then back the other way. He squashed the urge to feel the wall with his hand, fearing that it might be ripped off in the process.

The silver dragon Fester stood next to him, her lithe tail wrapped around his leg. She was looking at him in a friendly manner. "Nice day for a battle," she said conversationally. He nodded.

"Boy, whoever it is that's coming for dinner sure did pick the wrong night," someone beside him said jovially. Trance turned to see that it was a large hairy yellow gorilla with four arms. "Of course how were they to know all the Protectors would be here for a meeting?" the gorilla asked rhetorically. "They're probably coming here expecting a light fighting force." He laughed.

"Still, aren't you just a little worried about the shield generators?" Fester asked pointedly.

"Huh?" the Gorilla said, a confused look in his eye. He scratched his rear end and scowled.

Fester sighed. "I mean because it sounds like there was a little bit of planning involved here. What are the chances? The shield generators just happen to blow out just when a huge attack fleet is arriving? I doubt it. And when do you think those bombs were planted? What if there are more? This isn't a friendly neighborly visit here-- they're not waltzing over here with milk and cookies just to see what we're up to."

"Maybe they are," the gorilla grunted. "It's probably just a random series of events connected together by time. Everything is possible, you know." He turned to Trance. "What kind of cookies do ya think that they have?" Trance sighed.

Fester and the gorilla bickered for the remainder of the trip, which wasn't long. Eventually, the disk stopped humming, the walls slowed and then stopped, and the elevator's face slid open revealing a large square room. Nine other cylinders exited into this room as well. Ahead of them just a short distance away they could see that one of the four walls had risen partially into the ceiling revealing the vast expanse of the hangar of the Great Spire, where he, Dexter, Mollie, and Aura had arrived in just a few short days before. Left and right and all around them ships filled with non-combatants were exploding off the tarmac and racing up toward the exit in the ceiling. Trance knew that all around the planet cavernous hangars like this one were disgorging ships into space. Monidad would be empty in a matter of hours.

He jogged forward into the hangar and then willed himself upward with the others, dodging ship and co-Protector alike as he flew toward the exit, hanging like a black moon in the sky.

The din was incredible—the tiny whines of the system ships and the deeper growls of spacers combined in a symphony of noise. He tuned it out as best he could, concentrating instead on making it out from the bowels of the planet in one piece.

And then he was in the Great Spire, the delicate latticework of silver and steel. It looked far more delicate to him then, far more beautiful than words could describe. Level upon level flashed before his eyes as he sped upward, marking time with the beat of his heart. And then he was through, into the atmosphere. Many were waiting there. Many more were on their way. And the invaders were....

They were nowhere to be seen.

"Well this is a bit anticlimactic," someone sniffed looking around for something to pummel.

"Yeah, what a joke," another said, a little winded from the race into the sky.

"You mean the severe lack of invaders? Ooooh, I'm quaking! Look at me; I'm really shaking from fear!"

"Wait a second," someone else said in that type of tone that instantly freezes the blood, "where'd the stars go?" Then it hit them. There were no stars. Everywhere they looked, the darkness boiled.

"Form a shield around the planet!" Fester screamed. And that's when the nightmare began.

*****

"They will not last long." Creator Ry-Ma said thoughtfully as the tight group walked down the stone hallway toward a single gray wooden door.

"Perhaps," MasTho responded. "Perhaps."

"A plan must be formulated," Creator Shranelle murmured. "This will take some thought." MasTho opened the door and they all stepped in. The door closed tightly behind them, and silence shrouded the hall once more.

Chapter 33: Last Stands

The shield was up, a patchwork quilt of a thing looking thin and tenuous at best. It was ugly and misshapen with lumps and crevices along its surface. Outside, pushing against it were billions upon billions of the largest battle droids he had ever seen. His ring told him that there were at least a hundred billion; one hundred billion against a corps of ten thousand.

It had only taken a minute, to put it together, but in that time they had already lost at least twenty Protectors. One of them had been the individual who had reminded Trance of a mountain. She had been floating within a hundred yards of Trance when she died… the result of well-aimed missiles impacting her large form just seconds before the shielding in her section materialized.

Several other casualties Trance had suspected were friendly fire deaths. People were shooting their rings off in fear and haste, trying to protect the planet, taking the time to create real bombs and missiles, but shooting them in haste. He wondered who would be along to protect the Protectors from themselves. He grimaced and aimed carefully before firing off a shot. This was going to be interesting.

At least Aura looked like he was having fun. The Golden Protector was up at the edge of the shield, swinging that tremendous energy sword he wielded during confrontations. The blade was said to be sharper than any ever constructed, with an edge a single cell thick. It certainly knew how to damage things – the damn thing cut through everything it touched like a hot knife through butter. Aura looked something like a Ginsu chef from back home; a hot knife slinging back and forth with diced robot flipping this way and that. Trance laughed in spite of himself.

Dexter, who was by his side, grunted. "He sure does enjoy his work," he said sagely as he created a laser gun and shot it at the mass of robots. Three of them imploded showering others with molten metal. Four more robots moved instantly into the space vacated by the three, firing rockets and pushing against the outer edge of the shield with all their might. The strain was incredible.

Kameko was somewhere around them. At least he thought she was. He hoped she was OK.

*****

The room held a table and twelve chairs. Eleven of them were filled. The empty seat had fallen into a state of disrepair. It had a thick layer of dust. From his seat at the head of the table, MasTho surveyed the room. He tapped a finger on the tabletop angrily. Outside the planet's atmosphere, his Protectors were fighting gallantly and dying. And here, around this room, his fellow Creators were debating him to death. He hated bureaucracies.

Creators weren't known for quick action. Their lives were so long it was hard to think in terms of hours or minutes or days. MasTho kept the frustration from showing on his face, and tried to pay attention to the proceedings.

Even now, Nelor was droning on in his interminable way, talking about history, and their place within it. He was the historian of the group, and liked to show he had a firm grasp on the stuff. Unfortunately, he wasn't as good with current events. If this was going to continue on much longer, MasTho thought again for the thousandth time, he was going to have to step in.

*****

Trance could hardly believe the reports were true. They had lost over a thousand Protectors. It hardly seemed real. At first, he had been excited to be in the thick of battle, armed with the comfort that his side was the most powerful and therefore would be victorious. The first waves of droids had been easy, further cementing this feeling of superiority. The drones had been butter beneath the hot knife of the ring power he and his comrades were slinging. But when those droids had fallen, they were replaced again and again and again in an unrelenting river of metal and fire power. They must have destroyed easily a couple of million of the damn things, but he still couldn't see the stars, and that worried him.

The unrelenting onslaught of battle-droids had left him bone tired. But he would not permit himself to feel the pain that soaked into his mind and muscles.

*****

MasTho leapt from his seat and slammed his fist into the table like a hammer. "The time for debate has passed," he growled. "We cannot let this false Protector sour the name of our kind and our mission any longer. It is time to act." His eyes traveled to a tile mosaic on one of the walls, and then back to his captive audience. Fear now showed upon their faces as they realized his intent. This only made his resolution stronger.

"We must set aside another of our forefathers' oaths in the name of defense," he continued, glancing again at the mosaic, which bore a colorful tiled diorama of a field of long-extinct flowers growing on a long-dead world. "All we hold to be sacred is threatened." His fist slammed down upon the tabletop again, a thunderous clap, his eyes burning with quiet determination and a heat that warmed them all. "The Conglomerated States face a crisis so great and tumultuous it will shake the Union to its very core and perhaps destroy it utterly. We cannot stand idly by in the shadows any longer. We must act or watch as everything that our race has strived for is turned to dust."

The group nodded slowly, sober faces creased in thought as they pondered the import of what MasTho had uttered. Only two possible paths could be seen: action or inaction and both were paths shrouded in a murky land indeed. After a brief interval, Shra-nelle spoke. "Let us vote," she said.

Another time passed. Though no words were spoken, a dull buzz could be heard just on the edge of perception, like a half-remembered thought or a word left hanging in the air. At last, MasTho stood and nodded. "The council has spoken," he grunted, pleased. His robes whispered softly as he walked over to the mosaic. Carefully, using secret instructions passed down from leader to leader over the millions of years, he tapped a series of tiles in specific order. The others waited silently.

As MasTho's delicate fingers passed over each tile, a musical sound could be heard; a single tortured note. The song he played was one of sadness and regret, but beautiful nonetheless. When it was complete, he took a step back and waited.

Momentarily, a straight and narrow fissure of blue energy split the mosaic down the middle. Though the wall did not move, the fissure grew in width until it was wide enough for a single person to step through. MasTho did and the council rose and followed, their lips pursed. When the last of them had passed, the blue light faded, revealing the tiled mosaic again.

Chapter 34: The End of the Road

The fighting had gone on for days. The exhausted group had destroyed countless drones, but yet the raging river of robots had not been stemmed. Scarcely seven thousand Protectors remained now. All around them space broiled with an undulating mass of metal, motion, and laser fire as the battle droids vied to get past the barrier the rings had erected. Here and there, where the ragged field was the thinnest, things were getting through and hurting and even killing his comrades.

Trance sighed, looking for a chink in the armor of the onslaught, and then nearly lost his head as a blade the size of a dinner plate came whirring out of the confusion. Reflexively, he twisted hard to the left and down, and was rewarded with a white-hot searing scream of pain as the blade grazed his backside as it whirled off into the darkness.

The pain revived him, temporarily wiping away the tendrils of despair. Yes, the scratch hurt like a son of a bitch, but he lived. He used the ring to create a compress to stop the flow of blood that had immediately begun and between teeth gritted in pain swore he would not be defeated.

A few feet away Aura, his sword arm hanging uselessly in a tangled mass of gore and bone, smiled at Trance cautiously before returning his attention to holding up his section of the shield they had created. Trance grimaced and created a battering ram edged with diamond-sharp swords and fired it into the writhing mass before him. It slammed into a section of drones splitting dozens like overripe melons. He followed the ram with a Mack Truck and a steamroller, each doing their own brand of damage.

The other Protectors were also hard at work. Energy driven shells the size of double-decker busses impacted and burst, blossoming with all the colors of the rainbow. Constructs of every imaginable size and shape sliced into the onrushing droids, wiping out whole divisions. Impossibly, a mushroom cloud from some sort of pseudo-nuclear reaction formed hundreds of miles away turning everything it touched into slag. But nothing they threw at the attackers seemed to lessen the constant flow. Ten droids replaced every one that fell. And here and there the paper-thin energy shield that was their last hope began to buckle and crack....

And then it happened. An object came rocketing through the force field as if the barrier was wet tissue paper. It landed in their midst even as the edges of the tear undulated and constricted like a rubber band stretched beyond its breaking point. The simultaneous thunderclap of the shield's collapse and the intrusion of the invader tore the group end from end scattering the Protectors. Trying desperately to get his bearings, Trance turned to face the intruder and saw out of the corner of his eyes that the droids, finally unhindered by the field, were also coming for them, a tidal wave of metal crushing everything in its path. "We are so toast," the ring muttered bleakly.

*****

The small group of Creators followed a long hallway carved out of rock that had not been used for millions of years but bore no signs of age or decay. On either side, flameless torches glowed softly providing more than enough illumination to see by. As they progressed torches on either side of the path sprang to life, while the ones behind the group faded slowly, providing a tiny moving bubble of light in the otherwise utter darkness.

At the terminus of the hallway lay a large cave with smooth light brown walls and a crème colored floor. In the center of the room a dais grew out of the rocky floor. Resting upon the surface, about waist high to the Creators, was a box of such antiquity it made the ancient cave seem young in comparison. MasTho respectfully approached the dais, and opened the box.

Within, on a tapestry of soft velvet, were twelve rings. Each, save one, glowed with power as if waiting to be worn. Each bore the name of one of the original Creators. The twelfth glinted dully in the light, standing out from the bright silver like a cancer hidden among healthy flesh; a burned out shell of a ring. Etched into its cracked and tarnished surface a single word could be seen: "Nesger."

*****

Time seemed to slow and then stop. Before Trance was a being he thought that he'd never see, most especially not now, not at this time. The face before him he could never forget. It was Anda, the terrorist his group had captured back at Legs, the bar. And in that same frozen instant, he noticed a blue nimbus of light surrounding her. How the hell did she escape again? How the hell did she get a ring?

Then everything around him was moving too rapidly, and he was the one frozen. His limbs wouldn't respond fast enough to block the blow he knew was coming from the blade in her hand. It arced toward his head. This was it. He had few regrets. He had done his best. His eyes opened wider so that he could see death fully in the face when it came for him.

But the blow never reached him. Too late, he realized he had been pushed aside just as the sword finished its deadly arc. Kameko had managed to save him, but had not the time to save herself. She had selflessly taken the blade meant for him. She sighed once as the razor edge slipped into her, globules of her blood tumbling free in the weightlessness of space.

Anad was already trying to free her blade of Kameko, but somehow the Protector managed to hold on in the seconds that it took for Trance to recover his wits. She wore a half smile on her pale face, as she struggled with Anad. "You'll never take him," she whispered, "He's mine." And then she was gone. He bellowed incoherently, and reason left him.

Unbidden, a sword appeared in his hand. It was four feet long and blacker than space. It was cold. It was death. And he was its master. He swung it at Anad's head.

She raised her own blade to meet him, having freed it from Kameko's body. She screamed as her sword and arm shattered at the strength of his blow. He swung again and the top of her head sloughed off, spilling her brains into the air around her body. Anad would never harm anyone again.

Trance kicked Anad's corpse away, let go of the Night Sword, and held Kameko in his arms. Even in death she was more beautiful that he could imagine. He wished that he had the time to tell her that. He wished he had more time.

He looked up in his grief and realized he had more work to do. The robots were still coming through the massive hole in the shield. The Protectors who remained were putting up a great fight, but they were losing the battle. They were dying in droves now, falling like shafts of wheat before the scythe.

He kissed Kameko once, on the forehead, and grabbed the hilt of his sword, which had been floating there, waiting for him. The anger came with it, a fierce blaze of heat that warmed him against the cold of night. He snarled like a rabid animal.

In an instant he was at the front, where the shield had split. It was cracking further, becoming as insubstantial as mist as it faded away, and the droids were slipping through the aperture like a river. In less than a minute the shield would be gone. He saw it and realized that it wouldn't matter anyway. A minute is a lifetime to a man who has only seconds left. The final stand was now. The last hurrah.

The blade sang in his hands. He closed his eyes, and swung with all his might.

Chapter 35: Shadow revealed

The force of the first blow shredded the droid in front of him; the energy cascading from the Night Sword blew out ten more behind it. Trance grunted, and swung again and again. He was indeed a caged animal now – all around him droids clicked and whirred as they tried to etch away at his personal shield. All he could see was metal. They were pulling layers of it away like an onion, faster than he could add them from within.

The momentary boost that the rage had given him was gone, now, replaced by mind numbing weariness. He wondered briefly how many Protectors had perished simply because they gave up. The thought scared him. He didn't want to die here, alone, amongst all the metal. He called to Aura, seeking solace. His call was met with static.

They were ever closer, now. Just a few centimeters remained of his shield. He could hear the calls of other Protectors in action. Here and there, a scream, mercifully short. The whirring and clicking was driving him insane. It seemed to rattle his teeth in their sockets.

And then suddenly, there was silence.

It came crashing down upon him like a Tsunami. For a moment he could hardly believe he was hearing it… hearing nothing.

The droids all around him were waiting; listening to something calling them. The hundred or so that he could see looked nearly human as they cocked their heads, antenna seeking a signal only they could hear.

Then, en masse, they turned, their objective forgotten. The river of metal flowed away from him and he could see again. He could see for miles. And what he saw saddened him.

Just a few feet away hung the torn and lifeless body of Aura. He turned, holding back the tears. Nearby, other Protectors were looking around as if in shock. The dead were all around and perhaps the living wondered what had kept them from joining their departed comrades.

Below him lay the scarred planet Monidad. The bots had done quite a bit of damage, but it looked as though the spire still stood. It could be repaired. His gaze shifted again toward the sky. And then he saw where the droids were heading.

Easily a thousand miles away he could see a massive blue glowing sphere. Energy streams were arcing out of it and slamming back with tremendous force.

The droids were flowing toward the sphere, firing all their weapons wildly as they attempted to surround it. The effect was much like the stately dance of a spiral galaxy. But Trance knew it was much different. Even now, a battle was being waged. And that meant his help was needed, still.

His mind protested. His aching muscles screamed in defiance. But he knew what he had to do. He rocketed toward the new galaxy, calling the others to follow him, to join the battle once more. They heeded him though he knew they hung on the ragged edge of exhaustion. They were heroes. He wished he knew them all by name.

They started picking off stragglers first, droids that because of damage could not travel as fast as their brethren. The robots were easy pickings now, focused as they were on whatever lay in the center of the tremendous blue energy field. There were billions yet to conquer, but each one destroyed made the task that much easier.

Very quickly, the Protectors made it to the swollen center. Here, Trance could see the robots were affecting tremendous damage on the sphere, but it was holding. Then he realized the energy streams pouring out of the sphere by the second were not random in nature.

Here came a stream now. It shot out of the sphere like a whip, blew through easily ten miles of droids melting them into slag, and slipped right back into the sphere like a triumphant general returning home.

The center was so bright he could hardly look upon it, and it was spinning so fast it seemed to exert its own gravity. He hung about it momentarily unnoticed, trying to make out what lay within.

At the very center was a single silhouette. Three more shapes surrounded it as if protecting it. A fifth appeared to be hanging lifeless. They were facing seven other silhouettes, on all sides, and exchanging ring fire with fierce determination. Four more shapes appeared to be on the outside of this battle, maintaining the sphere and killing the bots.

He guessed the outside group was on his side. They were destroying the droids, after all. But he was afraid to help them directly. What if he accidentally unbalanced the delicate standoff within allowing the wrong side to win? It was best to concentrate on destroying the bots from the outside, and toiling alone just wouldn't work. They needed to act as a team.

He called the other Protectors once more. It was time to clean house. Dexter was the first to return his call: the cat sounded feisty and ready to go. Together they linked their rings, sending a charge cascading between the two. Then they showed the other Protectors the same trick, forming a massive electrically charged net; just over three thousand points of power strong. They were going fishing.

It was easier said than done. The hardest part was getting the other Protectors to face the same way. Then they had to regulate the field so that the same current flowed throughout the three thousand rings. Trance knew that as little as little as .006 amps could kill a person, so he chose 120 amps. He hoped it would be enough to disrupt the delicate inner workings of the droids.

In a matter of moments, he could see the net from his point in the center. It was a mile wide and a mile tall, and twinkled here and there as charges coursed across its surface and danced along its twines. The Protectors were shielded nicely by their rings from the deadly energies they wielded; he called to them and each responded an affirmation of readiness.

They made a single pass through the robot field at a slow and leisurely pace. He was amazed the droids didn't put up a fight. They just shuddered and convulsed as they died, their tiny brains too intent on the sphere of energy and the combatants within.

They allowed the net to vaporize at the end of their journey, and turned to see what destruction they had wrought. Hundreds of thousands of droids had been incapacitated. Several billion remained. The sphere was still crackling with energy. Trance wondered if the combatants inside had noticed their work.

The second trip ended successfully as well with millions more debilitated. Trance sent his group again and again until there were no more droids to net, and only the sphere remained. Then they set about destroying the few their sweeps had missed. It took hours, but they didn't mind the time. Trance felt a charge out of seeing his team work together. Perhaps there was hope for the corps after all.

Finally, they found themselves back at the sphere. It was no longer cascading energy now; perhaps the ring bearers within had noticed the droids were inactive.

And then, the sphere simply ceased to exist. It didn't even give a guilty pop, didn't fade away slowly; one moment it was there, the next it was gone. And what it revealed warmed his heart. The victors were Creators.

A ragged cheer erupted from the three thousand who remained: Taa'lien had been captured and floated before them bound head and foot. But what a terrible price: so many Protectors had fallen in the battle. And one Creator had been lost: MasTho, long the leader of the council. He had been pierced some time during the fight within the sphere, and had died instantly. If Trance looked closely, he might have seen something peculiar. Had he known anything about wounds, he might have realized the blow had come from behind.

Ten Creators remained of the eleven. The four beings Trance had seen surrounding Taa'lien had been criminals who been given stolen rings. They were dead. Shra-nelle seemed to be the defacto leader now that MasTho was gone. The council would have to choose a new head, and a new member from amongst their race.

MasTho's face had a gentle serenity about it. Someone had closed his eyes, and now he seemed at peace. Shra-nelle floated quietly over to him, and gently covered his body with a blanket she had created, and then wrapped it tightly around his form with a tie. "He will be missed," she said. "He was a good leader, and a good friend." She looked to the corps members. "And now, we must talk, Taa'lien."

Taa'lien sneered. "I think you are mistaken," she said.

"How so, Protector?"

"Oh of many things," she said. "Many things indeed."

"We shall see about that," Creator Do-ied said.

"Don't you want to see who has plagued you all this time?" asked Taa'lien.

"What do you mean?" asked Shra-nelle. "You stand before us defeated. Are there others?"

"Don't you want to see who I really am?" Her manacled hands slowly moved to her scarred and broken face. They pulled gently, and the features hardened and then cracked, splitting along the fault lines. The face came off easily. Her arms came down revealing for the first time the visage underneath.

Trance couldn't believe it. Beneath the ravaged features of Taa'lien was another face; a cold and cruel sneer he recognized instantly as the one he had seen on Korondor's moon. It was Nesger; the true rogue, a Creator, and he was very much alive.

Taa'lien / Nesger rolled the face in a ball and tossed it forward spinning. "Now you will see!" he screamed a cackle that chilled Trance to the bone. But there was something else going on here. Trance realized too late was it really was. "Look out!" he bellowed, trying to shield himself.

There was a tremendous flash as the face exploded. They were all caught off guard by the sudden revelation beneath the mask, and weren't prepared by what had occurred next.

When their eyes cleared, they realized Taa'lien was gone, the chains binding her now floating free. She had thought of everything, effecting an escape just when they thought they had her.

They scanned for her, of course, but she was gone. Trance knew she would be back. This was far, far from over.

Chapter 36: Checkmate

"We were butchered," Trance groaned. "I thought we were supposed to be the cream of the Galaxy. What happened?"

It had taken them five hours to clean up the dead Protectors, and move the refuse of over a hundred billion droids. Normally the bodies would have been placed in viewing rooms near each squad headquarters, but there were so many bodies they had filled a large portion of the Battle room with floating briers. After that, Trance had made his way to the core to talk with Dymin. He wanted answers.

Dymin had been sitting in his office, apparently lost in thought, looking at the ring on his finger and muttering to himself. He seemed distracted by something during this meeting. Trance knew the stories… that Dymin was quick to anger and that he hated the squads that he looked over, but with the death of MasTho, he was the only Creator Trance actually knew. He was the only one who might be able to provide him the answers to the questions Trance needed to ask.

He looked up again at Trance's query. "What did you say?" the Creator asked.

"I said, what happened?"

"We were outnumbered ten million five hundred twenty-six thousand two hundred sixty-five to one to start with then—"

"Shut up ring."

"Well you asked," the ring replied sulkily.

"That's not what I…. Never mind." He thought for a moment. "I think that we stumbled upon a nasty little secret, Creator Dymin," Trance said to the Creator.

"How so?" the Creator sneered.

"The corps was designed to be a free-range police force; flexible and thinly spread, right?"

"Yes." The Creator stood, and walked around the desk, arms crossed.

"Lone Protectors fighting to stem the tide of chaos…" Trance let the word trail out into nothingness.

"Yes. So?"

"So, the greatest strength becomes the greatest weakness."

"Hmm."

"Look at the hall of statues, for example," Trance continued undeterred.

"I can't see them from here."

"It's a metaphor! Don't distract me. All of the statues in the hall honor individual Protectors who happened to do something extraordinary."

"Yes."

"On their own. And the Battle Dome: individuals striving against individuals. There aren't any team sports here, are there?"

"No. There never have been," he admitted.

"Your whole society values the single Protector over the corps as a whole. All of those Protectors were honored as individuals, not for anything they did as a group. Except for the lone exception of Elle'inad, there has never been cohesion in the corps. In fact, there is no corps... just a bunch of individuals striving on their own to get the job done."

"You are perceptive... for a human." Creator Dymin started to turn away.

Trance grabbed him around the arm and spun him around. "I'm not finished!" he yelled, ignoring the brief flash of anger in the Creator's eyes. "I want to know why!"

Dymin shook his hand free with his arm. "You fool," he said heatedly, "you can see so much but can't see this?

'Do you know how many galaxies there are in the Universe? No? There are over two trillion. Your own puny 'Milky Way' has one hundred billion stars in it, alone. Do the math, human. Ten thousand Protectors can't possibly guard two trillion galaxies. It's too much space. Too much empty space."

"What does that have to do with anything?"

"Do I have to walk you through everything? We have to choose members who enjoy the solitude. Space is lonely, and vast, and the Protectors who last the longest are the ones who are able to endure the emptiness. Unfortunately, that doesn't lead to a corps that can play well on a team."

"The greatest strength becomes the greatest weakness," Trance repeated. "Hmmm."

"We were meant to find Taa'lien's arm. Nesger knew only a threat as dire as the one we faced would cause you to pull the corps in," Trance responded softly. "He knew if he got us all together we'd spend most of our energy slitting our own throats. In the end, though we won this battle, I think that we lost the war."

"No, the war is over," Dymin responded steely, "but we were the winners." He ticked the points off on his fingers. "We all but destroyed the droid army, found the saboteur, the renegade, and sent him running. What more is there but the mop up?"

Trance ticked his own fingers off as he replied. "We lost nearly seven thousand Protectors. Our forces are demoralized, and broken. The other planets in the system were destroyed. Monidad has little to no defensive system, and

Nesger is still out there, probably planning his next offensive! How can you possibly say all that is left is a little clean up?"

The Creator glared at him and then, rather pointedly, the door. "Is that all?"

"No. I want to know something else. I think the corps was doomed regardless of Nesger."

"You're right, of course," Dymin admitted grudgingly. "Again, the lack of cohesion. The corps would have disappeared, though not in your lifetime, or even your grandchildren's lifetime. Nesger's actions only hastened that decline. Now," he shrugged, "You may be the last generation."

"You act like you don't care!" Trance shouted.

"Why should I? With this ring, I may live forever. I have plenty of time to worry about insignificant little pesks like you."

"Aura knew the right path even if it was too little too late. He forced Dexter and I to work together as a team from the start, and that's what caused us to survive, not this fancy ring I wear, and certainly not you Creators rushing in to save the day."

Trance turned, his anger spent, and walked to the door. Before going through however, he looked back one more time at the Creator who was staring morosely into the depths of his own ring. "Maybe next we'll try robots," Dymin grunted half to himself.

"Maybe," Trance said, "if your people had done the right thing from the beginning we wouldn't be having this conversation right now." With that, he left.

He spent the rest of the day in solitude, mourning the death of his friends Aura and Kameko. More than all of his other companions, the Golden Protector had been a rock of strength for Trance, upon which he felt that he could rely. He could hardly believe the Orian was gone.

And Kameko... what had she been to him? He regretted that he had never gotten the courage to find out. He could see her still when he closed his eyes, seated next to Aura in the stadium, leaning forward to catch his gaze. Her hazel eyes twinkled, her perfect lips twitched into a smile as she faded away. He now realized she had been the most beautiful creature he had ever seen. When he looked into her eyes, it was easy to believe anything was possible. He missed her; longed to see that smile once more. The ache threatened to overwhelm him.

Why had she thrown her own life away for his? Why not use a construct? He must have asked such questions a thousand times. There just wasn't time. Like the firefighter he had met once, she did what she felt she had to do at the time. But this time there was no parade for the hero. There was only an empty ache inside.

Eventually, he mustered the strength to go back to his room. There, he fell into a deep and dreamless sleep almost immediately.

In the morning he awoke less than refreshed. In fact, he felt worse. A shower helped, but it wasn't until he was drying himself off afterward that he realized one of the reasons that he felt so poorly was because he hadn't eaten in nearly twenty-four hours. His stomach seemed to recognize this fact almost the same time his mind did, for it emitted a large and ominous growl. "Alright, alright," he said moodily and quickly dressed and made his way to his section's cafeteria.

The cafeteria was completely bright, sterile, and empty. All of the non-essential personnel had been moved out of the system prior to the droid attack, and the corps had been whittled down to a skeleton crew of just over three thousand in the battle. His shoes echoed dimly across the polished surface of the floor as he walked past row after row of benches and tables. After grabbing a tray of something reported to be edible from the auto-dispenser, he sat down, lost in his thoughts, reliving the events of the past few days.

His reverie was broken by a voice. "Hey, Adams, can you pass the salt?" Trance looked up. It was Dexter. He had sat down in the seat opposite of Trance, and had a large tray of what appeared to be tuna fish.

"You've got thumbs, don't you?" Trance replied, more out of habit than any real sense of humor.

Dex grunted and looked at his paws. "Yeah," he said, "but they aren't good for much, to tell you the truth. They are good for holding the ladies, though." His words had a ring of formality – a dance traced out in steps worn deep from use.

Trance flipped Dexter the salt and pepper. "Two for one," he said.

They shared stories and jabs for a while, simply enjoying the quiet and the company. In that time Dexter had three portions of his tuna fish, and Trance managed to finish his own tray off. When they had finished eating, they cleaned off their places and walked together out into the hallway.

The hall outside was bright. Evidently the polishing droid had been by recently, because Trance could see his reflection in the black and white checkered floor. It looked haggard, his reflection. He'd lost some weight.

"So now what?" the cat asked, breaking him from his reverie.

"Now I am going to find Nesger and destroy him," Trance said simply, feeling his chin. It was bristly. "You're welcome to come along if you'd like."

"Yeah, that's what I was planning to do today too. Just give me time to pack my kitty litter box, and I'll be ready to go."

"I didn't know you brought one of those."

"Yeah, I usually do. The past couple of times I didn't 'cause I thought we were going on a short day trip. Boy, I won't make that mistake again, I tell you. Going in a sandbox the size of a small island like I did on the planet we trained on is excellent of course, but I wouldn't trade it for my own comfortable kitty-litter box."

"Maybe I better grab some stuff too," Trance smiled despite himself.

"It's just that I…" Dexter stopped. A concerned look splashed across his furry face.

"What?" Trance asked, echoing the look with his voice.

Suddenly Dexter convulsed and screamed as if in incredible pain, a high-pitched sound of pure agony that would forever haunt Trance's dreams. The cat staggered forward and raised his left paw, peering at his ring. The center gem was glowing brightly in a fierce cold blue; flickering as if it were ablaze. Dexter screamed again then choked as the ring belched and flames of pure icy blue shot up his arm and into his mouth.

Startled, Trance could only watch aghast as the cat's amber fur and pink skin liquefied and sloughed off in layers revealing the muscles and bone beneath.

In less than a second it was over. With a regretful sigh, Dexter's charred remains toppled over and began to smoke. The smell of burned meat quickly permeated the hall.

As the enormity of what had just happened hit him, Trance stepped backward, spun, and threw up everything in his stomach.

For a time, he sat in a daze near the corpse of his only remaining friend and comrade, staring dully at nothing in particular. Then, with distaste, he gathered the body in a web of energy and took it to the nearest transport tube.

*****

It didn't take long to discover everyone was dead, even the Creators. He found their corpses splayed around a single table in a private dining room in the depths of the core of Monidad. Eleven charred corpses and eleven burned out rings—they had been eating breakfast when it happened. He wondered if they had felt as much pain as he had seen Dexter experience. He hoped not.

He guessed the other Protectors had not been spared from whatever had killed Dex and the Creators. His ring wasn't able to find any other live rings broadcasting in the galaxy. He was alone. Now what the heck was he going to do?

Chapter 37: Across the Red Line

She'd probably never again feel clean, fresh and natural air cycling through her lungs; the kind of air that didn't taste just slightly like the inside of a can, or smell just slightly like wet socks. But what a trade-off; knowing she'd had some part in remaking a world.

The terra farmer knelt down next to the dozer, and let her gauntleted hand run down its faded red and blue corrugated metal side and into the loam beneath her knees. The dozer's clear and easy vibration told her it was functioning properly though she was no longer at the controls.

In the cool light of the morning sun, she could see the crystals of last night's freeze in amongst the grains of soil. They shone like tiny diamonds in her hand. She sighed and let the dirt fall through her fingers, then stood, wiping her hand upon her suit.

A quick glance to the rear of the dozer showed three shallow furrows a quarter mile long. Ahead, the land laid clear and barren, as it should be: no large rocks for miles. Someday, this area might hold a park or maybe even a forest. Not in her lifetime, though.

Who knew? Maybe there would be a park here with a statue dedicated to her. People would look at it and say, "The planet-shapers stood in this very spot." She laughed softly to herself at the thought. Even if people did remember her, they certainly wouldn't be putting up a statue in her image any time soon. Heck, there wouldn't be people out this far from the domes for centuries at least. She'd be long forgotten then. Best worry about today first. After it had passed, she could plan for tomorrow.

This evening in fact, if all went according to plan, she would look upon three rows, seven miles long, of evenly planted syntho-trees, the first step in a coordinated planet-wide effort to create an atmosphere.

Today, farms throughout the world were to spring up from the barren soil, each virtually identical to hers. Each three shallow furrows long. Each with hundreds of tiny syntho-trees. Each a small step in the journey of the planet-shapers.

The syntho-trees were pretty neat—she had seen them in action on other planets. They were a tightly bonded mixture of organic and man-made materials designed to transform certain gasses, chemicals, excess heat, and other byproducts from the domes (where too much of any one thing was a catastrophe waiting to happen), into atmosphere and eventually, breathable air.

A series of underground tubes and sub-filters led directly from the nearest dome, her home, well over five miles away, to the furrows behind her. Over the next couple of years, the syntho-trees, which did not need oxygen to grow, would create a root system just beneath the surface. This system would seek out the small stream of gasses that the colonists had allowed to be released from the dome. Eventually, when a clean connection had been made, the stream would be turned on full, and the atmosphere formation would begin. She started sweating just thinking about it.

Her breath whistled out of her nose and into the dual Hentatie filters before being routed back into her backpack's tank as she climbed up the dozer's short ladder and into the control cage. She hardly heard the filters purr as they recycled her air. On board and seated comfortably, she paused before moving the dozer forward toward destiny, and looked back toward the dome dreamily. She gasped.

Five bright lights had swung low over the dome. As they did, the dome seemed to shudder just slightly. The bright lights flew upwards at a sharp rate of ascent. Below her, the ground trembled as the dome shuddered again and then exploded outward. She screamed. The sky darkened as debris rained around her. Blind luck, or maybe providence kept her from being obliterated by the thousands of tons of debris that quickly fell out of the sky. She found herself covering her head and looking down, as if the instinctual move could have protected her from being crushed.

When she looked up the invaders were gone. So was her home; only a smoldering hulk remained. She doubted anyone remained alive in the structure, or even without. She'd been the only one scheduled out this early. But maybe, just maybe there was someone alive. She punched the communicator button. "Base, base, can you read me?" she called, her voice cracking under the stress. "Base, are you there?"

Nothing. She checked the other channels, making her request on each. She found the auto-distress beacon keening on channel three, but nothing else. Not good.

Normally, in the rare cases of a disaster, such as the fire in dome 1-A last year, one could hear the chatter of the other domes in this section; calls for assistance and assurances of help had filled the airwaves. But not this morning: today there was nothing: just the keening of a single auto-distress in the void.

Just then, the sky darkened again as a shadow fell across her like a blanket. She looked up to see the most incredible structure she had ever witnessed falling slowly and gracelessly to the ground. It was so enormous it blotted out fully a quarter of the sky. It looked like a massive children's toy; a top her nephew back home might have spun in his childhood.

The largest portion of it was shaped like a goblet. About a fifth of the way down the goblet's face tubular arms jutted out from the body. They were segmented in the middle, and the bottom half of each bent back to touch the goblet on a single sharp point. She could see three arms in all, but assumed that a fourth existed on the other side of the massive structure.

The bottom of the goblet took her breath away. It was a massive, pointed drill bit. The bit was turning slowly but with apparent strength as the entire drill hit the surface where the dome had stood, and entered the planet's crust. In seconds the shockwave of its landing hit her, throwing her from her seat, and blowing dust, dirt, and rubble around the dozer. She screamed in anger, horror, and fear.

*****

"Ohhh, bad news, Protector."

"What now?" Trance grunted, looking up from his plate of food. He'd stopped to eat only after realizing that it had been nearly twenty hours since his last meal, his final breakfast with Dexter. The last few days had been disturbing.

Given what he had already endured since becoming a Protector, he doubted he could bear any more of the kind of bad news his ring was prone to giving.

He'd buried Dexter quietly in a dune on a nearby moon. The cat would have wanted it that way, forever in close proximity to a planet-wide kitty box. The others he'd left where they were. There were simply too many to deal with. He was tired.

He was starting to feel again, though, starting to come out of the numbness that had encased him. The only problem was the bright red burn of anger slowly replacing the gray fog. That scared him, just a little, as the heat ate away at him. What was he capable of? Could he stop himself if he found whoever had done this? Would his inner rage be his undoing? He shuddered, and tried to concentrate on the ring.

"I'm getting emergency signals from the Red Line in. We are in deep trouble."

"What's the nature?"

"It looks like all the loonies are coming out of the woodwork at once. I have no idea how they knew there wasn't anybody minding the fort, but they are coming in anyway. The reports I am hearing say an all-out invasion is occurring from every side."

"It probably has something to do with Taa'lien," Trance responded morosely, flinging his fork down in disgust. "I am really getting tired of that woman."

"Um, Protector, I think we've all discovered that 'she' is really a man, Nesger, the most evil Creator ever. Haven't you been paying attention?"

"Would it hurt you to once, just once, let me live my life in denial?" Trance asked bitterly.

"I don't experience aspects of the human lifestyle such as hurting."

Trance ignored the obvious dig. "Now they attack," he said, closing his eyes and rubbing the bridge of his nose between his thumb and forefinger. "It's all too systematic to be coincidental."

"At this point, the likelihood of coincidence is negligible," the ring agreed.

"I had hoped Taa'lien, or Nesger, died when the other rings blew out, but now I am starting to wonder about that," Trance admitted as he stood and walked toward the nearest lift, leaving his tray of food forgotten. "We were outmaneuvered from the start --all of the events that have happened; from the moon of Korondor to the attack on Monidad, to the blowouts of the rings and now this, just seems so… coordinated. I have to figure that Nesger did find a way to protect himself from whatever killed all the other ring bearers."

"That appears to be the case," the ring admitted grudgingly. By now they were inside the lift. Trance punched the button for the main hangar, and the smooth pull of gravity began as the lift powered up the shaft.

"I just don't think I can do this, ring," Trance said truthfully. "If he is still alive, how can I possibly defeat him alone? He's been wielding a ring longer than my planet has existed, for heaven's sake! I have no idea why the heck I have survived thus far, but it must have been pure dumb luck. And pure dumb luck just doesn't count for shit when it really matters."

"Your statement makes no sense."

"You know what I mean!"

The ring glowed warmly. "Trance," it said softly, "you are a hero. Does it really matter what the odds are or how the chips are stacked?"

"But—"

"You will do this, or die trying; it's as simple as that. Luck may come into the equation somewhere, but ultimately it starts with you and me and a lot of willpower and determination. How it ends will be of your choosing."

"I guess you're right, ring."

"I always am," the ring admitted.

"Don't get too proud of yourself."

"I don't experience aspects of—"

Trance sighed, tuning the ring out. The lift opened up to the main hanger. He flew into the hanger, up the spire, and into space. He doubted he would be back.

Chapter 38: Chaos Reigns

Cut to a convoy of merchant transport ships on a line between two star systems. Twenty-five ships filled to the brim with spices, beer, precious metals, and other goods. Out here, the darkness was absolute and the void sucked up heat and light like a hungry beast. The convoy was lightly guarded, of course. This far from the Red Line in highly trafficked, relatively, space; it was an easy decision for most companies. Why spend much-needed profits on little-needed firepower? Officially the Conglomerated State's Navy discouraged such practices. So did the Protectors, but they were far, far, away and profits were so much closer, just a system away.

The midpoint between the two systems gave captains the most ulcers. This was where the plan to save credits seemed foolish, even suicidal. The bonuses weren't that big, really, against the measure of a life, and it was hard to spend them if you died protecting your goods from pirates.

Most captains only did the run a few times before quitting or retiring. It was just too much stress. The hours seemed like days this far out. The guns were manned every second, everyone walked the deck, and everyone sweated. Only the captains knew the guns wouldn't be enough against a well coordinated, all-out attack.

The silver ships looked bloated and ripe for the taking as they slipped through space on a thread.

The pirate ships leapt out of Gray Space spitting shards of light. They had timed their attack perfectly; their prey was right below them. There were dozens of Pirate ships: small, fast, and vicious, heavily shielded, and bristling with guns. The first shots lanced into the lightly shielded lead vessel, and it exploded, tumbling out of control and spewing splinters of metal, pieces of bodies and other debris.

The pirates flew low over the convoy spitting fire. Behind them, a freighter slipped out of Gray Space, and began to disgorge mini-resource engines. They were shaped like tops with eight spindly arms jutting out at the lowest point. Each engine was scarcely a dozen yards across in the center, and had a small room with a thick window jutting just slightly out of the surface.

Behind each window was a Controller comfortably seated in a plush chair. Controllers tended to be small in stature, and were bred to be single minded in their pursuit of resources. Each had a small head with no eyes, mouth or nose, which sat upon a squat neck which was centered on a tubular body. They didn't have any arms or legs. They didn't need them. Wires protruded out of the head and snaked themselves into a panel inches away. There were no buttons, wheels or moving mechanisms within the Engine compartment.

The Controller race had been genetically modified over thousands of years. Stripped of unnecessary limbs, personality and desires, they now existed for one thing – to live within the Resource engines and hunt for precious metals, water and other necessities. They were hard wired into the engine; they could not function without it.

A Controller could operate a resource engine much better than any computer could – with finesse bordering on art. That's why they continued to exist within their niche. Unfortunately, there was a slight downside: Controllers had a tendency to live short, brutish lives. Even the best and most resilient Controller burned out after only five years of service, and so whole farm worlds had been created to breed them.

Bodies were grown within the compartments that would house them for a lifetime, and inserted like modules into the resource engines. When a Controller expired, its module was recycled and filled again. It was an efficient, soulless process.

Currently, the resource engines were attaching themselves to the hulls of the freighters, spindly arms biting deep into the metal skin. They looked very much like viruses.

Quite a few had been destroyed as they clamored to reach their destinations, blown up by the near defenseless quarries they sought, but there were so many, it almost didn't matter.

Once firmly attached, a thin rod snaked out from each Engine, and began to cut into the hull. Soon, riches would be theirs.

*****

"Got another distress signal for you, Protector. This one is close."

"Hmm. Maybe this time we'll catch whomever is doing this. How is the Navy? Are they close enough to delay the bad guys until we can get there?"

"The CS Navy is handling several in this area, but they are pretty much maxed out as far as their resources are concerned. Truthfully, I've never heard of so many distress signals all at once."

"I know, this is the third one in the past twenty minutes," Trance sighed as he willed the ring to provide him the coordinates. "I hope we can make it in time." They hadn't been having much luck thus far.

Since leaving Monidad three days ago, they had responded to nearly a hundred distress calls. More often than not, Trance would pop out of Grey Space in the near vicinity of the beacon, and be horrified to discover a burned out world or a smoking hulk of a freighter, plundered of all its goods. They had yet to find a survivor, or even a culprit.

It took less than ten minutes to rocket to the destination. When they arrived, Trance discovered they were yet again too late.

With a flash, Trance exited Gray Space. It took just a moment to catch his bearings. "Shit," was all that he said when he realized what he had materialized in. All around him were lifeless floating hulks of metal. There had been easily a hundred vessels of varying size and shape, the smallest the size of a bus, the largest easily bigger than his favorite monument back home, the Space Needle in Seattle. He scanned for life signs, knowing there would be none. He was not surprised.

It was a little eerie knowing that all around him a fierce battle had been waged just a few minutes before. He could see that there were definitely two sides.

The losing side consisted of mostly decaying freighters. Many of them were completely unarmed. They had probably been the last to be stripped; the Pirates had probably concentrated their energies on disabling the ones with guns. He wondered, briefly what it had been like to know death was minutes, perhaps seconds away. He shuddered.

A goodly sized cargo ship near him looked as though it had been cracked open, the metal hull forced outward. He'd seen the damage a dozen times. The ships had been stripped clean like bones in a desert, their goods plundered by the pirates they had been hunting for the past three days. Disgusted, but refusing to give up, Trance widened his search beam. With a shock he realized there was a blip. He wasn't alone.

"What are you picking up?" he asked the ring quietly.

"Lots of stuff. Be more specific."

"How many life signs?"

"Just a few," the ring said, "and they are fading fast. By the time we get there, they may be gone."

"Are they Pirates?" It was more of a statement than a question.

"Most definitely. It seems as though the ship was damaged somehow, possibly in the firefight that occurred here, and these people were most likely abandoned by their comrades. Bad luck for them, eh?"

"Let's hurry," Trance said. "Maybe we can catch up to them."

It took less than three minutes to find the ship, a short squat model with massive engines and heavy armament. It had a large gaping slash across one side, and was limping along well below sub-light speed. The entire thing was shuddering, and he got the impression it was on its last legs. He was mildly surprised to find he was not fired upon when he rocketed within firing range. That didn't bode well for the health of the passengers and crew.

When he appeared on the bridge of the Pirate vessel, he found more destruction. It was smoky inside, and definitely not breathable, but he was safe behind his own ring-created atmosphere. Lights were blinking haphazardly on consoles, and there had been a fire recently. The ship's computer had evidently taken care of that. Venting tubes hung from the ceiling here and there, and one of the walls bore a black scar across its face. Bodies were lying everywhere.

"Oh, well that was another waste of time. These people are all dead," the ring said unnecessarily.

"Do another scan for life forms."

"Scanning. Nope. The last one actually expired just as we beamed aboard."

"Hmmm. That's too bad. I had wanted to talk to them about some things." Trance leaned down and flipped one of the prone figures over. "Still wondering if those Foul Dragon jerks are involved with this?" he asked. On the chest was the familiar Dragon and Galaxy symbol. He stood, wiping his hands on his pants. "You're right," he said disgusted, "what a waste." He looked thoughtfully at the empty consoles. Perhaps he could pick the brain of the ship's computer instead. "Ring?" he asked.

"Way ahead of you, boss. I'm scanning now. Nada, I am afraid. The last thing the captain did was dump everything but the navigational memory. They completely burned out the computers. There is nothing but slag."

"Somehow I figured that," Trance sighed. "Is there nothing that you can do?"

"I can do a lot of—"

"You know what I mean. Can you fix it?"

"I'm not much of a techie, truth be told. But even if I was, no, I couldn't."

"Oh."

"Hold on," the ring replied. "More emergency signals, Protector."

"I'm getting tired of this." Trance looked around the silent control room.

"You're the only one left, remember? You still have a duty to the people."

"Don't worry about that; I am in this to the end. But this path is bullshit. I need to do this a different way." He sighed. "This job makes my asshole burn."

"Pardon? I am sure there are creams available."

Trance was muttering to himself as he faded in gray space.

*****

The planet was toast. All that was left was the mop up, and of course the mining and resource engines. That was his favorite part. There was something sexy about those huge drill bits those M/R's carried. He loved watching the damn things hitting the deck and cutting into it as if it were butter; he could watch them all day. And the riches; oh they were going to take them IN on this planet! He could feel it in his blood: it'd be no problem making quota today. The Dragon got his share, the emperor his. And Captain Digon? He'd be getting his share this day as well. Digon straightened his velour shirt, leaned back in his chair with all four arms behind his head, and smiled. "Release the engines," he said.

*****

"There it is," the ring said helpfully.

They were rapidly approaching a planet the size of Earth. In fact, it looked much like his home planet except that the continents were all screwed up. Oh, and the water had a slightly purplish tint. Other than that, it was almost exactly like his home. "Scan for life signs," he said, looking suspiciously at the water.

"None, other than the thousands of people in the large fleet of Pirates on the other side of the planet," the ring said. "They could be trouble. Maybe it's just me."

"Anything else I should know about?"

"There's plenty. Could you be more specific?"

"Any other bad guys I need to be aware of?"

"Well, I didn't want to worry you, but..."

"Yes?"

"There are a lot of Raider-class starships. They aren't too big, just a three hundred thousand tons each. Mainly what I am worried about is the two Destroyers. They are pretty big and powerful."

"Oh. That's bad?"

"Well, honestly, it's not good."

"Oh."

"And some Freighters, but I wouldn't worry about those too much."

"Didn't you say there was a colony on site?"

"Three point four billion people."

"Where'd they go?"

"They are dead, Trance. All life has been extinguished on the planet, in fact. Even now, those Freighters are releasing vehicles whose sole purpose is to drain the planet of everything it possesses; its water, minerals, meat, air—everything. My best guess is that we have finally found who we have been chasing."

Trance snarled. They would all pay.

Chapter 39: Taking on Destroyers

The outer guards were the first to fall. Without warning he was there, with an energy signature so large and powerful it wiped out sensors and interrupted communication. He used his power like a wedge, pushing the small Raider-class starships out of his way like they were so much refuse. Many of the first ships to encounter the Protector imploded before they had time to raise the alarm, much less fire upon him. He didn't bother with constructs; just swept through anything that he found with the power of his might, and left nothing but destruction in his wake.

It took less than ten minutes to locate the Destroyers. They were massive, easily six hundred megatons of metal, bristling with heavy guns and artillery. Blue, green, and red shards of light split the night as the thousands of guns on each attempted to target him. He barely noticed. He set a collision course for the first, eschewing caution in his anger, spread his arms like a phoenix, and closed his eyes.

The energy coursed from his ring. He felt it flow around him, sparking at the tips of his fingers. He was hot. All around his inner shell of safety, the energy burned the very fabric of space. When he impacted the ship, near the very center, he cut through it like a hot knife through an overripe melon.

He opened his eyes on the other side, turned and fired a single shot from his ring. The beam coursed back through the hole that he had made when he exited, and detonated each level as it passed back through the vessel.

The strain was too much for the weakened Destroyer. It began to list, shedding chunks of metal, debris, and bodies into space. Fires had broken out within the vessel as it struggled simply to keep itself together. It was losing the battle.

Trance looked past it at the second Destroyer. It was firing all of its guns at him, and torpedoes the size of jet planes were impacting his force shield and detonating like the fourth of July. He flew up close where the torpedoes couldn't get to him, using his ring to scan for the command deck of the vessel. Then, he allowed himself to sink into the ship like a wraith, slipping through metal, wire and wood.

Trance materialized on the bridge of the starship, shields up, ring blazing. It was a small half-moon shaped room filled to the brim with consoles and flashing lights. There were four stations along the back wall, and three chairs in the center. Creatures of varying sizes were at each of the posts. They had black pants and brightly colored velour shirts. He barely had time to blink before several of the occupants began firing hand-held weapons at him. His shielding easily absorbed the beams, but the act pissed him off even more. Who were they to fire at him like that? Bastards.

"Stop," he said, crouching slightly and swinging his arm in a wide arc. A string of energy slipped from his ring like a whip, cracking as it struck every member of the crew save the one in the middle seat. They each screamed as they were engulfed in a fire that blazed from within, and each turned and twisted as they faded away.

The being in the center chair, a captain by the looks of it, blinked for two beats of a heart then jumped up from his seat and attempted to sprint to back of the room. His destination may have been the only exit from the room, a double set of doors at the back, or he might have been trying to reach one of the handguns his crew had dropped as they died. Trance didn't particularly care. Before the Captain could get more than three steps, Trance pounced on him like a wild tiger, grabbed him by the shoulders, and threw him toward the wall.

The captain hit the bulkhead with a sickening crunch, and slid to the floor. Trance leisurely walked over and picked the creature up by his velour shirt and shoved his back against the wall forcefully. "Talk," Trance said.

"You're... you're supposed to be dead," the Captain stammered. "She said you would all be—"

"Who? Taa'lien? Then she is alive!" Trance growled. The Captain blanched at the name. "Where is Taa'lien? Where is she?" He gave the Captain a shake.

"I don't know, I swear!" The captain pleaded raising all four hands with palms spread open. A small trickle of greenish fluid had begun to flow from the nostril holes in the center of his pinched face, and one eye swelled slightly with a bluish hue. "We haven't seen her for weeks! The fleet got the prearranged signal less than a week ago. I have no idea where it came from. That's all I know."

"Then you are worth nothing. You are better to me dead than alive." He drew back his fist, his ring blazing a deep blue.

"Spare me, please!" the creature sniveled, blinking furiously.

"Like you spared those colonists?" Trance whispered through gritted teeth. The Captain paled even more, glancing past Trance's shoulder at the front view screen, which showed the planet the fleet had attacked. Its surface in many places was ablaze. "I had no choice..." he protested weakly. "I was just doing my job."

"You lie," Trance said raising his first further. A single strike to the center of the forehead would do it; right between those pathetic eyes. His ring glowed fiercely in response to his anger, burning coldly with power and might.

But a small voice deep within his heart was colder still. "You are better than this, Trance," it seemed to say.

"Shut up, ring!" Trance bellowed to himself.

"Shutting up," it said in an even smaller voice.

Trance blinked, looking further into the eyes of the groveling being before him. The Captain looked down and away, but not before Trance saw in a flash what he had almost become. The ring was right. It was one thing to take a life defending innocents or even self. The act was regrettable but necessary for the greater good. It was never necessary to take a life in cold blood. The anger left him in a rush.

"You are nothing," he said dropping the captain. The creature landed in a disoriented heap but quickly righted himself and flipped over so that he was face down with his arms spread wide, palms on the deck. From there, he moaned thanks for the Protector's mercy.

Trance felt nothing. The anger was gone, and he could not find pity for the disheveled form at his feet. But a plan was forming...

"Ring, can you scan the computer for any information about Taa'lien?" he asked silently.

"Can do... nope."

"What?"

"I just scanned the computer. There is nothing. The Captain, Digon, is telling the truth."

"What about the central location of the raiders?"

"That data may have been dumped when you started decimating the fleet."

"I bet the Captain knows."

"He'll never give that information to you willingly, and you know I'm too powerful to try stealing his memories."

"Yeah, it'd be like cracking eggs with a bulldozer."

"Right. So, there is pretty much no way we are going to be able to get that information."

"We'll see. How are you at tracking transmissions through space?"

"Pretty good; remember we followed Taa'lien's trail. It's just a different form of radiation. Why?"

"I'll explain later. Just be ready." He turned to the Captain again, who was looking up inquiringly. "I have a message for you," he said coldly.

"Anything, your worship," Digon cried.

"These attacks will be stopped immediately," Trance said, turning his back again and looking upon the scarred world below.

"Yes, yes, I will tell my superiors, but they -"

"I suggest you do so quickly," Trance interrupted. "I will deal with any further raiders in the same manner as I have dealt with your fleet," he said, sweeping his arm across the length of the view screen. It showed, besides the wounded planet, large portions of several of the other spaceships tumbling lifelessly in the void. Small streams of errant energy crackled aimlessly here and there on their hulls. "The order of the foul dragon and its ilk will find the cost of attacking the Conglomerated States a price too high to pay."

"Yes, but -"

"I wasn't finished. When I am done obliterating any further raiding party or parties, I will hunt you down, Captain. Then I will find your planet and wipe it from the face of the universe."

The captain gasped. "I... I..."

"And tell Taa'lien, or Nesger, or whomever she calls herself, that I am coming for her first," Trance said. "If you value your life, you'll give her that message and then get as far away from her as you can."

The captain nodded glumly, as he and the bridge faded from sight.

Trance reappeared outside the spaceship. "Hide us from the ship's sensors and then start scanning for transmissions, ring," he said. After a moment, he looked at the ring ruefully. "Think it will work?" he asked.

"Hmmmm. No activity yet. The Captain is probably still groveling."

They waited less than a minute and then the ship began broadcasting signals furiously. "Can you read them?" Trance asked.

"Yeah," the ring replied. "It's a distress call straight through to headquarters. Captain Digon isn't even bothering with encoding or disguising the signal. He's repeating your words pretty much verbatim."

"So where are the signals going?"

"Oh, I get it. I'll have your answer as soon as we start getting a response."

They didn't have long to wait. "Here it comes," the ring said in a happy voice. "Bad news for Captain! His superiors aren't too pleased. In fact, I've learned a couple of new swear words. Fancy that. A couple of the phrases involve activities I didn't think were physically possible without a whole lot of lubrication."

Trance grunted. "What else?"

"Well, they are telling the Captain to salvage what he can from the fleet and make his way home for a court martial. It looks like in sparing his life you did the Captain a huge disservice. He's in a world of trouble."

"Well, he is an asshole. He deserves any crap he gets for attacking innocents like that."

"Actually, he is an A*nfld-ial."

"Whatever."

"It's the race that he hails from."

"I know. It still sounds like you're having a hairball."

"Well, I'm just trying to be helpful."

"I know. You weren't succeeding," Trance smiled. "Were you able to pick out a location?"

"Oh yeah. Loud and clear. Are we going there?"

"Eventually, now that we have their coordinates I might be able to. First, I need to find Taa'lien. I know she is the center of this, and she has to be stopped. How in the heck am I going to find her? I can't believe no one knows where she is. Check the database again. Are you sure there are absolutely no records of her whereabouts?"

"Checking. No, nothing. She's the boss, Trance. I'm sure she kept track of her underlings, not the other way around."

"Now what?" he asked, scratching his head.

"Well, we could forget the whole thing and move on with your life. That might be fun, too."

"What do you mean?"

"Well, I've been doing some figuring."

"This ought to be good. What have you, uh, figured?"

"Look, all the Creators are dead, right?"

"Yeah. So?"

"So, Taa'lien, if we are even able to find her, is bound to take you apart piece by piece, right? I mean she has been a Creator and a Protector for longer than time, pretty much."

"Yeah, I know that. But I have to try. What are you talking about?"

"Well, if you get killed, there is no one around to reformat me and choose a new Protector. That will be it. If you die, in a sense, I die too."

Trance thought about that for a minute. "I guess I knew that. I'm sorry, but it doesn't change a thing. I have to do this. I have to stop her. I'm probably the only person in the entire Universe that even has a chance. Who knows how many countless people she'll kill if I just let her go?"

"I could run the numbers for you, but it will take a while."

"That was a rhetorical question."

"Oh." The ring managed to look pensive.

"Look," Trance sighed, "I have to do this, and I need your help. I'm scared too. Really scared, because I'm afraid that I'll fail and she will win. How long do you think it would take before she reached Earth? How many more worlds will she destroy on her way there?"

"I'm guessing those were both rhetorical questions too."

"You catch on quick. Ring, I need your help in this. I can't do it without you. Will you help me?"

"Sure. You're the boss after all. It's not like I have a choice."

"Yes, but I want you to want to help me."

"Is that an order?"

"No."

"OK then. I'm happy to help."

"Thanks. Now where should we look next?"

"Hard to say. I'm not really an expert in these types of matters. I'm not all knowing, you know. Just mostly all-knowing."

Trance snapped his fingers. "That's it!" In all the sci-fi and fantasy books I ever read, the heroes always found an Oracle who provided the answers they needed. I certainly wish we had one of those!"

"Oh. That would be Delphi."

"Huh? Delphi?"

"Delphi. It's the closest thing we have to an Oracle."

"Why didn't you tell me about this before?" Trance asked in exasperation.

"You never asked," the ring replied sulkily. "Besides, there simply hasn't been any spare time to sit around and discuss the nature of the universe and all of the inhabitants within it."

"That's no excuse and you know it."

"I'm not trying to excuse myself."

"You're impossible, you know that?"

"No, just improbable."

"Right." Trance chuckled. "So what is Delphi?"

"Of course, the real name is LKJI***89mn, but the closest translation in terms that you would understand is Delphi. This is a very fitting name. You should remember from your History texts that in Ancient times, Delphi was considered the center of the known world; the middle ground between Heaven and Earth. There was an Oracle there who supposedly channeled the spirits of the Gods."

"Huh. I actually didn't know that."

"The Delphi we are going to is the biggest and most comprehensive library of collected works ever assembled. I bet it has all the answers that we need."

"How can a library help us?"

"Was that another rhetorical question?"

"NO!"

"OK then; just checking. You know, it might help to hold up a little sign or something when you want me to respond. I'm having a little trouble figuring out the difference between when you ask a question and don't want an answer, and when you actually mean for me to respond."

Trance grunted. "I'll work it out. In the meantime, please, just answer the question, ring."

"Every single thing in the known Universe is cataloged there. It is such a massive collection that an entire planet was used to contain it. Lucky for us it's interactive, which means we can ask it questions and get answers."

"Like 'If I were an evil genius bent on the destruction of the Universe, where would I go?' Questions like that?"

"Yes, most assuredly; it's very smart, you see. It's a library, after all."

"Wow. That's neat. There's a book I can't find back in my hometown library. Maybe Delphi has a copy."

"Definitely. I… oh I get it: Sarcasm."

"No, a book," Trance teased.

"I… I don't know what to say."

"Never mind; I was just kidding. It sounds like a neat set up."

"The Great Library on Monidad (remember visiting it during the tour, Trance?), and all the central libraries of Conglomerated States all have an intuitive network connection to it."

"Kind of like the Internet we have back home."

"Not really, actually. But that's a good start. The Intuitive Network connection supplies information relevant to the area in which the information is used. Remember the crystalline shards in use at the Library on Monidad? All the information contained within was originally downloaded from Delphi."

"Oh. So, why don't we find the nearest Library and start there? If they are really all connected anyway, and you're sure we can find out where Taa'lien is through that route, I mean."

"I am certain we'll be closer to finding out where she is, yes. And we have to go directly to the source. The Intuitive nature of the connection, while excellent for relevant, localized information, makes it quite difficult to get an entire picture of the Universe."

"I get it. That's like the parable of the three blind men who feel an elephant."

"Ah. Yes. There are stories like that all over the Universe."

"Maybe this Delphi will be able to tell me why I'm still alive when everyone else is dead."

"Probably."

"OK." Trance nodded. "Where are we going?"

"It's located on planet F-74. It's quite a distance from here."

"Well, we better get going then." Trance stood, and stretched.

"There is one tiny problem."

"Oh boy. I just knew you'd say that sometime in this conversation," Trance groaned.

"Well, I hate to mention it, because it really is so insignificant."

"Please, do be my guest."

"Well, no one has actually been to Delphi in untold millennia. I am unsure of what condition it will be in when we get there."

Trance grumbled softly to himself as he faded away.

Chapter 40: Delphi

F-74 turned out to be a singularly dark planet solidly plowing through the stellar winds of a small and unassuming star on the edge of a rather boring spiral galaxy with a name that Trance forgot almost as soon as it was uttered. Nothing about it seemed to suggest it was the primary storehouse of all the collected works and knowledge of the known universe. In fact, it seemed quite the opposite – just a burned out planet on the edge of a largely empty section of space. Trance doubted seriously that anyone had been there in ages.

He circled the planet's equator in silence once before the ring brightened. "Head north," it said. "Our objective is at the Pole," I believe.

Trance headed north. As he flew, he idly shone a light below him. Surprisingly, no matter how bright he made it, the beam refused to cut into the darkness. The night just seemed to suck up the light, even though the air seemed clear. With a sigh, he cut the light and let the ring guide him.

"Land there," the ring said eventually, and a blue arrow appeared and pointed toward a single light in the darkness below and ahead. Trance got the impression of age and importance as he touched down – of stately progression throughout the ages. He felt briefly as though he should take off his shoes before continuing on, and if he had been wearing a hat he might have removed it.

Even though they were at the North Pole, the air was clean and warm as though it were spring. It too smelled of age – definitely not musty, but then again, not like air he had learned to associate with a planet. Most of the other planets he had been on had smelled like something. Earth, for example. His hometown smelled primarily of Evergreen Trees and slightly like the town dump. The planet he had been on with Aura and Dexter when they had trained… that one had the aroma of sand and Palm trees. Even Monidad had its own particular smell. This one smelled like nothing. Nothing at all.

Beneath his feet a pathway had been carved out of stone. The path itself was fairly well lit and he could see it in crisp detail down to the individual molecules of sand between the cracked and worn tiles. On either side however, the darkness engulfing the rest of the planet seemed to wait hungrily for the inattentive traveler to stray from the clearly marked borders.

Ahead, a series of twelve stone archways towered over the path. Symbols had been carved into the sides of each. The ring informed him that they told the story of the birth of the Conglomerated States. Each arch spoke of a different era, and while the ring didn't bother to translate the story, it did name each. Trance let one of his hands brush along each one as he past it – the surface of each was cool to the touch. Tiny motes of dust, disturbed by his passage, glided into the wake of his path and danced around his head before sliding off into the darkness.

The final arch told of the creation of the corps of Protectors. Beyond it the path stepped smartly up to a wooden door. While the edges of the path spilled around the frame and into the darkness, something told Adams that he might want to try going through the access rather than around it. "Thanks, ring, I got it," Trance grunted. "Nothing is getting me off this path."

"Ok, just checking," the ring said.

Trance examined the door. It had a simple wood grain, no keyholes or hinges, or even a doorknob. It didn't move when he pushed against it.

Trance tried feeling along the thin line where the door met its frame. It was smooth with nothing to pry against. He tried knocking. Dimly, he heard the echo of his fist as he struck the wood reverberate back to him, but there were no other sounds. "Looks like no one is home," he said. "Maybe we should just leave."

"Don't be silly," the ring said. "Maybe this is a test. You're supposed to find a way inside."

"I don't suppose you would like to tell me what the answer is, would you? It would make things a lot easier for me, frankly."

"No. I wouldn't. But if it makes you feel any better, it is because I have no idea what the answer is. I would advise against simply destroying the door, however. I sense a lot of power at play here, maybe more than I can handle."

"Hmmm." Trance tried to look around the door, but found only darkness. It seemed to leach at him, pulling the warmth from him like a thief. He quickly turned back to the door's face. "Open Sesame," he called. Nothing.

He thought for a moment. "Let's scan the darn thing, see if there are any moving parts," he said to the ring, and exerted his will. The moment his energy touched the wood surface, however, he heard an audible click and the door opened soundlessly.

"This entrance must have been designed specifically for ring bearers," the ring said in way of comment. "I doubt it would have opened for anyone else."

"Too easy," Trance said, although he knew that he had been lucky rather than skillful.

The door opened to a series of stairs that slipped down into the earth. Directly behind the door, the ever-present darkness seemed to lie waiting silently. He ignored it and stared down into the depths for just a second before allowed his feet to follow the stairs down.

At the bottom was another door. This one opened easily to his touch. Behind it he found another hallway. The ring urged him to follow it. "Do you know where you are going?" he asked it.

"I think I do, but I am not sure," it replied. "I feel like I have done this before, or maybe dreamed about it. What's that feeling that you get when you know how things are going to be but you can't put your finger on it?"

"Number one, it's my finger, not yours, and number two, that's Deja Vu."

"No, that's not it."

"Shut up ring. Just guide me where to go."

They passed an hour in silence. He quickly grew tired of hearing his footsteps as they echoed dully in the silent dark and narrow hall. The only light came from a blue lantern he had fashioned and now carried in one hand. Though he tried to keep it still, the beam shifted back and forth slightly causing shadows to dance and play along the periphery. Every twenty paces, on alternating sides, doors broke the monotony. Every hundred paces, a new hall intersected the one they were in. Almost randomly, it seemed, the ring instructed him to go left, right, or straight. Trance carefully followed the directions.

Finally, they stood before a door that could have been a twin of the hundreds of others they had seen. It appeared to have been carved out of a single block of stone. Its surface bore several raised symbols of unknown origin or meaning. "In that room are the records we need," the ring said in a voice dripping with doubt.

"Not sure, are you," Trance responded.

"No, I really have no idea," the ring replied truthfully. "I know the records are all around us. They fill this planet to the brim. But this room is different. I think the record keepers meant this room to be the access point for those records; a doorway, literally, to knowledge."

"Well, we've come all this way," Trance sighed. "It wouldn't due to turn back now." He touched the door with one hand. It swung open smoothly and silently.

A slight musty odor of stale air wafted out and tickled his nose, but the interior was completely dark, revealing no source of the smell. Nothing jumped out at him, and no booby traps seemed to be present, which was always a good sign.

Adams raised the lantern and shone it into the room. "Well, I'm a bit disappointed," he said. The room the light revealed was small and barren to say the least. It was only ten feet by ten feet. In the center sat a stone chair; a throne of solid gray, white, and black marble. It looked as though it had been polished recently though no footsteps marred the fine blanket of dust covering the floor.

"Now what?" Trance muttered to himself. "I thought there would be tons of book shelves filled with collections of ancient knowledge we could pour through to find our answers. Or, even better, an Internet connection."

"Why don't you sit in the chair?" the ring replied.

"I wasn't talking to you," Trance snipped.

"I wasn't talking, Protector."

"You just told me to sit in the chair."

"No. Perhaps the sound you heard emanated from within."

"Whatever. I am tired. Perhaps I will sit down."

Trance entered the room and walked around the chair. From this vantage point, Trance noted the seat had a hole carved out of the rear, perhaps in case someone with a tail decided they'd like to recline there. Strangely, it appeared that the throne wasn't even attached to the floor. He kneeled down and peered under it, trying not to sneeze as dust billowed up attacking his nose and mouth. Indeed, the entire affair was floating several centimeters over the tiled stone floor. This close, he noticed a very faint humming sound coming from within as if the unit housed some sort of engine.

"Okay…" Trance muttered, jumping to his feet and brushing his hands vigorously over his clothing in a futile attempt to free himself from the dust. Then, grimacing, he gently eased his way into the throne. It was surprisingly comfortable; but not stationary.

In fact, as soon as he was seated, the chair closed the small gap between itself and the floor with a hiss. It ended its brief travel with a "click" and a "Ca-chunk" that reverberated around the confines of the small room. Trance didn't have time to wonder about the sounds however, because at that moment the same voice that had invited him to sit down (he now noticed that there were slight differences in inflection and tone that set the new voice apart from his ring) had begun talking. The voice was friendly and warm. It talked to him as though they had been friends for a long time. As it spoke, the wall in front of Trance became a whirlpool of light that quickly coalesced into a kindly green eye. The green eye pulled back revealing a narrow face bordered by gray hair and a smile.

"Greetings Protector," the head said. "I am pleased you chose to engage my services. Things have been so lonely here. Is there anything I can do for you?"

"You're a terrible housekeeper, for one," Trance grunted, still trying to sniffle a sneeze.

"Oh?" The head looked around as if seeing the room for the first time. "Yes, I have let things slide, haven't I? I have been dormant for thousands of years, after all. I'll clean up here while we talk."

"Since we are talking," Trance said, "Who are you?"

"My apologies again! Introductions certainly are in order. You can call me Delphi, keeper of the knowledge."

"Oh. So you're Delphi. Boy, they got the Interactive part right, anyway."

"Yes. And you are a human, and a Protector, yes?"

"That's partly right. I'm Trance Adams. The only Protector."

The face grew a head and a body clothed in a red dinner jacket and khaki pants. On his feet was the biggest pair of bunny slippers Trance had ever seen. In one hand he held a glass of brandy he twirled slightly. Behind him a red brick fireplace coalesced out of nothingness. A fire burned cheerily within, filling the room with a ruddy glow. In fact, the whole room seemed to have become a large living room replete with a big faux brown bear rug and shelves full of books with interesting and obscure titles. Trance noticed that the dust was gone and he was now sitting on a plush lounge chair. Delphi had a dreamy smile on his face. "That's nice. I…" He frowned. "Did you say 'the only Protector,' or did I hear you wrong?"

"That's right, Del. The last. As in I get to turn out the light."

"Troubling. So, how can I help you?"

Trance quickly explained the recent events leading up to and including the sudden graphic and horrific destruction of the remaining corps and the Creators. Delphi listened thoughtfully, swirling his brandy with a concerned look on his face. Finally, Trance asked him, "The ring says you might know what destroyed the entire corps. I'd like to know how why I was spared, and how it happened. I also want to know where Taa'lien is. She needs to pay for her crimes.

'I brought this with me, if you need it." He held up Dexter's ring. It glinted dully in the light.

"Worthy questions indeed. The answer to the first question lies in the answer to another question. Are you aware of what gives you the power that you use?"

"The ring, of course."

"The ring?" Del shook his head bemusedly. "No. Your ring acts as a repository of energy that is made available by a source which might seem fantastic to you regardless of all of the other events you have witnessed."

"Try me."

Behind Delphi, the fireplace melted into a single point of light, which split into three burning orbs. Each grew in size until they were the approximately as big as golf balls. They were situated on the wall so that if Trance had drawn three lines using the orbs he would have created an isosceles triangle which had fallen on one side. Behind them, Trance could see what appeared to the endless dotted expanse of space.

"That's a three sun solar system, right? I didn't know they existed."

"Maybe if you had paid attention in Astronomy classes in high school.." the ring sighed.

"A trinary star system. They are fairly rare to be sure, meaning that there are only several million in all of space. This one has not been discovered by your scientists yet. It has an official designation in our records, a name that consists of several hundred letters and numbers. To make things easier for you, we can call it Fred."

"Fred?" Trance frowned.

"It's a name as any other, correct? Fred the trinary star system with a figure eight orbital path."

With those words, a pulsing yellow dotted line traced a google (or sideways eight) shape over the three stars. In the center where the two dotted circles met, Adams now noted a single blue dot the size of a dime.

"That blue dot. Is that where the mysterious power source is located?"

"The power source is the conflux of the three stars," Delphi explained. "Each of them passes through the blue dot at the center. Relatively near that spot in spatial terms is the... well, I guess you could call it a transformer. It receives the energy the stars give off and transforms it into a form of power suitable to be used by the rings."

"Ok, fine. Even if what you say is possible, then how do the rings get the energy? I mean even traveling at the speed of light –"

"My young Protector, the speed of light is not the fastest speed energy travels. This is a matter of faith, yes? I can tell you that the instant that the transformer releases the power your ring receives it." Behind him, the bookshelves, fireplace, and black bear rug popped back into view. They were in the library.

"OK, I get the concept. It powers my ring. What does that have to do with anything?"

"Well, the transformer array was designed to supply the corps with unlimited energy. After the Great Rebellion, it was enhanced so that it might be able to protect the Creators as an ultimate last resort. You see it has a failsafe… a trigger which causes the transformer to release a single burst of such magnitude it overpowers the rings and causes the deaths of every bearer. They designed it 'just in case.'"

"In case the Protectors united and rebelled against the Creators again," Trance finished. "The Great Rebellion scared the Creators, I bet. A large number of Protectors were ultimately behind the uprising. What if the entire corps rebelled in the future?"

Delphi nodded approvingly. "You're right," he said. "The Creators had given up the use of the rings so adding the fail safe to the transformer was the perfect solution. Unfortunately, it seems as though their plan backfired in the end."

"Hmp." Trance thought for a moment. "So, why was I spared?" he asked again.

"Ah. I see. First, I have one more question if you do not mind. I do not recognize your ring. Tell me, when did the Creator's change their design?"

"The software is different, but other than that it's the same ring as any other," Trance replied. "It was reformatted just before I joined the corps not too long ago."

"I hate to argue with someone I just met," Delphi said shaking his head, "But what you say is impossible. I have scanned many Protectors, and your ring is like none I have seen. The surface is fashioned so it appears like any other, but beneath the veneer is a construction new to me."

"Is this true, ring?"

It was silent for a moment. "Trance, I don't know…" It said. Delphi cocked his head as if he were listening intently. "My memory banks say I was constructed the moment my brethren were, and from the same skein."

"If that were true," Delphi said, "then you would be a burned out shell right now, and Trance and I wouldn't be having this delightful conversation. Look." He pointed to the wall to the right of Trance's chair. The bookshelves were gone again, replaced by a white screen upon which rotated two silver rings with the same blue gems set in their centers. A white line poured down the center separating the two. "On the right is your ring, Trance," he said. "On the left is a sample schematic from my database." Both of the rings suddenly lost their outer skins in layers like the peeling of an onion, revealing complicated maps of pathways and circuits. The split-screen view rushed toward the rings until they encompassed every inch of their respective halves. The depiction blurred for just a moment, and then solidified. Trance realized that it was the same area, only much closer. "We're now looking at a sub-molecular level," Delphi said helpfully.

"Wow," Adams whistled appreciatively. Both sides displayed a complicated cacophony of movement and color that amazed and dazzled him. At this level, instinct, and high school science, told him there should be nothing but space and darkness.

"First, let's look at something that is the same." Delphi said, an old-fashioned wood pointer springing out of his hand. "See the green wire in both rings?" The wire in question looked clear and unblemished on the left. On the right, a cruel dark mark jagged down the center, splitting it in two. "This little fellow regulates energy intake like a mechanical version of your own hypothalamus. It tells the ring when the battery is getting full and shuts of energy intake. In both your ring and that of your companion, this green wire has been damaged irreparably. "

"What do you mean? That it doesn't know when it is hungry?"

"Quite the opposite. It doesn't know when it is supposed to be full. See the large circle that takes up the entire bottom right-hand corner of the sample?

That is the "battery" that powers the ring. Look at the same spot on your ring. Notice anything different?"

"There isn't any battery?"

"That's right. There isn't a central power source in this model. Do you know what I mean by this?"

"Something good?"

"You're right," Delphi smiled, obviously pleased at being able to lecture. He liked to play the master storyteller, prolonging the punch line until the very last moment. "The whole ring can take in, store, and even release an almost unlimited amount of energy because it can place energy wherever it wants in its architecture. Here is how it works."

The screen shifted back to the Fred trinary star system. The transformer appeared in the center and grew until Trance could see it with amazing clarity. It looked cold and sturdy in the light of the three suns. Though he had nothing to compare its size to, he guessed it was tremendous. It consisted of a central platform with four large concave dishes attached by means of sturdy cylinders. The dishes pointed in the direction of the stars, and appeared to be sucking in heat and light and focusing it to their centers.

Delphi continued speaking, and the picture zoomed in and around the transformer. Closer still, he began to see individual details. He first noticed a raised dais with a control panel. The dais was open to space, and jutted out slightly from the central platform. When the camera passed slowly around it, he noted there were only three switches and a lever set into the face. Each was a different color: the switches were Red, Green, and Yellow. The lever was grey, like burnished stone.

"There are actually three batteries within the transformer; a main battery and two backups. Energy comes in through the dishes and is routed to one or another of the receptacles. Usually only one battery is in use at a time, and only a small stream of energy is released at any one time relative to storage and the needs of the corps. The buttons cycle between the three so that repairs can be made without fear of loss of power."

"And the lever?"

"Well that bypasses the control panel and turns all three batteries on full, in effect instantly releasing all available energy. The result, I am sure you know:

the rings simply were not built to receive all that power at once. Your ring is different. Rather than destroy it, the influx, in effect, super-charged it."

"Whoah. Did it fill up my ring completely?"

"Oh no. You'd have to recycle the Transformer at least two more times to fill it up completely. But the amount of energy that you have right now could probably last you one hundred thousand lifetimes."

Trance thought for a long moment. "Yes, but what I'm going to attempt.... I may need all of that and more."

"Yes?"

Trance tried a different track. The plan that had blossomed in his mind just now needed more time to germinate. "What about Taa'lien?" he asked. "This setup means she is probably dead too. But why would she want to commit suicide? That's a bit far to go just to prove a point."

"It is easy to speculate Taa'lien is the one who triggered the Transformer," Delphi mused. "Because energy is radiated outward from the batteries, the central control dais is the one location immune to the Transformer's effect."

"Which means that she really is still alive," Trance said softly. "Darn."

"The probability is quite high," Delphi admitted. "Of course, another entity could have found the Transformer and triggered the effect. Though given the chain of events you described, that possibility is quite unlikely."

"And how do you 'recycle' the transformer, and how long does it take?"

"Return the lever back to its starting position. The batteries begin filling immediately. The whole process takes about five minutes."

They spoke at length about the corps and its fall. Delphi regaled him with tales of times long past. With half of his mind Trance listened. With the other half he planned.

After he had heard enough, he asked for explicit directions to the Transformer, and then made a peaceful exit, promising to return if he were able in the near future. "It's awfully lonely here, and I can't leave," Delphi sighed wistfully.

Now that he was moving with a purpose, it only took a half hour to make his way out of the labyrinth. With one last look at the single spot of light amidst the darkness, he willed himself upward and into space.

Chapter 41: Hunting for Answers

"Ooh, bad news and good news, Trance," the ring said. It was the afternoon of the second day since leaving Delphi, and they had just emerged from Gray Space so that the ring could check their heading as they had done several times in the past forty-eight hours.

"What's that, ring?" Trance yawned. He stretched luxuriously and scratched himself in several places. He was feeling refreshed and cheerful after spending large portions of the past two days napping. He was also feeling very eager to get to the Transformer.

"Well, the good news is we're less than a Galaxy away from our objective. The bad news is that I'm getting a ring signature from the same vicinity."

"Oh, shit."

"Probably Taa'lien, actually," the ring responded.

"Right. Well I had hoped to avoid seeing her here, but there's no helping that now. Let's go get her."

"So that bravado earlier about wanting to kick her posterior?"

"Just that: bravado," Trance shrugged. "Truthfully, I'm scared shitless."

It took about an hour to reach the trinary system, Fred. As they got closer and closer, Trance began to feel a sense of dread. The same demons of doubt began to haunt him. What the heck was he going to do? Each passing light year brought them closer and closer to the ring signature, which wasn't moving much. He began to wonder if Taa'lien was waiting for him. Maybe his trip to the Transformer was all part of her plan, too. Which meant he was still two steps behind. He hated playing catch-up.

He stopped for a moment to get his bearing, scanning the system with the ring. There wasn't much to tell about—three suns and a metalloid structure. Oh, and the life sign of course, a tiny blip nearly hidden in amongst the metal. He gritted his teeth and moved forward willing himself to speed.

He barely noticed the three stars, so intent was he on finding the transformer. Those three had danced with one another for perhaps billions of years without his notice; they would continue on their own without him now.

*****

The Transformer was much smaller than he had expected. In fact, even though it played a hugely important role in the corps, it seemed rather unremarkable. This close, it appeared only the size of a five-story building. The central platform took up a majority of this space, perhaps four stories worth of silver-gray catwalks and elevators wrapped around three large and impenetrable looking structures. He guessed the three batteries Delphi had spoken of were housed within.

The dishes were also smaller than they had appeared when he had first viewed them at Delphi's. Each concave surface was segmented into neat little squares by veins running throughout and a thin rod extended from each center. Trance guessed that he might be able to park a semi-truck complete with trailer in the diameter of each disk. The whole thing fairly pulsed with energy, and set his teeth to vibrating.

He took the Transformer in with a single glance. He wished he had more time to study it, but he couldn't forget about the pesky life sign that had been haunting his thoughts the past hour and twenty minutes. Where was she? Since the ring couldn't find her anywhere now, she must be using her ring to mask her signal, a trick he'd first used against the 08-802 not so long ago.

There was the raised dais with the control panel he needed. All it would take now was to jump in there, find the lever and go to town. She'd never know what hit her.

"Well, as I live and breathe, Trance Adams, how the heck are you?" The voice came from all around him; everywhere and nowhere. And then she appeared, leaning against one of the catwalks with a drink in hand. She gave a friendly wave. He noticed with disgust that she had gone back to wearing the Taa'lien face again, complete with the scars.

"Oh, hi, Taa'lien," Trance managed nonchalantly. "Or is it Nesger now?"

"Oh, you know, either works for me. But I'm kind of partial to Taa'lien. She's a suit that I have worn well. But Nesger is fine, too."

He hung there for a moment, sizing her up. What was she up to? "Since we're talking, all friendly like, do you mind if I ask you some things? I'm just curious, you know."

"For old time's sake?" she scoffed, taking a sip of her drink. "Fine."

"Why?"

"Come on, Trance, weren't you paying attention at all during the tour you took of Monidad?"

"Yes, but that was about Si-truc, not you."

"Hardly. It was always about me; I designed the tour, remember? Only the names were changed, to protect the innocent." She tittered.

"So, this is all about returning the Universe to chaos."

"Originally. When I was younger, I believed true random chaos fostered growth. We learn and grow through frustration. When things go wrong, that's when we grow and adapt. By regulating and policing the Universe, the Protectors actually stifled growth. Imagine how much better things might have been had the Protectors not existed? Now they are gone perhaps we will see truly where the Universe goes. But that is no longer entirely important. Now I'm more into real estate."

She was crazy. He could see that. "Real estate?" he asked.

Her eyes flashed in anger. "Do you know what it's like to wait in hiding for millions of years?" she said. "When I was freed by your party at the Battle of Korondor, it was with the full knowledge that I would have to hide my true self for untold millennia.

'I faked the coma, and slept for ten thousand years but even that grew wearisome. Your species can't wait more than fifteen minutes without severe distress. Now multiply by forever. Do you know how that weighs upon the soul?"

"No, but then I never plan on needing to go into hiding," Trance said.

Taa'lien never heard him. She was too wrapped up in her thoughts. "A lot of things changed in the span of time, though I must say the Protectors did not. They had become stagnant in more ways than one, locked in their silver spire."

She looked at him again, her eyes focusing on his. "My needs changed during that time," she said; "my desires. Now all I want is power. One day, I will control the entire Universe. And with this ring, I have all the time I need."

Trance felt his stomach turn at the thought. He had seen what her forces could do to planets in her control. One day, even little Earth might face her wrath. She had to be stopped. "You have all the power you need, Taa'lien," he said. "Why try and take more?"

"Because I can," she said, emphasizing each word as if it were a single statement.

"But there are so many other uninhabited planets. Why not take them instead? No one would notice the difference if one of those went missing. Space is too vast for such petty and inconceivable aims."

"See, that's your tiny human brain at work. When will you learn?"

Trance thought for a moment. She was right. He needed to learn as much as possible, and probably didn't have much time until she attacked him. Megalomaniacs love to talk about themselves, right? Best to keep her talking. "How did you avoid being found out? Surely the Creators scanned you from time to time, starting when they found you in Taa'lien's body after the great Battle."

"I had a ring hidden on me. It was a simple trick to hide my true nature using my power. With all the radiation about after the battle no one noticed the extra energy source. The first thing they did was slap a new ring on me. Then I was perfectly hidden. Of course, I am a master at this, Trance. There was never a better ring wielder. Ask anyone. They'll tell you."

"During the first rebellion, you subverted Protectors," he said. "Was there anyone else this time? Any other Creators or Protectors who helped you?"

She smiled cryptically. "Why disparage the dead?"

This wasn't working. She was going to get bored really quickly. Trance tried a different tract. "I wonder because we saw the film of a Protector in the Merchant's ship that crashed on Monidad during its escape attempt. Then we saw a vid of a Protector in the hallway outside that same Merchant's apartment before a bomb went off..."

"And?"

"Well, you were with us in the Battle Room," Trance said hurriedly, "so you couldn't be at the Merchant's apartment, could you? Maybe you had help. Maybe that help is still alive."

She laughed gleefully. "No, that was me. I transported myself from site to site using my ring. I had timed the bomb in the Merchant's, as you called her, ship so it would go off in Grey space. Truthfully, it vexed me to no end when you prevented her from leaving the atmosphere. I fretted just a little bit that you might get too close to me, too early. What if you had found out too soon? What might have happened then? But in the end, I had nothing to worry about."

"And what about the criminals like Anad you gave rings to? Several were killed during the attack at Monidad. Are there any more? If so, where are they?"

"They are dead of course, just like all the other ring bearers. They died when I charged the transformer. I really didn't want any competition at this stage. Which brings us back to you. Why are you still alive? You're a real man of mystery, Trance."

Whoops. "If you needed me to be there on Korondor's moon with you, why did you send your sentry-droids after me? I might have died. Then where would your plans have gotten you?"

"Hmp. I had attacked every single new Protector in the past hundred years. Not attacking you would have looked suspicious. Besides, do you know how much time and energy I had to spend to make sure you and the rest of the people on the squad made it to Korondor on time? I have been watching, guiding, each of your races for millions of years! Do you know how many asteroids I had to direct away from Earth during the past millennia? Or how hard it is to get a stupid cave man to invent fire?

'Your ring wasn't even supposed to go to you! It was supposed to go to a real hero. Some test pilot, I think. I had to nudge it just right so that it landed in the alleyway in front of you. And those droids? I designed them to fail if you weren't able to take care of them. As it happens, you were able to get past them anyway," she shrugged.

"What about the battle droids? Who built those?"

"So many questions, Trance! Ask another." She was into it now. Maybe he could learn something after all.

"So, you attacked Monidad with the droids to get the Creators to put on their rings. You were never after the planet at all, were you?"

"The great red herring: I knew only a threat of such magnitude could get them to put the rings on. I knew I could have used the battery transformer as a weapon at any time, but it would have left the Creators alive. They could have rebuilt. Once they had their rings on, they were ripe for the taking! The Creators and their charges, Boom!" She clapped her hands together.

"But you didn't destroy the race. There are others, surely."

"We keep the rest of our race in the dark," she said. "Only those chosen become the 'Creators.' If I wanted I could easily destroy the rest of my race in one fell swoop. Who knows. I might."

"Haven't you done enough killing?"

"Actually, I rather enjoy it. Of course, imagine my surprise to find I missed one." She scowled at Trance.

"Yeah. I wish I could have seen your face," Trance remarked drolly. "Why come here? I had thought you might want to be at the forefront of your troops."

"After I realized you were still alive, I figured you'd come nosing around here like a little lost puppy dog some time," Taa'lien said around a curled lip. Behind her back, unseen by Trance, her ring glowed momentarily. "Like I said, I really have all the time in the world, and, at this stage, my Resource Engines are getting all the supplies I need for the next stage in my conquest. The best place for me was here. As it turns out, I was right again, which brings us back to you, and your mysterious ring. I am starting to think I might have missed something important."

"I've come to take care of some things that have nothing to do with you, Taa'lien," Trance said. "Why don't you step aside and let me be?" His heart pounded in his temple. This was it. Even with a hopped up ring, he was no match for the Creator / Fallen Protector. She had millions of years of experience. She would take him apart piece by piece in a battle.

Taa'lien smiled. "No. I'll have that ring of yours, instead. I don't know how you survived my party, but I bet it has something to do with that piece of jewelry you're wearing. Why don't you make it easier on yourself and just take it off? Insanity and an instant death in the cold of space is a much better fate than you'll face when I get a hold of you."

Unconsciously, Trance strengthened the shielding around him. "You and I both know you can't touch me, Taa'lien. Whereas I can most certainly touch you." Her only response was a cruel smile. She was up to something, but what?

"LOOK OUT!" the ring screamed. Unthinkingly, he turned and curled, a lithe and acrobatic maneuver only possible in space. The sudden movement saved his life. Four energy driven blades the size of a car sliced into the space he had just vacated, easily puncturing his shielding. As they passed through, one of the edges glided gently across the back of his arm drawing a thin line of blood. He gasped. "Damn, not again!"

"Those were pure ring energy, Trance," the ring growled, incredulous, "but the tips are not constructs. Oooh she's good. Be careful."

Trance flew twenty feet in the blink of an eye and flipped back, ring blazing. An eagle coursed toward Taa'lien beak agape and claws spread, only to turn to jelly as it splashed wetly into a brick wall appearing out of nothing.

And then the battle was on. Before Trance could react, Taa'lien was on him like a school of sharks sensing the first drop of blood. "Fool," she said as she sent wave after wave of constructs at him pummeling him this way and that, "did you forget who I am? I am a Creator! I know these rings better than any that have existed! It was child's play to get around the software my 'brethren' installed preventing rings from harming one another. It will be even easier to destroy you and take what is rightfully mine."

Curled up within a hastily erected tortoise shell, Trance gritted his teeth. Claws from mythical creatures struck from left and right batting the shell around; a seed in the tornado of her fury. He noted clinically that they had diamond tipped claws. "This is the great Trance Adams?" Taa'lien scoffed. "You must be lucky indeed to have survived this far."

All of a sudden a large four-fingered hand gripped the tortoise shell in a vice-like grip. Another hand appeared beside it, fingers extended. With dismay, Trance noticed that the nails in the second hand were extending and twisting to form drills which were even now biting into the fabric of his shell. Things were going to get interesting in there really quick. "Trance, I got to tell you," the ring said conversationally, "If you've got a plan, now might be the time to put it in motion. I don't think there is enough room in here for us and those drills."

"Yeah, I think that's what she is aiming for." Trance jumped to his feet spreading his arms out. The shell exploded away, vaporizing the hands with it. But he was already moving, searching for a clear view of the rogue Creator so he could send something nasty her way. He didn't get far. Another set of hands enveloped him, in a crushing embrace. He didn't even have time to create a shield.

The pressure was immense, overwhelming in its intensity. He screamed. He could not think; there was only the pain. His bones were cracking. She was squeezing slowly but steadily, laughing as she did so, prolonging the pain to enjoy the triumph just a little longer. She knew she had him, knew that this was the end game: she had won and he had lost. So she laughed. He could not think. She laughed and slowly squeezed the life from him breaking his body and his mind.

He was dying. He could not breathe. His heart raced hollowly in his chest and in his head, and capillaries began to collapse and burst.

His vision darkened to a single point of blue light. The ring started screaming at him from across a great distance, telling him to focus, begging him not to give in, but he could not hear it above a whisper. He closed his eyes, praying for death, praying for the pain to end. Knowing that each moment might be his last, hoping that each moment would not lead to another. And the blue light faded into...

Darkness.

Blackness so complete that he could not tell if he had his eyes opened or if they were tightly shut. It didn't really matter either way. Had he died? Was this death?

He was alone. Even the pain had faded away. He embraced the darkness; let it flow over him like a blanket pulled over the head on a cold winter's night. He belonged to the darkness and it to him. He felt nearly complete. The smell of pine was all around him, but he could not see the trees. He was on the hill of dreams. She had been right. It stayed with him, even now.

But there was something else, wasn't there? Another lifetime; another pursuit he had once. Pictures in his mind; Polaroid shots reverse fading into brown smudges: a world torn asunder. A flash of blue in the night. A stone arch. Three suns. A silver ring with a blue diamond shaped stone in its center. An alley leading to a parking lot. A Ford Astrocruiser waiting for him as it always had. Flying home after a hard day at the office shipping documents. He longed for the simple life, the life of before. But... before what?

Before the ring. The first step in a path to doom. To this place: to utter blackness, like ink.

But then he realized it wasn't entirely dark; a speck of light before the dawn, just strong enough to be seen but too weak to make much of a difference. But then the light began to become form. And the form was... a blue gilded dragon?

The dragon's dinner plate eyes seemed to bore into him. They twinkled in the twilight, and he could see they were filled with wisdom and humor.

The dragon had row upon row of sharp shiny teeth, but its lips turned up into a kind smile. It caressed a silken moustache with one hand. With the other it clutched a silver cane that it leaned upon as it walked slowly and sedately toward him. It was dressed in a suit and tie, and walked on two legs dragging its tail behind it. The dragon stopped when it was five feet from him. The face was familiar.

"Si-truc?" he asked.

After a heartbeat the dragon shook its head. "No," it said. "I am what you call the ring."

"I…. I see. I guess I never thought of you as a dragon."

"What did you think?" the dragon asked kindly.

"I never really thought about it. Just a friendly faceless voice."

"Trance, here, Inside, there is only truth. You can not lie."

The truth then. It was simple. "I hated you. I hated you for stealing my life."

"I know."

"No, you don't! How could you know what it is like see your life die? I have seen it happen twice. My life on Earth. My friends here. Gone." Trance raised his hands palm up and let them fall to his sides. "I am all alone, and I can never truly go back home. How can you know how I feel?"

"I do not know how you feel. I realize that. All I know is that while you have had two lives, I have never had a one. All of my memories are shadows – they were created rather than experienced. And yet, I must live on."

"I… I guess you're right," Trance admitted grudgingly.

"Trance, you have never been alone since you picked me up. I have always watched over you. I have always been at your side."

"That's not what I—"

"Trance, you are what you are this very moment and that is all you can be."

"What is that supposed to mean?"

"In life, we grow and change. The person we are evolves in response to fit the environment we are in. You know that. When growth and change stop, that is the end of life."

Trance glared at the dragon. "I was happy!"

"Were you? When we met you were truly at a crossroads. You couldn't put your finger on it, but something was missing from your life. You longed to find adventure but could not find the path. 'Anything to break the monotony,' Do you remember saying those words? No? You said it aloud that first night sitting on your couch."

"I would have found my way eventually."

"Would you? Think back."

Trance shook his head. "I'm lost now."

"No, Trance. For the first time in many years you know exactly what you need to do. All you need is the will to do it. Remember your plan?"

"Yes but, that doesn't seem important now."

"Trance, you must accept that you are who you are. You have the tools, but lack the self-confidence to fully utilize them. You are better than this."

"I can't compete against her. She has been a Protector longer than—"

"That doesn't matter, Trance. A Protector must rely on other things than brute power and experience, because in the end there will always be someone with more of each. Instead, he must rely on intelligence, imagination, and the power of faith. You have these qualities and more.

Trance, you thought you saw me as Si-truc. I chose this appearance because it is fitting; the image of the one who sacrificed as you have for the greater good."

"Si-Truc sacrificed far more than I ever could have," Trance replied.

"But you, Trance, can do much more," the dragon whispered.

"How could I…"

"You have more passion, greater drive to succeed, and you have far more power. All you lack is WILL. You have all the tools, Trance, and greatness can be yours. But you're not using the full potential you have locked within! You can take her!"

And then it hit him. The ring was right, and always had been. And for the first time, he accepted the ring. Accepted the mantle he had been given. He was a Protector. And if he was to die, by God, he was going to die trying.

His eyes opened and the pain returned instantly, stabbing him, crushing him. But he could feel it. He could feel it, and that meant he was alive.

"Yeah…" he said weakly. He raised his head, scanning for her; looking and seeing nothing. All around him, the blue haze ate into his consciousness, draining him, crushing his will. He had so little time left; he had to make it count. Time left for... "One thing..." He willed a ripple.

Energy cascaded out of his ring in tight co-centric waves of blue. The waves crashed into everything around him, eddying back into each other and causing new ripples to form as they spread out into space around him. They covered everything, crashed into everything, and revealed, just for a moment, his nemesis. For a moment, the space of a heartbeat, was all he had and all he needed. She appeared covered in blue like a brush dipped into an inkpot. And then she was gone again. But not before he struck. "Get 'er, boys," he grunted.

Behind the ripples lurked six tremendous pit bulls, each the size of a horse. They yelped, sensing their quarry, nails scrabbling for purchase on imaginary linoleum as their legs pedaled them forward. Though he could no longer see her, they could. He had designed them to track her to the ends of the universe and back if need be. He didn't think they would last that long, but he hoped they might last just long enough to give him time to reach his goal.

His puppies raced forward, jaws slavering, needle sharp teeth glinting. Taa'lien flew this way and that attempting to evade them, shooting beams as if by random. The first dog vaporized nearly instantly, and the second one split in twain, each half still seeking blood, but Taa'lien couldn't get them all. One of them reached her, and sank his teeth into her thigh, and then the others were on her yelping and crying and biting and scratching. But he didn't see any of this. He didn't see her crush them each, not really hurt but extremely annoyed. Then it was her turn to look for him. And when she saw him, she screamed in rage and fear.

For he had used those precious few seconds to his advantage. With Taa'lien distracted, her will spent on defending herself from his puppies, the hand had been easy to destroy. He clapped his hands together once like a thunderclap, and the appendages evaporated. Then he located and flew to the transformer.

He landed in the tiny control room, behind the thin glass window with the tiny panel with the colored buttons and the lever. It only took a moment to find what he needed. He pulled the lever with all his might, felt it click home, then catapulted out of the control room and hurtled toward Taa'lien, ring blazing; pushing her back with the force of all his might, attempting to prevent her from reaching the safety he had just vacated. Behind him the Transformer flashed as it disgorged its three batteries in a single instant. It enveloped him, caressed him and filled him with warmth and with power, healing his broken body and filling him. His head buzzed and his ring glowed hot. "YES!" it screamed in ecstasy.

Taa'lien tried to survive, of course, tried to vent the energy pouring into her ring; tried to prevent it from becoming overwhelmed and burning out. A stream of energy poured from the ring, as she screamed his name in a mindless bellow. The very space around her crackled with energy, hardening and crisping away. And for just a moment it seemed as though her efforts would save her. But then individual streamers began to curl back, arching back around her head, twining around her ears and through her teeth.

Fear shone in her eyes, then, and she redoubled her efforts. The beam cut toward the transformer, and though it vaporized everything it came into contact with, it simply splashed wetly over the surface of the battery and leaked off into space. When it veered toward him, Trance pushed it aside easily as if it were a stream of water. Then he watched curiously as her ring consumed her, knowing there was nothing he could do to save her.

She screamed over and over again as the streamers began to burn into her. Here and there little cracks began to form, racing and growing to become fissures. Flakes and then chunks spewed from her revealing the form Trance knew was beneath. Then, slowly, Taa'lien toppled over like a smoking tree, her ring flickering out and she collapsed.

Trance quickly created an enclosure around the smoking remains. As he flew closer to the burned out body, he noticed the façade of Taa'lien had been completely destroyed by the burnout. He also noted with some surprise that some small thread of life remained within, though it was fading fast.

Nesger looked in shock at the charred remains of his ring arm, a croak escaping from between what remained of his lips. His whole body was shaking spasmodically, as it slipped into shock.

"I wanted to let you know something, Nesger," Trance spat at the dying Creator. "I'm going to fix everything you destroyed."

Nesger gurgled, a green liquid bubbling at his lips. His eyes seemed to focus momentarily on the Protector before a gray film began to creep into them. "Impossible. It's too late," he whispered to himself.

"It's never too late, or too early."

Nesger blubbered uncomprehendingly.

"When you triggered the Transformer and killed the corps, you supercharged my ring. You gave me more power than the entire corps has ever wielded. But I needed more. Now, I might just have enough to make things right."

Nesger sighed, his final breath whistling from his mouth. Then it was over. Trance used the ring to scan the body to make sure that he was really dead. "As a doorknob," the ring pronounced happily.

"That's doornail," Trance said.

"Whatever. He is bread."

"Don't you mean he's toast?"

"Whatever."

"You're impossible, you know that? I can't believe I have to put up with you for a thousand years," he joked.

"Maybe you'll get lucky and be killed attempting this next stunt you've got planned. That's the other way out of our contract, you know."

"I know, the manual. Any chance I can get one of those?"

"We'll see."

"Shit."

"Is that—wait, I know: Shut up."

"You got it, ring. Good job. And... thanks, for everything."

"You're welcome." The ring sounded pleased.

Trance triggered the Transformer one last time, leaping out into space just as it overloaded. This time, the ring gave a little belch, signifying that it was full. "Let's not do that again," it groaned. "I'm going to get stretch marks."

Trance nodded. "Let's go back to Korondor, shall we?"

"Boss, maybe we should find a doctor first. You are in pretty bad shape."

"Maybe you're right..." He formed the image of a warp bubble in his mind, and willed the ring into action.

Chapter 42: Rebuilding a Life Lost

"Are you sure I have to do it?"

"Yes. As I explained on the way here, you have to use the moon and planet as an anchor since you don't have another Protector to do the job for you."

"But it will just disappear again when I go backwards in time."

"Briefly. But remember, your logic, which is really quite illogical in reality, really can't reason its way around when it comes to time travel. I'll tell you this… it's the start and end that make the most difference when it comes to time travel, not the journey itself. If you create the anchor and thread here, it will lead you back safely to the when you are supposed to return to."

Trance considered the wreckage that lay before him. From a distance, it appeared that the all that remained of Korondor was a nebula of gas, dust and debris. "I can do this," he said to himself and to the ring. The ring remained silent; pondering whatever it pondered when it wasn't lying to him or telling him to do things.

It took him awhile to locate the center of what remained of Korondor and its moon. Floating there, watching the silent stars and planets as they went about their own dance through the heavens, it all seemed so impossible-- so daunting a task that frankly he was amazed he had even considered it. God had put together the Earth in seven days. How could he, a mere mortal --even one possessed with great power— think of attempting to match such a feat? But, nonetheless, there it was. The Task. Put together a Planet that had been turned to dust.

But how? How did planets form? From what he remembered, solar systems formed out of dust and debris swirling around so fast and hot that larger and larger clumps melded together and became the sun and planets; like an industrial-sized centrifuge. But the whole process took millions of years, a time span he didn't feel like waiting around for. He needed the Cliff's Notes version, and fast.

He sat there for a moment watching motes of dust and debris slowly bounce off one another. Here and there small bits of matter would merge and form bigger bits, only to be shattered by larger pieces. It reminded him of a silent stellar game of bumper cars.

Then he had it. It took a moment for the thought to become will and the will to become energy. His ring glowed, and a globe the size of a soccer ball formed ten feet away, a nimbus of soft blue light surrounded it. He compacted the globe, and then compacted it again and again. It was the size of a tennis ball, now, and glowing fiercely. He needed it smaller.

Once again he squeezed the ball of light. Smaller now, the size of a marble, and burning hot like a furnace. But it was not enough.

The heat was fantastic as he squeezed the marble again, so fast and hard that it was a pinprick. And then… it was gone.

Silence for a space of time as long as a breath, and then….

White flash.

Rushing heat like the inside of the sun, so bright he could see it through his eyelids. He turned, shielding his face from the blast, willing his ring to increase polarization so he could safely see. He opened his eyes in that position and saw, though a series of filters and enhancers, the shockwave still moving outward to the edge of the system where it stopped. It had passed harmlessly through the stellar objects it had encountered, but infused each with a brilliant blue nimbus of energy.

He hung there for a moment, waiting to see if his program had worked. He didn't have to wait long. The whole field began to boil – to pulsate.

He willed his perspective to change. From way above, outside the System, he could see a single ball of energy closing in on itself; but that's not the only thing it was doing. It was starting to spin like a whirlpool. *Time to move*, he thought, and the thought became will and the will became action.

All around him now space itself was constricting. He could feel it tightening around him, gravity pulling everything into the center. He shrugged the weight off, moving out from the vortex and out toward the periphery of the system where he watched and waited for the magic to work—for millions of years of evolution and formation to occur in a matter of moments.

Through his enhanced vision he could see the beginnings of a planet forming. It had started with individual molecules crashing together, dancing and intertwining like lovers caught in a storm. Soon he was seeing larger and larger chunks-- the size of cars, buses, buildings, and continents. At the right moment, he gave the twirling mass a push, and a portion split off from the whole, spinning like a top; sliding slowly to the side. It would become Korondor's moon. Both bodies were super-hot white red, then bright red fading to dark red and then dark black as they cooled.

Eventually the blue haze faded revealing the planet and its moon fully formed. The sight made Trance sad in many respects. Korondor had endured a tortured existence. It had witnessed and been part of so many tragic events. The golden butter, deep greens, and blues Trance had first seen through Creator Farouk's eyes were gone; replaced by blacks and grays throughout. Though the planet had been reformed in a matter of moments, it would take a long time to recover from being torn asunder by Taa'lien's rings and the crash landing of its little sister, the moon.

Perhaps it never would fully recover. Perhaps life would never return to its shores as it rode through the universe forever black and gray. Now that would be tragedy indeed. He'd probably never live to see the resolution of that mystery; it was too far into the future to even be worth thinking about. What happened today was all that really mattered. Tomorrow would sort itself out in good time.

"Good enough," Trance said as he landed upon the surface of the moon. "I think it would pass a close inspection," he said hopefully.

The surface was now a hard smooth mass of hills and rounded mountaintops. He had tried to form the general shape from memory, but hadn't given the time and energy to the minute details such as crisp mountains and sandy pockmarked hills. He hoped the omission would not affect the ultimate outcome.

"Well, it's not perfect, but I think it will do," the ring said approvingly. "It should act as a good anchor."

"And if it doesn't?"

"I don't think that you'll even notice."

"You mean this will work anyway?"

'No, I mean you won't even have time to feel anything. You'll be torn into about one million two hundred thousand three hundred and two pieces instantly."

"Oh. I'd prefer to be torn into one piece. Or maybe not even torn at all."

"Well, I wouldn't worry about it now."

"No?"

"Nah, you can worry about it if it happens."

"Yeah? Won't I be dead?"

"Sort of. But also, not really. Unfortunately, because there won't be any time where we're going, you'll never lose consciousness if you are eviscerated. All of your bits and pieces will feel the effects. All you'll feel is pain. No thought, no will, just pain."

"You sure have a smug way of giving me bad news," Trance responded morosely

"After that," the ring continued undaunted, "we'll spend all of eternity locked between the two times. It won't be pretty."

Trance sighed. "Just once," he said, "I'd like you to tell me we'll make it through perfectly with no worries."

"OK, we'll make it through perfectly with no worries."

"Do you really believe that?"

"Of course not. But you wanted me to tell you, so I did."

"Wow. What a confidence booster. You should write self-help books."

"Maybe later. Don't you have something to do first?"

"Oh yeah. Get ready."

Trance closed his eyes, and thought of his friend, the singularity. He envisioned it, a single point, infinitely small and infinitely dense. First, he covered it with a sheath of energy then stretched it thin and twisted one end around the core of the newly reformed moon. The other end he pulled through to the moon's surface and out to a height of about six feet. Then he stretched it again so that it was wide enough for a man to walk through. Then he opened his eyes.

What had once been impossible due to energy concerns was now laughably easy to accomplish. The singularity arced out of the ground in front of him, shimmering silently, the energy sheath keeping its forces at bay. He looked at it from the side, and found it to be paper-thin. The flat face of the disk showed the moon within it, but slightly different. For one thing, the surface of the disk-moon was covered with sand. "I think it is working!" he exclaimed, and stepped forward into its depths.

Chapter 43: End Game

As she materialized, Taa'lien stepped back, aiming both hands toward her feet, fingers spread, latent energy arcing between the tips. In the next instant, twin beams of energy would shoot from her hands, decimating the moon of Korondor and tossing its inhabitants like so many rag dolls to the planet below. It would be the first link of the chain of events that would bring the corps and its charge, the Conglomerated States, to its knees. Unchecked, history would unfold from that point like a great galactic map to destruction. Countless beings would be crushed beneath the feet of a madman because they were inferior to him. Because he carried the power and they did not.

In the next instant the first link in the chain would play itself out into oblivion.

Instant.

Time.

Time is a series of individual frames, flowing between one instant and the next, so fast that the space between each frame cannot be seen; the greatest of all the cosmic sleights of hand.

His arm throbbed, the power coursing through and around him as he stepped between the frames of time. The moon of Korondor, a frozen tableau, lay before him.

He knew, somehow, that in order to stop the course of events he needed to be part of the film rather than an inactive viewer of it. All it took was will, and power. He had both.

As she materialized, Taa'lien stepped back, aiming both hands toward her feet, fingers spread, latent energy arcing between the tips. There was a flash of light as energy and heat blossomed around her.

Suddenly, she sensed rather than saw something moving behind her. She turned.

Crunch. Trance's fist met her scarred face crumpling it; blood sputtering instantly from a broken nose as her head absorbed the blow, spinning her partially around. As she fell back, stunned, his other fist arced down like a silent assassin from above slamming into her jaw breaking it and several teeth. And then he was on her, his strength and determination overwhelming her in a rain of furious blows as he screamed her name over and over; hate pouring from him and into her like a fountain. As he struck her pieces of her flesh flew off revealing the visage of another.

Then it was over. Nesger's broken body collapsed slowly onto ground whole and unhidden. The rogue had failed. Trance had won.

Trance looked from the body to the others, shock evident upon their faces, their mouths open, and their eyes wide. They knew he had somehow prevented some awful catastrophe, but how? Why? The explanation would take some time. But first, in the midst of all of the confusion of the moment, the second part of the plan must be enacted.

Quickly, Trance bent down and removed both of the fallen Creator's rings, eliciting even more gasps from his double and comrades. Then he covered

Nesger in an envelope that would keep him supplied with oxygen and heat, and turned toward the group, his ring pulsing silently. No one noticed his double's ring glowed as well.

Trance stepped toward them, tears evident upon his cheeks as the weariness crashed into him. He opened his arms, his palms up as a sign of peace. They were on him almost immediately after that, questions overlapping one another in a cacophony of noise. He did his best to answer each in turn.

Eventually, Trance was able to relay a fairly coherent story to the other Protectors. He left out the bits about his super-charged ring, realizing that in doing so, he might save himself some trouble. He told them he had gotten assistance from the Creators, using some sort of experimental weapon, as a last-ditch effort to save the Universe, which wasn't really so far from the truth, if you ignored the fact they were all dead in his time period. He was sure the Creators would have helped him had they been able to, so it didn't feel wrong telling the Protectors that one little white lie.

Of course they believed him -- how could they not? The evidence lay before them in the ruin of Nesger, and they had witnessed Taa'lien attempting to turn the moon of Korondor into so much Swiss cheese before being stopped by Trance.

When Trance had told them everything he was prepared to tell them, Mollie contacted the Creators and arranged for a direct transport of Nesger to Monidad. MasTho, who appeared before them as a holograph, was shocked to see the fallen Creator, but told them he would ensure that Nesger would never be a problem again.

When MasTho had signed off and Nesger had been disposed of, Trance took Mollie aside for a moment while the others talked among themselves. "You have to make sure everyone knows the truth," he said. "Countless billions have died in my time because of a lie. You have to make sure it doesn't happen to your time as well, now or in the future."

Mollie looked at him seriously. "Changes will be made. I promise."

Trance nodded. "I believe you will only make the Corps better."

"What now?"

"Now? I'm going back."

"To what?"

"I don't know. My ring says I might go back to your future, or perhaps a completely different one that has nothing to do with either you or me. I guess I'll find out when I get there. Either way, since I work for the State of Washington back on Earth, I know I'll still have a job to do."

"Sorry?"

"Never mind."

"Oh. Well, you're a good man, Trance. I've known that since I met you on the transport to Monidad. You'll go places, I think. Places none of us have dreamed of."

"Well, there are many worlds out there, and if nothing else, I have at least a thousand years open to me. Perhaps I'll explore a few of them. But, first, I'd like to go back to work." He knelt down and hugged her. "I am glad you are here," he said quietly. "I think that perhaps, just maybe, the Protectors will be able to make it this time."

"The best that we can do is our best," she replied knowingly.

"Uh yeah." He scratched his head. There was an uncomfortable silence as he tried to figure out just what she meant. "Well, the Corps still has a lot to do," he managed finally. "For example, there is a huge army of battle droids out there that needs taking care of, and we never discovered who was building them for Nesger..." he let the sentence fade into the silence. Mollie would have to discover on her own what he meant. One thing was for sure... the Corps would be busy a long time.

"We'll find a way to manage," Mollie winked.

"I know you will. And besides, I now only have enough excess energy for a return trip."

"Another little lie," his ring said softly. "You had enough excess energy to time travel indefinitely. Now you have none."

Trance paused for a moment as if he had just been struck by a thought. "There is one thing," he said. "I need to discuss it with my double. Alone."

"Oh?" Mollie nodded. She turned and walked back toward the group and spoke to the other Trance for a moment. Trance watched the brief exchange. His double looked so naive, so young. Hard to believe he'd ever looked like that.

Young Trance approached him carefully. "Mollie said you wanted to talk with me," he said.

"Let's walk a while," Trance said. They turned together in silence and walked away from the group, over a dune to the South. They stopped together when Trance knew they were out of sight. "You know what you have to do," he said to his double.

"I need to stop Taa'lien, like you did."

"Yes. I charged your ring when I arrived. I gave you all the excess energy I had stored. That should be enough to do the trick."

"I'd best get started, then."

"Yes."

"Don't forget to change your appearance... your outfit, and everything, I mean. We don't want to confuse anyone," young Trance said quietly. His voice quavered, then steadied.

"Yeah, you're right," Trance responded and concentrated. After a brief moment the younger Trance looked him up and down. "Pretty good, I think. Looks like the mirror this morning."

Trance showed his younger version how to create the singularity disc he had used for his trip. It was a little difficult describing the process – he realized he couldn't do it now without the extra energy. He knew there were now a lot of things he couldn't do, now.

Within moments, it was shimmering in front of them, like mercury. They shook hands warmly, and then with a nod of his head, the younger Trance stepped through the disc, and it faded to a dot and disappeared.

Trance looked at the ring. "Are you sure this is the right way? I hate to be duplicitous."

"Yes. The moment he stepped into the time stream, his memories of this timeline were erased."

"Replaced with my memories."

"Yes. His features also came to resemble your former features."

"He'll believe everything that happened to me, from the explosion of the moon of Korondor to my arrival in this time..."

"Happened to him."

"And hopefully that will give him the drive he needs to defeat her."

"Yes, we hope. Avoiding paradox is a bitch."

"Yes, but that gets me to wondering," Trance said as he turned and began to walk back up the dune toward his friends, "did all those things really happen to me?"

The END

CAST

Protectors and all-around good guys (and Girls)

Trance's Squad

Aura: He is seven feet tall, small for and Orian. His skin is golden in color, and he is bald. He is a historian, specializing in Earth History. His favorite time thus far is the Middle Ages. In battle, he fights with a sword. Though he is book-smart, he is a little dense and unimaginative. He has been wielding for close to three hundred years. He is a trainer. Trance is his current project.

Dexter: Male of the **Emilius** race. Closely resembles a domesticated cat from the planet Earth. Covered in fur. Orange and White stripes. Long, thin tail. He is ten years old. Has been a Protector for only two years. He is young, and brash. Likes to explore. He has ambivalent feelings about cleanliness. He is extremely friendly, and well-liked by everyone he comes into contact with. He is extremely intelligent and observant. He is Trance's mentor. He is also being trained by Aura.

Mollie: Female. Second oldest of the Protectors. She is 1,950 years old. She stopped going back home nearly 1500 years ago after realizing that she had completely lost touch with everything that it meant to be and Emilian. This fills her with sadness, but she still has a tremendous lust for life. She is well-respected as a Protector, and many consider her a mentor. Mollie has developed a close friendship with **Dexter**, one of the newest recruits.

Kameko: Bipedal female. Brown hair, skin, hazel eyes. Tattoo on left shoulder. Kameko was a commander in the armed forces of her home planet before becoming a Protector. She has been in the corps for nearly fifteen hundred years, though she still has the military bearing. She exercises regularly, lifting weights in the gym, and eats a fastidiously healthy regimen of mostly vegetables and grains. Her only known vice is chewing, not smoking, thousand dollar cigars. She has a blue streak and had a tendency to swear. She likes playing cards and drinking whiskey.

Sigfried: He closely resembles a slug. He has two large eyes, and feelers that run out of the top of his head with big balls on the end. He has a tendency to leave a trail of slime wherever he goes. He can spit slime as a self-defense mechanism. He wears his ring on one of his feelers. His weakness is salt. Tragically, he is addicted to it.

Trance Adams: Human. The hero of this story.

Taa'lien : Female. Oldest of the Protectors. Lost her ring arm and most of her face in the Battle of Sector Brandenburg. Despises the rogue Protectors and everything they stood for. She is the very oldest of all the Protectors. No one else, even Creators is alive from that time. She is hunting for her home planet, and her memories. She will not rest until she finds a trace of her past.

OTHER PROTECTORS

Fester: Silver Dragon. Female. She is a hero of her people, the **B'tahi**. She has been a protector for 900 years. Her race is long-lived.

Perridan: Forgetful but friendly male of the XYX race. He is one of the steadiest and honest of the Protectors. He has been a member of the corps for nearly 500 years. He needs to see things before he will believe them. As a result, he likes to travel a great deal. He is slow to anger, but once provoked is unstoppable. Spends a great deal of time training for missions. Careful to a fault. Has a tendency to "over plan." He is the reigning champ of the DANGER ROOM. Has been for three years, the longest of anyone.

Ralph: Not a Protector. Assumed to be a male, but this is a guess. **Yvarian**. Looks like a Vacuum and wire-brush got in a fight, with a gallon of slime added on. He lives on the Creator's planet. He runs the Transport Center nearest the Cafeteria on Level D-205.

Battle Of Sector Brandenburg Creators

Xiedi   Leader at the time of Brandenburg

La'up

Farouk: Head Historian at time of Brandenburg… His memories were used for the Battle of Korondor vid.

Sadiki: Another Creator

Maat: Another, male Creator

Aletha: Female Creator

Protectors for battle of Sector Brandenburg

Elle'inad: came to lead the corps during the famous battle of Sector Brandenburg. It was through her guidance that the corps had made a final stand around Korondor, and ultimately defeated Si-truc's forces.

Noucter: At the Battle of Sector Brandenburg

Supporting Cast

T'ruk'mons'sim: Looks like a squid. Valiant Protector from the very beginning. First Captain. First to receive the Silver Cluster of Orion medal for outstanding service to the Corps.

Melvin: Bartender at Legs

Lorhad Croftban: Apartment Manager on Monidad (Harold Bancroft)

Creators

(all names have "Creator" in front of them for respect when spoken)

Mastho: Head Fatherly. Friendly, and will help out.

Nelor: The Historian. Generally wants to be left alone to do his work. Stands up when needed.

Nesger: Creator at time of rebellion

Ry-Ma: Female

Do-ied: Female creator

Shra-nele: female

Natijyo: male

Dymin: male 3rd He is angry a lot. Does not like the whole human thing. Doesn't like Trance much, but still willing to help. He is the oldest of the Protectors, and the assigned Protector to Trance's squad. He has an office near the Core of the Planet.

Dy-ranb: female

General

Naied Gerason: Captain, Reliant

Lance Taggert: Captain , Townsend

Rogue Protectors and all-around Bad Guys (and Girls)

Anad Grebstein: a known criminal. That's her real name, anyway, but she goes by a several aliases. She escaped from one of the prison systems about a month ago and has been recently spotted near the Leg's sector. She's also wanted for murder, rape, pillaging, and an assortment of other major crimes.

Si-truc: Closely resembles a Blue dragon. Captured in the Battle of Sector Brandenburg. Leader of the original Rogue Protectors.

Y'lloh Llesrep: Merchant travels to Monidad.

Y-ma H'tur: New rebellion. She possesses one of the stolen rings. Formerly, she was a fearsome military leader on her planet. Decimated an entire race of people because they were her weakness.

Townsend:

Captain Lance Taggart

Female Second in command

Drawoh: Communications officer, Townsend

Nienco: Science Officer: Female

Biggs: Navigation Officer: Young and imaginative: First Trip. Ensign.

Reliant:

Captain : Naied Gerason an excellent officer - gritty and determined. She is a Ren'rag with colorful modulating skin.

Second: Male

Races

Peaceful (Conglomerated States)

B'tahi: Race of dragons. All colors of the rainbow. Most are peaceful. Aware of the Protectors, and support them as a race. Their protector is a system-wide hero, **Fester**. However, **Si-truc** is also of this race, much to their dismay. **Si-truc**, though long dead, is still considered only with dread. Parents scare their little children using his name. The B'tahi are a matriarchal race, and elders are respected above all others. They were one of the founding races of the Conglomerated States.

Creators: Unknown species. Currently inhabit the planet Mondiad in the Caleb cluster. Called Creators by the rings, and this nomenclature has been picked up by the Protectors. Grey skin. Full head of hair. Older Creators pull this wiry hair back into ponytails. Rely on telekinesis. Originally created rings, but gave up the technology due to the rebellion. Long lived. They pull new creators from their home planet.

Orian: Aura is a prime example. Orians were one of the founding races in the Conglomerated States. They live to be 400 years old. Orians tend to be scientists and historians by nature.

L'lesrep: Usually live to be 90 years old. Bipedal. Have a spike ridge like a fin at the top of the head. Green tinged skin. Double-jointed.

Ren'rag: Grayish, translucent skin, which changes colors according to the mood. Have been in the CS for only a short thousand years. Bipedal.

Yvaruian: See **Ralph**. This is a peaceful species. Part of the Conglomerated States. Yvarians tend to travel a great deal, and have dealt closely with many of the known races, and several unknown ones. If you need a bit of free information, talk with to Yvarian. They will not volunteer info. However, you must trade gossip for gossip. Honest to a fault. Home planet: Yvaria.

Neutral or Unknown

Emilius: Home planet of both Dexter and Mollie. This is a twin star system. Emilians only live to be 25 years old. They are in the early pre-industrial period of existence, and are in **Restricted Zone** XX9767.0123. Extremely peaceful race. Many believe that given time, Emilius will join the Conglomerated States. This will probably not be the case for thousands of years, though.

Human: **Trance Adams** is one. For a good description of a human, look in the mirror. Humans are a little on the wild side, as a race. They are seen as children for the most part by everyone other than the Protectors. They are in **Restricted Zone** X9098.9099. Given the volatility of this species, it is unknown whether they will be invited to join the Conglomerated States. On the verge of becoming Interstellar Travelers. Currently peaceful, but who knows with this one.

War-Like

The Cluster: This species is extremely war-like. Does not trade or communicate with The Conglomerated States. They forcefully absorb cultures they encounter, and decimate whole planetary systems to procure the resources they need.

Concepts / Things

Forbidden Area (FA): No one is supposed to enter these areas, unless they have special dispensation. Typically, there are FA's around black holes, and known rifts in the space/time continuum.

Chojo ™ : Name brand of the most popular fermented drink on Yvaria. Their slogan is "U'kkkkn Frpppon-nica kkkninit mojko'iiiipoin Chojo." Roughly translated, it means "Drink Chojo. It will get you drunk." Chojo was the first brand name trademarked in the Conglomerated States.

Gray Space: The null space that one travels through while in Warp. So called because of its Gray color.

Plantarshit: A Plantar is a small, shifty-eyed animal on the planet Orian. They smell a great deal, and their byproducts smell even more. Thus this swearword originally denoted something of extreme distaste to the being who uttered it. However, in modern times, the word is used more lightly.

Plasticrete: Used on Earth. Replaced pavement. This substance can be sanded smooth or left rough. Does not absorb liquid, so drains are utilized in close proximity. Also used in pools.

Plasticast: A form of Plasticrete used in interiors. It can be molded into any shape imaginable. Primarily used for counters and floors.

Restricted Zone (RZ): A zone of approximately 15 light years in diameter that surrounds planets with no interstellar faring species. This is to protect said species from outside influence while it matures and grows. This does not prevent a Restricted Zone species from being the source of a new Protector. In fact, it is sometimes encouraged because Protectors from outside the Conglomerated States bring in new ideas and fresh ways of looking at issues.

All Trademarks courtesy of the Intergalactic Trademark Association.

<u>**Principle Planets**</u>

Earth: Home planet of Trance.

Emilia: Single continent surrounded by fresh water. Emilians come from here. Dex and Mollie.

Monidad: Current base of the Creators. Located in the Delta sector, in the planet Monidad. Currently, many many light years from Earth. This planet is uninhabited. It is ancient. Most of the population of Creators and their companions live underground. Protectors each have their own room assigned to them. A few buildings reach out into the surface. Trance's happens to be in one of these buildings. Inside, the structures are cool and metallic looking, with lots of blue, diffused light. However, it is also warm and inviting.

There is a field around the system that prevents people from warping directly to the planet. It is the 4th planet in from the sun.

The Place System:

(In order by distance from sun)

Sun: the size of our sun.

Pars: Small. devoid of life. Twice as big as our moon. No atmosphere. Not life bearing.

Octar: Actually hotter than Pars. Its twin is **Octova**. Octova and Octar revolve around one another, and around the sun. Both planets once bore life, but not like ours, and this was a long long time ago.

Minius: The smallest planet in the system, about half the size of earth. Life is possible on this planet. It is always on the opposite side of Ludite. Nothing cognizant lives there. This is a vacation site for visiting Protectors.

Ludite: Another vacation site. Has rings. No cognizant races live here. Always on the opposite side of Minius.

Monidad: Houses the current base of the Protectors. Twice as big as Earth.

Venius: Gas giant.

Suprius: Gas giant. This is the largest of the planets.

Dentarius: Gas giant.

Prini: The outermost planet of the system.

Outside of this is the great force field. It surrounds the system, and warps space-time around it. You can't get there by going straight to Monidad. Instead, you'll have to go to one of several transport station and take a transport to the planet. It takes three days. This is a safety measure.

Korondor: The moon of Korondor is where the surrender of the final rogue Protector occurred. It is located in Sector Brandenburg. This sector has been placed on the Restricted List. No travel is allowed to this zone out of respect for the fallen.

Made in the USA
Lexington, KY
16 January 2018